THE BLUE MAGE

BOOK TWO OF THE **TEMPERED SOUL** SERIES

Jo de-Lancey

THE TEMPERED SOUL SERIES

The Crystal Shore
The Blue Mage

MW01624857

This is a work of fiction. Characters are products of the author's imagination

Return To Bodie

Return To Bodie

By

Rita A Weisheit

Dedicated to:

The westward bound who came before us
Those seekers who dared to forge new paths
The countless who took chances
The unfortunate lost along the way

"The living owe it to those who no longer can
speak to tell
their story for them."

— Czesław Miłosz

Prologue

Bodie, California, 1880

The echoes were dying down, the sound of the last ricochet was fading slowly. Newton slowly peeked out from behind the storage barrel to see if they were leaving. Sweat ran down each temple and down his forehead. He attempted to wipe it out of his eyes. It stung but he did his best to ignore it. He realized his hands were shaking; even the one without the gun. The ruckus was finally subsiding.

The men that had initiated the fray and fired the most shots had mounted their horses and were turning their backs. Leaving? Newton certainly hoped so. He rarely fired his own pistol and only kept it with him at the insistence of others. It was back in his pocket and missing only two cartridges; those he'd shot into the distant dirt as bluff, enabling him to run through the crowd and escape.

Two men were sitting on the boardwalk; one holding an arm, the other his shoulder. They had not faired well today. So far no one appearing to be a lawman had approached.

The commotion had been unnerving with over a dozen men involved. Newton was not experienced at gunplay, and would only have been trying to protect himself, after all. His part in the upheaval hadn't done him, or anyone else, much good. It had only served to garner unwanted attention from lawbreakers with no self-control. What had been the point?

He sat down and quietly exhaled, allowing the hot-headed gamblers time to simmer down. Some that had been on the scene had dispersed as quickly as they'd been able, darting into the nearest doorway or simply running up the nearest cross street. A few near the site of the recent commotion were tending to the injured, gathering to talk, leaning out of second floor windows to assure themselves that the majority of trouble was over or going about their usual evening.

From the murmuring going around, it seemed there had been an argument about someone having been cheated at cards. Newton had had nothing to do with the supposed card game gone wrong; he would have run or hidden sooner if he had not, to his chagrin, been caught in the flow of bodies exiting the surrounding saloons at the time of the argument.

It was at least a couple of minutes before he could summon the courage to hazard another look up the street. The three mounted men were leaving, heading north, a dusty trail behind them, and were now far enough in the distance to allow him a measure of safety in standing up. The cloud from the firing of guns still hung in the air, making it difficult to see well in the diminishing daylight.

He heard someone call from across the street. Lionel Bradley was waving to him, summoning him, but Newton wasn't about to abandon his position quite yet. He shook his head 'no' emphatically but Lionel waved him forward again anyway. If Lionel didn't get what he wanted Newton was afraid he would call out loudly and say something inappropriate.

The three riders were far enough away for open speech, but Newton felt no comfort in that. Too many others remained close at hand for what he suspected Lionel wanted to discuss. Newton shook his head again, frowned and pointed up the street in the direction of the retreating men.

Lionel's arms drooped to his sides, resigned to the fact that he would have to wait. Newton exhaled his relief and glanced up the street again to see the town's unwanted visitors galloping as fast as the mud in the streets would allow, the slight bend in the road and the buildings in his line of sight soon obliterating their presence.

He ventured across the wide street at a run. They couldn't possibly have seen him now, or cared, he hoped. In his haste he accidentally skidded in the slick mud and fell on his rump, scrambling up quickly and darting between the two buildings where Lionel waited.

He looked up the street again and no longer saw the three hard men that had most likely come to town to drink, gamble and fight. He was sure he did not know them but he had not seen them up close. Now they were gone; had moved further on, at least. He heaved a heavy sigh of relief, repositioned his hat on his head and looked up at Lionel, standing near. He asked calmly, "What did you want, Lionel?"

"I wanted to know if you thought they were gonna leave for good? Do you know, Newton?

Newton had stood up and tried his best to wipe himself off. Summer was at hand and the snow melt from the surrounding mountains was making the streets a muddy mess this year. He said with patience, "Yes, Lionel. I think they're gone. From this end of town, at least. But I honestly don't know for how long." Newton shrugged. Lionel seemed relieved and Newton smiled.

Slapping his friend on the shoulder, Newton spun him around and they cautiously returned across the street to the saloon they had previously occupied before the situation involving the three riders had begun. This was not his first choice of locations; he walked with his eyes downward in hopes of remaining inconspicuous. But with the riders heading away from them he thought they would be safe amongst the crowds, for now.

When they entered, Lionel went quickly to the bar and ordered two whiskeys and again summoned Newton closer. The piano music started up, having taken a break while customers had run for cover. Voices and laughter grew loud once again.

Lionel raised his glass in salute to Newton, Newton grinned at his friend and they each took a swig of the strong brew. Newton grinned at his friend, pulled his hat down further onto his forehead and turned his back to the room. Others present returned to previous activities. Some had recently come in off the street and several had been behind other closed doors waiting for the gunmen to leave. Most were relieved to be able to continue their evening.

A loud crack sounded from the other side of the room as someone sent the cue ball into the tightly packed billiard balls on the opposite end of one of the tables. Newton jumped inwardly, reminded of the recent gunshots. The breaker laughed and demanded his opponent buy him a drink for sinking two of the balls instantly. His opponent refused to buy anything until the game was over and there was a definite winner.

Two other men began arguing at the card table behind Newton. One accused the other of hiding a fifth Ace under his cuff. Their chairs slid out from under them with a screech as they stood to face each other defiantly. Newton looked from under the brim of his hat and said, "This was a bad idea. Time for us to go, Lionel."

As unobtrusively as they were able, Newton and Lionel wormed their way through the crowded room to the exit. Once outside Lionel started to say something, unaware of just how loudly he spoke, but Newton shushed him. No need to draw unwanted attention. A brawl had already begun in the saloon and he wanted them both far away before it spilled out onto the street again.

Still on the lookout for the men who had come to town to cause the usual type of trouble, they continued down the boardwalk, sticking close to the relative safety of the buildings. When they'd walked a sufficient distance Newton said, "What was it you were going to say, Lionel?"

Lionel looked at Newton with a questioning stare. He shook his head and said, "Don't remember." He chuckled, his voice gravelly. "Guess it wasn't important, was it?" He laughed again and began coughing. Newton slapped him on the back and grinned.

"It's okay. I think I'm going to head on home, Lionel. You okay now?" Newton asked with concern. His loyal friend could be skittish at times. Newton blamed it on Lionel's dangerous profession and the noise from the mine's dynamite blasts that Lionel hadn't ever gotten used to.

Lionel nodded and began to walk away. He crossed the street, barely glancing back and forth for safety. He was halfway across and surprised Newton by turning around. "Hey, Newton? he asked loudly.

"Yeah, Lionel?"

"I remember now, Newton. I remember what I was gonna ask ya." He paused, took off his hat and ran his hand over his graying, long hair. "Will you come over later so we can look at it one more time? I might be able to help you with it." He glanced around again, knowing Newton had told him not to talk about it too loudly.

Newton hurriedly met him in the middle of the road and took him by the arm to rush him to the other side. Once there Newton said, "Sure, Lionel. But you have *got* to stop saying things like that out loud. You know it doesn't take much for people around here to stick their noses where they don't belong. I don't want anything to happen to you Lionel. Okay?" Newton took Lionel's hat, reached up and plopped it back on his friend's head. "Okay?" he asked again, gently but insistently.

Lionel nodded. "Sure, Newton, sorry. I forgot." He paused for a second as if he had something to add. Then he simply said, "I'll see you later then. Tonight?"

Sooner's better than too late, thought Newton. "Sure, Lionel. Tonight. After dark, after supper." He patted Lionel on the back and they went their separate ways.

Newton had to cross the street once more and found himself still wary and on the lookout for danger; and newly worried that Lionel may have been overheard. It shouldn't have normally concerned him this much, but Lionel could be dim sometimes; there weren't many people that wouldn't take advantage of him if they had the chance. And Lionel was his friend. So, once again, he would go to see Lionel later, after dark, and see what he had to show him.

The difficult part was keeping Lionel from openly talking about it. The best thing for Lionel to do would be to leave this town and take the secrets, that had wound up as both of their problems, with him. But Newton didn't think Lionel had anywhere else to go. He lived alone and he had never heard Lionel mention relatives. At least none he seemed close to.

As Newton walked he sighed, wondering if Lionel would survive this town. It was big, rowdy, loud, wild and unsafe. So why was he here? Why were any of them here? The same simple reason. Gold. Maybe not so simple a quest, but certainly a simple motive to understand. The lure of gold and riches had tempted far better men than he.

Yet Newton was here as well. Not so much for the gold as for a unique opportunity created by it. An opportunity borne completely of pure accident. An accident that he didn't, and most likely never would, understand. But an accident he was going to try to make the best of. He was here, in Bodie, and that was that.

He was reasonably safe from speculation by virtue of the fact that residents didn't pay much attention to how or why people showed up in Bodie. Each had their own reasons. He didn't know why Lionel Bradley was here. He had never said, directly, and Newton had never asked.

Newton had his own family he wanted to return to; someday, not yet. If he couldn't be with his blood family at the moment, he would, for now, return to his Bodie family. At least he had that going for him. They may have heard the commotion and be worried about him.

The 'family' waiting for him was a hodgepodge of a family but it was a family nonetheless. When he had brought Lionel home for dinner one night he had been welcomed into the assemblage as Newton had known he would be. They were a group of misfits that seemed to fit together; most of them. But none worried about Lionel as much as Newton.

As he walked he thought he heard familiar sounds in the distance. He saw nothing in particular at first so continued walking toward home. Dusk was nigh, making it difficult to see well. The wind swirled around him as he heard the sounds again. Rustling, blowing sounds, more than just the noise from the people on the street or the pounding from the mills.

He stopped when he reached the edge of a building and peeked out carefully from around the corner. Then he looked the other direction but saw nothing of interest. The next sound that caught his attention was what sounded like horse's hooves, more than one. Newton turned around to look up the street and saw what he assumed was the approach of two of the gunmen that he thought had finally left. *I think that's them...*

It hadn't been long since their departure so Newton was surprised at their quick return. He wondered where the third man had gone. He wondered where everyone else in the street had gotten to as well. The saloons were full as was evident from the sounds emanating from within the multitude of establishments.

He considered warning someone that the men may be back and thought better of it when he saw them slow considerably and walk their horses to the front of a saloon. Tougher men than he were already in the saloon. Men with guns fully loaded and with worse tempers. Let them take care of the outlaws, he thought without remorse. He continued his walk, a quicker pace to his stride.

He stepped off the boardwalk into the mud of the cross street and was startled to find the familiar horse and recognizable form of the third gunman nearing him at a gallop. Newton stood there helplessly. He wasn't used to shooting so didn't react quickly enough to get his six gun out of his pocket before the man aimed at him with his own. Being on foot he could not outrun the man. At least the low light was making it more difficult for the man to see him. *I don't have any money, I wasn't the one at the tables...*

He realized he was going to have to duck into the nearest recess or alley if he had any hope at all of evading him so Newton began to run. Thoughts of Lionel entered his head and he hoped fervently that he was making it home safely.

Newton was nearing the back of a storage building and was planning on ducking behind it. The hoof beats of the stranger on horseback drew nearer. A gunshot; a brick over his left shoulder exploded. He covered his head and hunched his shoulders when he turned to run behind the building. He was still running along the back, looking for a place to hide, when there was another gunshot, after which he noticed the hoofbeats slowing. *Did he find me?* Newton caught his breath before daring a glance from his temporary shelter.

The horse was there, stamping his feet up and down agitatedly, riderless and beginning to wander away. The gunman must have dismounted. Newton quickly drew his head back in and crouched down low for another look. When he looked again he could hardly believe his eyes. There in the road, lay the gunman. Dead or alive he couldn't tell, but moving he was not. Newton looked on for several more seconds before venturing out a few more feet, afraid the man was playing opossum and waiting to rise up and shoot him anyway.

When he drew near and saw the motionless man lying in a quickly spreading puddle of blood Newton knew he need no longer worry about the gunman. His puzzlement as to who had shot the man dissolved when he spotted, across the road and only a little further down, Lionel Bradley; a rifle in his hands and a broad grin on his whiskered face.

1

Dubuque, Iowa, 1980

Phoebe rubbed her temples with her thumb and middle finger, trying to rid herself of the tension headache she'd acquired throughout the day. Again. Traffic was a little congested driving home, but fifteen minutes of it wasn't worth the ache behind her eyes that was becoming the norm for her lately. At the red light she took both hands off the wheel to massage her eyebrows and close her eyes for a moment.

After what felt like only a few moments the car behind her honked, letting her know with irritation that the light had turned green. She glared at the driver in her rearview mirror, slammed the heel of her hand into the steering wheel and yelled, "Okay, I'm going!" She took a deep breath, took another and realized her temper wasn't doing her tension any good. And it wasn't going to go away unless she did something about it.

Her days were becoming longer, not better, filled with impatience and fatigue. She kept telling herself this was what she had wanted. But lying to herself was a waste of time. Her father's words were filtering into her head, his comments winning out over her stubborn refusal to trust her own instincts.

"Stupid-stupid-stupid," she now admonished herself, as if this would do any good. But self-punishment took away at least some of her guilt. She had heard that as children in a family grow up they realize how smart their parents really are. Her twenty-six year old brain already knew it was true.

Many college graduates moved after college: better jobs, see the world, adventure with friends. None of these were why she ended up in the Midwest where she didn't know anyone and didn't really care to make new friends. There wasn't anything wrong with her current location. But it wasn't home. Ugh, that word. Home. People made such a big deal about the concept. Did that really matter? "Home is where the heart is," she said aloud, and realized she was talking to herself again, and repeating a phrase she had long thought trite. She shook herself and regretted doing so when she felt her head throb. *The heart,* she thought. Deep inside she knew what that meant but again pushed it down deeper. Guilt, family, missing her brothers Will, Tony and Troy. And Troy's new little girl she'd only seen briefly as a newborn. Another throbbing headache wondering why she had changed her major in school when everyone in her family knew what her first love was; wondering why it was so difficult to admit her father had been right.

Another stop light, only a half minute after the last one. She sighed. This time the honking driver pulled up next to her at the light. When it turned green he started to pass her. Phoebe could feel his eyes on her but she refused to look his direction. The car didn't pass. He stayed even with her. So that's how this was going to go. She accelerated a bit. He kept up with her. "Oh come on," she said aloud, still not looking over. Another light was up ahead and when she got to it Honker had stopped even with her again. She thought she heard him say something. She rolled her eyes and turned her radio on. He spoke again, louder. The light turned green, she accelerated and turned left the first chance she got. He followed her. *Just let me go home.*

Funny, but her father's face swirled before her mind's eye again. She envisioned one of her childhood tantrums, well that's what he had called them. She had just been treated unfairly that's all. Her father had tried to calm her down, speaking softly, being gentle at first then raising his voice enough to get her attention. It crushed her to upset him.

Later, she had been surprised to learn from her aunt that she had inherited his temper. He understood her more than anyone else in the family, with the exception of one person. But enough already. This honking jerk was getting on her nerves.

Up ahead and to the right was a moderately sized shopping center. She changed lanes to the right suddenly, without signaling. Honker continued to follow. She turned into the shopping center without warning, pulled into a parking spot near several other parked cars and near the frontage road where she would be visible to the public road, and put her car in park.

She got out quickly and reached into the back seat for the baseball bat she kept there. Standing with her back against the driver's side of her car she waited for Honker to pull alongside her, knowing he probably would, daring him to start something, anything,

As expected, Honker turned into the shopping center. He slowed when he saw where she had parked and stopped his car several spaces over from Phoebe's. She glared at him through his windshield, daring him to make the next move.

The hairs raised on her neck in the next instant when the thought, her father's shared common sense, popped into her head that maybe the guy was a lunatic and had a gun. Then what would she do? Nowhere to go, nowhere to hide except the other side of her car. Too far to run to a store, not near enough to call for help. He simply stared back at her. Her head throbbed, she frowned, she said to herself a second time, "Enough already," and walked toward Honker's car.

Honker rolled down his window and she approached, saying, "All right, jackass, just what the – "

Honker stepped out of the car before Phoebe got too near. "Phoebe?"

She stopped short, shock evident on her face despite how hard she tried to hide it. "You! You idiot, what was all that about? What a creep." Her voice rose in anger and Honker backed up just a step at her tone. Phoebe was feeling bold now and moved a step closer.

"You wouldn't look over, I was just trying to get your attention."

"Yeah, well you tried that already, and I don't want your attention. I see you enough. Following me at work, calling me at home. I still don't know how you got my number, but when I find out – "

Honker was somebody Phoebe worked with. Not somebody she liked either. He was a lech, or so she had heard from others, even though she preferred to shape her own opinions about people. Others seemed to be right.

He smiled a deceptively sweet smile and attempted a light laugh. "Oh, come on Pheebs."

"My name is Phoebe and I'm going home. Do not follow me." She turned around to walk back to her car but she heard Honker, she had a difficult time remembering his name, approaching her undaunted from behind. She also heard her father's voice again. Saw his face, heard his advice. It was always so confusing. *Which me should I be, Dad?* Stand up for yourself, but control your temper. Don't be intimidated by anyone or anything, but be polite. Those were opposites in her head.

He kept walking. Phoebe turned around. Close enough. Too close. "Look, what, exactly, is your problem? Go away. Go home."

He stopped walking but smiled his unattractive, snake-like smile. "Coffee?"

She was incredulous. "Coffee?" She felt her temples throb. "You want to buy me coffee?"

"Or we could go Dutch, your choice." He shrugged.

"That's it." She hoisted the bat on her shoulder, walked purposefully towards him, sidestepped him and walked straight toward his car. At the last second her intentions sunk in but it was too late for Honker to do anything about it. Phoebe raised the bat and announced, "Fly ball over the fence, and it's a homer," as she swung away and broke out the right headlight on Honker's Ford Pinto.

He stood in stunned silence as she once again shouldered the bat and strolled in his direction back toward her own car. She stopped near him and said, "I had a headache but it's gone now. Thanks." She smirked as she tossed the bat into her back seat, got in behind the wheel and drove home, leaving Honker frozen like a statue in the parking lot.

A block away, remorse overcame Phoebe. She looked in the rear view mirror expecting to see the police chasing her, ticketing her, sending her to jail. She dreamed that night of being of thrown in jail, dreadful things being done to her, things she deserved because of her temper. She saw her father's face, heard his voice. He didn't say anything, maybe because she didn't know exactly how he would have felt about what she'd done.

It wasn't always easy to tell how he felt about her actions. She just wanted to make him proud and was aware she thought about it much too much. She awoke at three o'clock in the morning afraid that was all the sleep she was going to get that night. But as she sat dozing the early hours in her only comfy chair she mumbled sleepily, "Sorry, Dad."

Carson City, Nevada

Hank Tucker's phone rang for the tenth time that day. He answered it in his jovial and patient way, acknowledging the fact that although he had assigned the RSVP name to his wife Bonnie he was getting all the calls anyway. After all, it was his grandfather that was having the birthday party so relatives were calling to say yea or nay and wanting to chat awhile with him in the process.

His grandfather, J. W. Tucker, born and bred in the Wild West, was still alive and kickin' and wanted a birthday party. Well who was he to turn him down. Especially since he was being so adamant about it this year.

He and his wife hadn't yet heard if their daughter Phoebe was coming back home for the party. Hopefully she would be, and would also decide to stay a bit longer, perhaps move back home. Not necessarily back to Carson City, but close enough to visit more often.

Phoebe's brother Will would be there, of course. So would her older twin brothers Troy and Tony and their wives. They all lived in or near Carson City and the siblings were close, especially she and her younger brother, Will.

Hank hung up the phone after a fifteen minute conversation with his sister in Albuquerque. She would be at the party with her husband. Her kids hadn't yet confirmed if they could make the trip or not; she would let him know later.

Hank's phone rang again as soon as he had hung up. He was surprised to hear J. W., his grandfather, on the other end, and said as much.

"You think I can't use a phone?" J. W. yelled into the phone.

"Not at all, Grandpa. I'm just surprised to hear from you. Is there something you need?"

"When is Phoebe coming?" Then there were some loud raps on the other end, as if J. W. was hitting the telephone receiver on something hard.

Hank held his own receiver away from his ear and winced. When the noise stopped he answered, "I'm not sure she is, Grandpa. But we all hope so."

"Can you hear me?" J. W. rapped the phone on a hard surface again. "Stop calling me that. It makes me sound old." J. W. was practically yelling into his end of the line.

Hank smiled, "Sorry, J. W. Stop hitting the phone, I can hear you just fine. I hope she's coming. I'll call her again and find out."

"Who?"

"Phoebe. I'll call and find out if Phoebe's coming to your party." At least he had stopped hitting the phone.

J. W.'s sigh on the other end combined with a little groan. "Of course she's coming. I just want to know when." He sighed again.

"J. W. are you all right?" Hank never would have thought he'd need to treat J. W. with delicacy. It was the last thing the elderly man would have wanted. But he was concerned by his grandfather's tone of voice.

"Yes, I'm fine, damn it." Hank thought for sure he heard J. W. chuckle and mumble, "Oh, poor boy, poor boy." Then he was mumbling something else and Hank had to get his attention, afraid his phone wouldn't be hung up properly and would be left off the hook, making it difficult to reach him. He didn't know who he was referring to as a poor boy. Hank's son Will, Phoebe's brother? But he'd never called him that before.

"Okay, J. W., I was just checking. Do you want me to have Phoebe call you?" Hank wasn't completely sure Phoebe was coming into town for the birthday celebration. And he wasn't going to ask any more questions of J. W. than was necessary.

He was easily upset over the phone. In person conversations were difficult enough with his grandfather; over the telephone was even more so. He would have Phoebe call her great-grandfather, which she would gladly do. They had always been very close. J. W. seemed so sure she would be at the party. He was going to be heartbroken if she told him she couldn't make it.

"You'd better. I have to talk to her. It's time."

Cryptic, thought Hank, but then again, that had always been J. W.'s way. He said what he wanted and left people asking questions. Some answered, some not. "Okay Gran – I mean, okay J. W. I'll have her call you. Do you need anything else?"

And the line went dead. J. W. had hung up. Hank smiled. When he was done talking, he was done talking. No need to take offense. He wondered what foibles he himself would acquire as he aged. And if his relatives would be as understanding of him as most were of J. W.

Dubuque, Iowa

"Now, please, everyone, do not, I repeat, do not forget that I expect the last chapter to be read by Monday." The groans, in multiple timbres, reverberated around the room. The teacher, Phoebe Tucker, ignored the protests. "And," she continued loudly, "we will discuss it and have a quiz on the information next Friday." The groans were followed by sighs, the scuffing of both lazy and hurried feet, and shouts, hollers and giggles of the students that had already forgotten the class discussion for that day; and, most likely, the class assignment for over the weekend. They were all headed out the door with other, more important things, on their minds.

Miss Phoebe Tucker picked up her few papers and couple of books she'd brought with her to the classroom and unceremoniously stuffed them into what her brother Will called her 'barf bag,' which was just her work briefcase, and began walking toward the door. *Brothers,* she thought. She turned off the lights, closed the door and headed down the hallway and back toward her office. She hoped none of the students stopped and asked for last minute help on her way out.

She was exhausted and glad it was Friday. She'd arrived just in time for the beginning of class that afternoon. She taught a business class, two days a week after school hours, to high-school seniors in one of the meeting rooms on the first floor of the manufacturing company where she worked. She had a degree in business and her boss had talked her into giving the seminar class because he had said she had "a way of speaking to kids that would get the point across." *Bologna!*, she had thought. *It's because the school got a grant, the company was getting paid for it and nobody else had wanted to do it.* But it got her out of her office a few hours a week so, *hey, why not*?

Now it was Friday, her busy and trying week was over, *why was every week so busy and trying and exhausting lately?,* and she was ready to go home; and found her normally bold self wary to venture into the parking lot. Of all her colleagues the one she most wanted to avoid an encounter with was Honker from the evening before.

Rick – Rich? was his first name, she remembered at least that much now. Was she nervous?, no. Afraid?, absolutely not, not her style. She supposed her emotions were mainly due to having stuck him with a car repair bill. But another confrontation wasn't what she wanted before she went home to a quiet weekend and called her family about her great-grandfather's birthday celebration. This had already been a difficult few months without making the situation worse.

She'd been with the company for over two years and had only agreed to take this temporary 'teaching' position because it was a break in a daily routine that had become a drudgery to her mind. It was a busy company to work for; always something to do, meetings to attend, calls to make, etcetera. But it was dreary nonetheless. And it had been her choice, so complaining about it wasn't optional.

She had an office, albeit a tiny one, was paying off her college loan and saving some money. She knew her co-workers thought she wasn't the best conversationalist, a mite rude, standoffish and, quite frankly, a bit intimidating. But it wasn't fair to build relationships when she wasn't sure of her future. Go home? Move on to another destination?

After all, this was her first 'real' job after college. Did she have to stay here forever? Summer was just around the corner; she hadn't looked elsewhere for another job; she hadn't told her family she was dissatisfied with her current position. Should she return home? Could she? All of this was in her head as she plodded unhappily down the hall to stop in her small office before leaving for the weekend.

She was also thinking about the night before and feeling a bit guilty. Rick – Rich? – had been nice at first. He was close to her age, dressed well and had been only a little rude to her. He had also been too friendly. Now that she thought about it he seemed too needy in his attempts to get her attention. But there was just no attraction there, hanging between them, that would ever lead her to date him, which was what she knew Rich – Rick? – wanted.

He had said he understood her (phoney) excuse that she didn't want to date from within the the building. He had subsequently asked her out anyway. Later, he tried again, pointing out the fact that he was in a completely different department and there wasn't any company policy concerning the two of them dating each other. She said thanks, but no thanks, and used another excuse, albeit a made-up one, that she didn't know exactly what her plans would be come summer. After their meeting in the parking lot she'd hoped she wouldn't run into Rich – Rick? – any more than necessary and he would forget about her.

Phoebe was walking across the parking lot toward her car, on her way home, when Rick – Rich approached her from behind. Usually prepared and ready for any surprise that may come her way, she had seen his reflection in the window of her car so knew he was coming. Was he angry about last night? Probably; she would be.

She turned her head and said, "Hi… there," quickly. *What the heck is his name!* She put her key in the door lock, turned around again and said with what she hoped would be a parting remark, "See you Monday," but he was standing very close behind her.

She was prepared for his anger, prepared for an outburst expecting payment for his car that she was fully agreeable to paying for. She was simply hoping to put off the conversation for another day. But he was yet again undaunted. This was not the first time she questioned his irrational behavior.

"Hey Phoebe, I was wondering if you wanted to go out to dinner with me tonight. Tomorrow's good too, if you're busy." The hopeful expression on his face caused her anger and resentment from the previous evening to resurface. The guy was nuts.

"Look Rich – "

"Rick. It's Rick." He smiled shyly, stepping closer.

If he thought she would acquiesce, he was mistaken. She stood her ground and said lightly, "Sorry. Rick. I'm sorry, but I'm just not interested." The innocent look on his face made her feel sorry for him; but only a little. "I'm trying to live without complications right now. I don't want to – "

He held up one hand. "It's okay, Phoebe, really. I get it. I didn't mean to bother you." Now she felt guilty. "Then I think that, since you won't be here much longer that we should, you know, get to know each other better." He moved so close she could feel his breath on her face when he spoke. He put his right hand on her shoulder. His tone was low and quiet when he next said, "Come on, one date."

She frowned, all previous guilt gone. Then, after only a moment's consideration that it took to recognize that the bashful veneer had been a ploy all along, she smiled patiently and moved to put her left hand on his right that was on her shoulder. As she touched his hand his eyes flashed with a triumphant gleam. Realization hit him quickly and the gleam faded. Phoebe gripped his first two fingers in her own and bent those fingers, and his hand, backwards over his right shoulder and held them there for a moment, his right knee beginning to buckle as he leaned into it. He grimaced in pain and cried out in surprise, stepping back a few paces and trying to wrest his hand from her painful grip. She let go and he wrapped his fingers with his other hand.

"Like I said, see you Monday," she said pleasantly before slowly unlocking her car, getting in and driving away. Rick was left stunned, gripping his sore hand and standing all alone in the parking lot. *Pay for your own headlight, jerk.*

***

Friday night, ten o'clock, pjs, drinking a glass of cheap and sweet red wine, one of her many beloved books open in her lap while watching the beginning of the Friday Night Creep Show: *pathetic*, thought Phoebe. *I don't even have a dog or a cat to snuggle up with.* She laughed to herself. A dog or a cat; her friends from college would say, *what do you need with a dog or cat, you should have a boyfriend!*

She pulled a face at the thought because envisioning her friend's comments made her remember Rick-from-work. Friends from college. Yes, she'd had a couple of friends in college. And a few in high-school. Not many, but a few. She had been in little contact with any of them since. What was wrong with her?

She had randomly picked a college, had literally picked the name out of a hat. She had written the names of a dozen schools on little pieces of paper and put them into a hat. She had told her parents that those were the schools she was really interested in and that she had a difficult time deciding which to attend. The truth was, she only knew about a couple of them. The others she had heard friends in high-school speak of so had written those down because the names and/or locations sounded interesting and her friends had sounded enthused about them.

When she picked The University of Illinois it had sounded like a good choice. Far from home, an adventure, a different atmosphere; just what every college kid needed, right? The discussion with her father after her first three years there had been one of the most difficult of her life.

"You're changing your major to what?" He had sounded incredulous over the phone.

"Now, Dad, everybody changes their majors. I guess history's just not my bag." She'd paused then, her face scrunched tight with tension against the disappointed reply she felt coming, her fists clenched in anticipation, expecting him to argue. He said nothing, there was silence on the other end of the line. Her palms had sweat even more, her heart had pounded with the waiting.

Then, very quietly, Hank asked, "You want to go into business?" Several seconds passed and he had added, "Okay."

That's all he had said, that's it. That bothered her more than if he'd yelled at her or gave her a long lecture. The Dad talk about her future and if she was really thinking this all the way through. If she was making the right decision. On what was she basing this sudden change of heart? She'd gotten none of that and it had been deep in her conscience ever since. "Okay? That's all you're going to say?"

"Yes. It's your choice. I'm just surprised. But if you want to go into business that's fine. There are plenty of opportunities, it's up to you. As long as you've really thought it through, and as long as you think you'll be happy." And then he was quiet again.

"Look, Dad, don't be mad. I mean, my friends are behind me. A bunch of people are taking the same classes, I think I only have to add a couple more semesters and everything, and – " she realized she had run out of reasons and excuses and they weren't good ones.

Her own brain had given herself her own version of the 'Dad talk' that night and for several more after that. Still, she had switched from a bachelor's degree in history to a business degree. It had added more than a year of school and she had graduated behind two friends that had initially said they were changing their minds with her but in the end decided four years of school was enough and had stayed their original courses.

"I understand, sweetheart, if this is really what you want." She thought she had heard a sigh, but hadn't been sure. "Just remember who you are inside. Just don't forget," he had said before they'd ended their phone call.

'A bunch of people are taking the same classes,' she had said. 'My friends are behind me.' Why had she said all that junk? Who had she been trying to convince? He had been so quiet; he had known.

Now as she sat sipping her wine watching the Creep Show and trying to concentrate on her book at the commercials she felt like a guilt, angry idiot. Her dad's cryptic words were winding round and round in her head. Again. *Remember who you are... What did he mean by that anyway? I'm Phoebe-the-invisible from a big family in Nevada, whoop-di-doo.* She finished the last couple of ounces of wine in one gulp of frustration, nearly choking herself in the process.

She rubbed her eyes, feeling tired, and glanced at her clock. Ten-fifteen p.m. Her wandering mind had already made her to miss the beginning, thereby missing the point of the movie. If she had another glass of wine she would fall asleep in her chair. So what? She got up, closed her book, clicked off the television and went to bed. Another exciting night in the world of Phoebe Tucker.

As she lay in bed she couldn't help but wonder: if her father's calm words long ago had been so innocuous, why had they stayed with her for years? And why did they continue to haunt her to this day?

2

Phoebe awoke at nearly nine o'clock in the morning. She glanced at the clock and rolled over to face the other direction. Another fifteen minutes passed before she got out of bed, put on her favorite worn robe and shuffled lazily to her tiny kitchen to make a full pot of coffee. "I can't believe I slept this late when I went to bed so early," she said aloud as she watered her small houseplant that sat in the sliver of sunshine on the kitchen windowsill.

Coffee and cinnamon toast in hand Phoebe yawned and shuffled into the living room to re-shelve the book she had so easily abandoned the night before. Putting it in its place she ran her fingertips over other titles in her collection that were sadly collecting dust on her floor to ceiling bookshelf. She hadn't picked through any of them in at least a month, a long time for her.

She frowned; history books, archeology books, books on western life, the major wars. Some from before she had changed her major that she couldn't bring herself to resell at the college book store, most she had purchased herself. She slapped the backs of the books with her hand and spun around. *Stupid books, next time I have a bonfire you're going in.*

She went to her sitting area and switched on the television. Then, knowing she was pouting, she pulled her feet up under her and absentmindedly watched a travel show that would make anyone want to set sail to and experience beautiful blue seas and white sands. However, her mind was elsewhere this morning.

Toast gone and coffee needing warming, she poured herself a refill and sifted through some mail that had sat unattended for the last few days; junk, bill, junk, advertisement of a new store opening. She sighed and tossed it all aside. She turned off the television, grabbed a change of clothes and headed to the bathroom for a quick shower.

Once out, her mood improved. Then her telephone rang.

"Hello?"

"Hey, Phoebe." It was her brother, Will. She at once brightened then drooped.

"Hey, Will. Wait, what did I forget?"

He laughed. "What does that mean?"

"How often do you call? Usually when I screw up and forget something. So what did I forget this time?" She sipped from another warmed refill.

"Nothing that I know of, but I talked to Dad." Phoebe tensed. "I think he's going to call you about J. W.'s birthday party. Just wanted you to know. I hope you're coming. J. W. will have a fit if you're not there."

She relaxed, not completely understanding the reason for her initial reaction, and not taking the time to think about it. "Not fair, he will not. Stop acting like he's so fragile. I mean, just because I'm the favorite," she left off, grinning a grin she knew he couldn't see. Phoebe and her 'little' brother were very close and she missed him desperately at times. He knew she was teasing.

"Yeah, yeah. I don't know why he likes you, I can barely stand you. Anyway, I hope you're coming, Pheeb." Funny, she thought, Rick-Rich had called her that and she had yelled at him for it. "Most of us will be there and we miss you. It'll be fun, you know."

"I know," she said, leaving an easy moment of silence between them. But he knew she was over-thinking the situation.

"What?" he finally asked.

Phoebe groaned. “Ugh, I don’t know. Why is it hard to come back when you think you’ve made a mistake?” she mumbled, but he had heard her comment.

Phoebe had only been home once since college graduation and now maybe Will would get the answers as to why. “I heard that Phoebe. Mistake? You? ” he teased, lest she stop talking to him about it completely. “Is that really it? Maybe you’re afraid of something?”

“No,” she answered sharply.

Will was smiling on the other end of the line. “I thought that would get you.”

“Oh, shut up,” she replied, both of them knowing neither was serious.

After a few seconds Will asked, “Hey Phoebe?”

“Yeah?”

“Dad’s not mad at you, you know. He only wants you to be happy.”

Phoebe sighed audibly. “I know, Will, I know.”

“So,” he paused, not because he was afraid to ask her but because he was giving her time to think about the answer to the question he was sure she knew he was going to ask. “Are you? Happy?”

Silence. Just – silence.

“Phoebe?”

“I’m here. Maybe things are different than I thought they were going to be but, you know, yeah, I’m fine.”

“I’m fine? That’s it?”

She laughed lightly. “No, actually I’m terrible, how’s that? See, I’ve got this dreadful little brother who just won’t leave me alone and – ”

“All right, all right. I see you’re just as snarky as usual.” He didn’t push, knowing that’s all he was going to get out of her at the moment. “Hope we see you at the party.”

“Thanks, Will. I’ll see.”

“Okay. Gotta’ go. Later, gator.”

“Yep, later.” The siblings hung up their call, Will hopeful he would see his sister at the family get-together soon, Phoebe dreading the feelings of doubt and regret that had been with her since college that always came back to haunt her at the prospect of revisiting her childhood home.

The phone rang again after Phoebe had just finished washing the few dishes that had stacked up in her sink from the last couple of days. This time it was her dad, Hank, calling to talk to her about J. W.'s upcoming birthday party. She knew he had been going to call. She was always happy to hear from her dad and held nothing against his good wishes for her happiness. She was also mature enough to understand what she was feeling was the result of her own actions and that blame did not rest with him.

"Good morning, Kiddo, hope I'm not disturbing some important business," Hank stated good naturedly.

Phoebe smiled. "Oh, very. I had a dozen cups and plates and spoons that needed washing. When that's done I don't know *what* I'm going to do with my day. What's up?" even though she knew.

"I heard from J. W." He paused. Phoebe smiled. "He asked when you're coming to his birthday party. Not *if* you're coming. Does he know something I don't?"

Phoebe couldn't help but chuckle a bit. "Sounds like J. W. is being J. W. I haven't talked to him if that's what you mean. Does he want me to call him?"

"Yes, I think so. I suggested it anyway. You know how he is, he wants clarification for everything."

"I know. But it's okay. I haven't talked to him in awhile so I'll give him a call today if it'll make him feel better."

"I'm sure it would. And just so you know, he said something strange. He said 'oh poor boy' when we were talking. I don't know what that was about. Who knows if he knows. It made me wonder about his memory of late. I wanted you to be aware of it when you talk to him.

"Okay, Dad, I will be. But, can you answer one thing for me? Do you have any idea why he's having a party for his birthday a month early?"

Hank laughed lightly. "Not really. He set the date and we simply went from there. Maybe he doesn't want to interrupt everyone's summer vacation. I didn't ask, actually." Her father added, "He's getting up there, Phoebe. It would be nice if you came to the party. We would all love to see you, but I'm not sure how much longer J. W.'s going to be here. I know it's not a pleasant thing to talk about, but, you know what I mean."

There was silence on the phone for several seconds, a hot sensation stinging Phoebe's throat. She cleared her throat and said, "I know, Dad. I was planning on coming all along. I'm sorry I didn't say so earlier. I can stay at the house with you and Mom, right?"

"Nope, sorry, I turned your old bedroom into a home gym and threw all your old stuff away." Phoebe laughed.

"That's what I thought," she said lightly. Then quietly she said, "Thanks, Dad."

After another short pause Hank asked, "Driving or flying?"

"Hmm, I haven't decided yet. I'll let you know, okay?"

They hung up on a cheerful note. Phoebe would call J. W. and talk about his upcoming birthday party. She would decide when she would be arriving at her parent's house. She would figure out whether she would fly or drive, then notify work that she would be leaving for a... vacation? Break? Sabbatical-because-she-hated-her-job/life-and-needed-to-run-away-from-Rich/Rick?

Then she would have all the time in between her decision and actually leaving to wonder how she would feel when she once again encountered the sights, sounds and smells of the land she had turned her back on years ago.

***

The phone rang several times and Phoebe smiled, wondering what J. W. was up to. He'd been relatively active at the old-fashioned, two-story boarding house where he'd lived with four other gentlemen until Phoebe's grandparents had moved him home to live with them. J. W. refused to go into a typical nursing home just as adamantly as Phoebe's grandfather, Henry, refused to put him in one.

J. W. was quite elderly and his family was concerned for his well-being and happiness. At home with Henry he had his own bathroom and a telephone in his converted room on the first floor, along with the addition of a small kitchen cupboard, counter top and walk-in closet. And with the worry that J. W.'s memory was diminishing and that his temper occasionally flared, putting him in closer proximity to family was a priority.

At the boarding house he'd always found someone to chat with, or found someone with whom he could start up a poker game so he could win his share of their M&Ms. He could also have had the landlady cut his hair, but he said she clipped hair as if she were shoeing mules. So her grandfather Henry had picked him up every few weeks for that. It had given them a chance to have lunch and spend some time together. Now he didn't have his boarding house cronies to spend time with and that made family visits extra special. Although Henry would occasionally drop him off at his prior residence for the day for a poker game or two.

So far, in the years that J. W. had been back at the Henry Tucker home, the situation had worked out well. J. W. feigned resentment at times, but he enjoyed being back with family. He missed his wife Grace, of course. She had passed many years previously after sharing a long, loving life with J. W., their four children, a host of grandchildren and getting to know some of their great-grandchildren. He didn't dwell on the pain of her passing, but he thought of her often.

Phoebe hung up, waited a few minutes, tidied her small kitchen, then dialed again. Someone other than either of her grandparents answered the phone on the other end. Initially concerned at the stranger's voice on the line, the girl identified herself as Abigail, her grandmother's helper that came in a couple of times a month to help straighten the house. She also said she was going to be helping with the upcoming birthday party being planned in the family as well so Ms. Julia wouldn't have to work so hard. She sounded young, teenage-ish. Phoebe relaxed, knowing her grandmother had probably taken pity on a local high-school girl or a friend's granddaughter looking for extra money for the upcoming summer.

Phoebe told Abigail who she was and who she was trying to reach. Politely she said, "Hold on, please." Phoebe heard her calling out, "J. W., your great-granddaughter is on the phone." A pause. "No, this phone. But this phone is the same line as the one in your room." Some shuffling noises, then, "Oh, for heaven's sake, J. W., she's on this phone right here. Are you coming?"

Phoebe waited another minute in silence. Then Abigail said, "Hello?"

"Yes."

"I'm sorry, Ms. Tucker, J. W. said he didn't want to talk to anybody *out here*, so he's going to call you back."

"Did you tell him it's Phoebe?"

"Yes, I was writing it down when I answered. He was out there on the porch, looking through some old travel magazines." Phoebe smiled. There was no impatience in the girl's voice, only a degree of amusement at the temerity of an elderly man roaming the house and still doing as he pleased.

"Okay, thank you. Did he tell you to call him J. W.?" Phoebe asked curiously.

"Oh, yes. He said he didn't want me getting him mixed up with his son and daughter-in-law."

"That sounds like him. Abigail, where are my grandparents?"

"Oh, they went out to the grocery store. J. W. said he didn't want to go with. He did tell them to make sure they brought home some ice cream though. And some whiskey." Phoebe detected the lighthearted nature of her remark, and appreciated it.

Phoebe laughed lightly. "Yeah, that sounds like J. W. Okay, thank you. If I don't hear from him soon I'll call back. Thanks again."

Phoebe hung up and laughed. She was picturing the teenager, maybe she was a little older, waving J. W. closer and J. W. stubbornly shaking his head and holding up a magazine as if to say, *Nope... busy!* She realized how much she missed her great-grandfather.

After waiting twenty minutes she tried again. The phone rang five times. At the beginning of the sixth ring Phoebe held the receiver away from her ear, experience having taught her to expect the loud voice on the other end. "Phoebe, that you?" J. W. practically shouted into the phone.

Phoebe smiled at the sound of his voice, feeling more guilt than she had expected at not having spoken to him in several months. "J. W., you're shouting. Stop it. Neither one of us is deaf and you know it." She smiled again. She was the only one who got away with speaking to him in a matter-of-fact way. Their special bond had begun as far back as she could remember and had never faded; no one understood it, not even themselves. It just existed.

J. W.'s volume decreased a mite but he still spoke louder than normal. Phoebe knew he was a bit hard of hearing. She also knew that he knew it. It didn't matter.

"Don't think you're such a big bug, little lady." Phoebe stifled a giggle.

"I would never. So you're having a party, huh? Can I come?"

"Hmm..." As if he were thinking it over. Phoebe heard some noises, clunking, some static, and wondered if J. W. had accidentally hung up the phone. Then she heard him breathing into the phone again, heard him exhale a deep sigh.

"J. W.?" There was obvious concern in her voice.

"Oh, what? Can't an old man sit down to talk on the phone without the world thinking he's dropped dead? For crying out... What?" He yelled.

About to question him, Phoebe paused, hearing someone speak at the other end of the line.

"I don't know. I'll let you know when I'm good and ready." More shifting, rustling. Phoebe waited. He mumbled something to himself about not knowing what he wanted for lunch yet and that he wished she'd stop bugging him.

"Hey J. W., back to the party," she stated simply, never one to patronize him.

"When are you coming?"

Phoebe smiled into the phone. She closed her eyes, pictured J. W.'s face and could easily envision his light layer of whiskers. Memories: tickling her with that five o'clock shadow and making her giggle, frowning and pointing his finger at her in mock admonishment from across a crowded room to elicit a giggle, smiling when no one was looking when she revealed her fearless bareback skills, sharing the same taste in foods that most others in the family thought odd, the random few words to calm her after a childhood disaster.

She opened her eyes, not wanting to keep him waiting for an answer. An answer she knew bore no serious consideration. It was J. W. and there could be only one answer. He had to already know it, but he also needed to hear it.

"I'm coming, J. W. I'll be there a couple days ahead of time, okay?"

"Good," he said gruffly. "I'd hate to have to put you over my knee." The call ended on his end with a crash.

Phoebe laughed. And laughed. And realized she had tears in her eyes for the great-grandfather she missed, adored and loved so dearly.

3

Henry Tucker's home was situated on the northwest side of the small town of Minden, Nevada, just south of Carson City. It had been a rural property when he and his wife had acquired it from it's previous owners a year after their marriage and it remained a rural property today. On it was built a sixty-year-old, four bedroom farm house situated on close to forty acres. The main barn no longer held horses or other animals, neither did the smaller, secondary barn. Since his grandchildren had grown older, Henry now used the larger barn and outbuildings for storage instead.

Phoebe had enjoyed riding, had been a natural on horseback. Will, not so much. The twins, Tony and Troy, the oldest of Phoebe's siblings, had ridden too, but just as an occasional pastime when they were kids. Henry's wife, Julia, had never been especially enamored with the beasts despite having grown up in a rural area. Of all the grandchildren of Henry Tucker they had lived the closest. They still did, except for Phoebe, and her siblings visited the most often because of it. The family was a close-knit one nonetheless.

The home of Henry John Tucker, son of J. W. Tucker, was to be the location of the birthday party for J. W. Since it was a family party, that is, quite informal, Hank and his wife, Bonnie, were sending out the invitations and taking note of who was able to attend. Henry and Julia were simply supplying the location. They had room in the old farm house, places for parking, for family that wanted to spend the weekend and J. W. now lived there. It was all very low key, casual and, well, Tucker-ish.

It had been J. W.'s idea for his own birthday party. He had told his family a few years ago that he wanted to have one more big family birthday party but he would choose the timing. As mysterious as that had sounded, no one thought it odd, not for J. W. At his age they supposed he could do as he pleased, and having a birthday party wasn't an outlandish request. He said he would notify them when he thought it was time. He had said the time had come, albeit a month before his real birthday, so let the planning begin. He stated simply that he wanted 'everybody to come,' and that he wanted barbecue. He had even insisted it be at his son's home, what he now called home. No one had truly argued the point.

Thinking of it now made Henry chuckle, knowing the salient point was true; at this point in his life J. W. could ask for whatever he wanted; and he would always get it.

This wasn't the only family that Phoebe and her siblings had. J. W. and his wife Grace, now gone, had had four children in total. His oldest son was Henry, Phoebe's grandfather. Then had come a son that had died in infancy. Next was a daughter, Joanna, who had passed away a few years ago. She'd been married and had three children of her own, was also a grandmother, and had become a great-grandmother not long after she had passed away. The youngest of J. W.'s children was William who currently lived in Texas. He was married, had two children and was also a grandfather.

Some of Phoebe's aunts, uncles, and cousins were attending the party as well, although Phoebe wasn't sure which ones had returned positive responses yet. Family gatherings tended to be extremely casual in their family. There was usually a different group every time the family met. Whoever couldn't make it to one gathering usually ended up at the next one.

But this time was different: a special gathering and important to the family. J. W. was aging. Every gathering with J. W. present was special to them. And like her father Hank had said when they'd last talked on the phone, who knew how many more times she would get to see J. W.

Phoebe had asked her great-grandfather his age when mention of the party had been broached. But she'd been told a couple of different wandering answers that didn't include numbers. She didn't think J. W. really wanted anyone to know exactly how old he was although she couldn't think of a good reason why not. Surely he knew, she thought with a smile.

Phoebe remembered when her great-grandmother Grace had passed away. She herself had been young. Her great-grandmother had been near eighty. Not that unusual. She retained small memories of running into Grace's arms when an uncle or cousin had been playing with her and chasing her. She remembered the perfume she'd worn and how she always had open arms for hugs.

Her thoughts shifted again to her great-grandfather. J. W. had an impeccable memory. But sometimes she wondered if he found it difficult to concentrate on the present. Sometimes his mind seemed to wander, as if he were repeatedly reliving events in his past. It was at those times, when she was aware that J. W. was in a moment of reflection that must include warm memories of his wife Grace, that Phoebe disliked bringing up the past. Remembering must bring such sadness, especially when one lived to be as old as J. W. and saw so many acquaintances leave you behind.

And it must be a strange feeling to see your kids grow up, have kids of their own, see those kids grow up and have kids of their own, and so on.

At times he looked sad, despite the fact he said he wasn't. He would be lost in thought, staring out the same window of the old farm house, with what she took as a reminiscent smile on his face. It had been years since Phoebe had seen her great-grandfather with that look on his face and heard the ramblings of a lonely man.

She shook herself to rid her mind of the vision. And of the guilt at having been away from home so long.

Mind shift again, a to-do list. So much to do. She plopped down in her comfy chair again to make a list. First a mental list then write it down.

Jumbled thoughts, thrown together in a hazy fog. A galloping horse stopping suddenly to look at her wide-eyed. The sound of gunshots echoing off canyon walls, or was it a car backfiring. Surely Phoebe knew the difference. Pounding, banging, what *was* that? Just a noise in her head, demanding to get out, to get her to wake up. Someone at the door? No, louder that that. Running, soggy shoes and cold feet. Yuck, what an uncomfortable feeling. Squishy socks that would take forever to dry out. Put them by the fireplace, but be very careful. The urgent need for a drink of water, to get that awful taste out of her mouth. She licked her lips, so thirsty. Someone pushed her and she fell...

Phoebe woke with a start, jerked awake, feeling like she was falling, almost feeling the pain of the hit from behind, landing on the palms of her hands and banging her forehead on the ground. Frowning in consternation she stood up quickly, dizzy, not quite awake from her quick nap in her comfy chair. "I hate when that happens," she said aloud, frustrated and not able to shake the feeling that the dreamy visions had felt real and that she had left something undiscovered.

She'd begun her to-do list in her head, a pen and notepad in her hands, not a single word written on it. The daydreaming had begun, like thoughts of leaving her job and never seeing what's-his-name-with-the-broken-headlight-that-will-probably-call-the-cops-on-me again. *Maybe I should send him a check for twenty bucks before I go.* She'd started looking forward to seeing her family, her brothers, her parents, everyone. Then she'd drifted off to sleep. *I did not have enough coffee this morning.*

Dreams are weird. They rarely make sense. She was thinking about home too much. She'd been looking up at her wall of books when she dozed off. That was it, her history and anthropology books. She knew what all the titles and subjects were even without reading them all again. Her books she couldn't bear to be rid of, books she'd poured over endlessly, unintentionally memorizing pictures and captions, charts and text interesting to few others. Those books were to blame for her rambling dream. A dream like so many others she'd had of late, since J. W.'s party had risen to the forefront of her brain.

Those books really did have to go.

She paced a few laps, tapping her forehead, once again attempting to organize her thoughts. Notify work; why hadn't she already done that? Attending the party was a foregone conclusion. J. W. was counting on her. Drive or fly; she needed to get an oil change or an airplane ticket. *Pick one already.* Pay her bills ahead of time, the rent wouldn't be due for a couple of weeks. Put a hold on her mail at the post office. How long would she be gone? Put her houseplant in the car with her? She couldn't take it on a plane. Give it to a neighbor? Ask a coworker to water it?

Absentmindedly plopping some cubes from the freezer into a glass and filling it with water, the details of her wandering mind coalesced. Simplify it; *I'm going, there, done.* "As if they'll miss me at work anyway," she scoffed aloud.

She set her glass in the sink, stowed her pad and pen in the junk drawer and called to make arrangements to get the oil changed in her car. Better to have her own transportation when she got where she was going. She put her plant on a table by the front door to take to work for a coworker to care for. Take it early lest she forget. She then wrote a check for twenty dollars to give to that idiot, refusing to even think his name, so he wouldn't have any reason to look her up. And a check for her phone and the electricity to mail at the end of the week.

She would tell work she would be gone at least two full weeks. The time was due to her. And perhaps she wouldn't go back, who knows? The rest? Pack a bag, get money from the bank, lock up, and there you go.

A gift for J. W.? Good grief, what do you get a great-grandfather? She'd think about that later. Maybe ask her brothers, or her parents, what they thought.

The prospect of her trip home was overtaking her mind, distracting her, actually exciting her. And making her apprehensive at the same time. *But why*? she asked herself. Anticipation of an adventure? Having time off work to see friends and family? Well, family anyway. Or was it simply a change in schedule that threw her off balance and gave her too much too think about.

Her brother Will's phone call, helping her, prodding her. Then her Dad calling, his patience and understanding, always more than she felt she deserved. And her talk with J. W.; he had known she was going to be at his birthday celebration. But he was more than simply sure. It was as if they had spoken about it previously. She smiled; J. W. knew her better than she knew herself.

No matter, she told herself. If only I can be so self-assured when I'm a great-grandmother. She smirked to herself. *Me, a great-grandmother. Not when I spend Friday nights watching the Creep Show all by myself, falling asleep with a stupid book in my lap.*

***

The Monday morning drag-yourself-into-work syndrome should be a common ailment in today's Modern Medical Science books, was what Phoebe was actively thinking as she parked her car. She was halfway to the entrance when she had to return to her car just to lock it. And already five minutes late. So be it.

Nobody spoke to her in the mornings until she at least had her coffee in hand. If they did she simply held up a hand and walked on. It hadn't taken them long to catch on to her need for additional morning caffeine. One cup before she arrived simply wasn't enough. Today she'd been rushed and was still waiting for cup number one.

First stop, bosses office. A two minute conversation took care of her two week vacation request. She hadn't taken a single day off since she'd arrived. In fact, her boss had suggested she take a few days off before she accepted the extra assignment for the high-school business class. But she'd been saving her paid time off; she didn't know for what at the time but was now glad she had. Only a couple more weeks until school was out for the summer, and the class ended before that. Then she would be free from that obligation.

Next, asking about her plant. Her closest work friend, Karen, was in her office. Karen was cheerful and friendly and gladly accepted the huge responsibility of plant sitter when it was time for Phoebe to leave. Phoebe did feel obligated to explain why she needed a caretaker for her plant. But the sense of gratitude she felt was mixed with a guilt that passed through her mind at wanting to tell Karen it was none of her business to know where she was going. *What is wrong with me?* So she sat down, explained, and accepted an offer of a quick in-house lunch later that day, just because.

Last stop, dropping off the check to dumb-dumb's office. Quick peek, not in, put the check on the desk, something heavy on top, out fast. *Oh, crap, he's coming.* They passed each other in the short hall. Rich-Rick glanced up and looked away just as quickly, adjusting his tie for a distraction. Phoebe kept walking. There was a notation on the memo of her check for what it was for. If he really wanted to talk to her about it, he knew where to find her.

Her day passed quickly. Lunch with Karen turned out to be a surprisingly pleasant half hour and she was out the door by 5:10, making up for her late start to the day. No business class today. So distracted was she by her upcoming trip out west she wouldn't have noticed if dumb-dumb was following her this time or not.

Tuesday, Wednesday with a class in the afternoon, then Thursday. Then another Friday with a class. And the weekend had rolled around once again. Payday. Always a good day, no matter how much money you made or who you were. The day you feel free, powerful and in charge. Then in the next few days you pay bills, buy groceries and have to start all over again. She shrugged. Still, it's more money than she'd had before she'd graduated college. More than she'd had in her whole life. So where was the pride, the feeling of success, of accomplishment?

Shaking her head, she drove home, away from her stark, tiny office she'd never felt like personalizing, her files and folders, away from dumb-dumb and the dozen office gossips whose names she couldn't even remember, away from a tedious yet well-paying job. She drove home, toward her own belongings, her book shelf and her very comfy chair.

4

Phoebe hurried to get through the door, fumbling with her keys, barely getting to her phone while it was still ringing. She grabbed it quickly, "Hello?" expecting the person on the other end to have given up.

There was a crackling noise and distant mumbling, allowing Phoebe time to set her things down, reach to close her door, then smile, automatically knowing who was on the other end. "J. W. are you there?"

"Yes, I'm here," he said gruffly. "What took you so long?"

"I'm sorry, J. W. I just got home from work. I couldn't find my key."

There was a pause. Then, "Uh-huh, well..."

"Are you okay? What's up?"

"Yes, I'm fine." He paused again. "When are you coming?" He coughed. Concerned about his cough, Phoebe wanted to ask about him again but hesitated, knowing J. W. greatly disliked coddling.

"Soon, J. W. What's with that cough I hear? You been on a five mile jog again?"

She heard a raspy, short laugh. "Don't think I can't if I want to. Your grandmother made me some tea. Some tea, for God's sake. Been choking on it since lunch." He paused to cough again, to show her the culprit was indeed the tea.

"Well, I'm sorry about that. Go get a water chaser." He chuckled at that. "So, J. W., I'll be getting ready to go this evening and leaving in the morning. I'm driving so I'll have my own car. I'll see you in a few days, okay?"

"Are you driving that hunk o' junk you call a car all the way out here? You been paintin' your nose again?"

"J. W., there is nothing wrong with my car. It's five years old and no, I have not been drinking." She smiled at his colorful word choice. "I'll be fine. I'll check in along the way, how's that?

"Sure, sure you do that." He didn't sound convinced.

"Besides, I think I'll enjoy a little time on the road by myself. I need a break."

"Enjoy your peace and quiet while you get it, kiddo." He chuckled again. "All bets are off once the shooting starts."

Now Phoebe laughed. J. W. and his crazy phrases. But she supposed once her family was gathered together they could be a garrulous bunch. "Yes, I suppose it will be quite a party, won't it."

"Party? Oh, yes, the party." J. W. coughed again. This time Phoebe could tell it wasn't quite real.

"J. W. what – "

"I have to go. See you soon."

And that was that.

Tossing and turning in her sleep had never been a problem that belonged to her; tonight it did. Not a good thing when she wanted to start her morning bright and early at five a.m. No concrete thoughts told her what, precisely, was bothering her. Was she dreading going? No. She was looking forward to seeing her parents, Will, her twin brothers Tony and Troy and J. W., among others, including a beautiful niece she'd only seen once when she'd flown home for a quick weekend a little over a year ago.

She was really looking forward to getting away from work. No facts and figures, no more classes, no more dumb-dumb-Honker to avoid. He never did mention getting her check for the broken headlight. But he'd cashed it, so she guessed he wouldn't be turning her in. Had she forgotten to pack something? To turn off something? To turn *in* something? No, that wasn't it. She was thorough, to a fault sometimes. She'd left nothing undone. *Go to sleep!*

She finally drifted off, exhaustion taking hold. When she woke with a start her first thought was that she'd slept through her alarm. No real problem, since she was on her own time table. But a sleepy brain concocted all sorts of disasters from a simple misstep. She stared at her clock and let out a relieved sigh. Four-fifty a.m. Curling back up on her side she drifted off to sleep again for another few minutes. It's amazing how soundly one can go to sleep in just ten minutes.

When she woke to the alarm she smacked it several times to shut off the blaring music that sounded like it was coming from a distance. Dragging herself out of bed to her coffee pot she made a half pot. A full one would have made her stop at the nearest rest stop once she was on the highway. She drank some to perk up, took a quick shower, filled a tall to-go cup with the rest of the coffee, put on a necklace, the one piece of jewelry she wore most often, threw her favorite, many-pocketed, olive-green Army jacket over her arm, ate the last of the grapes in her fridge and she was ready to go. She'd set her bag by the door the night before.

As she was taking a last look around she spied her bookshelf full of treasures. She wouldn't admit it to anyone else but that's what they were to her. Walking toward it she looked them over, knowing where each title and subject was by heart. She took down two of them, quickly stuffed them into the outside pocket of her suitcase and zipped it up all in one fluid movement, as if in doing so she could secretively hide the action, even from herself. Then she was out the door and on her way home.

A few hours on the road and Phoebe arrived in Des Moines, Iowa, a good place to stop for breakfast and gas. It was still early morning and she filled up on pancakes and eggs. And, of course, more coffee. A handful of grapes hadn't taken long to wear off and her belly was growling for more. Energized for a long day of driving she filled her to-go cup again and was back on the road, already enjoying herself. She popped in an eight-track tape and daydreamed her way down the highway.

She stopped for gas again later and grabbed a drink and bag of chips. Maybe her choice of car hadn't been the best; the mileage wasn't great, only a little better than the big boats from a decade ago. But it was a cool car, high off the ground, big tires, and it got her through the winter snow. Her brother Will had been jealous; he'd wanted one a few years ago. Maybe she'd let him drive it when she got to Carson City. She grinned, thinking what she could possibly trade him for the privilege.

She switched back and forth between the radio and different tapes for music. When silence was preferred her mind was, for a time, lost in thought.

Her last stop for gas had been an adventure in the junk food isle, something she seldom shopped for. But hey, this was vacation. Her front passenger seat held a wide variety within easy reach while the floor in front of it held the remains in a paper bag that served as her creatively classic trash can. Not wanting to take any longer than necessary at this point, she stopped for a fast food dinner and kept on.

She stopped for the day in Rock Springs, Wyoming. It had been a long day, and evening, and she'd been ready to call it quits a few hours ago. But this was over half way to her destination and she had no desire to spread this into a three day drive. It was time to find a room and relax for at least a little while. She would check in with family to let them know everything was fine, that she was still alive. A good night's sleep would do her good.

The hotel was a moderate affair, priced right and with a restaurant next door for breakfast the next morning. A time saver. She called her dad and asked him to relay the message to J. W. that she was A-OK. Then she got some ice from the ice machine, grabbed a snack she'd brought in from the car and turned on her television. Relaxing on the bed, alone in the hotel room, nothing from her apartment to distract her, her mind wandered.

Her eyes landed on her suitcase. She unzipped the outer pocket and pulled the two books out halfway. She closed her eyes, imagining her dad, seeing his face, asking her if she was making the right decision about school. She quickly shoved the books back into the pocket and zipped them up with force. *I need sleep.*

She turned off the television, puffed up the pillows, pounded them as if they were guilty of some transgression and buried herself in the covers, pulling them tight under her chin. She closed her eyes tightly against memories as she drifted off to sleep.

It had been too long since she'd been home for a vacation. Phoebe said she had reasons; Will called them excuses. Either way, it became easier the longer she was away. A new job doesn't allow time for getting away easily, especially when that job is on the other side of the country from the place you'd like to visit.

Her various part-time jobs while in college hadn't allowed her to save much money, so she couldn't afford traveling far. Yes, her parents had paid for a couple of visits back then, but Phoebe figured that since college graduation and being on her own, really on her own, the obligation to pay for trips was hers alone. She had insisted. *Stubborn girl,* she now called herself. Will had called her an idiot. *Brothers.*

In her heart and mind she knew she needed to go home. Was it really a vacation when it was returning home, to family, to a place that felt so familiar? To a place that was going to remind her of her mistakes? No, she had done the right thing, she was sure of it. She was good at what she did, disciplined, exacting, meticulous, organized. All the traits of a business person. But when somebody asked her what she did for a living why did she feel her face screw up into an odd sort of smile, a grimace of doubt, and avoid the answer by asking her own question or pretending she didn't hear in the first place.

"So, what do you do? Something interesting, I'm sure."

The grimace: "I'm sorry, what did you say, is that a dog barking? I really like your shoes, are they new?" My friends are behind me... A bunch of people are taking the same classes... Why hadn't she just answered, *"I'm in business, doesn't that sound tragic! Well it is, it's God-awful, if you really want to know..."*

With an audible giggle Phoebe woke herself up. She'd been dreaming again, envisioning herself at a dinner party, oh yes, she attended so many of those, and answering personal questions posed by the elegantly dressed hostess. The shocked look on the face of the hostess had prompted the giggle which woke her at three a.m. She walked to the bathroom, got a quick drink of water and turned on the light beside the bed. Then, not being able to help herself, she retrieved one of the books from her suitcase.

The hotel front desk telephoned with Phoebe's wake-up call at five-thirty a.m., sharp. She answered it sleepily, sounding more grumpy than she intended. She thanked the clerk, absentmindedly thinking they must hear many grumpy people on the other end of early morning calls. Yawning and stretching she was ready in fifteen minutes, having only spent the night. Her book from the prior evening lay open at the foot of the bed. She closed it carefully and placed it back in the zippered pocket. Check out. Breakfast. On the road again by six forty-five.

She stopped in West Wendover, Nevada for gas and a quick lunch at a local cafe. She was welcomed with a warm smile and a hot cup of coffee and a waitress that asked how her day was going as if she were a neighbor that stopped in every day. As Phoebe waited for her breakfast and enjoying her view out the cafe window she realized that even though she was still hours from home, this didn't look like Illinois or Iowa anymore.

Yes, she'd been driving westward for over a day now. No, she hadn't paid attention that closely to the view out her front windshield. Was she driving like she lived her life; with tunnel vision? Putting on blinders as to the big picture that was life going on around her? Was she simply going through the motions day to day, not investing too deeply in emotional or physical attachments?

It was late spring, or what kids already called summer because school was out. Early June. No more winter coats, no more boots, no gloves and hats or shoveling of snow and scraping of ice. Yes, it got cold in Carson City. No, not as cold as where she'd just driven from. Yes, the change of seasons was colorful in Illinois and Iowa. No, the rolling green of farmer's crops didn't cover the landscape from east to west and north to south in the higher elevations and arid regions of Nevada where the ice age had neglected to deposit mother nature's beloved black earth. She saw the differences when she looked, really looked, and thought about the new life she had slowly become accustomed to.

She couldn't see the Carson range from here but she knew it was approaching as she drove. She knew it was up ahead; the division between Carson City and Lake Tahoe. The scenic backdrop to her hometown. Smooth and green this time of year, the little snow they received having melted with the warmth of the sun, the rolling mountains keeping one company when traveling from north to south as the mountains joined their parent, the Sierra Nevada range.

She remembered the smell of the clear spring air, the touch of the prickly sage near her parent's home, the feel of the thick, lush grass under her feet where her grandparents lived in the valley. She couldn't describe any of these specific sensations from Dubuque. Nor did she possess any truly fond memories associated with her new place of residence. Why would she? She hadn't been there that long, after all. And was that so bad? *Nothing wrong with starting fresh, right?*

The waitress plopped down her lunch of a turkey sub with a side of fruit, chips and a cola, and asked if Phoebe needed anything else. "No, that's enough, don't you think?" she asked with a light laugh.

The waitress smiled back and said, "Well we have some great cheesecake at all hours. Just let me know." Half an hour later, having passed on dessert, Phoebe headed to her car to continue her westward journey. But not before leaving a large tip on the table for her friendly waitress.

Trying to time her stops just so, seeing as she knew the distance between stations was greater here than it was in the Midwest, she stopped for gas in Winnemucca, Nevada, called her dad to check in, and continued. She switched her eight-track tape once again, turned it louder, and rolled down her windows a few inches to let in some fresh air.

The noise from having the windows down forced her to turn up the music and with her hair blowing all around and a candy bar in hand she sang along at the top of her lungs. A car passed her on the left, eyeing her as she flipped her hair out of her eyes and bopped her head up and down to the rhythm of the song. She smiled at the other driver, he drove on, and she laughed. If Rick-Rich-Honker could see her now she suspected he wouldn't even think about asking her out.

When she had listened to the tape make it around twice she turned it off, rolled up the windows and drove on in the quiet for awhile. The road passed quickly beneath her tires now. It was flat, mostly straight and she daydreamed her way through many more miles, feeling more and more that home was just around the bend.

She pulled into a gas station and convenience store just past Fernley with only a little over an hour to go. So why was she stopping? Get a drink, bathroom break, stretch her legs... No, not any of those. She did walk around a bit. It had been a long couple of days. Before getting back in the car she leaned against it and stared southwest. Carson City was over there, not far now. Before long she would be driving down highway fifty, past the gun range where she'd excelled as a teen, into the center of town, turning south and then west toward the canyon and pulling into her parent's driveway. She was stalling and she knew it. Sighing, she got back into her car and pulled back onto the highway.

Even closer now. Phoebe knew the Carson River was snaking along beside her, on her left, even though she couldn't quite see it from this distance over the flat land. A broad curve left, then a broad curve right, and the straightaway leading into Carson City was before her.

This was the once famous Highway 50, also named Lincoln Highway. It was the longest highway in the nation leading east to west, coast to coast, and had once been known as, "The Main Street Across America." The road remained, now merging with others, renamed as it narrowed and broadened or was detoured to re-emerge elsewhere. But it was the same road. A grand achievement of early nineteenth century engineering.

The Carson range was clearly in view, had been for many miles now. She supposed some thought it easy to get lost in this sparsely populated part of the country. But the landscape, hills and mountains were always there to guide a visitor. Yet if a person found themselves turned around and disoriented they could also be unforgiving. Even this close to home her mind was wandering instead of enjoying the coming couple of weeks with her family.

Carson Street, a stop light. Phoebe felt conspicuous. Two pedestrians were crossing the street in front of her. They smiled and waved a hand in thanks. She smiled back, remembering how easily people here thanked drivers for stopping when it's what they were supposed to do in the first place.

She was turning left and realized the light had turned. At home she might have been honked at from behind for the delay. She held up her hand in apology and was greeted with a similar greeting from the car behind her. It was no problem. A small kindness much appreciated.

Through town, a couple of more turns, a right turn on King Street, one of the original, historic streets in Carson City. It didn't look quite the same as it had a hundred years ago, but a few of the buildings remained. This area was where the historic homes and buildings were, before the town spread out in later years. The old mint on Carson Street was now the Nevada State Museum, open to the public and tours. The Governor's Mansion was a huge affair in the middle of a neighborhood and the Nevada State

Capital Building had remained in its original location for the last one hundred and nine years.

Now a couple more miles on King Street, which became Kings Canyon Road once out of town. Almost there. Phoebe's parents, Hank and Bonnie, lived off the main road, ahead a bit, out in the desert. They were waiting for her, expecting her. She noticed the tight grip of her hands on the steering wheel and took them off one at a time to wipe the moisture that had developed there on her pant leg. One last right turn, up the dirt road, into the driveway.

Phoebe pulled to a stop in front of the house, a large sprawling ranch with a patch of watered green grass in front and flowers in pots around the front porch, both a touch of mother nature arranged by her mother in the dry, arid region.

No sooner had she shifted her car into park and removed her keys than her parents burst through the front door and flung themselves at her as if they hadn't seen her in years. With guilt she realized it had been a long time. But here she was, back to where she grew up, closer to family.

Her mother kissed both cheeks and squeezed her so tight Phoebe giggled. Her father wrapped his arms around her in a warm, gentle bear hug that she gladly accepted. Quietly, he said, "You're home."

"Yeah, Dad, I'm home."

5

Walking into her parent's house, the house she had also lived in not all that long ago, brought back warm memories for Phoebe. It also brought her suppressed guilt closer to the surface. While away it had been easier to avoid thinking of the household climate the week she had left for college, and after she had made certain decisions without consultation. Being home, so close to her dad, hearing his voice, seeing his face, his expressions... It was still good to be home.

She carried her suitcase into her old room, put her favorite jacket over one of the two new guest beds, and went back out into the kitchen. Pouring herself a cup of coffee her mother had brewed on seeing her pull up the road, she walked back and forth, stretching her legs, not wanting to sit quite yet, although driving all day had indeed exhausted her.

She and her parents talked while her mother put the final touches on a quick dinner for the three of them. Phoebe closed her eyes, inhaled and smiled. When she opened her eyes her mother was looking at her, so she said, "Why does it smell so good when someone else is doing the cooking?" Bonnie laughed.

Around nine o'clock the front door opened and closed loudly. "Hey," someone called out.

Bonnie scowled, Phoebe grinned and called back, "Hey, yourself. Stop yelling and come in here to talk." She looked at her mother, who had always told her children to enter a room before speaking or go to someone before calling them for dinner, and winked. Of course, they had still yelled down the hall, through the house or out across the yard. Now they did it for fun.

"You're not even going to get up to give me a hug?" said her 'little' brother Will, smiling broadly and spreading his arms wide.

Phoebe shrugged. "I'm tired. You come hug me." He laughed and yanked her up from the couch. Phoebe yelped, and he gave her a brotherly squeeze. Then he shoved her back onto the couch.

"Hey, Mom. Where's Dad?"

"Hey, yourself. Outside. Didn't you see him? Oh that's right, Phoebe moved her car round back. He's looking at Phoebe's Scout. He's been obsessed with those things since she bought it, same as you. Go on." She excused him.

"You I can talk to later," he pointed at Phoebe. "There's a car waiting." Will left through the back door. They heard him say, "Dad, there you are..."

Phoebe and her mother talked awhile longer, Phoebe reclining on the couch on a couple of comfy pillows, tired from the last couple of days. The fresh breeze coming in through the open windows was relaxing her and making her sleepy. Her father and Will came in from outside, chatting easily. "Time for pie?" her dad asked hopefully.

Bonnie said, "I think Phoebe's too tired."

Will picked up a pillow from a chair and flung it at his sister. "Phfft. Nobody's ever too tired for pie." The pillow hit Phoebe in the face.

Phoebe, tired and a bit cranky at this point, retrieved the pillow and flung it back at her brother, frowning. She sat up, yawning and rubbing her eyes. "Thanks, Mom. I'd love some dessert."

She stood, walked past Will, stuck out her tongue at him and walked into the kitchen. "Darn, I wanted your piece," he said.

An hour later Phoebe was dozing on the couch to the sound of her family talking. Will had stopped by to see his big sister on the night of her homecoming. He now told his parents he would see them soon and went home. The party for J. W. was in a couple of days and he would catch up with her before then, and in the days following, before she returned to Iowa. He wished she didn't live so far away.

***

The smell of coffee, the sunlight filtering through the curtains on her old bedroom window; both aided Phoebe in slowly waking up, snuggling under the covers because she had left her window open a few inches last night. She never did that in her apartment in Iowa. Her bedroom window had balcony access and her building was in a busy area of town. Was Dubuque a trustworthy Midwestern place to live? Yes, or she wouldn't have moved there. But here, out in the Canyon, away from town, in her old house... She supposed it was just because it was where she had lived when she was small, her parents were here and that she loved the smell of the country air. The cool air moved through her room and she wrapped a thick sweater around herself as she went to the kitchen for some wakeup coffee.

Her mother had made a big breakfast, something she did when people visited, but there was also a box of assorted pastries on the counter. She headed directly for it, oohing and ahhing. Her dad, reading the newspaper and sipping coffee eyed her over the top. "The breakfast of champions," he teased.

"You bet," she mumbled with a mouthful of glazed donut. She got a plate and accepted a couple of pancakes, eggs and bacon and sat across from her dad.

"You going to eat all of that?"

She frowned. "Um, yeah. Get your own." She scooted her plate closer to herself and he smiled.

"I see you're used to living on your own. Did you see that, Bonnie? She nearly took my finger off," he said as he went back to reading his paper.

Phoebe smiled. Yes, she had missed her dad. When they had finished with breakfast and Phoebe was helping her mother clean up the kitchen, she asked, “Taking off work today, Dad?”

He shook his head, “No, just going in a little late. They can do without me for a couple of hours. Taking off tomorrow and a couple of days next week though. I wanted to see you this morning.”

“You’re stuck with me until I go home, you know.”

“Yes, I know, but once the family gets together, there’s no talking to any one person for long. You know that.”

She nodded her head and smiled, remembering fondly. “Yes, I know.”

“Come on, let’s take a walk.”

Oh boy, she thought. *Maybe I’m going to finally get that Dad Talk.*

They stepped out the back door onto the brick patio. It was a large rectangle surrounded by a low brick wall enclosing a central table and chairs, a couple of small tables and a few of her mother’s planters overflowing with flowers. An awning stuck out from the house at one end allowing escape from the direct sun. No trees here, in this yard, like there was in Iowa. Phoebe perched on the low wall while her father stood, looking out over the land at the back of their home. They couldn’t see their nearest neighbor.

“Okay, what is it, Dad? Get it over with.”

“Don’t be so defensive.” He turned toward her. “I just want to know that you’re happy.” He paused, looking at her, holding her gaze until she looked away. He sat down in one of the patio chairs.

Sighing, he began, “When you were little you had two older brothers who were the same age. Being twins I wondered if they would pick on you, leave you out. I was ready to step in, if I had to. As was your mother. But they loved you so much. It was like you were their new little doll. That is, until you learned to talk.” He paused, remembering, and smiled. “They started coming to us to tell on you, instead of the other way around. I stopped worrying about you, at least at home. Then along came your brother

Will, you started school and all of you together were one great, close group of little monsters."

Phoebe smiled. "But?"

Hank shook his head, afraid he was losing track of his message to her. "There's no but." He paused. "As you all got older, well, you had twin brothers that stuck together like glue. You had a younger brother who wanted to do everything they did. Then there was you. At first I was worried about you, afraid you would feel left out."

"Why, because I was a girl?" He didn't miss the tone in her voice.

He shook his head quickly, "No, no. Because you were so determined not to fit in."

Phoebe started to speak but her father held up his hand. Wait. She did.

He continued, "Your mother said to let it go, it was part your personality, and parts of it would change a million times before you grew up. She was right, of course, she always is." He smiled again; so did Phoebe. "By the time you graduated high-school I wanted to be sure you were making choices for yourself, not only to defy someone or someone else's beliefs. Do you know what I mean?"

Phoebe walked over to sit in the chair next to her father. She scooted closer, looped her arm through his and leaned her head on his shoulder. "I think I do, Dad. I – " She paused, thinking her next words over carefully, something she should do more often. "You're still worried I did the wrong thing."

Another minute passed. She said nothing more so Hank asked, "Did you?"

Her father had rarely had talks with her. He usually got his point across in a sentence or two. Obviously this subject had been on his mind for as long as it had been on hers. And now that he was discussing it with her, bringing up what she had thought a subject long dead, here she was, the girl who usually couldn't hold her tongue, finding it difficult to get the words out of her mouth that she had wanted to say to him long ago. She inhaled, paused, then said quietly, "No."

They sat in silence a moment longer until Hank said, "I was just talking about you eating too many donuts." Phoebe laughed, her voice shaking with relief, confident in knowing their lines of communication hadn't been shut down after all.

She turned in her chair and hugged him, still finding it difficult to find the right words. "I thought all this time you were mad at me, even though Will told me you weren't. I was afraid, I don't know why."

"Mad at you," he stated quietly, shaking his head 'no.' He pushed her back to look at her. "You know it's not like you can't change your mind again."

Quickly considering this and all the implications, Phoebe said, "But that's not going to happen. What's done is done, and I think it turned out for the best."

He looked down at her hands and held them a moment. He seemed to want to say more but all he said was, "Okay, Phoebe. But like I said once before, as long as you've really thought it through, and as long as you think you'll be happy."

Phoebe spent the rest of the day with her mother, looking at the checklist of RSVPs and catching up on the lives of those that would be coming for the weekend that she hadn't been in touch with in the last couple of years. Phoebe saw the latest pictures of her niece, Kimberly. Sandy hair, brown eyes, button nose; Phoebe had her six-month and more recent one-year picture on her fridge at home but couldn't wait to see her in person for the first time since she'd been a newborn. Her brother Troy and sister-in-law Diane had been married for several years and had been beyond excited to welcome little Kimberly. She suspected, juvenile as it seemed, that Tony and his wife Clara would soon follow suit. Twins you know.

As it turned out, most everyone in the immediate family would be coming, some staying with Phoebe's parents, some with her grandparents at the farmhouse in Minden, and most of the others would be in the hotels in Carson City, not far away. With guilt, Phoebe found out through conversation with her mother that day that her aunts, uncles and cousins had been in touch regarding J. W.'s upcoming birthday party more frequently and thoroughly than had Phoebe. So distant had she been, both physically and emotionally, that remorse took hold of her now, causing a pain of dereliction in her gut.

Surely her family had known she would be there. J. W. had known she was coming. Her parents had probably made excuses for her lack of communication. She held her forehead in her hands and apologized to her mother. "Phoebe, you're imagining things. What's on your mind?"

"Mom, do you think I ran away when I went to college?"

"Where's all this coming from?" She sat down across from Phoebe at the kitchen table. "Because you're busy?"

"And across the country, and don't keep in touch much." She fidgeted with her coffee napkin.

"No. I don't think you ran away. But I do still think you have things to figure out. And only you can do that." She patted Phoebe's hand and stood up do something else.

Phoebe nodded, acknowledging her mother's words. "Dad said you're always right."

Bonnie turned quickly to face Phoebe. "He said that? Well... He could tell me that once in a while, don't ya think?" She winked at her daughter.

In the late afternoon a commotion outside drew their attention. Mary, Hank's sister from Albuquerque, and her husband George, arriving from the airport in Reno, had pulled up in front of the house honking and yelling, "Hey, anybody home, we're here."

Bonnie and Phoebe rushed outside, eager to greet family, and Phoebe was delighted to see that her cousin Jody had come with her aunt and uncle on the same plane. Greetings, talking, carrying bags, laughing, hugs. Phoebe insisting Jody would be sharing her room as she had done on other visits.

Later on, when Hank returned home, they ordered dinner for pick-up, talked of the party, of other family joining them and looked at some of the family pictures

Bonnie had had out on the coffee table. Bonnie had called her sons earlier to tell them of Mary's arrival and Will walked through the door just as they were getting out dishes.

Tony and Clara, and Troy and Diana with little Kimberly in tow, entered in one loud group together about fifteen minutes after that. Phoebe jumped up to rush to greet them all. Diana was holding Kimberly, who held back a bit from the stranger strangling her daddy. But it didn't take long for her to warm up to the household.

The assemblage spilled out into the other rooms and onto the patio after Phoebe's mother made coffee. Kimberly was choosing her favorite rocks from the edge of the yard and collecting them in a plastic bucket her Grandpa Hank kept handy just for her. She brought a shiny one to Phoebe for approval. Phoebe laughed. "Oh, I think you've found gold in this one for sure." The little girl smiled and mumbled something incoherently, placing it in Phoebe's lap.

Troy said, "She likes you. The shiny ones are her favorites." He paused and sat down by Phoebe. "So where've you been stranger? Forget about us?"

She knew he'd bring up her absence from home eventually. "Do you really have to pick on me right now?"

"Do you really have to avoid talking about why you moved across the country? We miss you, you little runt." He took a drink of his coffee and she saw the whimsical look in his eyes.

She sighed and looked away but he saw the small smile first. "It's – " she stopped and gestured all around her with an arm, "this place."

He raised his eyebrows, questioning, waiting for more.

She pointed a finger at his chest. "And you." She stood up and walked away but her brother laughed.

He followed her across the patio and said from behind her, "Nice try. But I know you've always loved *'this place.'* And some day," he started to walk away, "you're going to admit it."

She hadn't meant to stir up anything with with Troy. She was very happy to see all of her family, to play with little Kimberly, hold her little hand and get a big goodnight hug from that sweet-smelling, sleepy little angel when they left for the evening. It had been a great evening, with several more days and nights just like it ahead now that she had several days off and more family to see.

Once again her words and actions hovered just out of reach of reasonable explanation as she lay in bed staring at the ceiling. Why did her return home trouble her so?

Tomorrow was Friday and the rest of the family would be arriving throughout the day. Many were taking the day, the weekend and extra days off for J. W.'s party. It was going to be busy. Fun busy. Phoebe, her mother, her aunt Mary and Jody were going to Minden to see about last minute arrangements, take supplies and see if Phoebe's grandparents, Henry and Julia, needed any last minute help. A few others would be there to help with the set-up as well. The party was on Saturday. And Phoebe couldn't wait any longer to see J. W.

6

"Rise and shine, sweet cakes." Phoebe remembered, too late, how Jody was a bright and shiny type of morning person. She thought perhaps her cousin would have slept in, having been tired from a day of travel. No such luck.

A pillow landed softly on Phoebe's face. Not in the mood, Phoebe lay motionless for a moment, then rolled over to her side without removing the pillow.

"Oh, come on, cous', get up. Lots to do today." Jody plopped on the bed at her cousin's feet and set the bed shaking.

Phoebe sat upright, flung the pillow from atop her face across the room, and scowled at her younger cousin. "Don't ever wake me up like this again, got it? Now get off my bed, and get out," she said with irritation. Phoebe grabbed the blanket edges, threw herself down onto the bed and pulled the covers over her head.

"Geez, you're still a grouch in the morning." Jody bounced off the bed and went to the door, picking up the pillow from the floor. "First donut's for me," she said before the tossed the pillow back at Phoebe and closed the bedroom door as quickly as she could.

Phoebe didn't move for another half an hour.

When she emerged from her room her hair was a ruffled mess, her soft sweater was hanging from her shoulders loosely and she shuffled to the coffee pot. She took a donut from the box, took a bite that was too big for her mouth, glanced at her dad, saw he was looking at her over his newspaper and said "Wha'?"

Hank grinned and shook his head. "Good morning, sunshine."

She shuffled out to the patio and took a seat in one of the chairs, and, wrapping her sweater around her in the cool morning air, looked out on the open land. Hank walked up from behind and kissed her on the cheek. "I'm leaving on an errand for your mother. I heard you're going to your grandpa's today."

Phoebe, still sleepy, simply nodded. "Good. I know they'll all be happy to see you. And lighten up on your cousin, would you?"

She didn't say anything on that subject but decided perhaps she could have been a bit more patient. Then her father told her, "Jody's brothers, Roger and James, are meeting you over there too. I think Tony and Troy might be there later. See you in a bit."

"Hey Dad?" she asked before he walked away.

"Yeah, Pheeb."

She hesitated but her honest streak caused her to blurt out, "In Dubuque I had a co-worker that wouldn't leave me alone."

"Okay." He waited for more.

"Does that worry you?"

"You'll always be my little girl, I'll always wonder if you're all right." He stood waiting because he didn't think she was finished with the subject. After another few moments he asked, "So what did you do?"

"I bashed in one of his headlights with my baseball bat." She sipped her coffee.

"Did he leave you alone after that?"

"Yep."

"Good. See you later, then." He patted her on the shoulder and walked toward the house.

Phoebe grinned into her next sip of coffee. Her conscience was clear. At least with regard to the subject of the car headlight. His words, '*as long as you've really thought it through, and as long as you think you'll be happy,'* bounced around in her brain. Since the approach drive into Carson City those words hadn't left her alone.

Bonnie got word a little later that more of the family had arrived and had checked in at various places in town. Her cousin Jody's brother was staying in town with his wife and her other brother, James. Jody was the youngest in that family. The rest of the extended family would catch up at the party.

Around ten they put a few things in the car for the drive south to Minden. Phoebe had offered to drive and grabbed her Army jacket at the last minute to ward off the morning chill. Seated in the back seat behind Bonnie, her cousin said as they bounced along, "I can't believe you drove all the way here from Iowa. Why didn't you fly?"

Phoebe shrugged. "I like to drive. I have my car now that I'm here, I can come and go as I please. Why not?"

Jody made a face, clearly not fully appreciating the freedom. She was several years younger than Phoebe, still lived at her parents home, had a part time job and an old car of her own. Cousins they may be, but their differences were many. "Well, I like flying. It's fun. That was my second time. Have you flown before, Phoebe?"

"Yes, a few times. The last was when Kimberly was born. I flew home for the weekend to see her." She remembered having come home then, a little over a year ago. It had been a quick trip, congratulating her brother and sister-in-law, delivering a baby gift, getting to see and hold her beautiful new niece who was as perfect as perfect could be.

She had been distracted from her own problems, enticed by what real life was and how the future was a tangible thing to be seen through the eyes of a baby. No time to think about anything else before heading back to the airport and getting back to a job that paid the bills.

They talked for a few minutes about Kimberly's advancements, her adorable toddler achievements, the way Troy had somehow turned back into a boy when she had come along. The subject made her wish she lived closer, if only to see Kimberly more often. She was a cute little thing.

The drive to Minden wasn't long. Soon they left the city limits of Carson City, began the drive through the Carson Valley and Phoebe rolled down her window to let in the wonderful early summer air that she loved. The forecast didn't change much here this time of year, and the weather was mostly predictable. The next few weeks ahead the temperature would rise a few degrees slowly during the day, the nights would be cool and refreshing. There wasn't much rainfall in the month of June and the days were sunny. Perhaps this break was exactly what she had needed.

They passed the Carson River, driving by herds of meandering cattle grazing in the sun. Soon they neared the turn for her grandfather's house on the north side of Minden. She pulled onto the side street off the highway, the house already visible.

Phoebe's hands gripped the steering wheel tightly when she saw the big farm house in need of painting but not desperately so, the rich green grasses surrounding the farm in all directions, the dilapidated and disused outhouse ready to fall down, the large red barn and the smaller barn that didn't quite match the rest of the farm. There were two ancient Sierra Redwood trees in the front that shaded the house and yard and one along the side with an old rope and tire swing attached. All were tall and majestic and standing guard, landmarks of the property.

There was a shed in the back, random items collecting at the sides, and a couple of smaller trees and scrubby bushes that needed either trimming or cutting down altogether, just as any other old farm house. But her grandfather had kept the land and yard relatively tidy compared to some other farm houses in the area. He had recently mowed a large swath near the road to enable visitors to park. Phoebe pulled onto this space and got out, eyeing the place.

In some ways this felt as much like home to her as her childhood home in Carson City; she had visited often. A warm breeze blowing the field grass around her; the tire swing lazily swaying, waiting for someone to hop on; birds flitting branch to branch, startled by her arrival, waiting until the humans disappeared to return to one of her grandmother's several bird feeders hanging within sight of the windows. The rich land surrounding the large, old house was a welcoming site that warmed her heart with indescribable sentiment.

"Phoebe, you coming?" her mother asked from the door. She hadn't realized she'd been daydreaming.

"Um, yes." She grabbed her jacket, closed her car door and joined the others just as her grandparents were coming to greet them.

As she received a hug from her grandmother Julia, closing her eyes and smelling her familiar perfume, her grandfather wrapped his arms around them both, his jovial laugh filling the air. He patted her on the back with his large, workman's hand, and gave her his own hug when her grandmother finally released her. Jody received similar treatment, all grandchildren were loved, but Phoebe felt as if her greeting was special. She knew she was the one who wasn't home often.

Only moments after they walked in through the side entrance and into the large country kitchen did Phoebe hear a familiar voice coming from the living room on the opposite side. He was sitting in his comfortable chair, a black and white Western movie on TV. But he wasn't watching now. He was banging his walking stick on the floor loudly, trying to get someone's attention. Phoebe walked to the edge of the room and leaned on the side of the built-in book shelf.

"Hey, Mister, who's making all the racket in here?" J. W. looked up at her, frowning, and banged his stick twice more. They stared at each other only a moment, Phoebe raised her eyebrows, and J. W. let a slip of a grin cross his face. Walking over to him she kneeled down in front of his chair, put a hand on one of his and said, "Hi J. W."

She thought for a moment the elderly man might be speechless. He put his other hand on top of hers and patted it. He then said, "'Bout time you got here." Phoebe laughed. Loudly enough that it drew everyone else's attention for a moment.

Phoebe leaned forward and kissed him on the cheek. "I missed you too."

J. W. put out his hand, reaching toward her throat. Gently he fingered the necklace she hadn't taken off since leaving her apartment in Iowa. The necklace he had given her as a gift when she'd graduated from high-school. He smiled and looked into Phoebe's eyes. "You still have it."

"Of course I do, silly. It's my favorite." He looked at it again, holding the miniature gold horseshoe between his finger and thumb. He seemed lost in thought. "What is it?"

He let go of the necklace. "You know, it was difficult to find one that hung upright when I got that for you."

Phoebe smiled. "It's a good thing, or I'd have blamed you for all my luck going bad."

Henry walked in, his voice a baritone timber, matching his size and handshake, "What're you two planning now? J. W.?"

"Get me something to drink, why don't you? And none of that poisonous tea, Julia, God love ya. I want whiskey."

"No you don't," called Julia from the kitchen. "I'll get you some lemonade."

"Hmph, it's not like I've already got a brick in my hat."

A quick hour later Phoebe's father Hank and her brother Will came through the kitchen door. They had brought a few folding tables, borrowed from Hank's workplace, to set up outside on the large cement block patio. Another half an hour and Phoebe heard another, louder pickup truck pull up outside. Moments later Tony and Troy came through the door as well. They were delivering a truck bed full of folding chairs to go with the tables.

Phoebe went outside to help unload the chairs. Jody watched, directing foot traffic, saying watch out for that rock, that bush, that... oh sorry, I didn't see that. Phoebe told her to go back inside and said they would be done soon.

They readied tablecloths to set out the next day before everyone arrived and also arranged napkins, forks, knives, spoons and cups to help her grandmother and Abigail. Decorations they would hang later. Another half hour and Jody's brothers, Roger and James, arrived with drinks to put in the extra fridge plugged into the detached garage her grandfather had built a couple of decades previously. Roger's wife had stayed at the hotel in Carson City to greet other family members coming that afternoon.

Phoebe's brothers took the truck and went to Minden to pick up something quick for everyone to have for lunch. When they returned, as many as could fit sat at the long farm table. Julia got out the guest list and she and Bonnie checked the names one last time. With only a few exceptions, all invited would be in attendance. Hank's brother Charlie, along with some of Hank's cousins and their kids, would arrive the next day. All of Phoebe's own cousins would be there, as well as her Uncle Charlie's two grandchildren. Yes, it would really be something. She hoped J. W. knew what he had asked for.

The relatives nearby were bringing desserts to go with the J. W.-requested barbecue. Henry and Julia were supplying the meat to cook. Julia had baked a large cake; two in fact. And Abigail had been helping get the house cleaned and ready as well.

Phoebe glanced at J. W. a couple of times during the party discussion to gauge his reaction. He heard, he was listening. But mostly he seemed distracted by something else. He shifted in his chair, glanced out the nearest kitchen window, played with a phantom object in his pocket. "J. W., is there something bothering you?" Phoebe asked him. Julia glanced at Phoebe, a crease on her brow. Phoebe might be the only one who didn't tiptoe around him, but also the one who usually got straight answers out of him.

He scooted his chair back with a couple of tries, stood up with the aid of his walking stick and walked to the large window at the back of the house in the living room. "No," he stated defiantly. Phoebe followed him.

"Well, you're acting kinda weird. This is your party we're talking about. Just us, family, just like you wanted. What's the matter?"

He reached down into his pocket and pulled out a pocket watch. He opened it and showed it to her. "See this?" She nodded. She remembered having seen it before. It was very old but she didn't know anything about it. "Time," he said, and closed it, replacing it in his pocket. She waited patiently, knowing there was no hurrying J. W. when he had something to say. He looked at her and turned back to look out the window once again.

"J. W., what is it? I don't want you to be sad. The party is going to be fun."

His eyes grew wide and he looked back at her. "Sad?" He grinned at her then, nearly chuckling, bringing about a cough. Shaking his head he looked outside and looked searchingly for something. In a moment he held his finger to his lips and motioned with his head to come closer to look for herself. "See that?" He didn't have to whisper, he just didn't want her to move quickly. She would scare it away.

She said, "Yes, I see it. What about it?"

"Don't you recognize it?" He made her wait for his next words again as they watched the small bird flit from branch to branch to branch, waiting its turn at one of her grandmother's bird feeders.

"It seems impatient."

"Hmm. Yes."

"Okay, what? What is it about the bird?"

"I remember Henry telling you the name of that bird long ago. Don't you remember?"

"J. W. you're giving me the creeps. No, I don't, and I'm sorry. I just don't remember. It must have been a long time ago."

"Yes, a long time ago. That doesn't mean it doesn't matter anymore." He looked outside again. The bird was at one of the feeders now, hopping around, flying back to a branch and back to the feeder. "It can't decide what to do. See how the feathers on its head stick out a bit when it sits there, as if in annoyance. And the face is a little darker around the eyes. It's frowning, concentrating, thinking."

"J. W., it's a bird. Do you really think its got all that going on in that little brain?"

He ignored her. "Do you remember the name now?"

Something in the way he asked her again made her feel as if she should, but she didn't. But the feeling his questioning gave her was familiar. Anticipation, expectation. She shook her head.

"It's called a Says Phoebe." At the surprised look on her face he smiled. "I can't make up my mind, I'm betwixt and between, all you other birds should keep your distance... Says Phoebe."

"Hey, that's not fair..."

He reached into his pocket for the watch and held it in front of her face. "Time, Phoebe. You've been dilly-dallying long enough. It's time."

Phoebe didn't know what to say and simply stared at J. W. He returned the watch to his pocket, looked back out the window and didn't say another word on the subject. Julia intervened then, taking J. W. by the arm and asking him if wanted anything else for lunch. She escorted him back to his comfy chair. Phoebe watched him go and looked back out the window for the Says Phoebe bird. It was gone. She glanced back toward J. W. He was looking at the television as if nothing had happened at all.

She walked up to him, hands on hips, and asked, "What was all that about?" He ignored her. She stepped between him and the television. He looked right through her and used his walking stick to push her out of the way.

"Don't get all huffed up, now," he said. "I'll see you tomorrow. It's gonna be a long day. Stay outta my closet. And wear good shoes."

She sighed. "Okay, J. W." She bent down to kiss him on the cheek. "I'll let you know when we're ready to leave. You watch your show."

Phoebe went back to the kitchen table, the look of concern obvious on her face. Henry asked, "Everything all right in there?"

"Has J. W. been okay lately? Healthy, I mean? How's his memory doing?"

Henry smiled. "You know J. W., Phoebe. He's always been a little difficult to understand. He marches to the beat of a different drum. Kind of like a certain grand-daughter I know." His eyebrows went up.

Phoebe felt a certain measure of relief. Her grandfather and grandmother saw J. W. every day, lived with him. If they were unconcerned, so should she be. She would put it out of her mind, would let it go, knowing his quirks had always been part of his personality and were also now part of his age.

The conversation about the birthday party continued. Everyone was expected to arrive around eleven in the morning. Family was, of course, welcome at any time throughout the day. There would be food into the night.

Phoebe and Jody helped clean up the kitchen while the others decided where to put everything. Some decorations were hung or set about and still J. W. watched his Western. When they were finished they heard J. W. bang his stick on the floor once again. Phoebe went to him, but he waved an arm toward the kitchen to signal he wanted them all to come.

Phoebe knelt down beside him. "What is it, J. W.? Can I get you something?"

He looked around at the faces before him and cleared his throat. "Tomorrow's my birthday party, right?" They nodded. He pointed a finger at them as a group. Phoebe was amused in anticipation of what he might say. "It's my day, I get to do what I want." He waited another moment, as if to let that sink in.

Phoebe heard Henry mutter "Oh, boy," under his breath at the same time as Bonnie said, "Uh-oh."

"Well, I don't want to just sit around here all day. After lunch we're going on a road trip." At the gasps that escaped the mouths of her grandparents and her mother, Phoebe covered her mouth to hide the grin.

"What!"

"Road trip? At your age..."

"Where...?"

J. W. held up a hand to silence the protests and exclamations. "Don't get your knickers in a twist. Just for a little while. If you want to come, fine, if you don't, fine." He looked directly at Phoebe. "You're coming."

Phoebe smiled at J. W. "Count me in." When the others in the room started to protest all at the same time Phoebe and J. W. ignored them all.

J. W. leaned close to her and said, "Wear good shoes."

7

After those gathered had exclaimed, shook their heads or simply rubbed their temples in consternation or humorous frustration and walked away from J. W., Phoebe asked, "So, where are you going?" She had a feeling she already knew. If it was where she was thinking, she wished he would change his mind.

He looked at her but didn't answer right away. She could see he was thinking something through, his lip twitched, his eyelids moved in a fluttery motion before saying simply, "You'll see."

Phoebe sighed. "Okay. I'm going back out there. Need anything else?"

He directed his gaze back to the television and shook his head.

Her grandfather Henry noticed her concerned demeanor and said quietly, hoping J. W. didn't overhear, "Don't worry about him, Phoebe. He's aging, you know. He's going to say some strange things now and again. You know that. Tomorrow he might not even remember what he said. We're taking good care of him. There's nothing else you can do."

She wrapped her arms around her grandfather. "I don't doubt that, Grandpa. I feel bad I haven't been back to see him, all of you, in so long. He seems okay, but then says goofy things, and..." She hated how she was starting to sound. She cleared her throat and went to the fridge for a can of soda. Her brother Tony was leaning against it. He was grinning at her.

"What?" she asked, irritation in her voice.

He put his hands up in surrender. "Touchy, touchy. I just saw you hug Grandpa. Getting soft in your old age, sis?"

"Oh, shut up. Maybe I shouldn't have come back after all." She closed the fridge and plopped down in one of the kitchen chairs, next to her cousin Jody. A safe place?

"Hey, Phoebe, I'm trying to decide which classes to take in school next year. I took a year off after high-school, then went part time this year. So I can pretty much do whatever I want at this point. But I thought I'd ask you, since you took a bunch of different classes, at least that's what my mom told me, and it's community college so I just wanna see what I like first, and well, since you did a couple of things..."

Phoebe had gotten up, put on her Army jacket and walked out the back door on the far side of the kitchen that led to the porch, letting it slam on the spring. She truly hoped no one followed her, that they would leave soon, that whatever conversation continued inside did not include her to the extent she would have to clarify her position to anyone.

Crap, too much to hope for. Phoebe heard the screen door shut behind her. Then again. Footsteps, several. She looked up and saw her mom, her dad, her brothers Tony and Will. The inquisition. Phoebe got up to sit on the porch railing. Higher ground, a getaway on either side.

They all sat in chairs on the porch. Each had brought something to drink. Hank had brought Phoebe's soda she had left at the kitchen table. "You forgot this." He sat down next to Bonnie. And the guilt settled in... again.

She sighed. "Thanks."

Tony asked, "So what're you going to tell Jody?"

She looked up and saw Will smiling. She answered, none too seriously, "Drop out. Drop out now, that's what." She took a drink of her soda.

Jody came out with Phoebe's grandmother, Julia. The group started talking amongst themselves and soon Phoebe felt on the outside, just where she'd wished she'd been only moments before. She walked to her grandmother and apologized for slamming the screen door. Julia chuckled and said, "Of all the times that door has slammed, I doubt once more is going to matter much."

Phoebe hugged her grandmother, and said loudly, "Hey, Tony, I just hugged Grandma too." He looked at her and raised his eyebrows, not being goaded into the challenge.

"So Phoebe, what classes do you suggest I take? What were your favorite?" asked Jody again, clearly unaware of Phoebe's prior agitation.

Will groaned, Tony laughed, Hank rubbed his eyes. As patiently as she could, Phoebe said, "Jody, I have no idea. Whatever you pick, you'll probably change your mind. You'll love the idea, then hate the class. Love the concept, then hate the outcome. You'll have grand ideas then realize you can't make a difference. So pick something, anything. Or go to Vegas and play craps. Same process, same outcome." She walked across the porch, grabbed Will by the front of his shirt and said, "Come with me, I need to let off some steam."

They went through the kitchen and into the living where the remainder of the day's helpers were gathered and listening to a baseball game on the radio. J. W. appeared to have dozed off watching his Western. "Grandpa, can I ask you something?"

He looked up, "Well sure, sweetheart, what is it?"

Will and I wanna go out back to the hill and practice. It's been awhile. Do you mind?"

"No, I don't mind. I got 'em all ready for you, just in case," he winked.

"I thought today would be better than tomorrow."

"Just the two of you?" Phoebe nodded, Will stood next to her, silent, going along. Henry stood and headed down the short hall, past J. W.'s room on the right, to a room at the end. He unlocked the cabinet inside and asked, "Rifle or pistol?"

"One of each for me, please," said Phoebe. "I need practice."

"I'm just here for the show," said Will, smiling at his grandfather. "She's the sporting nut." Henry grinned. It wasn't the first time he'd heard such words when these two were together.

"Here ya go. I think this was your favorite once," Henry said, handing Phoebe the Winchester repeater he'd taught her to shoot when she was a young teenager. "And how about my Colt?" Henry grinned as he handed her his prized possession. "I always loved that Old West gun," he said with a hint of nostalgia in his voice. It's an original, but you know I baby it." He turned the gun over in his hand, admiring it. "And before you blame me for the scratch on the grip, it was there when I got it," he grinned. "Dad gave this to me after your grandmother and I got married. He said it was time to pass it down. Hopefully I'll do the same one day," he said with another wink at Phoebe.

"Wow, J. W. gave up one of his prized possessions," she said, smiling, handing Will the pistol to carry. "Where did he get it?"

"He never said," Hank said with a shrug.

"Big surprise. We won't be out long, Grandpa. Any cans in the garage?"

Henry retrieved some ammunition, the same size used for both in this instance, and handed it to Phoebe. She put it in one of her Army jacket pockets. He said, "Your grandmother wanted me to tidy up a bit so I moved anything I had from the garage to the big barn. More room in there than the shed. There's some paper targets in there too if you want. On the left on the shelf." He faced her. "I saved them for you. You're pretty much the only one who used to like to come out here and use them." Guilt again. So many years away from home and the people she loved.

"A dollar on a perfect target? First ring or better at eighty?" she challenged him.

"Hmm," he pretended to mull it over.

Will said, "I'll keep her honest Grandpa."

"Then you're on," he said, smiling and patting her on the shoulder.

“That’s why Will doesn’t want in. He’s a lousy shot,” Phoebe teased, winking back at her grandfather.

Henry went back to the baseball game on the radio as Phoebe and Will exited the house through the rear kitchen door. They crossed the yard to the big red barn. Phoebe handed Will the Winchester so she could unlatch and swing open the heavy door. Once inside she weaved her way around and through the lawn tractor, other lawn equipment and some old farming equipment to the row of shelves on the left side. She found a bucket and filled it with the cans her grandfather had said were there. The paper targets were rolled in a cardboard box nearby. He really had saved them for her; everything was together and easy to find.

Phoebe gave the barn door a shove with her foot, closing it most of the way, then took the Winchester back from Will. “Come on,” she said, as they walked along the back of the yard, past the porch, past the staring faces, and on toward the field at the far side of the open land that belonged to her grandparents.

When they had walked approximately one hundred yards through the back field, they came to a flat area covered with gravel. Grass and weeds had begun to invade the area a bit, but it was still visible as the space once used as a private range. The land was flat from here but another eighty yards out a hill of land rose up, more than fifty yards wide, creating a natural backdrop for safety.

“Here.” Phoebe shoved the bucket of cans at Will. Go stand those up on the crates.” She took the paper targets and started walking toward the hill. She called over her shoulder, “Please.” She walked to the hill, picking up some small sticks along the way. She posted 4 of the paper targets on the hill, several feet apart, attaching them to the dirt hill with two sharp sticks apiece. Will did as his sister had asked, or rather, commanded, and propped the soda cans on the wooden crates at uneven intervals, halfway to the hill. He was back to the gravel area before she was, sitting on one of the tree stumps that had been used for chairs for years.

Phoebe knew her grandfather kept his guns perfectly clean and in working order, so when she came back from hanging the targets a quick check was all that was required before she loaded first the Colt pistol. One gun at a time. Half-cock the hammer, expose the cylinder, slip in one .44 cartridge at a time. Six in all. Release the hammer, gently. So far Will had remained silent. He knew his sister well. She would talk when she felt like it and not before.

Like riding a bike... or so the saying goes. Phoebe held the pistol, her grandfather's Colt Single Action Army revolver, SSA for short, down at her side, closed her eyes, inhaled through her nose, held her breath a second or two, then exhaled through her lips. The world went quiet. Her grandfather Henry's words from another time were all she heard now. *Never fire a gun in anger... find that quiet place in your mind... shut out the world and there is only you and the target in front of you...*

She knew her family was watching from behind her at the house. She also knew they trusted her and her grandfather's lessons of safety and restraint, at least when on the firing range. Phoebe raised the Colt, aimed at the third can from the left, angled at twenty degrees to her left. Inhale – exhale, and fire. A little kick, not much. In a steady succession of shots one second apart, she fired at the third can, the fifth, the first, the fourth, the second and sixth can. She missed the fifth and second cans.

She put the pistol down, stepped back a few steps and exhaled sharply. Then she picked up a large piece of gravel and threw it as hard as she could in the direction of the cans. Will quickly covered his smile with a hand, hoping she didn't see him. Too late. "Funny, huh?" she asked angrily.

Will held up his hands in capitulation. "The missing? No. How long has it been since you've been to a range, anyway? Thinking you could hit a can with a rock at forty yards? Yes, that was funny." He shrugged.

Hank, Bonnie, Phoebe's twin brothers and Jody meandered to the gravel flat. Phoebe snatched the Winchester from her younger brother. Checking to be sure the hammer was in the half-cocked position first, she tipped it on its side against her leg and loaded it through the slot in the side, filling it with the fifteen cartridges it would hold. She grinned at him. He was right, it had been a long time, and it had made her feel better. "Okay, smarty. Sure you don't want to bet?"

"On you and Grandpa's Winchester?" His eyebrows went up. "No way. You're on your own." He crossed his arms, signaling he was here for the show.

The family had arrived behind the gravel area now and were standing around watching. Phoebe glanced at them briefly and turned to face the first paper target. *Find that quiet place in your mind... shut out the world and there is only you and the target in front of you...* Pull the lever to release the lever lock. Release the hammer into the dropped position. She remembered the sound, the feel, the small kick of the smoothly manufactured gun as she lifted the rifle, adjusted accordingly, exhaled, and, unlike what many others had told her, opened both eyes.

The gun was old, her grandfather had had it for years. A famous model 1873, an original, manufactured until 1923, known as "The Gun That Won The West." Henry Tucker's gun since he'd been young; and he let her use. A privilege.

Cycle the lever, putting the first cartridge into the chamber. Pull the trigger, first shot off center, a quick inhale, exhale, pull the lever, fire, second ring out, a hint of a smile, no inhale, no exhale, lever, fire, bullseye, Jody exclaiming from behind and so easy to ignore right now... lever, fire, edge of first ring, lever, fire, second ring, lever, fire, bullseye...

Fifteen shots in all. Phoebe returned the hammer to it's half-cocked position and lowered the rifle to her side. She stepped back and looked over to Will. "You owe Grandpa a dollar," he stated.

"That was one target. I've got three left." Will shook his head in wry amusement. Without speaking, Phoebe loaded the rifle a second time, stepped forward, released the hammer, cycled the lever, shifted her stance to the second target, closed her eyes a moment, breathed deeply, exhaled, opened her eyes and raised the rifle to her shoulder. Four bullseyes in a row, one in the second circle, three bullseyes, one in the first circle, three bullseyes, one in the first circle, two bullseyes.

Phoebe put the rifle down and turned to look at her family still standing behind her. Troy was scratching his head. She had had competitions in her youth at the gun club she had passed when driving into Carson City. Tony and Troy had never been able to outshoot her. Will had had other hobbies. They appeared to be patiently watching and waiting to see what happened next.

Third round, third target. Six bullseyes, one in the first circle, three bullseyes, one in first circle, four bullseyes. Jody jumped up and down, and clapped and squealed with delight. Phoebe couldn't resist grinning at her cousin. After putting the rifle in the half-cocked position and locking the lever once again, she picked up both guns and walked to Will. "Hold these," she said, as she first picked up the spent cartridges, put them in another jacket pocket, then walked to pick up the cans and put them in the bucket. She also plucked all of the targets off the hill in the distance and re-rolled the one she had not used.

When she returned Will asked, "Only three?"

Phoebe shrugged. "I found out what I wanted to know. I'll save the fourth for next time."

"No second try with the Colt?" He sounded surprised.

Phoebe shook her head. "Not this time. Good thing I didn't bet Grandpa on the cans."

Will was glad to hear she sounded more like her old self again.

They turned to walk back toward the house. Hank walked alongside her. "Feel better?"

"You know I never shoot angry. I know better. But yeah, I do. I – " She paused and she and Hank stopped walking. "Dad, I – " The others had kept walking. It was just the two of them now. "Dad, I love the way this place smells, the way it looks, the way the breeze sounds in the grass, the mountains." She sighed. "And I've missed everybody so much."

Hank hugged his daughter. "Then what's the problem?"

He could tell she was shaking her head on his shoulder. "It reminds me."

"Isn't that good?"

"No. Everything that life here makes me remember is what I've been trying to get out of my head."

"Which is?"

They started walking toward the house again, feeling frustrated. "Dad, we've talked about this before. You know."

"So why do you keep bringing it up, if not for someone to try to change your mind?"

They all made their way back to the house. Phoebe put her jacket back over a kitchen chair and returned her grandfather's two guns to the gun cabinet, knowing he would insist on cleaning them both later. Will had volunteered to put away the cans and three of the targets, the winning one taken inside the house with Phoebe. She collected her dollar from her grandfather. He had put it on the refrigerator under a magnet before she had returned to the house. He pointed to it with a grin and a smile. She retrieved it, waving it in the air from across the room in thanks. He knew she would do it.

J. W. called to her from the living room. His Western was over, as was his nap. Her cousins and grandfather were seated nearby, rehashing plays from the game. Phoebe took a seat close to J. W.

"I heard the shooting. It was you, wasn't it?"

"Yes, it was me. Just getting in a little practice. Nobody had the guts to bet me, except Grandpa." She glanced at her grandfather and winked.

"How did you do?"

"With the Winchester, fine. With the pistol, terrible. Must be the gun, can't be me, right?" She teased.

"That thing was always pretty accurate. Maybe raise your sight up a bit, especially in the open with a breeze."

Phoebe raised her eyebrows. "Now you tell me."

"I'm surprised you did that well with the Winchester. That one pulls to the left a mite if you're not expecting it."

"Maybe for you," she teased.

J. W. continued, "Now, a scattergun. Hard to miss with one like that."

"Hard to hunt a dear with a scattergun," interjected her brother Tony, as he entered from the kitchen.

"Bah," J. W. waved his hand at the comment. "Not many deer break into your house."

"I think even Phoebe might be able to hit a burglar with the Colt if they broke into her apartment," her brother teased her.

The group laughed good-naturedly.

Then Troy asked, "Do you have a gun, Phoebe."

She said simply, "No."

"No? I'm surprised. Why not?"

She shrugged. "What for? I don't compete anymore."

"I'm sure there are ranges in Iowa where you could still shoot."

"I'm sure there are," she said, shifting in her seat on the couch, hoping somebody would change the subject. "But I don't want to."

James and Troy started discussing gun ranges in other parts of Nevada. Phoebe looked over at J. W. and found him staring at her. She frowned but said nothing, asked him if there was anything she could get for him, then got up to get a glass of water.

In the kitchen her cousin Jody approached her. "I've never even shot a gun, Phoebe. Do you think you could teach me sometime?"

"Sorry, no. When the party is over I'm going back to Iowa. It's a long way from Albuquerque."

"Oh," said Jody, sounding disappointed. "I thought you were staying a few extra days."

"I am, but I didn't think you were. Besides, that was just for fun. I haven't done it for a long time. Sorry."

"That's all right. I understand." But she walked away, sounding deflated, and Phoebe felt to blame.

J. W. was standing close by. She hadn't seen him come into the kitchen after her and he startled her when he spoke. "Is that how you talk to your friends back in Iowa?"

"What?" Phoebe was taken aback, not knowing how to respond. "I – I don't have many friends in Iowa, to be honest."

"And why do you think that is?"

"It doesn't really matter." She took a drink of her water.

"Doesn't it? Why did you leave Nevada?"

"Really, J. W., what's this all about?"

He looked her in the eye, serious now. "Answer the question. I would like to know."

"To go to college, you know that."

"Why did you really leave Nevada?" he asked again.

Phoebe didn't recall her great-grandfather having ever spoken to her so sternly before. She couldn't move her feet, couldn't leave the scene, couldn't run away; because he had never given her any reason not to merit the utmost respect. She cleared her throat. "I did leave to go to college. But I ran away." She fingered her necklace. "I picked the furthest place I could. It was an excuse." She looked down into her glass of water, feeling rebuked by one of her favorite people in the world.

"What were you running from?" he asked simply

She shrugged. "I don't know."

"Yes you do. And it's time to stop putting responsibility on someone else for your mistakes. As soon as you do that, maybe you'll finally stop chasing away relatives that love you and do what makes you happy." At that he banged his walking stick once on the floor and shuffled back to the living room, down the short hall and into his room.

***

Back in Carson City, after dinner, Phoebe and Hank were sitting on the patio enjoying a cup of coffee and looking at the stars. They recalled her mother's reaction to J. W.'s announcement of his plans the next day. She had been flabbergasted recounting J. W.'s desire of a road trip. "A road trip, at his age," she had said as she had splashed bubbles in the sink. Hank had let her talk. "Where does he think he needs to go when everyone will be in town to see him!"

"Did he tell you where he wanted to go?" Hank asked Phoebe now.

She shook her head. "Nope. And I didn't ask. For all we know it's down into Minden to the boarding house he used to live in just to say 'hi,' who knows. I don't see why they were so upset. At his age he can do whatever he wants, I would think."

"I agree." They sat in silence another minute.

"Dad, can I ask you a question?"

"Always."

"J. W. showed me something today. It was out Grandma's window. A bird, eating at one of the feeders."

"Okay."

"Was I named after a bird?"

Hank laughed, a hearty laugh, full of warmth and humor. "The Says Phoebe?" His laughing slowed and he smiled at her. "It figures he would show that to you. Phoebe, you are a particularly unique person. I think the bird was probably named after you."

8

Phoebe was up at eight, yawning. She hadn't gotten much sleep the night before. After Jody had gone to sleep she had snuck under the covers with a flashlight and the two books she had packed in the pocket of her suitcase. *Why can't I part with them?* She read parts of them for the bazillionth time, studying details of the photographs and captions below. The faces stared out at her; *what were you doing just before and after this picture was taken?* Sometime in the night she woke, turned off the flashlight and put her two books away, dreaming of the faces after once again drifting off.

In the morning, with the light of day bringing order to her brain, she had a leisurely coffee and toast on the patio, enjoying the morning sun. Soon it was time to go. Initially dressed in pants and a light sweater, she exchanged this for a below-the-knee summer dress, something she seldom wore. Purchased two years ago, she had to take off the store tag before putting it on.

She smiled as she switched the shoes she had been about to wear. Sandals weren't walking shoes. She swapped them out for her knee-high soft leather boots. They were well worn but she loved them and took great care of them. Before leaving she grabbed her favorite jacket from her room. It was still cool this morning and she might need it until it warmed up. The color wasn't a bad match with her dress. But the fact that it was an Army surplus olive green meant the style was, well... It was her favorite jacket, after all.

Her father drove today, as did her aunt and uncle in their own car. Phoebe felt odd being driven, it hadn't happened in a long time. Bonnie talked on the way to Minden, wondering aloud of the possible destinations of J. W.'s supposed 'road trip.' It seemed not to bother her as it had done the day before. Phoebe supposed she was resigned to the fact. She herself looked forward to the day much more than she had before.

Her dad was looking at her in the rear view mirror. "What?" she asked.

"I was just wondering what your plans are once the party's done with. I know you're staying for a few days, but then what?"

"Then I'm going home. What else?" She paused. "Sorry, Dad, I didn't mean to snap. I meant, what else is there? I'm here on a little vacation, to see everybody, then it's back to work."

"Hmm," he nodded. "I see."

"What would you like me to do? Quit? Get another job? It's what I do, and it's a good job. Really."

"No, I didn't say that. I was just asking." He paused. "I never heard you say you like it though."

Phoebe had no answer to that and stared out the side window the rest of the way to Minden. She saw her mother glance at her father. They were worried about her. "Look, you guys, I'm fine. That's why I'm here. I really need a vacation, and to see all of you. That's all."

Her mother turned to her. Changing the subject, she asked, "Any idea what J. W. has in mind?"

Phoebe shook her head. "Not really. I have a suspicion, but I hope I'm wrong."

They pulled in at her grandparent's farmhouse to see they were not the first to arrive. Her aunt and uncle were in front of them, but there were a couple of other cars present. Phoebe loved her family, her aunts, uncles, cousins, second cousins and so on. Many would be here. If there was a group in which one could be comfortable, where else but with family? So why was she feeling pressure as she walked toward the door, as she saw faces smiling back at her, heard voices begin the endless chatter that would go on into the night as stories were told and retold, old photos were pulled out, memories were relived again and inside jokes were bantered back forth.

She took a deep breath, looked up, heard what she thought was a Says Phoebe bird flitting through the trees and said, "Oh, shut up."

Once inside, there were greetings, hugs, how-are-yous and laughter. People made themselves at home, grabbed a drink, meandered, found a seat, remained standing, went outside, found a lawn chair or a picnic bench. But not before finding J. W. and wishing him happy birthday, bringing a balloon, a bunch of flowers or a small gift. He hadn't forgotten a single name, despite his odd behavior at times. A half an hour into the day and all family that had been expected had arrived.

Phoebe pulled up a stool and sat down next to J. W., seated in his favorite chair. "So, happy birthday. Great-grandpa," she teased.

He did a double-take glance at her and frowned. "What are you wearing?"

She looked down at herself. "What does that mean? I put on a dress for the first time in years for this party."

"No, I mean that green thing. What is that?"

"My favorite jacket. I wore it yesterday for a little while, didn't you notice? It's a Vietnam, Army surplus jungle jacket. I like the pockets."

"I guess that could come in handy," he said.

A couple of relatives walked across the room to talk to Phoebe. She got up to hug them and they talked for a few minutes before all going in the kitchen to get a party snack. She squeezed J. W.'s hand before she left with them. *See you soon.*

Phoebe's cousin, Beverly, her uncle Charlie's daughter, greeted her in the kitchen. She was a few years older but the two had always been close growing up. Beverly was married and had two kids who bumped into her legs as they ran through the kitchen toward the back door on their way outside. "I'm sorry, Phoebe," Beverly apologized.

Phoebe laughed. "That's okay. They're having fun. At this rate they're going to be exhausted by tonight, though. So, how've you been?" And they caught up, at least on Beverly's end. Married nine years now, a daughter that's five, a son that's seven.

"How about you? I heard Iowa? That's far."

And Phoebe's first stumbling explanation of the day commenced.

"But I thought I'd heard you were going to college for... what was it again? History? Did I get that wrong? Really, there are so many of us."

"I guess I lost interest. You know, teenagers, right?" Phoebe found herself spinning her glass round and round in her hands. "What I'm doing is interesting. It's all about what's going on right now, every day. Real life. Not things that are past and gone." Phoebe looked up to see her brother Will watching and listening to her from across the kitchen. The flush crept up her neck and cheeks. Beverly didn't seem to notice.

She gripped Phoebe's forearm affectionately for an instance. "I'm happy for you. Anybody special in the picture? Any cute guys at work?" She teased.

Phoebe felt her face grimace unintentionally, the first name and face coming to mind being that of Rick-Rich-Honker. "No," she stated sharply. "I mean, I haven't made a point of meeting that many people. I work a lot."

Beverly took the last swallow of her drink and said in parting before moving on to another group of family members with whom to chat, "Take my advice, cousin. Live a little."

When she'd gone, Phoebe glanced to where her brother Will had been standing. He'd moved on and was nowhere in sight and Phoebe walked outside. Was there anywhere to go to be alone for a minute? She wandered over to the small barn, opened its big door that faced away from the back of the house, slipped inside, and closed the door from within. It was darker inside so she felt around until she felt a wooden crate to sit on. And sighed.

Then jumped. "Still running away?" someone said from the dark.

"You're one to talk. Why are you in here at your own birthday party?"

"It's my barn," was all he said.

Eyes now accustomed to the low light, Phoebe saw J. W. sitting on another crate just opposite her. "But why are you in here?"

"I came in to look for something and stubbed my toe. I sat down to rub it and then you came in. Why are you in here?"

Phoebe grinned. Truth. "I was running away again." She leaned her chin in her hands.

A few seconds passed and she felt a thump against her ankle. J. W. had hit her with his walking stick. She rubbed the spot. "Ow, what was that for?"

"Time to go. No more hiding." He stood and opened the barn door.

"Hey J. W.," she asked before getting up from the crate. "What do you mean this is your barn?"

"It's *my* barn. I moved it here, it's mine." He continued out the door.

She didn't think she'd ever asked why it looked distinctly different than the other barn. She figured it had been built by someone else, at a different time. "Huh. Weird. Most people move with their pets or their plants. People don't usually bring their barns with them," she said sarcastically, earning a chuckle from J. W.

"Good one," he said as he swung the door closed.

"Did you find what you were looking for?"

"Wouldn't you like to know?" Phoebe shook her head, knowing it was the response she deserved.

Her grandfather Henry had prepared chicken and pork on a huge grill on the patio in preparation for the family lunch. Not long after arriving anyone who was hungry helped themselves, family style, to heaps of barbecued meat, roasted potatoes, grilled vegetables, beans, and other picnic fare. One folding table alone was devoted to desserts. Phoebe found a seat at the far end of the patio with her dad's cousin Adelia and two of her kids, close in age to herself. Also there was Adelia's brother Hugh and his son Tom, sixteen.

Word had spread of Phoebe's shooting a near-perfect target the day before and Tom was quite interested. He was a high-school athlete and, while he didn't shoot, he appreciate competition of all sorts. It was an enjoyable talk with her younger second cousin about her previous competition experience.

Phoebe offered to get anyone a refill and walked into the garage to the spare refrigerator. On her way back she bumped into Tony rounding a corner. She laughed and apologized. "Look who's having fun," he teased.

"Oh come on, do you really think I'm that crabby?"

"Not when you peel off all the regret."

She frowned. "Don't start."

"Just joking, kid. Have you seen Dad? J. W.'s asking anybody who wants to go on his little drive to gather inside."

"I was beginning to wonder if he'd forgotten."

"Nope. But I don't think it's a big deal. He knows everybody's here. I don't think we'll be gone long."

"You're going?"

"Yes, and I know you are too."

"Of course. I told him I would. And I'm not letting any of you talk him out of it," she said.

"Wait 'til you hear where he wants to go." Tony smirked and edged around her, saying over his shoulder. "Don't forget you promised to go."

Phoebe delivered the promised drinks, said she needed to go inside and briefly explained why.

On entering the kitchen she saw J. W. sitting in a kitchen chair talking to his youngest son, William, her grandfather's brother who lived in Texas. William's youngest grandson, Eric, thirteen, was there as well. The last time Phoebe had ever spoken of her extended family to anyone was to a couple of friends in college. They marveled at how she remembered her family member's names and associated relationships.

J. W. looked up as Phoebe approached the table. He said, "Are you ready to go?"

"Road trip, huh? You're still doing that?"

He banged the tip of his stick on the floor once. "Yes, I am. My wheelchair's by the kitchen entryway. I'm riding with you." He pointed his first finger at her.

"I didn't drive today, Dad did. Wheelchair?"

He didn't say anything else, just stood up and crossed the living room on his way to his bedroom. Phoebe followed him. "J. W." He walked into his room and stopped, turning to her.

"What?"

"Where are we going?"

"Out."

"Out? I want to know where we're going."

He closed the door in her face. Phoebe couldn't resist smiling at the eccentricities of her elderly great-grandfather. She heard noises from within, shuffling, a bang and silence. She put her ear to the door. Then opened it. The door to J. W.'s large walk-in closet was open. She called out, "J. W., are you all right?"

She heard scuffling again and J. W. shouted, "Out."

Startled, Phoebe didn't move. "Are you hurt? Do you need help?"

J. W.'s face peeked out from around the door jamb. "Did you hear me call for help? No. I'll be out in a minute. Now, out." He was frowning, out of breath. But she respected his wishes. "And I told you to stay out of my closet."

Phoebe left and closed the door behind her. Henry was in the other small room at the end of the hall. "Just making sure I locked the cabinet last night after I cleaned the guns. Everything all right?"

"J. W. chased me out." She shrugged.

Henry smiled at his granddaughter and shook his head. "He'll be out soon. He won't want to miss a minute of this day." He started to walk down the hall to the living room.

"Grandpa, what do you mean?"

"You'll see."

I've had about enough. Phoebe knocked loudly on J. W.'s door and called out, "Hey, Great-grandpa, come on out. You wanna' go on some road trip, then let's get going. Stop leaving us all in suspense."

The door opened and J. W. said, "I said stop calling me that. It makes me sound old." Phoebe tried to look over his shoulder into his room. *What is he hiding in there?* He turned to close the door behind himself, hustling Phoebe into the hall.

Back in the living room, J. W. cleared his throat to get everyone's attention. It failed, as there were so many simultaneous conversations the sound was lost. He banged his stick on the floor. That didn't seem to work either. He then picked up a bell he kept on the end table near the chair he sat in to watch television and shook it hard.

People turned to look and one by one people stopped talking, seeing that J. W. was intentionally trying to get their attention. "That's better," he said, putting down the bell. "By now you've heard it's time to go. If you haven't, well, it's time to go." He started to walk toward the front kitchen door, waving to Phoebe to follow him.

A few family members questioned his meaning, but by the time they reached the door word had spread to all of his desire to go for a drive that afternoon. A few wanted to come along, most would stay behind and wait for him to return. The small group gathered outside by the trucks and cars and decided whoever owned a truck should drive. They then discussed who would drive and who would be riding along in which vehicle.

Phoebe's parents were going, as were Will and Tony. Jody wanted to go because Phoebe was. Adelia's brother Alfred wanted to join them, as did his daughter Laura. And Phoebe's great-uncle William's daughter Kathleen and her nineteen-year-old son Daniel would go as well. The remaining family members would wait at the farm. They didn't mind as they all knew J. W.'s propensities for spontaneity.

Phoebe saw her father talking to J. W. for a moment. Hank glanced up at her mid-sentence and the hidden dread she'd been feeling since J. W. had said he wanted to go on a 'road trip' on the day of his party hit her; that apprehensive feeling in the pit of her stomach. She joined the group that was beginning to get into vehicles and J. W. looked at her, grinned and asked, "Are you ready?"

"Ready for what, exactly?" she asked.

"Are you ready to return to Bodie?"

9

J. W.'s face looked jubilant, gleeful. She noticed the flicker of amusement cross his expression when he finally told Phoebe where he wanted to go. She knew what visiting Bodie meant to him. She also knew that he knew it would annoy her. *Old rascal.* But she wouldn't let him down.

Hank sighed as they started driving. "Grandpa, do you realize how long it's going to take us to get there? Over an hour and a half, then back again. There are people at Dad's house for your party. Why do we have to do this today?"

J. W. scooted around in his seat, seemingly to find a comfortable position. Phoebe figured he was stalling giving an honest answer. "Because I want to, that's why. We've got all day. Them people ain't going nowhere." He looked out the window, a look of determination set upon his face.

A few minutes of driving and they approached the town of Minden. "Look at this. People building new places all the time," J. W. said on seeing new construction out his window, shaking his head in disgust. "What's wrong with using the old stuff all over again?" he asked rhetorically. Out of Minden, into and through Gardnerville and Phoebe saw him shake his head again.

Soon they were out in the country again, open land all around them, heading southeast, then south. Before long,

Topaz lake was on their left, long and shining in the early summer sun. Truck and camper traffic picked up here, families heading to and from the lake for a few days leisure as Phoebe and her family had done a couple of times when she and her siblings were kids. She felt her father's gaze on her face from the rear view mirror as she reminisced. At the lake they crossed over the state border into California.

Many more miles down the road cane the curve in the road that Phoebe remembered well. Usually thought of as flat, dry, boring and full of sagebrush, the west could surprise a newcomer with a hidden twist and turn in the road or a swollen river or stream that would make a crossing difficult and slow down travel. The West Walker River in this location was one such curvy stream and surprising bend in the road. Phoebe sat up higher in her seat to get a better look at the fast-flowing river. It wasn't extremely wide but the water broke over the rocks in bubbly rapids in its hurry.

They drove along in sight of the river for several more miles as Phoebe looked out the windows at the beautiful Sierra Nevadas and green flowering sage. Soon the grade on either side grew steeper and the hills were dotted with pines as the sage dwindled. Then the forest pines were left behind and the sharp hills on either side of the road became lower, the sage returning in force as it spread itself before them and flowed over the rolling hills. They drove over a bridge that crossed over the West Walker River, the river finally leaving them behind as it flowed on westward and they continued south, curving east.

The mountains were behind them now, the snowcaps in the distance, the land becoming flatter, dustier, more brown then green. It looked more like the desert people thought of when they thought of the middle-of-nowhere-Nevada. At least that's what Phoebe thought from her own conversations with people that hailed from elsewhere. Now she was seeing it with fresh eyes. From the perspective of a visitor. But she held in her heart the will to defend it to a stranger.

Another turn south and they came upon flatter land similar to Minden with green land for ranching. Phoebe sighed audibly, unaware she had. She noticed her father look at her again in the mirror. Another canyon, more sage, more pines, then another change and the land flattened again, spreading out wide before them, fewer trees, more green, cattle again. This part of the road she also remembered well. An eastward turn onto the last straightaway before heading into Bridgeport. Historic Bridgeport, with it's original buildings, used today as they had been one hundred years ago.

Once known as Big Meadows for its wide-open, fertile grazing land due to spring snowmelt runoff from the mountains, Bridgeport became the official county seat of Mono County in 1864. Six years later the town relocated to the west side of the East Walker River. A new county courthouse, initially slated to be completed by December 1880, was finally completed in early 1881. It remains in use today, having undergone a restoration in 1974 to its original condition and being placed on the National Register of Historic Places. This year would be it's centennial celebration.

As they slowed their drive through town Phoebe looked left and right at the buildings on either side that had stood through nearly one hundred years, not all in the same location as they had originally been built.

The Bridgeport Elementary School, set back from the highway and now a large modern building, is across from the original, that one having been moved to its current location in 1964 when in danger of being torn down. It serves as the first county museum now. It can be seen in its original location nearby, however, in the 1947 Hollywood movie *Out of The Past*. The 1948 movie, *Belle Starr's Daughter* had been filmed in Bridgeport as well.

Across from the courthouse is a former hotel relocated from Bodie years ago. And there is The Brick Saloon, now known as Ken's Sporting Goods, where a famous murder trial of a Chinese businessman accused of the cannibalistic murder of a Paiute Indian had taken place in 1891.

The Bridgeport Inn, once the Bridgeport Hotel and originally the Leavitt House, had been built in 1877 as a stage coach and buggy stop to and from Bodie. It continues as an Inn, one of the rooms having been named in honor of Samuel Clemens, aka Mark Twain, as he is legendarily known to have stayed there.

There were other such buildings, Phoebe had visited them, read about them, been inside them, talked to the people here... So long ago, when it mattered.

Phoebe found herself daydreaming as she viewed Bridgeport. The street was wide, as most towns in the west were whose growth had been due to rich land and cattle herds being driven through town. The dirt roads were gone, replaced with pavement and traffic signs. She pictured the way it had existed once, envisioned women in long dresses made of dark, easier to wash colors, men in mustaches and hats, children running about after chores were done.

"...Phoebe?"

Her head snapped to attention, realizing the truck had pulled over to the side of the road. "What?"

"We're stopping to get something to drink. Want something?" Her dad asked, already opening the door to get out. "I'll get you something."

"Sure, anything is fine."

After several seconds she could feel J. W. looking at her from his seat beside her. She looked at him and frowned, frustrated at the grin that spread across his face. "What are you up to, Mr?"

He shrugged and turned to face out the front of the truck. "I don't know what you're talking about. But I do know what you're thinking about," he stated quizzically.

"Yeah? And what's that?"

Hank returned to the truck with cans of soda. The jug of water they'd brought from the farm was at Phoebe's feet. She didn't get her answer.

On they drove, around the curve in the road and turning south. Sage and rough land on the eastern side, the flat grazing land of Bridgeport on the west, and the ever present snow-topped mountains in the distance, guiding, watching, living on and on. If her family chatted while they traveled Phoebe hardly noticed. She'd leaned back into the seat, pushing against it, as if that would keep her from arriving at their destination. Her feet were planted firmly against the mat on the floor, muscles tense in her legs and back.

The land rose on either side; they would be at the turnoff soon. It came up quickly, too quickly for Phoebe. J. W. was craning his neck to see around Bonnie in the front seat and was trying to see out the middle of the windshield when they turned left onto highway extension 270. This was a highway mainly 'to nowhere,' Bodie National Historic Park being the only thing at the end of it, thirteen miles ahead through sharp turns, sudden curves, narrow lanes and steep drop-offs on the sides.

Hank was adept at such driving, as were many native drivers in this part of the country. Through conversation with college friends Phoebe knew some of them hadn't been out of their local area and would have found this part of the country intimidating. She had had an acquaintance in college whose home town was Denver, Colorado. For him, driving through the Rockies was a mere inconvenience. For flatlanders it could be terrifying. Phoebe's plastering herself to her seat had nothing to do with the roads or her father's driving. It was the inability to stave off any longer what was she advancing toward.

The rough road began, the last three miles remaining unpaved to lend to the realism of originality to Bodie's visitors; dirt, rocks, large ruts, some holes, and occasional drops to one side that would plunge a visitor to sure mechanical failure or death, depending on speed. They were almost there. Phoebe worried about J. W. being jostled around but he seemed to be enjoying it. She glanced at him, he glanced back, winked at her, and continued hanging onto the headrest in front of him with one hand and the edge of the seat with the other. She hoped his brittle old bones could take it.

Last curve, Hank slowing down, all of them peering ahead, blue skies, mountains far to the right, the west, the hills of Bodie, still full of gold, ahead and on either side of them as they drove into a valley. J. W. let out a whoop and Phoebe smiled for him.

Bodie, California, ghost town, lay ahead of them, quiet, still, waiting for life to go on around it. It had all begun in 1859 when the first prospectors, a group of four, arrived. Some argue the spelling, but W. S. Bodey, one of the four, had frozen to death after being lost in a snow storm. The future town was named after him. Some gold was found then, but after a cave in and a major strike was found the rush was on and the town grew exponentially.

A state park since 1962, it now stood frozen in time, in a state of arrested decay, maintained but unchanged. Phoebe had been here several times. In fact, she thought she would never see it again. But J. W. had brought her back.

They approached the small building to pay for entrance to the park. One at a time the family trucks went through, turned left on the access road that curved wide around the town and cut between the town and the cemetery. A little further on was the park parking lot. The air was dry so they all took one last drink before getting out of the car.

Hank retrieved J. W.'s wheelchair from the back of his truck and helped him into it. J. W. complained a bit but Hank reminded him that to see the park required more walking than J. W. was accustomed to. He still brought his walking stick, carried flat across his lap.

Everyone met at the front of Hank's truck and headed down the walk to the nearest street. Phoebe held back. She looked out over Bodie, turned left to look toward the road leading north out of Bodie and to the even older town of Aurora with an even older cemetery. The area was covered with sagebrush now, green with new growth after a few weeks of warm, early summer sun that had finally melted the last of the heaps of snow Bodie was known for collecting. That area had been full of homes and buildings once. Most had been small ones, but homes just the same. There, also, had been Chinatown, the red-light district, opium dens and saloons.

Her gaze panned right, Bodie Bluff across from her, scarred from the mines, the tailings area from early excavation still visible at the bottom if one knew what to look for. The stamp mill stood there against the bluff, huge and powerful, the inner workings still inside. It had once operated around the clock until production slowed. Later, stamping hours were reduced to first light until dark, pounding, banging the gold and silver from the ore brought up from the mountain. Now it was silent, speechless.

Her gaze continued to the right, more scars on the hills, all the way to the top with more she couldn't see on the other side. Over one hundred buildings remained of the several hundred that had once lined more than a dozen streets. There was barely a sign of the south end of town, more green sagebrush growing in its place. It took a strong imagination to envision what had once been a large town full of life. Fire is deadly in more ways than one to a town made of wood.

She looked to the far right, seeing the cemetery with its small stones and low fences. A few larger stones stood up tall; testament to costly memorials.

The family group had moved on ahead of her. Her parents were aware she knew her way around. Will had held back a bit and was only a dozen yards down the path ahead of her. She sighed and began her walk into town. Approaching Will, she continued walking and he joined her stride. "Having fun yet?"

She walked on a few paces. "You know, I used to love this place."

"I know." He paused, taking his chances by asking his next question. "What happened?"

She turned to look at her younger brother, shook her head, and turned her gaze to where her family had gathered ahead of them to stop and look at one of the buildings. "Look around. It's gone. All of the things that went on here, it's all gone." She paused but Will knew she had more to say now that she was finally getting her troubles off her chest. "So what difference did it all make? The past is over. Why get stuck in it?"

They continued walking, strolling now, keeping pace behind their family. "I changed my major to business because all I ever thought about was history, the past, studying what had already happened and why, the people, the places, their things. Then I met people who were interested in the present, the future, my future."

They stopped walking when J. W. had stopped the group to point something out. He glanced back to see what Phoebe and Will were up to and continued whatever explanation he had been involved in. "I realized I needed to stop living in the past. Stop studying people long gone, stop spending so much time wondering what had gone on before I was here."

They walked in silence a few more seconds. Will finally said, "So you let others decide what you loved. Doesn't sound like my sister."

Phoebe halted, inhaled sharply to protest, looked at Will with a hint of anger in her eyes and stopped herself from stating the heated denial that had come to mind. Too many thoughts whirred in her brain, knowing he was right, knowing her father had been right, that doubting her college decision had been the warning she had blatantly ignored. But still unable to admit it aloud. Frustration bubbled inside of her. "You don't understand." She walked on ahead of him but he caught up.

"Explain it then."

"I have a job that's moving forward, that matters, that helps people right here, right now, in the present. Look around," she spread her arm wide. "This was here, and now it's gone. People come here to see how people lived. Good for them, fine. But the present is my time, our time." Her explanation quit midstream and she sighed heavily.

"The people that lived here, and other places just like this, didn't they have day to day lives just like us?" Will asked.

She smirked. "I'm sure they did. But it was a different world. Very different. Like Mars and Earth and I just lost interest in the past. It's over."

"Okay," he shrugged. They walked toward the family group, finally ready to join them on the walk around Bodie. "But for somebody so sure of one decision you're certainly behaving like you should have made another."

Will walked on ahead of her, leaving Phoebe with nothing to say. Probably a first, thought Will. He rarely spoke that bluntly to her. If they'd been kids she would have given him a sock in the nose, but she needed to hear it.

When they had both caught up to the family J. W. poked Phoebe with his walking stick. "What took you so long? I was pointing out the church and the red barn."

"I was talking to Will for a minute. I've seen them before. But I'm sorry."

"Hmph," he grunted. He pointed forward down Green street, indicating the direction he wanted to go. They walked on, slowly, passing the J. S. Cain residence, the man instrumental in Bodie's preservation later on, the Boone General Store built in 1879, the Wheaton & Luhrs Store, the Swazey Hotel and the schoolhouse that had originally been the Bon Ton Lodging House until the first school had been carelessly burned down.

Peering into windows was interesting even though dust and filtered dirt settled everywhere. Victorian wallpaper was still visible. Furnishings and belongings of another time were in every building, awaiting the return of the owner. Items of every type remained from the last residents to have lived and worked in Bodie. Some thought it eerie, some saw ghosts or felt spirits of Bodie's rough past when the gold mining town saw tribulation in this remote area, hours of travel from the nearest town. But Phoebe saw only desertion and desolation, heard only the quiet breeze blowing through the valley. Bodie was dead.

When they reached what J. W. said had once been the cross street of Wood street they stopped. It wasn't more than a walking path now, a dirt trail that narrowed and ended, no traces of the street remaining at the end. They only walked a few feet since there was nothing to see here. But it had once been a narrow street lined with homes and families. Further ahead and on the left had been the Catholic church, built in 1882, but it was gone now too.

There had been many fires in this town made mostly of wood, and what hadn't burned down in Bodie in the first large fire in 1892 had been taken in 1932, the second and most devastating fire in Bodie. Over time some structures had been removed to other towns, preserving existing lumber and bricks, and saving money on new construction. Most of the residents left for more practical locales. The hopeful still seeking their fortunes and the Bodie faithful had remained until its full decline.

J. W. poked at some sagebrush at the side of his chair. "Aren't we supposed to stick to a path to see the buildings on the guide?" asked Jody, her first comment since arriving.

"Bah." J. W. waving his hand was Jody's answer.

They stood silently for a few moments, looking southwest over the sagebrush. The mountains rose up in the distance, the cemetery to the far right. Hank knew why they were in this particular spot. So did Phoebe and Will. Respectfully, they allowed J. W. his personal reflection.

J. W. reached for Phoebe's hand to help him out of the chair. He walked carefully forward, took a few steps to the right, and turned to face his family. Softly he said, "This was my home." The family had heard the tale, but a rare few had visited with him and seen the look in his eyes when he spoke of it.

Phoebe felt a strong tug at her heartstrings now, looking at her great-grandfather. He turned back and looked out over what remained of Bodie, his head held high, a slight breeze ruffling his graying hair. Phoebe saw him take a deep breath and let it out. Then he lifted his walking stick in the air and pointed. "Over there. I lived right over there with my parents."

10

J. W. looked proud standing there, gazing out over a ghost town that was a burned-out shell of its former self. This was perhaps his last visit here, he knew that, he wanted everyone here to know that. Phoebe felt selfish and guilty for putting her misgivings ahead of what was obviously something very special to him. He hadn't talked about his parents before, not to her recollection. She wondered how much her grandfather Henry or her father knew of them. She'd never seen any pictures of them, if any existed.

He walked the few steps back to his wheelchair and said, "Back the way we came." They turned around, facing north and headed toward Green Street.

Pointing ahead at a large building complex on the hill, Jody asked, "What's that?"

J. W. pointed at Phoebe. Taking the hint she explained to Jody and any others that may not have visited before that what they were seeing was the Standard Stamp Mill where the quartz rock had been crushed after being brought out of the mines of the surrounding hills, and where the gold and silver it contained had then been extracted. Her father's face displayed a smile of pride when she talked about the history of the mill company. Jody walked up beside her and asked, "So how do you know all this stuff, anyway?"

"Long story," she told her cousin. "Hey Jody, I want to apologize to you for yesterday. You were just asking for advice, about college, and, well, I was short with you. I shouldn't have been. Pick what you're interested in, something that'll make you happy, whatever that is. Go from there." She bumped her cousin in the shoulder with her own. "You'll be fine."

Jody's smiled ear to ear. "Thanks, Phoebe. I appreciate that. Is that where you learned all about this place? In school?"

"Some. The rest was on my own."

"You must really love it then." Will walked past and glanced toward Phoebe with his eyebrows raised, having overheard. Phoebe had no comment.

They turned left on Green Street, heading back the way they'd come, but stopped at the intersection at Main Street. It ran north and south, or nearly so, meeting up with the Bodie Road they'd taken into town and leaving the other direction north to Aurora, an older ghost town that had been abandoned earlier than Bodie. They turned right, north, and wandered along, chatting, some members of the family peering into an occasional window, reading their guidebooks and musing about what had been here and what had been over there. If J. W. knew more information he revealed none of it.

They'd walked some distance before reaching the next building, nothing but open space and sagebrush in between. Jody spoke up when they reached what was left of the Bodie Bank; the vault. The vault had been built within a brick enclosure and had survived the fire. The bank building had not. Only a partially wise decision it seems. "Why didn't they build the whole town out of bricks?"

J. W. snorted with derision and shook his head.

Jody, puzzled, looked to Phoebe, who said with more patience, "Some buildings were. There was a limekiln for mortar to the north and there was a brick yard south of town.

But it was slower to build that way, and more expensive." She shrugged.

Jody looked around. "But this place isn't all that big? Wouldn't it have made more sense to make the whole place out of bricks?"

Phoebe continued, "Jody, the population at one time was over eight thousand strong. Main street was a mile long, full of houses and businesses and livery stables and storage and so much more, from there to there." Phoebe gestured from one end of Main street to the other and at the width of the valley between the hills. "It grew quickly, it was built quickly. Just because you don't see it doesn't mean it wasn't once here."

J. W. snorted again, this time directing a look to Phoebe. She glanced from J. W. to Will to her parents, who were all staring back at her, and the import of her last statement struck her. She stepped forward, to escape the scrutinizing looks, but J. W.'s walking stick stopped her. "What?" she asked quietly, looking down at him.

He looked up at her from his chair, squinting in the bright light of the day. She noticed the lines around his eyes and mouth, the thinning gray hair at his forehead and temples. The once bright color of his eyes had begun to fade to a pale shade. She waited for him to say something but he seemed to question his own reply. Finally he put the walking stick back across his lap, looked down and rubbed his eyes with his other hand. "J. W.?"

"Push me," he said, and Hank moved off to walk with Bonnie.

"All right."

"So it was cheaper and easier, I see. It's a shame about the fires though," said Jody, moving to walk with Laura. Kathleen and Will joined J. W. and Phoebe.

Just ahead was the intersection with King Street. They turned around to head back south on Main Street. Turning left on King to walk uphill and view the structures there would have been bumpy and uneven for J. W. in his chair. Apparently more willing to hear information from others than to read her guidebook, Jody asked, "What's that building?"

At this Phoebe smiled. A little scandal was always fun. "That's the jail." At Jody and Daniel's reaction the adults present smiled.

Daniel hurried up to it and peered inside its wire window. "Where are the big iron bars on the door?"

"Most jails then had heavy wood walls and doors and bars on the windows," answered Phoebe.

Daniel nodded. "It looks creepy. Just imagine, being locked up in there. But then a pretty lady from the hotel would bring over your dinner, and – "

J. W. shook his head, muttering, "No, no, no..."

"What?" Daniel asked innocently.

"That's *Gunsmoke*," was all he said, gesturing to be taken back south.

"Wait, was there anything over there?" Jody asked, pointing toward a large open area north past the jail. "Nothing's there now."

Again, Phoebe grinned. "That would have been the red-light district, There was a street there called Bonanza Street."

Jody frowned, then raised her eyebrows.

Will laughed and Phoebe noticed Daniel's face turn a shade of crimson before turning his head away. J. W.'s head bobbed up and down in a silent snicker. "There were several tiny little houses all in a row, small as cribs."

"How much room did one really need?" Will muttered out of earshot of his parents and Phoebe backhanded him on the arm.

They returned to Green Street and turned right, back the way they'd come. One of the family asked where they were off to next. They knew they could spend all day looking in buildings, asking questions of the rangers and volunteers, visiting the Museum Center. But they didn't have all day.

J. W. pointed straight ahead with his stick. When they had walked just past the church they veered left, took the path crossing the bypass road that curved around town and continued up the incline toward the Bodie Cemetery.

Daniel was looking bored and Jody seemed squeamish about tramping through a graveyard. They decided to wait outside the perimeter, have a seat and lean against the large brick building close by. However, when Phoebe said, "You know, that's the building where they used to store cadavers in the winter when the ground was too frozen for burials," they both decided to come along for the cemetery tour after all.

Three cemeteries in all, the burials were spread out on the western slope at the edge of town. They'd been moved early on in Bodie's history from the southern part of town; originally establishing a cemetery where the spring thaw waters collected had proven to be a poor idea. The hill was a much more appropriate option. Ward's Cemetery, named for furniture maker and undertaker Henry Ward, Masonic and Miners Union cemeteries combined to make one large area.

Entering through the gate in the fenced area, they followed the path where one existed. At times they carefully negotiated overgrown or narrow areas with J. W.'s wheelchair. They had gone ahead to a cluster of old graves, wooden, granite and stone when J. W. put out his stick to halt his driver. Phoebe put on the brakes and helped J. W. get out of his chair. Arguing with him about walking on the uneven ground would be useless.

"Where are you headed, Grandpa?" asked Hank.

"Don't call me that," he sighed. Then he pointed. "Over there." He shuffled toward a tall stone, engraved on two sides. His family stood respectfully nearby as J. W. paid his respects with Phoebe at his side. "Solomon," was all he said. He pointed at the tall, white stone with his first finger.

Phoebe hesitated, but asked, "Did you know him?" The dates read '*Died Jan. 13, 1904, Aged 49 yrs, 16 days.*' J. W. nodded, revealing precious personal information. On the other side of the stone was the engraving of Solomon Burkham's wife, Kathryn.

“That’s a big one,” said Jody from behind them. “Wasn’t that expensive?”

J. W. moved to walk on but Phoebe answered. “Yes, larger markers were more expensive. And the more engraving there was, the more that cost as well. Bigger budget, bigger stone. Sometimes the stones were shared for that reason.”

“What about these?” Kathleen asked about the wooden slabs placed here and there, faded and weathered, the wood split from the rays from the sun and the freezing temperatures in winter.

J. W. answered Kathleen’s question with a kick to the small ring of stones around a wooden arch sticking out of the ground at a slight angle.

Hank exclaimed with an intake of breath, “Grandpa!”

“What was that for?” Phoebe asked, incredulous at his behavior.

“Dang fool, had to go and get himself killed,” J. W. said, frowning, sounding angry and upset at the same time.

“Wait, what? You know who this is?” Hank asked.

J. W. turned around to face his family, a look of consternation on his face. “Yes, I know who it is. He got shot. On Main Street. I saw it with my own eyes.” He turned back around to face the grave. His rubbed an itch on his chin thoughtfully, his lips moved as if he was about to say something else, his eyes twitched a bit in the bright sunlight. Clearly thoughts were swirling around in his mind.

Finally Bonnie said, “But, J. W., it’s been so long. Are you sure?”

He faced them all again, a red tint burning in his cheeks. He pounded his walking stick into the ground and stated with a forceful voice, “When you get old you forget things, you don’t make them up.” He then took Phoebe’s arm and turned to keep walking.

Those assembled were taken aback at the short but sudden outburst, and felt suitably reprimanded. J. W. mumbled to Phoebe as she escorted him onward. “They think I don’t remember so good. I remember fine. They think I'm old and crazy. I may be old. But I'm not that crazy." He looked at Phoebe and winked.

"You're not that old," Phoebe said and winked back. He stopped further on and she asked, "That marker back there, who was it?"

He didn't answer right away, just looked out at Bodie. "Someone who was nice to me. And he didn't listen."

They waited for the others to catch up to them after having stopped to look at other markers. Phoebe leaned close to J. W. and whispered, "I'm sorry," and squeezed his arm. He patted her hand in return.

Several yards up the hill they stopped in front of a medium stone, dark, engraved and easier to read than most. J. W. stared at this one as if he remembered something but couldn't quite reach back into the proper corner of his mind. Jody stood alongside them and said with delight, "Hey, this one's got a poem. An expensive stone, right, Phoebe?"

"Right," Phoebe said, grinning at Jody's enthusiasm.

"But no fence around this one. Let's see," Jody leaned close so she could to see the letters. "*'To Live in Hearts We Leave Behind is Not to Die.'* That's so sad." Jody stood back and crossed her arms.

Hank said, "Isn't that a saying or something, by somebody?"

"Well said, Dad," Will teased.

Kathleen spoke up, "Yes, it is. It's part of a poem by Thomas Campbell, Scottish poet. Either the deceased was well read or the person who commissioned the stone was." She shrugged.

"You know about this stuff?" Jody asked.

"Just the poetry," Kathleen said.

"What's the rest of it say?" Daniel asked, moving forward to investigate. J. W. grinned as he remembered how Daniel and Jody hadn't wanted to come into the cemetery in the first place and were now asking questions about its inhabitants. Daniel leaned close and read the stone without touching it. "*'Newton L. Sanford, Died June 19, 1880, Aged*

29 yrs 3 mo.' Wow, twenty-nine. Jody, any name on the other side? Was he married too?"

She looked. "Nope, just his name. Wonder what happened to him."

Daniel shrugged. "Don't know. Weird, huh."

"What?" Jody asked.

"Thinking that this guy was here, right here. And now he's gone and we have no idea who he was. And there's just this stone to tell us."

Will moved to stand next to Phoebe. "I think your influence is rubbing off on those two," he teased.

"Don't worry," she shrugged. "The real world will greet them soon enough and they'll forget all about this place."

"Such cynicism, tsk, tsk," he clicked his tongue in mock shame.

They turned around to go downhill to the opening in the fence that separated the three cemeteries, then walked uphill again. Hank pushed the wheelchair along in case J. W. wanted to sit at any time. They split up in small groups or singles and meandered amongst the stones and wooden markers. The graves faced different directions and looked as if they had been placed haphazardly on the hillside.

"Why are they just up here all over with no order, no rows or anything? This is the strangest cemetery I've ever seen," exclaimed Jody, putting her hands on her hips and turning a circle. "Not that I've see that many," she admitted. Daniel looked around as well.

"There are a some in rows but we can't see them anymore. And there are more graves here than we realize. They're lost," stated Phoebe simply.

"Lost? Lost where? What does that mean?"

Phoebe continued, "It's been a long time, you know. Like that wooden marker back there. Some markers may not have survived the weather and the years. Maybe vandals destroyed some of them, or took them, I don't know. There are records of the people that are buried here but not every person with a record has a matching marker."

"You mean we could be walking around on them right now? That's awful." Jody's look of dismay was so sincere Phoebe hadn't the heart to tease her now.

Kathleen said, "It's a shame we can't read the wooden one's anymore. At least the one like the twenty-nine year old's back there is in stone."

"Newton L. Sanford," said Jody sadly. "I'm going to try to remember his name. Somebody should."

The group continued walking. J. W. stopped once again by a stone marker. He looked down on it, no sign of emotion on his face. Phoebe squeezed his arm out of sight of the others, acknowledging his memories. Hank asked, "J. W.?"

He pointed at the marker with his stick and read the stone aloud. "*'William Hick, Died Nov. 24, 1901, Age 54 yrs. Native of Cornwall England.'* Kids were fascinated by the way he talked," J. W. grinned.

Nobody spoke, allowing J. W. a moment once again.

Walking further south into the Miner's Union Cemetery took them a distance from the parking lot. They day was moving along and they still had a drive back to Minden ahead of them. "Do you want to keep going or have you seen enough?" Phoebe asked her great-grandfather kindly.

He gestured forward. They kept going, following one of the paths.

They reached a tall stone on a square base. J. W. stared, a crease between his brows. The front read, *'Arthur McQuaid Died Dec. 26, 1890, Age 18 Years.'* Directly underneath that it said, *'Hugh McQuaid Died Sept 7, 1888 Age 16 Months.'* On one side was *'Mother,'* with the details, and on the other side was *'Father,'* with those details.

"Is there something special about this one, J. W.?" Phoebe asked. "It seems very old."

He shook his head, not in the negative but to motion that the loss was a shame.

Bonnie said, "Sixteen months," and put her hand on her heart. "I just can't imagine."

"It says the parents died in 1909 and 1899. Did you know them?" Kathleen asked, not wanting to sound repetitive, but wondering why he had stopped at the marker.

He gave a simple nod and turned to continue on. He waved a hand for Hank to pull closer with his wheelchair and Phoebe helped him get seated. He stumbled slightly, and would have fallen to the ground. But he landed on one outstretched hand due to Phoebe's aid of an arm part way around his waist and Hank's hold on the other arm. Once balance was restored he stood up slowly, wincing and clenching his fist tightly as if he had injured it. Phoebe didn't ask if he was all right. He would tell her if he needed something. But she and her father exchanged worried glances.

Once seated, J. W. motioned to keep going but they went downhill and turned back around north. They stopped when J. W. pointed to a white, slender, rectangular marker, smooth at the center and engraved, *'Peter Noonan Feb. 25, 1848 – July 10, 1894.'* He glanced over at it momentarily, grinned, and motioned to continue.

No one wanted to ask what that had been about.

A few feet further on they stopped again at a white fenced-in marker, tall, rounded at the sides and pointed on top. It read, *'Mary Louisa Moore March 23, 1871 – April 26, 1891, Age 20 yrs. A precious one from us has gone, A voice we loved is stilled: A place is vacant in our hearts, Which never can be filled.'* The family looked at one another with questioning gazes, some shrugs, some shakes of the head indicating 'don't ask him again.' If there was significance to this grave they did not know what it was. Perhaps Phoebe would ask him later.

They had to wend their way back through the three cemeteries to get to the path back to the parking lot. But walking in a straight line without the meandering and reading didn't take them long. At the cemetery gate they were greeted by a park employee also leaving this area and heading in the same direction.

"I was just answering some questions for that couple up there," he pointed behind himself. "Is there anything I can do for you while you're here?" the man asked. "My name is Jeremy. I work with the Park Service here." he smiled, friendly and ready to help.

J. W. didn't even glance his way and Jody and Daniel were too self-conscious to answer. Hank struck up polite conversation on the walk back down the path. Phoebe saw their mouths move, their heads nod, saw the ranger smile a time or two. Hank and the ranger stopped to wait for the others when they reached the fork that would take them back to the parking lot.

Addressing J. W., the ranger said amiably, "So, you used to live here, huh? That's amazing. We have a few past residents pop in from time to time to visit and tell us stories. If you ever want to do that, we'd be more than happy to hear anything you can tell us."

Alfred, Bonnie and Phoebe held their breath, hoping J. W. didn't decide the man was being condescending. He eyed the ranger, considering, mulling over what he'd said. The ranger, mistakenly thinking J. W. hadn't heard him, leaned forward and repeated his statement in a louder voice. J. W. frowned. Phoebe saw his knuckles go white as he gripped his walking stick. *Oh boy,* she thought, thinking the ranger just might get a smack in the head for his troubles.

Hank, stepping between the ranger and J. W. spoke up for his grandfather. "Thank you for the offer. Yes, he used to live here. But that was a long time ago, and I don't really know for how long. So I'm not sure how many stories he has to tell. But we'll keep that in mind."

"Great, great," the ranger said. "Here's a Bodie Park card with my name and telephone number on it. If you ever want to meet with us out here, just let me know. I can throw in a tour for you. During good weather, of course," he laughed lightly.

"Of course." Hank and Jeremy-the-ranger shook hands. Jeremy touched the brim of his hat in a friendly farewell to the rest of the assemblage. “I hope you enjoyed the park today.”

When they turned to walk up the path to the where the trucks were parked Phoebe noticed that J. W.’s knuckles were turning whiter as his grip tightened on his stick. He muttered something inaudible.

“What’s the matter?” Phoebe asked matter-of-factly.

He grunted. His knuckles gripping his walking stick remained white and it shook in his lap. He was angry. “J. W.?”

“‘I’ll give you a tour, during good weather. I hope you enjoyed the park today.’ Hmph. I don’t need a tour. And this wasn’t a family picnic where we came to swing on the swing set.”

“I’m sorry, J. W. He doesn’t understand, I guess. How could he?”

“No, he doesn’t. This was a place, a home my home. But you understand.” Phoebe parked his wheelchair near her father’s truck and set the brakes. “You just don’t care anymore,” he said sadly.

11

Phoebe slid into the seat on the other side of the truck from J. W. She didn't look him in the eye. She couldn't. First she had the guilt from her college decision and disappointing her parents weighing her down. Now she had the guilt her great-grandfather had placed on her shoulders practically pushing her through the seat. Yes, she understood. He had lived here once. And the park ranger had made him feel like a feeble novelty.

He never went into details with her, or any of them, about his life here. They had talked of that subject amongst themselves on occasion but no one knew exactly why that was. Perhaps he harbored bad memories and details brought them back up? Saying people's names brought back the pain of those lost? Or maybe he hadn't lived there long at all and he simply held an affection for the place because his parents had lived there with him. Phoebe could understand that concept. Carson City would always be special to her and her brothers.

The three mile bumpy ride back seemed shorter than the ride in. And the ten miles to the main highway felt a great deal smoother after that. Oh, the invention of pavement.

She was turning to J. W. to speak, to break the ice she felt had developed. He turned to her in the same instant. His hand reached across to hers. Rarely did J. W. blatantly show affection so Phoebe didn't turn it down this time. She put her hand on his and squeezed. When she looked at his face he was looking out the front windshield, peering around her mother's headrest in front of him. She smiled. That was all she was going to get. But it meant she was forgiven.

Hank drew her attention when he asked, "Phoebe, have you ever heard of the Bodie Curse?"

She smiled. "Oh yes, I have. Why do you bring that up?"

"The what?" asked Bonnie.

"The Bodie Curse," replied Hank. J. W. withdrew his hand and looked out his own side window. "When I was walking with the ranger he mentioned it to me. He said some people believe if you take anything from Bodie, anything at all, that you will be visited by misfortune of some kind. That it will only go away when the object or artifact is returned." He chuckled and looked at Phoebe in the rearview mirror.

"Yep, that's what I've heard," she said, glancing again at J. W., who was still looking out his window. "Not that I believe it." She saw J. W. move his head and heard a little snort come from his direction.

"Okay, Mister, what do you know about it?" Phoebe asked, poking J. W. in the shoulder. He turned to look at her and raised his eyebrows.

He shrugged. "Sounds like downright shecoonery to me."

"Shecoonery? You mean chicanery?"

"I mean what I mean. Curse, hmph. Of all the... watch out – "

Hank had been listening to J. W., seeking revelations of new information, and had taken his attention off the road for an instant. The pair of Pronghorn Antelope dashed across the road ahead. None of them had been in real danger, but he inhaled sharply, gripped the steering wheel, and regained his composure. The antelope were across safely and the car was moving down the road.

Phoebe said, "Somebody must have taken something. That looked like the Bodie curse in action back there."

Bonnie said, "Well it's silly, of course, but it's fun to think about." She turned in her seat to face Phoebe. "What kinds of things do people take?"

"Oh, anything at all. Glass bottles, buckets, cans, random pieces of metal on the ground. Before it was a park the abandoned houses were locked. But some buildings were broken into and antiques from the homes and stores were stolen."

"That's terrible. No wonder they spread a story about a curse. I hope it stopped people from taking things."

"When the story spread about bad things happening to people it helped," Phoebe grinned. "Some people reported strange or unfortunate things happening to them. But people can be very superstitious."

They drove on toward Minden, chatting lightly on the way. The return drive was more pleasant for Phoebe than the drive out. Bodie was behind her now. She didn't need to see it again. J. W. had had his road trip. Now they could go back to her grandparent's home and enjoy the rest of the afternoon and evening with the family; eating, playing horseshoes, swinging on the old tire swing. She inhaled deeply and sighed.

She felt J. W.'s eyes on her and asked him, "How's your hand?"

He looked down at it. He'd folded his pinky finger under and, wiggling the other three fingers and his thumb in front of her he said, "Oops, seems I've lost one." She laughed.

"I'm glad you're okay." He nodded.

Hank turned on the radio and an old, favorite song came on. He and Bonnie hummed along, singing a few words here and there. Phoebe had to smile at the happiness between the two of them. It was delightful to see. Now they were on their way back to her grandfather Henry's home where he and her grandmother, Julia, lived. They were another happy couple, together for dozens of years now. *An anniversary party coming next?* Phoebe wondered, trying to think of specific dates. She glanced at J. W.

He was, in a way, alone.

Her great-grandmother, Grace, had passed away years ago. J. W. mentioned her now and then. There was a picture of them at her grandparents house, taken only a couple of years before she passed away. The family was large and they gathered as often as possible. But Phoebe knew he missed her. She had seen him staring out the kitchen window, probably thinking about her, wishing she could have been at his party with all of her kids, grandkids, and so on. But who didn't remember with fondness the moments that give life meaning?

I remember wearing my favorite dress the first day of first grade; I remember when Will was teasing and tried to push me off my horse and I hung on and ran away. J. W. has many more years full of memories than I do. Reliving them isn't necessarily a bad thing. Then why doesn't he tell me about them?

They arrived back at the farmhouse a few minutes after five o'clock. As Will walked past her in the yard he said, "Time for round two," and rubbed his stomach. He and the others headed back to the buffet.

Although J. W. looked tired, he seemed to have gained a new energy with the ten minute nap he'd managed to take toward the end of the ride home. Julia offered to bring him something to eat and drink as soon as he walked through the door and said his chair was waiting for him. He took a glass of water, complained that it wasn't a whiskey, and vowed to come get one later. Accepting the offer of of a delivered dinner, he said he would be right back and went directly to his room. And closed the door.

Phoebe helped herself to something to drink then went to the porch and filled a plate with food. Then she found time to visit with family she hadn't had a chance to speak with earlier and filled them in on their afternoon.

Phoebe was in the middle of a second round of a game of horseshoes with her second cousin Steve, Hank's cousin's youngest son, when she glanced up and saw J. W. looking out the kitchen window at the rear of the house. She caught his eye, smiled, waved a little hello, and saw him lift his hand in reply. She threw another shoe. It glanced off the metal post and missed to the left. She groaned, knowing if Steve ringed his shoe she would lose. She hated to lose.

Steve's throw. He aimed exaggeratedly, one eye closed, tongue sticking out; his mother Adelia laughed, roll her eyes, and said, "Teenagers."

He drew back his arm and pushed the shoe forward. It arched in the air and Phoebe said, "Oh, no, no, no," as it landed inches in front of the post and slid into place around it. "No," she yelled, jumping up and down. Her twin brothers clapped for Steve's victory over their sister.

Steve's oldest sister, Lori, said with a smile on her face, "I think that was his biggest win, Phoebe." No one had taken the match too seriously.

Phoebe dug a quarter out of her jacket pocket and slapped it in the palm of her second cousin's hand. "One of these days I want a rematch."

"You got it," he answered.

Glancing back at the big window, Phoebe noticed J. W. had moved. He was coming outside through the side door, letting the screen door slam behind him. Nobody was going to tell J. W. to apologize to her grandmother for that. Someone went to him to assist him to a chair. He growled that he needed no help, but his actions belied his words when he leaned on the helping hand and sat down in a lawn chair on the porch. He waved his hand for Phoebe to come over.

She went over and took the seat next to him. "I lost. I can't believe it."

"I saw. Do you always win?"

She sighed. "No, of course not. But I like to," she chuckled.

He was staring at her, nearly expressionless, a particular look on his face as if he had something to say.

"Do you need something? What is it?"

He turned his head, looking out over the back yard, past the trees.

She ventured into territory she knew was dangerous, that may get her censured for sticking her nose in the wrong place. "Maybe we shouldn't have gone today." She held her breath.

He turned to look at her. But his eyes crinkled, his lips parted and his chest moved up and down. He was beginning to laugh. At the look that must have been on her face he laughed more until a slight cough made him stop and he sighed. "Now what made you say a crazy thing like that?" he asked.

Taken aback, it took her a minute to formulate an answer. "I – well – you – "

He raised his eyebrows, waiting.

Phoebe frowned, feeling silly. *Just say it.* "You looked so sad when we were riding in the truck on the way home. You looked sad just now. We go to Bodie, you think about the past, the people you knew, Great-grandma Grace, and you get sad. I hate it. That's one of the reasons I didn't want to go to Bodie. The past is gone and it makes you sad."

J. W. took one of Phoebe's hands in his. He reached up with his other hand to the necklace he had given her as a high-school graduation gift. Its gold shined in the light of the early evening sun. "I'm not sad," he sad matter-of-factly. He let go of the necklace and looked her in the eye. He cleared his throat. "I've lived a long life," he started.

"J. W. – "

"You don't know what I'm going to say. Now let me finish," he snapped, "and don't tell me what I'm thinking. I've lived a long life. People have come and gone, a few of them I've like," he grinned. "I wish you'd known your great-grandmother better. She appreciated being called that.

She was beautiful. I miss her, yes. But she would have anointed me with a blinker if I'd sat around and pouted my life away after she died."

At Phoebe's quizzical look he pointed to one of his eyes. "Black eye." Phoebe nodded, smiling and finding it difficult to believe Grace capable of such a thing.

"And don't lie. That's not why you didn't want to go."

"I said it's one of the reasons." She looked down into her lap.

"So you're the only one allowed to have something on your mind? Hmm." He let go of her hand and turned back to look out at the yard.

"Okay, what then? What's on your mind? Tell me."

He picked up his walking stick and placed it on the ground between his feet, both hands holding it. "I've been waiting. I told you already." He took his old pocket watch out again, opened it, nodded, closed it, put it back in his pocket and said, "It's time." He stood up, Phoebe's hand on one elbow, assisting. He took two steps and turned to look at her and asked, "Coming?"

They crossed the yard to the large barn but walked past it to the smaller barn. Walking around the right side to the front, J. W. nudged the door open with his walking stick and walked to the right side to a shelf. He picked up a flashlight, flicked it on and told Phoebe to close the door. He sat on the same wooden crate he'd been on before and gestured for Phoebe to have a seat across from him.

"Do you know why I call this my barn?" He asked her.

He had called it that before. She shrugged. "Because you moved it here, right?"

"Yes, I did. I wanted it so I moved it," he stated simply.

"Okay. What does this have to do with anything?" Phoebe didn't ask for more. If J. W. felt like adding details he would. Whenever he chose.

"You were talking about Bodie today. Answering questions. You know some buildings were moved when the town declined." She nodded. "This barn used to be in Bodie."

Phoebe was surprised but not shockingly so. J. W. rarely talked about details of the people he had know, the places he had lived, or when he'd lived where. "I don't think I've ever heard you mention that before. Why not?"

He didn't answer her directly but moved on. "Have you ever heard of something called The Doorway to the Gods? In Arizona?"

This was unexpected, but J. W. had a habit of surprising people. "No, I don't think so. What's that?"

He leaned forward, speaking quietly, "It's a mysterious place in southern Arizona. There's a stone arch there. People have said for generations that it's a portal to another time." He sat upright and nodded, settling the matter.

"What? You're kidding me, right? What has this got to do with anything?"

He shook his head. "I'm not. There are stories that are quite convincing. I'm surprised you've never heard of it."

"I haven't heard of everything, you know. Well, what is it? What does it do?"

"It's an area full of land formations and geodes, and some people say lost mission gold and silver. In 1800 Indians were passing nearby and one of them went through the arch and disappeared. A body of an Indian was found in the 1940s. What he was wearing was ancient but he didn't look like he'd been there for over a hundred years. They said it was like he'd gotten lost in another time."

Phoebe's eyebrows went up in disbelief. He waved his hand for her to wait and keep listening. "Mind you, I've never been to that area. However, people have seen the arch shimmer, as if with heat, when it's chilly outside. And they've felt vibration in their ears when close to it. Wild horses were heard running nearby, but none were seen."

J. W. let all this sink in. Phoebe didn't say anything at first, knowing J. W. wouldn't tell her these random facts without having a good reason. After a moment she asked, "Okay. So now tell me why you're telling me this?"

He smiled. "Do you believe me?"

"I believe you, yes. I don't know if I believe the other people that told the stories or not. It's sounds a little – out there. Don't you think?"

J. W. stood up slowly with the help of his walking stick. He walked in a slow circle, around and behind Phoebe. Shuffle, shuffle, shuffle. Stop. He looked at her. Shuffle, shuffle, stop. "Get up," he said and shuffled toward the back of the barn, into the darkness and away from the two small side windows. He lit the way with his flashlight until he was standing in the corner. This barn wasn't used much and Phoebe had to swat away cobwebs in order to walk under the loft that was above their heads. He propped the flashlight on a nearby bucket.

"It's a good thing I trust you, Mister. Now what are you doing?"

J. W. had his back in the corner, Phoebe was a few feet opposite him. Using both hands he reached up to a nail on the wall, took down a rusty metal rim from a very old wagon wheel and placed it flat on the ground between them. It wasn't a usual wagon wheel rim; it had a shimmer to it in the dim light from the flashlight. Phoebe squinted, trying to see why it shined. J. W. answered her inquiring glance. "Gold dust," he said. Before Phoebe could ask about that he stepped into the middle of it. "And, I'm not sad. I have something to show you. But now my mind is clear."

"J. W., this is weird. Are you feeling okay?"

"Stop asking me that. I'm fine. You need to ask yourself if you're okay." Slowly, he reached over and put his arms around her in a gentle hug, his old limbs moving with care. Phoebe couldn't remember the last time he had given her a hug like this. If she wasn't worried about him she would be suspicious. But she hugged him in return, hoping he wasn't losing his mind.

He pulled his arms back, gently kissing her forehead as he withdrew. The light was dim here in the corner, the only light from the sideways flashlight a few feet away. He removed a small object from his pants pocket. Light shined off the small object in his hands as he stepped back to the corner, leaving the metal rim between them. "Step into the rim, please."

Phoebe frowned. "What the heck, J. W. – " He put his finger to his lips. She took one step into the rim and waited. J. W. took one of her hands and put the object into it, closing her fingers around it.

He picked up the flashlight and turned it off and on several times before leaving it on and returning it to the bucket. A minute later the door opened and Will walked in. "Back here," said J. W., "and close the door."

"What the – " Will started to ask, not knowing why J. W. had told him to keep an eye out for a flashing light at the barn window. Will joined them in the corner.

"Step in," J. W. said. Will laughed at the scene before him but shrugged. Believing his great-grandfather was playing some trick on his sister he went along.

"Okay." He stepped into the circle, shoulder to shoulder now with Phoebe. "We've played some crazy games before but what – "

"Don't lose that," J. W. glanced at Phoebe's closed hand. "Remember, I love you, Phoebe. And be careful." He looked at Will apologetically and winked. "You too," he whispered. He reached down and grasped the metal rim on the barn floor, lifted it up quickly, keeping it horizontally level as best he could, and raised it up and over the heads of his great-grandchildren. As soon as it cleared the top of Will's head he pulled the metal rim to his side, hung it back on the nail on the wall, reached down to retrieve the flashlight and sighed. J. W. picked up his walking stick and made his way back to the door. He turned and gave one last look to the empty barn before he closed the door.

12

Darkness surrounded her, so black she instinctively opened her eyes wide to let in more light, but to no avail. She was overcome with a lightheaded feeling and reached out to keep the dizziness from tipping her over. Her hands contacted an arm, then a hand, then another hand grabbed onto her upper arm and a sense of panic evoked a surprised sound close to a squeal. The hand slipped away, scraping her arm in the process. A whirring sound was in her ears, filled her head, so much so her hearing faded and she felt as if she were going deaf with the pressure of it. A strong wind was blowing and she squeezed her eyes tight shut. Then the pressure lifted, the whirring slowed, the dizziness ebbed and the ground once again felt solid beneath her feet.

Someone was calling her name; so far away. Opening her eyes as wide as they would go she searched left, right, up, down, afraid to move her feet because she still couldn't see anything in the blackness. She was remembering being in the barn, with J. W. and her brother Will. Had it been Will that had reached out for her moments before? "Will?

Are you here? Will?" She called out, reaching out with arms extended. So much empty space.

A muffled reply came, "Phoebe? Phoebe." It was Will. She was relieved and annoyed at the same time. Will was here but why was he so far away? What had happened? What had J. W. done?

Her hand contacted something, someone. Her hearing cleared, a bit of light was visible and she saw Will's face in front of her. She was flooded with relief. Will must have felt the same for when he finally came into focus she saw the tension ease from his face and he sighed heavily. He held both of her upper arms in his hands for a few moments, collecting himself. Phoebe calmed quickly and raised her voice, "J. W.! Where are you?" she yelled. No answer came.

She looked down to see they were still standing inside the rusty metal wagon wheel rim. How? There had been a peculiar emptiness surrounding her, arms flailing about searching for something or someone to hold onto. Now Will was directly in front of her.

When no answer came she turned around to look toward the barn door. She took a single step over the metal rim of the wagon wheel but instantly stopped. Something had changed. Drastically. The light was changing, becoming brighter, the utter darkness from before now gone. No lights were on, no flashlights or candles. Just dim light filtering in through the two small windows at the sides of the barn.

Turning her head to check on Will, she saw alarm in her brother's expression. She walked slowly forward to look out the window on the right, afraid now, nervous. This couldn't be J. W.'s barn. This didn't look like the same barn they had been in only minutes ago on her grandparents farm. There *were* two windows, one on each side. The barn door *was* at the front, straight ahead. The loft *was* in the back extending over one third of the floor below. But this one had implements of all sorts hanging from the walls. This one had dirt and straw on the floor and three horse stalls in the back near where they had stood inside the rim. This one was in current use; but it was indeed the same barn.

She whispered, “Are you coming?”

Will stepped forward out of the metal rim without speaking, still too apprehensive to form words in response. He approached Phoebe at the window, squeezing next to her to peer outside. He inhaled sharply, dumbfounded at what lay before his line of sight. He shook his head, rubbed his eyes, covered his face, looked out the window again and groaned. “What is – where – ”

Phoebe turned her back to the wall and slid down to the floor. She put her head in her hands. “Oh dear Lord, J. W., what did you do?” Will joined her on the floor, wanting to ask, afraid to ask, waiting for Phoebe to tell him what he wanted to know. They sat like that for another minute, breathing deeply, shaken, recovering from the experience inside the metal rim. “Okay,” Phoebe finally said, “It’s clear J. W. has deserted us.”

Phoebe had never seen her little brother panic; until now. Will jerked upright, hands flying in the air, voice raised as he looked her in the eye and said, “That’s all you’re going to say? He’s deserted us? Where the hell are we, Phoebe? What did he do? One second he’s telling me, ‘hey come into the barn in a minute, I want to show you something,’ and the next I’m whirring and buzzing and spinning my head off, I can’t see, I can’t hear, I’m lost in the dark, I’m yelling for you, you don’t answer, can’t hear me, I don’t know, maybe I couldn’t hear anything, no idea, and the next minute we’re exactly where we were before except we’re *not* where we were before and, and,” he looked around, “is this even the same barn? I mean, when did Grandpa get horses? J. W. doesn’t even like horses, at least I didn’t think so, but who really knows what J. W. likes, he never talks about anything, just ‘do this,’ ‘don’t touch that,’ and, holy cow, it smells like dirt in here, do you smell that? Geez, I think I’m sitting on a fish hook – ”

Phoebe pulled her arm back and soundly slapped Will across the face. He inhaled sharply, putting his palm on his cheek and staring open-mouthed at his sister. His breathing slowed and he leaned his back against the wall and groaned. "Thanks."

"Sorry," she said quietly. "But that wasn't helping. Stay right there." Phoebe stood up slowly and peered over the edge of the window again. Using the edge of a sleeve cuff she rubbed the smudged window, enabling her to see more clearly. Dirt covered both inside and out but it helped a little. Still reeling from the dizzying experience inside the rim she rubbed her eyes as well, hoping to clear her vision, hoping she had fallen, had bumped her head, was dreaming, having a nightmare, or some other reason than might explain that what she was seeing and hearing looked so very real.

"I think my hearing's back," said Will. Phoebe glanced down at him, still sitting on the barn floor and rubbing one of his ears with the end of his finger as if to unstick it. "What is that noise?"

Phoebe's gaze returned out the window. She felt like crying, like screaming, like panicking as Will had. She inhaled deeply, exhaled slowly. Panicking was not her thing. *No, but running away is, isn't it?* a phantom voice asked from within her head. *Time to face your demons, Phoebe.*

Will asked from his place on the ground, "Where are we Phoebe? Do you know?"

She turned around again but remained standing. "Yes, I know." She paused and looked down at her brother. "I don't know what happened, or how, or why, but somehow, somehow J. W. sent us, sent us – "

"What? *What?*"

"We're in Bodie, Will. We've somehow returned to old Bodie when it was still a town." Phoebe saw Will's eyes roll back in his head and he dropped to the floor like a sack of potatoes.

"Oh for heaven's sake," Phoebe said as she sat next to her brother and made sure his head hadn't hit anything too hard on the floor. She tapped his face with the palm of her hand. "Will, Will, wake up. Good grief, wait 'til I tell Tony and Troy about this." She shook his shoulders and Will started to move.

He breathed deeply and jerked himself upright. Rubbing the side of his head where he'd fallen he asked, "What happened?"

"You passed out."

"I did what? No way."

"Yes you did. I can't wait to tell Tony and Troy."

"Don't you dare." Then he groaned, remembering what Phoebe had told him. "What are we gonna do? This is insane."

"I agree. But J. W. must have had a reason."

"A reason? A reason? How? I want to know how in the hell does somebody do something like this? Wait. Are you pulling my leg? This sounds like something the two of you would cook up together." He stood up, still a little wobbly but regaining his balance quickly, and turned to look out the window, smiling, sure of himself now. His confident smile disappeared instantly. "Oh my God..."

"Will, I'm glad you never became a serious poker player. You only swear when you freak out. And right now you are freaked out. Calm down."

"Calm down, she says. We've got to get out of here. I deliver medical supplies for a living. I don't know how to live in a place like this. I drive a car, not a buggy. I use a telephone, not a telegraph. I drive across the country in three days not three months."

She interrupted, "When have you ever driven across the country?"

"What difference does that make? Now I can't do it even if I wanted to." He sat back down and put his forehead in his hands. "And I like drive-through burgers"

Phoebe gave him his moment to calm down. Then she added, "Sorry, but it takes a lot more than three months to get across the country." When he looked at her sharply she shrugged. "Unless you take a train."

"This is your thing, Phoebe, not mine. We've only been here a few minutes and you already fit in better than I do." He groaned again.

"You think I like this?" she snapped. "This is as much of a surprise to me as it is to you. I told you I was happy where I was. Now this."

"No you didn't."

"What?"

"You didn't say you were happy. I asked you. You avoided answering me. When we went, came, to Bodie with J. W. and you started answering Jody's questions, *then* you looked happy. You don't like your new job and you know it."

"Enough of this. We've got to figure out what J. W. did and how we can get out of here and get home." Phoebe began crossing to the other window on the opposite side of the barn. Noises from outside ceased her footsteps and she froze. She motioned to Will to come with her back to the corner of the barn. He shook his head no, wary. "Oh come on, would you?"

"No," he said, glancing at the metal rim on the floor.

Phoebe moved to the corner quickly and bent to pick up the metal wagon wheel rim. She remembered now that she had noticed a strange glimmer coming from the rim in the scant light from J. W.'s flashlight earlier. Picking it up she realized it did indeed, as J. W. had stated, have minuscule gold specks embedded in it. *Gold dust,* he had said. Phoebe angled it so more light reached it from the windows. Yes, it was more than just metal.

She hung the metal rim on a nail on the side of the barn. *The same nail?* Whispering Will's name she waved him back to the corner and pointed that she had hung up the wheel rim. He nodded and joined her in the corner. "I feel better with that thing out of the way."

"Me too," said Phoebe, eyeing the rim.

Whatever footfalls had sounded nearby failed to enter the barn. They both saw shadows outside one window and both were fearful of being discovered. Phoebe felt they would have to leave to find answers, that they couldn't just stay put and expect that the mysterious answers as to what had happened and why, and how they would get back home would suddenly pop into their heads. But she wanted to postpone stating the facts to Will as long as possible. He was an intelligent person; with a little perspective he would soon calm down and see reason.

The shadows were no longer visible from the corner of the barn. The footfalls no longer audible. Whoever had been directly outside had moved along, they hoped. But now what?

"What if we just try to step inside the rim and reverse whatever J. W. did? What was he doing before I walked in?" Will's suggestion was worth a try.

Phoebe tried to remember what had happened before Will had come into the barn. "Let's see, we were just sitting up there talking, then he told me about this mysterious arch thing in Arizona, then he told me to come back here and then he said 'here hold this' and handed me something. Then he gave me a hug and said – "

"He gave you a hug?" Will asked, eyebrows raised.

"Yes, he gave me a hug. He likes me. And yes, I thought it was weird too. But then he took the wagon rim off the wall and put it over my head – wait – or was it already on the ground when I walked back here? Geez, I don't remember."

"You're not going to panic now, are you? If you do can I slap you?"

"Shut up, I'm trying to remember." Phoebe tapped her forehead with her fingertips, trying to bring the memories to the forefront, like bringing bubbles to the top of a container.

"What did he give you to hold?" Will asked, having just heard what she'd said.

Phoebe opened her hands and looked at both palms, remembering that J. W. had said 'don't lose that' when he'd place an object in her hand. "Oh no, what did I do with it? I was spinning, I reached out. Where did it go?" She pushed straw out of the way with one foot then the other, searching.

"What are you looking for?"

"I don't know. J. W. put something into my hand, said not to lose it and then, well you know the rest." She ran the toes of her boots over the ground, slower now, in the low light in the dark corner of the barn. "There's nothing here, nothing." She plopped down on her rear and sighed. Will sat with his back against the wall, his forearms resting against his bent knees.

"What exactly did he say to you, Phoebe?"

She thought about it. "I've been worried about him. I told him I didn't like that he seemed sad. He said he's not sad, and then I think he said something about having something on his mind, that he had something to show me so he brought me to the barn. His barn. You know, the smaller one on Grandpa Henry's farm. He told me it came from Bodie, that he moved it from there." She paused, trying to remember more of what he had said. "Then he gave me something, told me not to lose it, and said to be careful."

"That's it? That's all? How is that helpful at all?"

"I don't know," she said, exasperated. "That's what he said to me. And I lost it." She hung her head, shuffling her feet back and forth on the dirty, straw-filled floor in agitation.

Her scuffing of the floor created a small cleared space and a thought occurred to her. "Will, all that's here is wood and dirt and straw. That's all I see. Help me look, maybe we can still find what J. W. gave me." She moved to her hands and knees and began searching.

Will joined in the search but said, "But we don't know what we're looking for."

"Just look for something that looks like it doesn't belong."

Their hands moved straw back and forth carefully, wary of slivers, not sure what lie underneath. Phoebe's fingers contacted an object about the size of an acorn. It was shaped like a pyramid with the pointed end rounded off, yet had no sharp edges. It was light gray, nearly white, and made of some kind of stone.

"I think this is it. Why else would this be here?"

"What is it?" Will asked.

Phoebe held it tight in her fist, imagining it when J. W. had handed it to her. "Yes, this is it. And I have no idea. Looks like stone but I don't know what kind." She shrugged. "Okay, you grab the wagon rim and put it here," she indicated the place on the floor it had been before.

"I don't know, Phoebe..."

"It was your idea. What have we got to lose?"

Will looked worried, apprehensive. Frustrated, Phoebe unhooked the rim from the nail in the wall and placed it on the barn floor.

"Okay, now step in."

"Then what. You're some kind of time travel expert now?"

"Get in," she said sternly. Will slowly stepped across the edge of the rim, wincing as if expecting an electric shock or hard blow.

"Didn't he lift it over our heads? How are we going to do that?"

"Together. I'll get this side, you grab over there."

They each took hold of a side and lifted it until they could reach no higher. Nothing happened. They lowered it and lifted it again, slower, then tried it again but lifted it faster. Finally, after a few attempts at varying speeds and angles they put the rim back on the nail on the wall. Neither could remember what else had occurred.

Noise from outside, scuffling, a horse nickering, its feet stamping the ground, a small voice. Wood rattling. Someone was opening the barn door.

"Don't lose that thing again. I don't know for what, but if J. W. said you need it, you need it," Will whispered hurriedly. She quickly slipped it into the lower left pocket of her Army Jacket and heard it clink with the other items she had accumulated in the last couple of days.

Phoebe and Will stood up fast and pulled themselves tightly into the corner of the barn. They would still be seen when the light came in through the door.

Its wide door swung open and they could see a horse waiting to enter. They saw its escort, a boy. A small boy, no older than six or seven, struggling with the heavy door but managing in his stubbornness to push the door and hold the hungry horse at the same time. Once the door was stationary the boy led the horse inside and headed for the stall in the corner adjacent to them.

The boy jumped when he saw Phoebe and Will and stopped. Will held up both palms to show he meant no harm. Phoebe attempted a smile, but feared her caution made it come across as more of a sneer. They stared at each other for several seconds before Phoebe spoke first and said, "Hi. We're, um, we're lost. Do you think you could help us?"

The boy stared for a few more seconds, looked the strangers over and finally nodded. He pointed at the horse and Phoebe nodded. He needed to put the horse in its stall first. They waited. He was quick, he had done this before. The boy led the horse in, tied him up, his feed and water already there. The boy climbed up the stall wall and down the outside of the one next to it, and walked out to face them.

"Who're you?" The boy asked, hanging his thumbs in the sides of his overalls.

Phoebe and Will took a timid step forward from the corner. "I'm – I'm – " Phoebe caught and corrected herself before making a casual mistake in her introduction. "I'm Miss Tucker, and, and this is my brother Mr. Tucker." The boy stared and frowned. "And you are?"

"Walter. Come on." He turned around and headed out the barn door.

They followed the boy out of the barn and stood aside while he closed it. They didn't help him as he seemed quite capable. And the frown on his face hadn't yet gone away. They needed a friend right now, even though it may only be a little boy.

Will said, "That noise. I thought it was my hearing, but look." Will nodded ahead of them and on the hills to the right.

Phoebe looked and inhaled sharply. It was the stamp mills, in full operation, pounding away at the ore that had been brought in for gold and silver extraction, da-da-da-da-dum, over and over and over, in rapid succession, creating a sky-filling cacophony. She saw the Standard Mill, the one that remained of the Bodie she knew, the one she had spoken of to Jody. But there were others here now. Many others.

The boy walked ahead several feet, through a short wooden gate in the middle of a horse fence that connected to the house, and around a corner. Phoebe nearly lost him as she looked about with wide eyes, not fully believing what she was seeing. Will grabbed her upper arm and jerked her toward the boy. They were at the side of a neat little house painted white, two stories on one half, a single story on the other half. He took this chance to whisper in her ear, "Miss Tucker? Mr. Tucker?"

"Yes. Kids don't call adults by their first names here."

"Look how we're dressed. Good thing that's not weird," he said sarcastically.

"Nothing we can do about that right now, is there?"

She smiled at the boy when he looked around to see if they were still following him. They rounded another corner to what was the front of a house facing a narrow road. The boy went up a few steps and opened the door.

Phoebe and Will followed the boy into the small but neat room full of Victorian charm. A woman came into the room as they entered, wiping her hands on an apron, a look of curiosity and concern on her face. Walter closed the door behind the three of them. Will was out of his element and looked to Phoebe for help. Phoebe spoke up but was hoping they weren't thrown out in the first seconds after their introduction.

"Hello, I'm Miss Tucker, and this is my brother. We're lost. We met Walter outside and he said perhaps he could help?"

The woman nodded once and said to Walter, "Go wash up for supper." Then to her two new visitors she said, "I'm

Mrs. Barrett. Welcome. We're about to have supper. You can stay if you'd like."

"That's very generous of you," said Phoebe.

"Follow me, I'll show you where you can wash up."

She turned around and walked back the way she had come. They followed. Walking forward through the doorway they entered a short hallway. Directly right from the hallway was the kitchen, directly left was a stairway that went up to the second floor. "There are three more bedrooms at the top, one on the left and two on the right," Mrs. Barrett pointed out. They passed this and reached the end of the hallway and two more doors. One on the left in the corner and one straight ahead that opened into a room situated at the back of the house.

Mrs. Barrett opened the door on the left in the corner. "For you," she told Phoebe. Nodding for Will to follow, the woman walked a couple of steps ahead to the other door. She opened that one, stepped aside and gestured for Will to go inside. "You can use this room." Will thanked her and stood just inside the door, unsure of what to do. He was waiting for Mrs. Barrett to leave the two of them alone so he could ask Phoebe what was going on.

Phoebe thanked her and nodded to Will to go inside, stepping back into her assigned room and closing her own door. Will started to thank Mrs. Barrett, following his sister's lead, when he heard someone call Mrs. Barrett from the other end of the hallway. Footsteps followed the voice and Mrs. Barrett excused herself. Will heard Mrs. Barrett say something, and the other person, a man, gave an inaudible reply.

A few moments later Mrs. Barrett returned, accompanied by the voice. "Mr. Sanford, this is Mr. Tucker. He and his sister, Miss Tucker, will be joining us for supper. This is Mr. Sanford," she said to Will.

The man's smile was only slightly visible beneath his horseshoe mustache as he held out his hand for a handshake with Will in a most friendly manner. "It is a pleasure to meet you," said the man. Will shook his hand in return and did his best to mumble a polite greeting.

13

Will stood just inside the doorway, uncertain and unable to move. Mrs. Barrett excused herself and the man named Sanford asked, "So, you're staying for supper?" Will nodded. "I have a spare coat if you would care to borrow it," he offered.

Will was informed enough to know his pants were shaped all wrong and the wrong color for where he was now was. And he also wore a tucked-in, button-down shirt with vertical stripes and palm tree on the chest pocket, and a brown belt around his waist. He thought momentarily of those movies when a guy walked into a high-class restaurant and had to borrow a black suit jacket just to sit down at a table with his date. So that's why the man had stayed to talk for a moment.

Will managed to mumble, "Um, yes, thank you. That's nice, yes."

"Are you well?" the man asked, standing just at the doorway. "Perhaps you should have a seat." He gestured toward a chair in the corner of the small room.

“I don’t know. Again, thank you.” He rubbed his eyes with the heels of his hands.

“You look about the same size as I am. I’m sure one of mine will fit you just fine. I’ll retrieve it directly and bring it to you. Supper is in a few minutes. Don’t be late, it would be rude to our hostess.”

Will nodded and Mr. Sanford walked out and closed the door, leaving Will alone to gather his thoughts. At least alone he could wash his face, rub away the daze, and rub his neck muscles that were so tight they were beginning to give him a headache.

A few minutes later there was a knock on his door and he jumped. It was Mr. Sanford with his loan of a coat. Will would have simply called it a jacket, but he put it on and it fit nicely. It was black, the sleeves were long enough, and the shape was straight, the length to mid-thigh, with four buttons in the middle. *Not the best with the khakis but...* Will shrugged. Phoebe would probably be horrified. *Phoebe!*

Left alone for a few minutes to wash face and hands, Phoebe was able to collect her thoughts. They had gotten a lucky break, at least for now. She felt as if only a short time ago she had eaten at her grandparents home. But everything that had happened in the last couple of hours had made her stomach growl. And who knew when they would get the chance to eat again.

She splashed some water on her face, picked up a clean hand towel from the washstand and looked at herself in the small mirror above the stand. *J. W. what did you do? And why did you do it? How are we going to get home?* Useless questions, she knew. Only worth something if they made it home so she could ask him herself.

Her reflection showed her the dress she was wearing underneath her olive green Army jacket. Too bright, too much neckline showing, and she couldn’t take off her jacket because her arms would be exposed by the short sleeves. She buttoned the top three buttons, hoping that would do. She and Will were going to stick out like sore thumbs. *Will!*

Phoebe inhaled deeply, in with the courage, out with the tension. She had no choice, after all. She turned the knob and opened the door, Will having done the same thing at the same time in the room next to hers. She saw him peeking out when she stepped out and closed her door behind her.

They stood near each other and checked to be sure they were alone. Phoebe whispered, "Did I hear voices out here? Who was it?"

Will nodded. "Yes. Mrs. Barrett introduced me to someone else, a man. He loaned me this," he fingered the lapel of the coat."

"Hmm, very nice," she said, feeling it with a couple of fingers. "Weird, but nice," she teased. "Who was it?"

Will shrugged. "Stanton...Stanley...Sandine... I forgot already. I got nervous and don't remember what he said his name was." Phoebe rolled her eyes at his answer.

They walked forward down the hall toward the doorway to the kitchen. They both heard voices from the front room grew louder. Will grabbed Phoebe's forearm, his grip growing tighter when they saw bodies step into the kitchen. She shook him off, glaring at him, saying quietly, "Calm down. They're people, not aliens. Just be polite." He gave a quick nod.

Mrs. Barrett smiled at the two of them and touched the tops of two chairs at the large kitchen table in the center of the room. "Please, sit down." She turned to the stove. The boy Walter came in next and began putting dishes on the table. When he saw them he frowned again and resumed his duties.

Three other men were standing on the other side of the table. One was Mr. Sanford. He had been chatting with the second man, the third stood alone. When the siblings entered the room they all went quiet at the sight of them and waited until Phoebe was seated before seating themselves. Will followed suit.

Mrs. Barrett turned from the stove and said, "Gentlemen, we have guests for supper. Miss Tucker and her brother Mr. Tucker will be joining us."

The unidentified men both looked to be thirty or so and nodded to Phoebe. "Pleasure," they each said in turn, nodding at Phoebe. The first reached across the table to shake Will's hand. "I'm Albert Griffin."

The second man, slender, perhaps a bit younger now that Phoebe had a moment to look closely, said quietly, "Hello," and put his hand out to Will. "I'm Chester Murphy." He nodded to Phoebe a second time.

Mr. Sanford nodded at Will and said to Phoebe, "It's a pleasure to meet you, Miss Tucker. You brother and I have already met. My name is Sanford. Newton Sanford." The man smiled at her, his bright eyes sparkling, full of mirth.

Phoebe stared at him, thinking, remembering, *Where have I heard that name?* She knew she was staring. *Rude!* "Thank you, it's pleasure to meet you all." She had to look away. *Think, think.*

Mrs. Barrett set down a heavy pot of stew at the center of the table. Then she returned to place a plate of sliced bread beside it before sitting down herself. She looked at Phoebe, waiting for her to make the first move. Phoebe handed Will her bowl and asked him to fill it for her. He did so, stiffly, nervously, being sure he made no eye contact with anyone else in the room. Then Mrs. Barrett picked up the plate of bread and passed it around the table.

Phoebe tried to relax, going with the flow. Ears open, pay attention, learn the room, go from there. When she opened her mouth to speak Will's eyes opened wide and he shot her a glance that said, *What are you doing?*

"I'm sure I speak for my brother when I say we can't thank you enough for your hospitality this evening, Mrs. Barrett." There, that sounded proper, didn't it?

Mrs. Barrett nodded her appreciation. "You are both welcome, Miss Tucker. After supper we can sit down in the parlor and discuss your predicament. Walter, stop staring and eat your supper."

"But Ma, they look – "

"Walter," his mother snapped and the boy was quiet. Phoebe wondered what the boy had been about to say.

Albert Griffin took a few bites of his stew and said to Will in a conversational manner, "Walter told us he found you in the barn. That you said you were lost? Lost how, exactly?"

Will looked up, a look of alarm on his face. He looked from Mr. Griffin to Phoebe and back, and swallowed hard. "Well – I – we – we were looking for – um – and then we – I wasn't feeling well and – I – "

"I think he's still not quite himself," Phoebe said apologetically. "We were dropped off and I'm afraid I took a wrong turn. We were looking for a hotel. My brother wasn't feeling very well so we found a quiet place to sit down for a few minutes. I didn't have long to explain, I'm sorry, Mrs. Barrett. We'll pay you back for supper as soon as we can."

At that statement Will kicked her in the leg under the table. *How?*

"Yes, it's not always easy to find what you're looking for is it? I'm sorry you didn't get better directions. I trust you're feeling better by now, Mr. Tucker."

Phoebe kicked him back and he cleared his throat. "I am, thank you."

"It seems you stumbled into the right barn, after all, Miss Tucker," said Newton Sanford. At Phoebe's puzzled expression he continued, "You see, Mrs. Barrett runs a first-rate boarding house here." He raised his glass of lemonade, a silent toast to their hostess. Mrs. Barrett grinned. "Mr. Murphy and I have two of the rooms upstairs. Mr. Griffin has the other."

It was becoming more clear to Phoebe; Mrs. Barrett had readily let them come in for supper, she was doing all the cooking, she had let everyone else sit down before she did, there were fresh towels on the washstands, only she and the boy Walter seemed to be related and no one had so far mentioned her husband. Was she the lone adult in this venture?

"I understand now." Phoebe had been about to blurt, '*thanks for letting us crash your party,*' but stopped herself.

She was going to have to concentrate before speaking from now on. "I appreciate your thoughtfulness."

Two of the men shared a few minor comments and complimented their hostess on the meal. Albert Griffin didn't say much at all. Phoebe and Will were nearly silent for the remaining time at the table, even through chocolate cake for dessert.

When everyone was finished eating, the three men cleared their own plates and each picked up an additional item from the table to help. Going off of this clue Will did the same and walked to the parlor after Phoebe waved him in that direction. Phoebe stayed a few extra minutes to ask Mrs. Barrett if she could help with the cleanup.

Mrs. Barrett accepted graciously and directed Phoebe on what she wanted her to do. Phoebe didn't mind helping, and she thought it might give her some idea as to how she could pay the woman back for her generosity. *What have I got to lose for asking?* "Mrs. Barrett, may I ask you something?"

"Yes, what is it?" Her tone was clipped. Her break was over, back to efficiency.

"Have you any idea if any of the stores in town are in need of sales clerks? Or the hotels?"

"Perhaps, yes. It's always busy here," was the only answer she received.

After finishing in the kitchen they met Will in the parlor where he was sitting with two of the other men. Mr. Griffin was absent. Will looked uncomfortable and overly happy to see Phoebe. The two men stood when Phoebe and Mrs. Barrett entered the room. Will did the same, a little late, and Phoebe grinned. This world was going to take some getting used to for him.

Mr. Murphy and Mr. Sanford excused themselves and left the two newcomers and their hostess to discuss their situation. Mrs. Barrett had correctly assessed Will's reluctance in handling matters and Phoebe's equally opposite confidence in doing so.

She said to Phoebe, "If you would like to rent a room here you are welcome to. You may each have the room I let you use." She paused a moment, kneading her hands. "I must confess, instead of simply offering to help you find what you were looking for, I invited you in in hopes that you would rent the rooms I have here. Bodie has many rooms available, and I currently have only three boarders." She seemed embarrassed at the confession. "Meals are included, such as they are. I expect payment once a week," she said hopefully.

Now Phoebe was glad she had broached the subject of looking for a job. Mrs. Barrett had no idea of their financial situation; now she knew that they were in need of money and had still invited them to stay. Perhaps they could postpone payment for awhile. Walter called to his mother from the other room and she excused herself.

Will said, "What are we going to do? We have to get out of here, we have no money, clothes, nothing."

"I know that, and you saying it all the time won't change it. I think we can probably find jobs to get us by until we figure out how to get out of here. There has to be a clue, something. J. W. sent us here for a reason."

"Jobs!" He hung his head in his hands once again. "Oh Dear God..."

"It's not going to kill you."

"Look where we are. It might." Phoebe rolled her eyes. "Bet you a quarter we never get out of here," Will said, pouting again.

"Only a quarter? I'll bet you a hund – " she started to tease but then her eyes opened wide.

"What is it?

"A quarter!" She said, but her hands went to her pockets of her Army jacket she still wore. "I had some money in my pocket. I bet Steve a quarter in horseshoes and I lost and had to pay him."

"And that's helpful because? You can't pay for something in 18-whenever-we-are with a 1980 quarter."

“Because that’s not the only thing I have in my pockets,” Phoebe was excited now. Her jungle jacket had four pockets total, two on top and two on the bottom. She skipped the two top pockets; she knew she had a Chapstick and a Kleenex in one and who knew what else in the other. But she stuck her hand into the bottom right pocket first and pulled out a handful of spent cartridges from when she had been shooting in the back lot at her Grandpa Henry’s farm.

A second try and she pulled out a candy bar, two paper clips and a small pocket knife that Tony had given her when she was sixteen. She also had the strange stone that J. W. had slipped in there, a ten and five dollar bill and another quarter. Modern. No good.

Will was looking disappointed. Phoebe, undaunted, pushed her hand into the bottom left pocket. It jingled with the sound of spent cartridges as well, but when she pulled out her hand the fresh cartridges she had neglected to return to the gun cabinet were still there. She had only shot one cylinder with the Colt and had used only three of the four paper targets. Phoebe smiled. Will didn’t understand. “If I have to I can sell these. Grandpa’s Winchester is the the same gun they would have used here. Get it?”

Will nodded, looking hopeful.

She reached into her pocket again, feeling something else. Paper, and something clinking in the corner at the bottom. She didn’t remember what that could be. Filled with apprehension she pulled out the small bundle of printed paper.

Will looked closely, “What is that?” he asked quietly.

Phoebe unfolded the sheets of crinkly paper and gasped, softening her laughter with a hand over her mouth, but unable to stop laughing altogether. She pushed it toward Will for his inspection.

“Is that – is that...?

Phoebe nodded, “Yes, it’s money. Lots and lots of money.” She looked closely at several of the bills. “Nineteenth century, United States bank notes, dated 1878, 1879. J. W. must have slipped it into my pocket. I thought it was weird that he hugged me." She remembered the clinking and reached into her pocket to retrieve the last items at the bottom. Her laugh trailed off but her smile remained and she shook her head in continued disbelief. "Gold. Gold coins. Four twenty dollar gold pieces. This is worth so much more in 1980 yet he stuck it in my pocket. Oh J. W., what am I going to do with you?" Feelings between frustration and amusement bounced around in her brain thinking of him. "He planned this."

"The bills look... weird. Are you sure it's real?"

"Yes, I'm sure. Paper money was bigger then. And the Bodie banks had charters so they'll take these."

"I don't know what that means – " Will pushed at Phoebe's hands when he heard Mrs. Barrett coming back into the room and Phoebe quickly placed the items back in her pockets. Mrs. Barrett sat back down and said, "I trust you've had time to discuss your situation?"

Will and Phoebe exchanged glances and Phoebe answered. "Yes, thank you. We would be delighted to stay with you."

Relief spread across their new landlady's face. Perhaps she had been running short of cash as well.

"I'm glad. Your weekly room for the two of you will be five dollars. If you care to eat here as well that will be an additional four dollars per week per person for two meals per day. That includes use of an oil lamp, washtub, water and towels in your room. I trust you will find that satisfactory?"

Phoebe certainly was relieved she had found J. W.'s money in her pocket. It's a shame he'd saved it for her instead of having once spent it himself. And it's a big shame that he couldn't have gotten more money out of the gold coins instead of holding on to them all these years. But that was his own fault, she reasoned, for sending them back here in the first place.

"That will work out just fine, Mrs. Barrett."

Their new landlady stood up to leave them alone. "Oh, I'm in the front room here," she pointed to the room adjacent to the parlor, "with Walter. If either of you need anything, please let me know. I've already put your keys in your rooms, on the table. There is a second key for the front and rear doors if I'm out. Please lock up if I am." She stood to leave and turned to them. "Again, I apologize for any deceit. I meant no harm." Phoebe smiled at her reassuringly.

When they were alone again, Phoebe sighed and flung herself back against the small sofa. She wished she had her comfy chair to sit in and a cola to sip. But that would have to wait. Will said, "Now what?"

"Now... we take a breath, think, then look around and try to find some clues, something, anything that tells us what we are supposed to do while we're here." She sighed.

"This was supposed to be a vacation." Will snorted, the closest thing to a laugh for him since they had arrived in Bodie. "I have to work on Tuesday. I took Monday off to spend more time with you. I think I'm sick of you already. And I'm fired for sure."

Phoebe saw something out of the corner of her eye and sat upright. It was a thin, flat item, approximately a foot square, on a table by the front window. She stood up to go look at it and picked it up to bring back to the sofa. "It's a calendar," she said, showing it to Will. "And someone marks off the date every day. So unless the efficient Mrs. Barrett is like much of the rest of the world and forgets to mark off a day or to change the month of her calendar, it appears it is June. Monday, June fourteenth; the same date for us, Will, the fourteenth. But it's Monday. And the year is 1880. Oh my God, 1880. One hundred years exactly." She looked at her brother, eyes bright. "One hundred years."

"I heard you," he answered simply, sounding understandably despondent. "Yep, I'm fired for sure."

That name! I remember! "Oh no, no, no, no...."

Alarmed, Will looked at her, his back stiffening. "What? What!"

"That name, Newton L. Sanford. I remember, don't you? The cemetery. The trip with J. W. and everybody. Oh no, Will. This is terrible.

Will whispered, "Newton Sanford, Newton Sanford," to himself. "It sounds familiar. Why?"

"The stone in the cemetery. The one with the line by that poet Kathleen recognized. *'Newton L. Sanford, Died June 19, 1880, Aged 29 yrs 3 mo. To Live in Hearts We Leave Behind is Not To Die.'*"

Will realized what she was saying. "It's him, Phoebe. It was his stone."

"Yes, Will." They couldn't say it aloud, it was too terrible now that they had met him. Phoebe looked down at the calendar again and realized, with a sadness pulling at her heart, that in less than one week Newton Sanford, a smiling, friendly man who had been a helpful stranger, was going to die.

14

Phoebe returned the calendar to its place on the table and turned to face Will. “This is terrible. Now I won’t be able to get that out of my head every time I see him or talk to him.”

“Is there anything we can do? Warn him or something?”

She sat back down beside him. “Oh sure, that’s a great idea. ‘By the way, Mr. Sanford, we’re from the future and we know the day you’re going to die. So if you could just, you know, not... that would be great.’” She raised her eyebrows at Will.

“Not exactly what I meant.”

“Look, this isn’t like *It’s a Wonderful Life* or *Dr. Who*. At least I don’t think it is. This is real life. At least I think it is.” She punched her brother in the arm.

“Ow,” he frowned, rubbing the spot. “What was that for?”

“Just checking to see if we’re really here,” she grinned. “Look, Will, I don’t have any more answers than you do.

But I feel like whatever has already happened, well, happened. It's done, you know? We're merely accessories, observers that get to look in from the outside and go home soon, if you get what I mean."

"Not really."

"I don't think there's a lot of real-life source material on the subject. So who knows?" She shrugged. "Either way, there isn't much we can do about it."

The front door opened then, and Newton Sanford walked in. He wore a hat which he took off when he stepped inside and when he saw Phoebe he said "Ma'am," politely. He then nodded to Will and when he spoke he addressed them both. "I spoke to Mrs. Barrett outside. She's taking some wash off the line. She said you have both decided to stay on as boarders. It will be nice to have some new faces at the supper table. Welcome." He nodded once again, said, "If you'll excuse me," and walked through the parlor to the stairs to his room.

Phoebe felt an ache in her gut as she watched him walk out of the room. Less than one week until he lost his life.

"What do we do now, Phoebe? It's getting late and it'll be dark soon. What's a daily schedule like around here, anyway?"

"People are up early, to bed late. The saloons and some restaurants are open all night long and you can probably find an opium den open too. It's like Vegas, baby, except you have to pay for the drinks. At least the banging stops at night," she smiled.

"What about on Sunday?"

"There are dozens of saloons and they are all open on Sunday. This is Bodie," she raised her eyebrows. "If anyone here attends church it's at the Miner's Union Hall on Main Street."

"Why not the church?"

She whispered, "Neither one is built yet."

"What are we going to do?"

"Get a good night's sleep, if we can, and maybe our brains will function better in the morning." At this she stood up and walked toward her assigned room. Will went with her.

He was standing in her doorway when Newton Sanford came down the stairway that let out at the other end of the hall. He smiled at them and asked if there was anything they needed before he went out.

Will took one step closer and asked, "Um, could you tell me, um, where..."

"Where the necessary is? Certainly." He pointed toward the back of the house. "There's a side door that exits through the kitchen. Turn left and it's on the right side of the barn."

Will felt his face flush. "Thanks, um, thank you." Newton Sanford slapped him on the shoulder and continued on his way to the front door. "The necessary? Oh, geez."

"Don't you remember using the outhouse at Grandma and Grandpa's before they put in plumbing? I do." She shrugged. "Grandma Julia had us all over for dinner when they had the new kitchen and bathroom put in, she was so excited to show them off."

"Back then I didn't have to ask a stranger where it was."

Phoebe faced him in the doorway. "Will, go take off your coat, try to relax, get some sleep and I'll see you in the morning."

"Already?"

"What else do you suggest we do? Go out looking like this at this time of night? Tomorrow we'll be rested, have clear heads, do some shopping, feel more like normal and start figuring out how we can get back home. Okay?"

He nodded, knowing she was right. Almost right. "Feel like normal?" He turned toward his door shaking his head, mumbling to himself.

Phoebe closed the door, locked it, took off her Army jacket, put it on the bed and flopped down on top of it. She wasn't going to let it out of her sight until she had a secure place to store the belongings that were inside of it.

An hour later, wishing she had a flashlight, Phoebe put on her Army jacket and unlocked her bedroom door. It was dark outside now. No nightlights, no streetlights. And the first quarter moon was upon them. Wait, the lamp. She felt around for matches and there was a small box of them on her stand by the door next to an oil lamp. Will had used their father's kerosene camping lantern, surely he could figure out this kind. She struck a match, lifted the chimney, lit the wick and adjusted the flame.

Opening her door carefully, she peered down the hallway. She didn't know what she expected to see but hoped no one was out there. She tiptoed down the hall, turned left into the kitchen, and crossed to the door. She opened it as quietly as she was able and walked down the few steps to make her way to the outhouse. *Why didn't I do this before it got too dark?* she asked herself.

To the left of the stairs there was an area where Mrs. Barrett had hung the wash. She moved to the rear of the house, saw the barn and kept walking straight until she saw the outhouse there. It wasn't far; land was prime at this time in Bodie. She grinned to herself knowing she wouldn't find one of those handy little red-green 'occupied/vacant' signs on the outside. No light coming from within; close enough.

On her way back to the house she heard a noise that caught her by surprise. She jerked and inhaled sharply when she nearly collided with the noise. "Miss Tucker?"

She exhaled with more calm. "Yes, who is it?"

"I apologize. It's me, Albert Griffin. I didn't see the light until I almost ran you over. I'm sorry to have startled you. Again, my apologies."

Phoebe's grip on the lantern tightened, especially when she noticed the distinct smell of liquor about him. She believed her lantern light to be quite visible so she sensed he was not being truthful. And she trusted her gut implicitly. It had never let her down before. "It's quite all right Mr. Griffin. If you'll excuse me," she said as she moved around him toward the back door.

"Goodnight, then."

"Yes, goodnight." She moved quickly, keeping her eye on him until she closed the door, leaving it unlocked, unsure if she was supposed to lock it at night. Then she went to the water barrel she had seen in the kitchen corner, took out a ladle full of water for a drink and returned to her room, locking her door. Not daring to knock on her brother's door to talk to him, she listened and heard no sounds from within. She was unwilling to wake him to declare a suspicion since he needed sleep as badly as she did, or more so.

As comfortable as they were, taking off her boots felt good. She then put out the lamp, pulled down the covers, checked her jacket pockets to be sure Mr. Griffin had not indeed been a nighttime pickpocket, put her jacket underneath her, covered up and tried to relax and go to sleep. She hoped Will was all right.

***

Bright sunlight came through the window in the morning, waking her. It was a north-facing window. *Thank goodness,* as there were no room darkening curtains here. She groaned and stretched, wishing desperately for a cup of coffee. Looking around her room, she realized she definitely felt better than she had the night before. A couple of crazy dreams could be dealt with, but she had slept comfortably. She was rested, they had a new day before them and she was going to explore Bodie in the daylight.

Noises were coming from the kitchen. She splashed water on her face and combed her fingers through her hair the best she could, *Oh, my hair!* I do look out of place. I should have it up or out of the way, or something. She looked at herself in the mirror. *Yes, up, too old for braids, I'm not a school girl.*

A shopping trip was one of the first things on their list. Phoebe sat down for a moment and counted the money from J. W. This should be plenty to do them for several weeks if they were frugal. Otherwise...

She buttoned her jacket, made her bed and put her room and front door keys in one of her pockets. The smell of freshly baking biscuits greeted her when she entered the kitchen. Mrs. Barrett was finishing at the stove and turned to see Phoebe. "I'm sorry, Mrs. Barrett, I should have been out earlier to help you."

"That's fine, Miss Tucker," she answered, moving brusquely "Walter and I are off on some errands this morning. We're going to visit some neighbors first. So if you wouldn't mind just clearing your dishes I'll clean up when I return." She put two plates, biscuits and fried eggs, and a bowl of strawberries on the table. "Coffee is on the stove there," she pointed.

Her landlady moved with efficiency, and headed out of the kitchen before Phoebe could think of anything suitable to say. Was she supposed to have been up to help? She was a boarder and was paying for services, although she hadn't paid anything as yet. Had the other two men been in to eat yet? Did they help out? Where was Will?

Before checking on her brother the call of the coffee was more than she could resist. She took a cup off a shelf near the stove and used a towel to pour from the metal coffee pot. Boiled, strained and strong, the old-fashioned brew brought an audible "Mmm," from her. So distracted had she been to first get her burst of morning caffeine, she hadn't heard the footsteps come into the kitchen.

"I see you've tasted Mrs. Barrett's delightful coffee?" It was Newton Sanford. Knowing what she did about his inescapable fate Phoebe was hoping to keep her contact with him to a minimum. Like not naming a farm animal you're planning to sell for slaughter; don't get too attached or it hurts too much to see it go. Will walked into the kitchen behind him.

"I have. It's delicious. I don't mean to," she had been going to say *'hog it all,'* "take more than my share. Would you like some?"

Will grinned, accustomed to her true manner of speech. "Thank you, your brother and I have already had a cup. But I'll have another if you'll sit and drink it with me."

Phoebe turned to the cups. *What the...? Go away! I don't want to spend time with you, I don't want to get to know you, you're going to die in a week, you idiot."*

"Certainly. Will?"

He said casually, "Sure, thanks," confounding her. Maybe she should take her own advice and relax.

"Have you gentlemen eaten breakfast?"

They answered simultaneously, Will saying 'no,' and Newton Sanford saying 'yes.' Great, now she would have to eat in front of him while he stared at her.

"Mmm," said Will, biting into a biscuit with fresh butter. "My grandmother used to make butter," he glanced at Phoebe, "like this.

"Where are the both of you from? You said you were, 'dropped off.' Was there someone you're visiting? Looking for? Perhaps I can help." At this Will looked down at his plate of eggs and wouldn't look back up. "I asked Will this morning and he said – " Then Newton Sanford stopped talking, noticing the glare Phoebe directed at her brother. "My apologies, I didn't intend to be intrusive."

"What exactly did you say, Will?" Phoebe's vexation was obvious.

Silence.

"Mr. Sanford – "

"I would be pleased if you would call me Newton, Miss Tucker." He smiled, his eyes shining like they did the first day they had met.

Phoebe pursed her lips, then continued, "Mr. Sanford, we have traveled a long distance and are here on an errand. That is all I, we, care to discuss." She look hard at Will, hoping he could feel her annoyance.

Newton Sanford took a last sip of his coffee. "Again, I apologize for my intrusion." He stood to go, placed his cup in the washstand and turned to them at the kitchen door. "If there is anything else you need while you are here, don't hesitate to ask." And he left.

"Why are you always so rude, Phoebe?" Will finally spoke.

"What's wrong with you?" she snapped. "We aren't here to make friends."

"We don't know *why* we're here. And I didn't tell him anything, really. I tried to put him off but I always just stutter and sound stupid. I told him to talk to you, that's all, I swear."

"I'm sorry."

They sat in silence another minute. Will reached out to touch Phoebe's wrist. "We'll figure this out, Phoebe. But like you said, it's a new day. I couldn't go to sleep forever last night, I was miserable. But then I remembered, you said you used to love this place. So now's your chance, whatever happens, to get to see it. You can walk the streets of Bodie, the way they used to be in the books you used to look at. You can see the buildings, hear the sounds, walk into the stores. I'm out of my element here. Big time. But you're not. I trust you, Phoebe. We can do this. But take advantage of the chance you've been given."

His words had tightened her throat. She put a hand on top of his and whispered, "I have a confession to make. I *still* look at those books."

***

Phoebe and Will weren't sure what to do with the leftover biscuits. They wrapped them in a towel and left them on the table. Phoebe finished off the pot of coffee.

Will's hands were nearly shaking as he stood at the front door ready to step outside and into the daylight. Phoebe put a hand on the doorknob, waggled her eyebrows at him, grinned and said, "Let's go shopping."

"So now you enjoy shopping?" He asked with a snort of laughter.

"Not really. But look at you. You look like you're going to an Duran Duran concert and I don't want to be seen with you," she replied with a mockingly haughty tone. "And you need to return that jacket and get one of your own, don't you think?"

When they opened the door the first thing they noticed was the increase in noise from the stamp mills, pounding away, grinding the gold and silver from the ore taken from the surrounding hills. Bang bang, pound pound, thump whump, over and over and over...

The job was dirty, dangerous, difficult; but the job of a miner paid well; four dollars a day. The men knew the strikes wouldn't last forever and took their chances every moment of every day. The young and foolish worked hard for their pay and often spent a chunk of it in the saloons and gambling halls. The more mature sometimes did the same but often had homes and families on which to spend their hard-earned wages.

They walked down the few steps and stepped into their new world. Will was stiff, nervous, his face screwed up in a wince of pain, as if he were wearing shoes two sizes too small. Phoebe was trembling, she felt a flutter in her throat, had a difficult time swallowing, clenched her fists and clamped her hand onto Will's upper arm in a grasp so tight he couldn't pull away. She had sensations bubbling up inside her similar to those she had experienced on the drive into Bodie with her parents and J. W.

Will looked down at his sister, only a few inches shorter than he. Trepidation: that's how he would describe her demeanor. He offered her his arm and she took it. "Mr. Victorian Gentleman," she teased.

Then Will stepped in a glob of mud and grimaced. "Everything is muddy, yuk, why, and it's so noisy, if I have to wear a wool jacket every day I'm going to sweat like a pig..."

At least that brought a genuine smile to her face, he thought.

There was a neighbor across the narrow street that was outside shaking a small rug. She waved and smiled at the strange, oddly-dressed brother-sister couple walking down the street. Phoebe forced a smile and waved back. Will waved his hand but his smile was still befitting of someone with too-tight shoes.

He mumbled, "This is just too weird. We were here yesterday. Yesterday..." His voice trailed off; he had wanted to say more but had no idea how to put his thoughts into words.

"I know, Will. I understand. I don't know what we're supposed to do next, or what J. W.'s reasons are. It has to be something we can handle or he wouldn't have done it." She shrugged. "So let's stop thinking about J. W., about not fitting in. Let's see what happens, okay?"

She saw him nod and glanced over to see he was already distracted. Not far ahead of them was what appeared to be a main thoroughfare. "Pioneer Brewery," he said, reading the name of a business ahead. "Huh." They turned left, keeping to the side of the road as there was mud in the center. A right turn would have led them uphill and toward the mining.

Phoebe inhaled sharply and stopped walking. Looking around, behind, left, right, she looked at Will and whispered, "Green Street."

Failing to see the significance he shook his head and raised his eyebrows.

"Look," she said, and pointed ahead and to the right.

Will recognized what he was seeing. "The schoolhouse? Is that the school?" Phoebe was nodding and Will noticed her grip was firmer on his arm.

"And look at the houses. The homes. Much of this area was residential; the new part of town." She began walking, her arm looped through his, her grip still firm. Other people were out walking. Some stared at Phoebe and Will but they were oblivious at the moment, so enthralled were they by their surroundings. A home or two on the left, one on the right, an empty lot here and there as families moved in and decided where to live; businesses and other boarding houses dotted the area as well.

"Just where are we going, Phoebe? How much further? I feel like I stick out more than a sore thumb; more like a hand with no thumb at all."

Phoebe smiled and said, "We've got to go downtown. Downtown Bodie, to the business district." She spoke as if to no one, her eyes searching her surroundings, looking, studying, thinking, remembering.

"Oh, geez," he mumbled, putting his head down but keeping his eyes up to see where he was going. "Is it far?"

"You were just here yesterday. And you've been here before. Don't you remember anything?" She was incredulous.

"It looks a little different, okay. And there's a bit less sagebrush than the last time I saw it. You're the one who knows where everything was – is – ugh."

"Chill, would you." They walked a dozen more yards. "Watch out," Phoebe told him, jerking his arm to keep him from stepping in more mud.

"Why is it so muddy?"

"Wait 'til we get to Main Street." More people were gathering here so she stated quietly, "Last winter was one of the snowiest in Bodie's history. So when the snow melted this spring, well," she gestured with her left hand, "mud everywhere. It was a real problem. They wrote about it in the newspaper." A few yards further along she steered them right at the intersection to cross the street, looking for the highest parts of ground to step on. "Main street."

Just then a carriage rounded the corner, moving toward them from the opposite end of Green Street. It turned north on Main street, going the same direction they had turned. The wheels spattered mud in the air even as it drove at an even pace, the horse's hooves making a sucking sound in the muck. The carriage slowed and stopped in front of a building on the right. The driver stepped down and opened the door for the passengers within. Out stepped a man and a woman, both dressed nicely. The driver closed the door, the man tipped the driver and the woman took the arm of the man as they began walking toward Phoebe and Will.

When they passed, Phoebe noted the woman's haughty expression, mentally deriding Phoebe for her choice of clothing and hairstyle. The man tipped his tall black hat politely and the couple walked past. "Do I have to dress like that?" asked Will, sounding miserable.

"No. I don't know who they are but they are very dressed up. Probably rich, or here on business of some sort."

"Good." He scratched his chin. "I need some stuff to shave with too. I'm itchy."

"Why don't you grow a mustache?"

"And a beard too? No thanks." He scratched again.

"Stop that," she snapped. "People will think you have fleas." Will laughed. "And whatever you do, don't get hurt, or cut yourself, or... how long has it been since you had a tetanus shot?"

"Tetanus... Oh geez, I'm going to die here, aren't I," he groaned.

"Don't worry, there's plenty of whiskey here to bath you in. You'll be fine."

Will began looking around at the buildings and businesses of which he had only ever heard stories. "So which kind of store are we looking for, anyway."

"Duh, a clothing store. But there are several. One of the big ones is back that way." She used her thumb to point back the way they had come.

Will glanced over his shoulder. "What? Then why are we going this way?"

"Because I want to go up here first. I need a milliner."

"A what?"

"Milliner. I need a hat, and something to put my hair up. I look like I belong on Bonanza street with my hair hanging down all over the place."

"If you belong on Bonanza Street you know that makes me – " He quickly removed her hand from his arm. "Ew, gross, Phoebe."

She laughed at his response. "Sure, now you remember one of the facts I told you."

They walked a little further, side by side, their eyes wide with wonder at what lay before them; the wide street, many buildings painted white, the wooden boardwalks, businesses with living quarters above, signs, advertisements.

There were hotels, stores, markets, laundries, barbers, butchers, drug stores, bakeries, attorneys, a stone cutter, booteries, saddlemakers, breweries, hardware stores, fruit stands, a furniture store, newspaper printers, banks, livery stables and more. And oh, the saloons...

"I can smell fresh-cut lumber," Will said, sniffing the air.

"Yes, the sawmill is up there," Phoebe pointed to her left, west.

A moment later Phoebe spotted a store she'd been looking for and pointed. "There, I'm going in there. Wait or come with, but I'm getting a hat."

Phoebe boldly strode forward, passing several other businesses on her way. One of the doors opened as she walked purposefully forward and the person exiting collided with her, sending her tripping and stumbling off the boardwalk, into the street and into a slushy quagmire of mud.

15

Will rushed forward to assist Phoebe out of the street. Phoebe lifted herself up to a sitting position and the person who had caused her tumble stood casually nearby, observing. She stood up unassisted, not wanting to smear Will's hands with mud, told him thanks, and turned to the perpetrator. Will stood aside.

Stepping up on the boardwalk Phoebe advanced toward the man, her consternation obvious. "Why don't you watch where you're going? Look at me, this is all your fault. I was walking along and you burst through the door like the place was on fire behind you. How dare you – "

The man held up both hands in a plea for reprieval. "Ma'am, I do apologize." The man took off his hat and held it to his chest. He glanced at Will and looked back at Phoebe whose face was streaked after pushing her long strands of hair aside. A small crowd had gathered because of the commotion that was underway and because Phoebe, Will and her assailant were blocking the boardwalk. The mud was a deterrent for stepping around them.

The man reached into a pocket and attempted to hand Will a gold coin. He did not take it, confused by its meaning. "Here, Sir, perhaps this will make up to you for the pleasant day you had ahead of you now ruined."

Will had no time to react. Phoebe reached out and slapped the man across his face, hard, sending his hat tumbling down the boardwalk amidst the feet of the gathering crowd. Reeling at the unexpected blow the man held his burning cheek, his eyes wide. "This is my brother and we were out shopping, you simpleton. Take your gold coin and shove it – "

"Phoebe!" Will moved quickly now, picked up the man's hat and handed it to the closest stranger. He then pulled Phoebe forward through the crowd, trying to put space between them and the man behind them. Twenty yards further on they stopped and stood to the side, letting others pass them by. "What was that all about?"

"What? He accused me of being a hooker. And assumed you had purchased my company. What a jerk." She was attempting to shake off the mud around the bottom of her dress and brush off the drying dirt on her jacket and hands. "Look at me, what a mess."

Will made a face. "Did you have to flip out? I thought we were going to try and be inconspicuous? Geez, your temper."

She didn't have a chance to reply. A man was approaching, closer and closer, preventing further conversation.

"Miss Tucker, Mr. Tucker. Are you all right? I see there's been an incident. May I be of service in any way?"

Phoebe groaned audibly. *I just wanted to buy a hat.* Surprisingly, Will spoke first. Phoebe faced away, attempting to rub the dirt off her face and straighten her hair. "Mr. Sanford, hello." The two men shook hands. Will looked to his sister for the next cue.

She turned to Newton Sanford with a smile, spreading her dress to show the mud and said, "So, you witnessed this did you?"

"No, not exactly." Newton Sanford seemed unsure of his next words. Perhaps he had seen or heard Phoebe's reaction. "I saw the crowd there," he pointed, "and asked someone what had happened. I thought perhaps someone had suffered an injury."

"And what answer did you receive, pray tell?"

Newton Sanford looked between Will and Phoebe. He seemed bewildered. "I – well I – "

"Go ahead. I want to know."

"The women said you slapped a gentleman that suggested you were Mr. Tucker's, um, associate."

"How very diplomatic. What did the gentlemen have to say on the matter?" She was goading him now.

Newton Sanford grinned, glanced once more at Will who seemed to be enjoying the exchange, and said, "Excuse me, Ma'am, but I do not care to have this discourse resolve in a similar fashion."

Phoebe opened her mouth to talk but was interrupted when Newton Sanford held up a hand. "I assure you, Miss Tucker, I witnessed enough of the aftermath to have full appreciation of your annoyance."

"I would hope so. Now, if you'll excuse us." She turned to go, expecting Will to follow her. The milliner she had been intent on patronizing was behind her. Not knowing where there was another did not stop her from proceeding. Momentarily discovering another across the street, she looked both ways before crossing. She was already tiptoeing to the other side before she noticed that both Will and Newton Sanford had followed her. *Great.*

For a moment she had forgotten where she was, had forgotten she was on Main Street in Bodie, had forgotten she was here only yesterday and was now walking into a store that had burned down long ago in her world. Before entering she turned to see her brother and Newton Sanford waiting in the center of the wide street for a carriage going south to pass. Newton Sanford. smiling in an easy manner, saying something polite to Will. Her brother, out of place, nervous, hesitant with uncertainty, yet relaxing in the other man's presence. *June 19, June 19, June 19...*

She entered the store and was greeted by a young woman who seemed slightly younger than herself. The young woman stifled a giggle and said, "Oh, my, I see the street came up to meet you." Phoebe like her instantly.

"Yes it did." She shrugged and returned the smile. "Can you help me, please? I am in desperate need of a hat or two and something to pin up my hair."

"Do you have a color preference?"

"No, something that I can wear with anything, I suppose."

"Grand idea. Here..."

Phoebe chose a straw hat with four different color ribbons she could tie around the top of the hat. She also purchased a few smaller ribbons for her hair, a hairbrush and a small tin of hair pins. The woman in the store helped to brush her hair, most of the dirt coming out of it now that it was drying. She showed Phoebe how to braid it, wind it up behind her neck and pin it. Phoebe chose the brown ribbon for her hat and said, "It matches the mud," making the clerk laugh.

While she was sitting in front of a dressing mirror getting her hair brushed, the young woman said, "You have pretty hair." Phoebe looked up at the woman's reflection and she followed up quickly with, "I apologize if that was impertinent."

"Oh no, not at all. Nobody's ever told me that before. Thank you," replied Phoebe.

"Really? I think it's lovely. It's brown but has a beautiful reddish hue to it, like it's been kissed by the sun. And it's long and soft, and... oh listen to me."

"It's all right. Thank you." After her hair was braided and pinned and the hat was atop her head, a thought came to her. "Do you happen to have purses here, I mean bags. Perhaps a reticule or chatelaine bag of some kind. Something simple?"

"I have both. Here." She showed Phoebe two beaded reticules and two chatelaines. Both were big enough to carry the money from J. W. and the gold coins. The chatelaine would attach to a clip that would hang from a sash or chain around the waist. The reticule had a simple drawstring-topped enclosure.

"I'll take the big chatelaine, please. With a chain if you have one."

"I do. I'll go get one for you." The young woman returned. "I own one similar to this."

"I think they're a spectacular idea. It makes it harder for a thief to make off with my millions," teased Phoebe, finding it easy to talk with the clerk, who stifled another giggle at the comment. "If one attempts to I'll have to – have to – " she borrowed J. W.'s phrase, "anoint him with a blinker."

At that the woman laughed aloud. "I would like to see that."

Phoebe paid for her purchases and thanked the woman again. As an afterthought Phoebe turned when she reached the door and asked, "Do you mind if I ask your name?"

"No, not at all. I'm Mary. Mary Jacobson."

"I'm Phoebe Tucker. It's been a pleasure, Miss Jacobson."

"Likewise. Stop by anytime if you'd like anything else. I live upstairs with my parents. They own the shop." Phoebe nodded and Mary waved goodbye.

When Phoebe emerged from the store Will was standing just outside on the boardwalk. He looked relieved to see her. "It's about time," he said. "You took forev – nice hat."

"Oh hush, I think it's cute," she said, glancing around.

"He's gone." At her questioning look he continued. "Mr. Sanford, he's gone. He said he had to continue on his way and he left." Then, in teasing reply to the downcast look she displayed he said, "Don't tell me you're disappointed?"

"No," she answered too quickly. "I'm relieved. Now we can continue our shopping trip in peace. Come on." They continued north, not far, to a dress shop. "Coming in this time?"

"Should I? I shop so often with you at home it's always so hard to tell when – "

She yanked on his arm and pulled him through the opened door.

Will stood near the door, feeling overly exposed. "Hopefully I won't be long," Phoebe tried to assure him as she walked over to find someone to help her. Will saw Phoebe talking to a middle-aged woman in a long brown dress. He looked around the store. There was a lot of brown fabric. Some blue, some green, deep red; but most was dark. A few had bright inserts or stripes. He even saw a few plaid designs. But he supposed white wouldn't go over well with people like his sister falling in the mud.

Phoebe checked in with him, stating that there were some nearly ready-to-wear dresses she was going to try on. "They'll measure me and stitch up a last seam or two. Otherwise I would have had to make them from scratch, and ugh, we know how that would turn out," she said, rolling her eyes, getting a grin out of her brother. "Be back soon." She left again and walked behind a large curtain. A woman came out, went back, came out, went back, working her patience with his sister where, he knew, patience was sometimes greatly needed.

Thirty minutes later Phoebe emerged from behind the curtain in a long blue dress with thin vertical stripes, snug fitting around her ribs, high at the neck and down to her ankles. She had taken time to affix her chatelaine chain and bag around her waist and put the items from her jacket inside of it.

Her Army jacket was over her arm; the woman who had assisted her eyed it as if it carried a disease. The jacket and the other dress she had worn were placed onto wrapping paper and tied with string. She had purchased one more dress, one skirt and two blouses that were wrapped separately.

"How do I look?" She asked Will, doing a spin near him by the door.

He looked her up and down. "Hmm, not bad." He shrugged. "You look like you're getting your old-timey photo taken. But I always pictured you a-stetson-and-holster kinda girl"

"Maybe next time. At least I can still wear my boots. You're not wearing those," she said, pointing at his feet.

Before leaving the store Phoebe took a moment to look around. High ceilings, wooden floors swept clean, wooden counter at the side, some shelves with merchandise, a mirror on a stand, a velvet couch and chair. Not unlike a store where she was from, but so much more elegant and well-crafted. She sighed; and it was gone.

Leaving through the door she said, "Okay, your turn."

They headed south now, back the way they had come. She glanced across the street and saw a bootery, a jewelry store and a barber. All were open, all were painted white. Some were one-story, some two, in some cases owners worked the store below and lived above or behind.

The false fronts, rounded or rectangular, gave the owner room to paint or hang a large sign for advertisement purposes. Awnings with wooden posts were common, keeping rain and sun off passersby and out of interiors on a hot day. Many building were built against the next in line. Exceptions existed; when a building was moved or replaced or when space was needed in between for water drainage or animals. In Bodie the cost per foot was expensive; buildings were close together.

When they passed by where Phoebe had been pushed into the mud, she halted their progress and looked across the street. She noticed that the building where the man had burst through the door and collided with her was a saloon. Next to that was a sign for a gunsmith within the hardware store. She turned to her right and saw another saloon just a few feet ahead on their side of the street. She really needed to slow down and relax. There was so much around her to see.

"You're right, let's stroll," she said, looping her arm through her brother's once again.

"I'm right? I didn't say anything."

"In my head you did. Now let's find you something to wear. People are staring."

Will looked around quickly and saw no one looking at him. "Very funny."

People were out and about on this Monday morning, as they were every morning in Bodie. Businesses were open, the mills were in operation, the people in the mines were going down, coming up. They passed a restaurant with a sign out front that said 'Meals all day and night,' and heard voices coming from within. A group of men walked out, talking in friendly conversation, saying "Pardon me," to Phoebe and Will as they moved along on their way to their jobs or homes or saloons.

A few minutes later they drew near Green Street again. Phoebe gripped Will's arm tighter and said excitedly, "Ooh, Will, let's go in here first." They were standing in front of the Boone Store, one of the buildings that had withstood Bodie's fires and still stood in modern Bodie. Her brother looked it over and shrugged. Phoebe asked, surprised, "You don't recognized it, do you? It's the Boone Store. It's here, I mean it's in the Bodie we know. Let's go in."

He nodded, curiosity in his expression now. "Sure, why not?" They stepped from the boardwalk to the angled entry and recessed front door and walked in.

"Did you know that Harvey Boone is a descendant of Daniel Boone?" she whispered. Will shook his head 'no.'

The store had a few other people inside so they were not immediately greeted upon entrance. It gave Phoebe and Will a few minutes to look around without being noticed. She drew in her breath at the organization of all the items for sale in the store. Everything was lined up, neatly arranged, the shelves were stocked full of daily items. Looking up she saw the tin panel ceilings that were so popular in the nineteenth century. A long counter along the right side had shelves above it filled with items. Barrels and boxes containing merchandise were lined up on the floor. There was a large coffee grinder, rolls of parchment paper and twine for wrapping parcels, more shelves on the left side of the room, and storage toward the back.

Phoebe nudged Will. "A razor, you can get that here. Look at everything..." Phoebe was looking around and began doing circles while moving forward. Will grabbed hold of her sleeve just before she bumped into someone who was walking out the door. "Excuse me," she smiled apologetically. The man and woman couple smiled back at them and continued on their way.

"Look at this," Phoebe said, picking up a long metal object. I wish I could buy all of this stuff, but how would I, you know, get it home?"

"What is that?" Will made a face.

"A curling iron," she laughed. "You warm it up on the stove or over a lamp. And portable," she wiggled it. "No cord."

"Who knows, Phoebe? Maybe these kinds of places are where all the missing persons really go when they disappear. Maybe we'll never get home."

Ignoring him she said, "Look," and pulled him forward. "Penny candy." She pointed at a display of sugar candy sticks standing in canning jars on the counter. "Just like we used to get when we were kids. Weird, they look the same. Want one? I'm buying," she said as she picked up two labeled sassafras. And Whitman's Chocolates Samplers?" Phoebe picked up a box and showed it to Will, raising her eyebrows. Will laughed.

"Is there anything I can help you locate?" A voice spoke close to Will. Again, he turned to Phoebe. He was never quite sure what verbiage to use or what to call things. His sister was well-versed in proper etiquette of the times, her slapping of the stranger notwithstanding. And if she misspoke she simply didn't care.

Phoebe was still fascinated seeing all the items available for purchase in a general store. And this one wasn't nearly the largest in Bodie when compared to Gilson & Barber on North Main Street.

She spoke up, as Will had known she would. "My brother needs a razor. And I need some soap, if you please."

She smiled sweetly, then added as an afterthought. "And two toothbrushes and some baking soda too, please."

"Why, certainly." The man showed two folding straight razors to Will. He gulped, glanced at Phoebe and mouthed the words, '*this is a razor?*' She nodded and he picked the smallest, most compact. He hoped he wouldn't need to use it for too long. He did not look forward to a bare blade in close proximity to his face and neck.

Their package of items was wrapped in a small square of paper and tied with a string.

"Did you buy the Whitman's Chocolates?" asked Will.

"No. I wouldn't want to run out of money and force you to go to work or anything," she stated sarcastically. "But I got two stick candies for later."

"Can I still afford new clothes?"

Phoebe laughed. "I think we'll manage," she said as he opened the door to Boone's store for her. They exited and she looped her arm through his once again, crossing Green Street and sticking to the boardwalk.

"Hey, I don't remember that building. This looks different." Will pointed to the Bodie House Hotel on the corner.

"*That's* what looks different?" She glanced up at him. "It's not there anymore if that's what you mean. And the mortuary," Phoebe said, pointing beyond the hotel, "isn't there now but it will be moved here later."

"I don't know how you keep it all straight in your head," he said. They turned right, walking along Green Street, attempting to stay on the far left of the road, out of the mud, puddles and wagon wheel tracks of this, one of Bodie's main roads.

"Up there is Fuller Street. Remember the big red barn? That's up here." She pointed and they walked past it momentarily.

"Fuller Street? I don't remember that one."

"It's almost gone in nineteen eigh – " she looked around, suddenly self-conscious. "You know." He nodded. They passed the red barn and Fuller Street was just on the other side of it. She pointed to the opposite corner. "That corner is where the church will be built. They're raising money for it now."

"Where are we going? Are we almost there?"

"Yes, turn left here."

Will was amazed at the number of buildings and people on Fuller Street. "Everything looks so..." he said, waving his hand around, unable to articulate what he was seeing. He turned his head to look from where he had walked and back again.

For a moment Phoebe felt an old pain in the pit of her stomach. One she hadn't felt in a long time. Her last visit here, before coming with her family, had been before she had left for college. When she had shown a new college friend an article featuring the gold mining town, she had allowed that friend to see her infatuation of the subject. That friend had sneered at the ludicrous idea of wasting one's time on people and ideas long dead; and a bubble had burst within her. Always independent of nature and not easily influenced, that had been the beginning of her annoyance at the mention of her previous passion, pushing people that knew of it away and deviating her life's course in school. Deep down her gut told her she had been lying. If not to others directly, then to herself.

"Hmm, yes," she replied, distracted by reflection.

"So where are we going? I don't know where anything is."

"Sorry, it's up here. A men's clothing store. Reinstein & Wolf."

"Never heard of that one, but, okay," he said, letting her take the reins once again.

They approached the store, a relatively large one, the name painted on the false front at the top. "No, I'm not going to wait outside. I don't trust you," she said. They walked into the store and a clerk immediately offered to help.

He asked Will how he could assist him and Will looked to his sister. She nudged him, urging him to answer for himself. "I – I need, um, I need clothes." *Yep, that was dumb,* he thought. "More precisely, I require a pair of pants," Phoebe nudged him again, "or two, and, a shirt, or two. And a coat," he remembered.

The man told him to come with him so he could measure him. Phoebe said quietly, "and you need a hat, a vest, and suspenders, and a tie."

He was following the man and whispered back to Phoebe, "Suspenders? A tie?" She nodded and he turned back to follow the man.

Phoebe sat in one of the chairs to wait for Will. She heard his voice and grinned, picturing his unease in his present situation. He probably hadn't been this uncomfortable since being measured for a tuxedo for their brother's wedding. Another man was buying clothes and another husband and wife pair walked into the store while Phoebe was seated. She did feel better, and less obvious, in her new dress.

Phoebe set her packages down in the seat beside her. When she did so a shadow crossed her as a person stepped in front of the light from the window. She looked up then, curious, and inhaled in surprise when a man stepped toward her, smiling. "Miss Tucker, this is a pleasant surprise."

"Hello," was all she said, and pursed her lips in silent annoyance.

"I didn't mean to startle you – "

"You didn't startle me. I don't startle that easily."

He paused. "I didn't mean to catch you unawares." He wondered if that was an acceptable phrase for her. Phoebe nodded once.

"I'm here with Wi – my brother." *That was a genius thing to say. Why else would you be here, sitting in a chair in a men's clothing store?* "He's purchasing a coat, he should be able to return yours to you soon. Thank you, again, for the loan."

"It's quite a coincidence that you chose Reinstein & Wolf."

"And why is that, Mr. Sanford." Newton Sanford stood opposite Phoebe now, looking down at her. Phoebe looked past him to see if Will was going to be much longer.

"I am a clerk in this retail establishment." At that statement Phoebe returned his stare and wished she'd shopped for Will on Main Street.

"I see. Yes, that is a coincidence." *Walk away, now, if you please.*

"If it isn't too forward of me to say, I see you've made some purchases as well. You look rather lovely."

She looked down at her dress and remembered that her hair was up and she was wearing a hat. The last time she had seen him that morning she had been covered in mud. There was still some on her hands and boots, but access to water soon would take care of that.

"Thank you, and, no, it's not. I appreciate your kind words." She allowed herself a small smile but couldn't look him in the face.

Will came out from the back room then, seeking Phoebe's approval. He was wearing a black sack suit; a pair of black pants, a white shirt, black vest, and a simple crossover tie. And looking downcast at his appearance. The other clerk spoke to Newton Sanford for a moment and after a nod from Phoebe proceeded to wrap up Will's old clothes in one parcel and his other new clothes in another.

Newton asked, "May I help you find the perfect hat?"

Will looked relieved. Phoebe looked, once again, annoyed. They picked a black felt Derby and he modeled it for his sister. "Now this I like," he said, looking at himself in a mirror on the top of a table. He was only in need, now, of a pair of sturdy shoes or boots.

Will and Newton Sanford stood talking a few moments longer while Phoebe walked to the first clerk and paid for Will's purchases. She then walked to the door, ready to be on her way, cleared her throat, waited, and repeated the ritual. Both men turned at the sound. And both men walked to where Phoebe was standing near the door.

"Are we all done?" Will asked.

His sister nodded and said, "Except for shoes. We'll find a bootery." She turned the knob and pulled the door open.

"See you later, Newton," said Will, shaking the other man's hand in parting. Phoebe noticed how quickly he had dropped the "Mr." title in that gentleman's name.

"Yes," he replied. In a louder voice he called, "Miss Tucker?" Phoebe turned from the doorway.

"Yes, Mr. Sanford?"

"I took the courtesy of asking your brother if the two of you would like to join me for supper this evening?"

"Did you?" She looked at Will. "And what did my brother say?" Will had the sense to look sheepish.

"I – I said, well, I thought it was a nice gesture, Phoebe."

"Did you? What about Mrs. Barrett? Isn't she cooking supper for us this evening? It would have been nice for you to have consulted me on the matter?" Will knew she was choosing her words carefully and inwardly winced.

"I apologize, Miss Tucker," said Newton Sanford, looking, if she were to name it, hurt. "I didn't realize it would offend you. I spoke to Mrs. Barrett when I saw her earlier and proposed the idea to her at that time. I asked her to join me as well. Again, my apologies."

He dipped his head to her and she felt riddled with guilt. Will's words were stuck in her head; *Why are you always so rude, Phoebe? Because he's going to die, Will, and I don't want to get to know him, that's why.*

"No, Mr. Sanford, I apologize. I was very rude," she looked directly at him; he did the same. His mustache twitched and she suspected a hint of a smile underneath. "I – we would be delighted to join you for supper. Since Mrs. Barrett already knows, I suppose we won't be putting her out, will we?" She didn't notice the smile Will was attempting to hold back.

"Wonderful. Perhaps we can walk together? I will see you back at Mrs. Barrett's at eight o'clock. Will that suffice?"

Will was nodding and Phoebe replied, "Yes, that's just fine. Thank you."

As they walked along Fuller Street toward Green Street once again, Phoebe said, "You seem able to talk to Newton Sanford just fine. What's up with that?"

"I don't know, Phoebe. He's nice, that's all."

Nice! That's the problem, Will. June 19, 1880, 29 yrs, 3 mos, To Live in Hearts We Leave Behind is Not to Die.

16

Phoebe and Will retraced their steps and went back to Main Street. "Why didn't we get shoes last time we were here?" her brother asked.

"You're not a miner, so you're getting one pair. I wanted you to get your suit first and you didn't know what that was going to look like, did you?"

He hadn't thought of that, and shrugged. "Oh. No, I guess not."

"They're expensive. We don't how long we're going to be here, so we're buying a minimum of clothes."

"Do you think we can take anything back with us? I kinda like the hat." He took it off to look at it closely and put it back on his head.

"You mean like in a dream and you try to hold tight to something, hoping it's there when you wake up? I don't feel like we're dreaming, but that would be nice. Otherwise, I have no idea."

"You do that, don't you? Try to take things back with you from your dreams?" He gave her a quizzical look.

"Oh shut up, I know you do too." He grinned down at her and she smiled.

They found a bootery on Main Street. Will purchased a pair of short, black boots. "Aren't these kind of, dressy?"

"They're just regular boots. Like I said, you're not a miner. Or a mucker, a blacksmith, a livery worker, a carpenter, or a banker. Any place else you might go or work, those are the shoes you would want."

"So, no Adidas? And what's a mucker?"

"They shovel the ore into the mine cars to move it to the stamp mills for crushing."

"That sounds fun," he said sarcastically. "Maybe I wanna be a mucker, you don't know."

They were standing outside the bootery now, deciding what to do next. "I'm getting hungry. They have food here, right?"

"All the time. Remember, Vegas. And me too. Let's find a restaurant."

Will looked as if he might panic again. "You mean go in and eat? We can't just, pick something up?"

"Do you see any drive-throughs? And what's the big deal?"

"What do we do?"

"Do? Go in, find a place to sit, order off a menu, wait for our food, and eat. Does that sound too complicated for you?" She had begun to steer Will up the street again. "What's the matter with you?"

"I guess really being here is, well – you know I feel like a fish out of water."

"I know, sorry. But it's not that different. People are people. And they have come here from all over the place, different states, different countries. They all have different routines, hobbies, traditions."

"Ha, the last time we were here you said it *was* different, like Mars and Earth," he reminded her, looking superior.

"I don't want to talk about it." She turned from him and began walking "You told me to enjoy myself. Now let me. Let's find a restaurant."

Will couldn't decide if he felt more noticeable in his new clothes or the ones he'd arrived in. At least nobody was giving him funny looks now. He certainly felt conspicuous; the only hat he ever wore was a baseball cap. He felt more dressed up than many he saw around town. He supposed it was because his clothes were all new; and because he wasn't a mucker.

"Here," Phoebe said, and pulled him into a doorway. They entered the establishment and went to sit down at a small table along the side.

"Where are we?" asked Will.

"The Nevada Restaurant and Chop House," Phoebe replied.

"Chop house?" Will asked, unfamiliar with the term.

"You'd call it a steakhouse, but that's not what it's called here, now. This one was supposed to have been a good one. I want to try it." She looked around at the Chop House, then closed her eyes to breath in the scent of cooked meat. There were wooden tables and chairs with white linen tablecloths, polished walls, high tin ceilings. *And it's all gone.* Before someone asked what they would like to order Phoebe rested her forehead in her hands a moment, collecting her thoughts.

"What's wrong, Phoebe?" Will asked.

She opened her hands and gestured around the restaurant before looking at her brother. "It's all gone, Will."

"Yes, Phoebe, I know." She shook her head, as if he simply did not understand. "But?"

"I don't know. I get distracted, forget where I am, then I remember and it hits me, Bam, and I get this sinking feeling in my gut that just, that just – "

"Hurts?"

She nodded. "Yeah. I always thought, 'wouldn't it be cool to see what it really looked like back then,' or 'I wish I could visit an old town and see the people in person.' But now that I have, that we're here... I don't know, I feel sick about it."

"Why?" He leaned forward, not fully understanding her reaction.

She shrugged. "I don't know. Maybe because not only is their town gone, and their way of life, but they themselves. All dead and gone."

A man walked up to the table and handed them menus, saying he would return momentarily.

"I think you're taking this all the wrong way," he said. She frowned at him, doubt clear in her expression. He continued, "If someone were to show up at your house or job, Zap, and meet you, and live with you and talk with for a day, two days, a week, and then Zap, return back to their own home, would all your days leading up that encounter, and all the days remaining of the rest of your life never happen?"

She sat back in her chair and relaxed, contemplating her brother's rationalization. "You're right." She looked at him sharply and continued, "And I hope you write down the date because I don't think I'm ever going to say that again." Will smiled.

"And you thought you were the smart one." He brushed at imaginary dust on his shoulder in an elitist fashion.

"Thanks. Now take off your hat."

***

After they had ordered chopped steak and baked beans, one of the cheapest combos on the menu, and coffee, they relaxed for the first time since their arrival. Siblings having lunch; how much different was that no matter where or when? And just like at home the waiter asked if they would like dessert. They shared a slice of lemon cake, delivered daily from the bakery just down the street, they were told.

"Now what? I don't even know what time it is." Will asked, looking around for a clock.

"You could've bought a pocket watch, I suppose. But there are clocks everywhere."

"It's all right. I have a feeling they cost too much anyway."

Phoebe left money on the table and they stood to leave. When they exited, traffic in the street had increased considerably. Two freight wagons were slushing through the muck in the street, one heading south full of lumber, one heading north full of supplies to fill the stores on the north end.

"Now I see why the street was made so wide," said Will, looking left and right and back, watching the drivers work their teams with skill. "Hey, look, it's your friend from this morning," he said, pointing across the street.

"Great," Phoebe muttered. The man spotted them standing in front of the Chop House and stared as they turned to walk south on Main Street. "Coming out of another saloon. Why am I not surprised?"

"I think you have a fan."

"Keep your eyes peeled for him from now on, Will. I'm not kidding. This is not a safe place right now."

Will grabbed her arm, but kept walking, and said close to her ear, "Don't look now but it looks like you and I and that guy have a mutual friend."

Phoebe's steps slowed at the pressure on her arm. She turned, pretending to speak to Will, but looking past his shoulder instead. A man was talking to the slapped-in-the-face stranger, a man they both knew. Albert Griffin, one of the other boarders at Mrs. Barrett's.

They stepped around a small group that had gathered on the boardwalk to talk. "I can't say I'm surprised by that either," said Phoebe, and explained how she had encountered him the night before while outside, how he had smelled of liquor and had been behaving suspiciously.

"Why didn't you tell me?"

She shrugged. "I don't know. I didn't think about it once the morning came. But now we need to keep an eye on him too."

"Seriously?"

"Yes." They walked on, past the same hardware store and tinsmith they had previously seen from across the street. It advertised weapons and ammunition for sale, as well as the skills of the gunsmith. Phoebe stopped in front of it and glanced at her brother. She continued walking but was considering her options.

They turned on Green Street, going back to the boarding house. Phoebe looked behind them to see if they had been followed by Albert Griffin and his companion. She saw neither and relaxed somewhat. Up ahead was Wood Street. On they walked, passing homes, businesses and hotels. They passed Pioneer Brewery when they arrived at the corner and turned.

The front door was unlocked. They walked to the rear of the house where Phoebe opened her door with her key. They both went in and she locked the door behind her. She put her packages down, sat on her bed and fell onto her back to relax. Will sat in the chair in the corner, unbuttoning his coat, taking off his new boots and wiggling his toes. "New shoes," he said.

They sat silently for several minutes, Will leaning his head against the wall with his eyes closed, Phoebe staring up at the ceiling. "Hey, Will?"

"Yeah," he said, keeping his eyes closed.

"What do you think J. W. had in mind sending us here?"

He snorted in laughter. "You know him better than I do, I think. So I have no idea." Then, "He said he used to live here with his parents. Do you think it has something to do with them?"

She pushed herself up on her elbows. "I don't know. He never said when that was. Or where, or what their names were, or anything, now that I think about it."

Will opened his eyes. "I'm going to take my stuff in my room and put it in that tall thing against the wall." He stood to go.

"You mean the wardrobe?" she teased.

"Whatever it is, yes. Then I think I'll go to the necessary," he smiled, giving the word air quotes.

"Okay. You know where to find me." Phoebe re-locked her room after Will left. She heard him do the same next door. With Albert Griffin in the same house she didn't feel safe leaving it unlocked. She unclipped the chatelaine bag from her waist and took the opportunity to mentally measure it. At the store she had chosen the largest one; perhaps there was room for a Colt in there too.

Feeling refreshed after splashing some water on her face, Phoebe was ready to use the outhouse herself and unlocked her door. She looked toward the front of the house and didn't see anyone but heard sounds from the kitchen. She walked through the door to see Mrs. Barrett making a pitcher of lemonade. Her landlady seemed surprised to see that it was Phoebe walking into the room.

"Miss Tucker, hello. I didn't expect to see you. How are you?"

"I'm well, thank you. I'm actually on my way..." she pointed to the door leading outside and Mrs. Barrett nodded, smiling. When Phoebe returned, Mrs. Barrett was still in the kitchen. "May I speak with you for a moment?"

"Of course, Miss Tucker, sit down." They sat at the kitchen table after Mrs. Barrett poured each of them a glass of lemonade.

"I wanted to pay you for our first week's charges." She had folded the necessary amount separately so she needn't rifle through her bag in her landlady's presence.

Mrs. Barrett seemed surprised, but accepted the cash from Phoebe. "I see. Thank you. I apologize, but I was under the assumption you may not be able to pay me right away. I'm sorry if that sounds rude."

"No, no, it doesn't. You could have turned us away, and you didn't."

"Did you meet up with your acquaintances, then? Did everything turn out all right for you?" She seemed curious. Phoebe hated to lie but she truly had no choice.

"My errand was successful, thank you." The landlady asked nothing further, but her face was full of curiosity. "I appreciate your kindness."

Mrs. Barrett smiled then, a thin, dour smile, sticking the money inside her apron pocket and resting her arms on the table between them. "I must confess. With all the hotels and other boarding houses in town I needed you to want to stay. I told you previously that I had only three boarders. With you and your brother I now have five. I had two different boarders before, but both of them perished in a mining accident last year."

She looked down at her hands and fidgeted with her fingers. "It was my husband's idea to run this boarding house." She looked back at Phoebe, who was patiently waiting for the woman to continue. "He was a store clerk at Reinstein & Wolf before he died from pneumonia seven months ago. Now it's just me and Walter."

"I'm so terribly sorry, Mrs. Barrett." Phoebe had a chance to look at the woman closely now, for the first time. Sitting across from her she saw that, if she had her hair down, hair that was similar in color to her own, she would look much younger than she did with it pinned up. Phoebe didn't think she looked more than late twenties or so, nearly the same age as herself, and was momentarily stunned at this realization.

"My brother and I spoke with Mr. Sanford at Reinstein & Wolf earlier. Will, my brother, needed some clothes. Is that how you met Mr. Sanford?" *Now why did I ask that?*

"No, actually, Mr. Sanford hasn't lived here long. The store needed another clerk and I recommended him. He is a fine and honest gentleman and he was looking for work." She looked down at her hands again. "And I was looking for a boarder."

"Did he mention to you about having supper at a restaurant this evening? He asked us to supper and he said he spoke to you about it?"

"Yes, he did. I was on errands this morning with my son, Walter. Mr. Sanford saw me and stepped outside to speak about it."

"But what about the other boarders and their supper? I don't want to be an interference to their routine."

"Don't worry. Mr. Griffin rarely eats supper here. But I have left instructions for my girl to cook something for them."

"Your... girl?"

"Yes, my helper. I pay her for sometimes lending a hand. She is a Paiute from near Mono Lake. Her family lives south of here now and they work all over Bodie. Her name is Wyanet. It means Beautiful. Her mother and her tribe weave the most magnificent baskets."

Phoebe had forgotten about the Paiute baskets that were in the museum in Carson City. She had seen many pictures of the different designs and sizes that the Paiutes had produced for generations. They were true pieces of art, some antique baskets selling at auctions for tens, and even hundreds of thousands of dollars. She didn't think it hurt to say, "Yes, I've seen the baskets. They are masterful."

At that moment Walter burst in through the kitchen door, winded, out of breath, about to say something to his mother. When he saw that Phoebe was there as well he glanced from one to the other and held his tongue. Mrs. Barrett stood up, facing Walter, moving toward him. "Walter, what is it? What's happened?" The boy glanced at Phoebe again and needed further prodding from his mother. "Go ahead, what's the trouble?"

He pointed outside, toward the rear of the house. "The barn. The horse. I was watering him and – and – " his hand still on the doorknob, he looked back outside before continuing. "There's a man about to take him. I told him not to, that it's Mr. Griffin's horse, but he pushed me aside, and I fell, and – "

Mrs. Barrett frowned, her voice rose, she reached over to the counter, picked up a cast iron skillet and moved to the door. "He pushed you?" She moved past Walter and went down the steps with purpose driving her. Walter had stepped out of the way and Phoebe walked out the door behind his mother. Walter, curiosity getting the better of him, followed moments later.

A wooden fence connected the house with the barn on each side of the house and ran along the back behind the barn, allowing any boarder's horse a little room to roam when released. Each side had a gate with a wooden latch. Mrs. Barrett unlatched the gate, walked through without closing it and proceeded quickly into the open barn. Phoebe and Walter caught up to her but stayed a few steps behind.

"You," they heard Mrs. Barrett say. Phoebe and Walter looked at each other, staying silent, waiting. "I'm responsible for the safety of that animal, as it belongs to one of my boarders. I suggest you leave it be and vacate my property immediately." Phoebe noticed Walter take a step backward. He knew his mother's tone, her manner and her temperament. Phoebe took note.

There was no reply. Rustling and hoof beats could be heard from within. It sounded as if the man, whoever it was, was ignoring Mrs. Barrett and going about his business, whatever it was. The horse walked out, being led by a man, his face hidden from Phoebe and Walter on the opposite side of the horse. Mrs. Barrett moved to stand in front of him, challenging him. "I said you will leave the horse. Unhand it immediately or I will notify the authorities, you ratbag, and have you hanged as a horse thief."

Ratbag? I haven't heard that one, but it sounds like it would have been an appropriate slam when I encountered Rich-Rick-Honker back in Dubuque.

The man stopped walking the horse and said, "Now, now, I'm not stealing this horse. Ma'am," he added. "I've come to fetch it for your Mr. Griffin. He's waiting for me, so if you'll just move aside..."

Mrs. Barrett didn't move but gripped the skillet with both hands now, her gaze boring into the man, not taking her eyes off of him. The horse, beginning to fidget, stepped back a few feet, allowing the man to see Phoebe and Walter standing to the side. He glanced at them and grinned. Phoebe frowned now as well, recognizing him. He said, tipping his hat in her direction, "Ma'am."

Phoebe stepped forward and stood beside Mrs. Barrett. "Release the horse."

"I cannot abide by your amiable request. Good day, Ladies." The last word was directed toward Phoebe. Remembering that the last time she had seen the man's face was directly after she had slapped it, Phoebe sneered at him, said, "I wasn't asking," and walked to her left to the gate. She stood in front of it, preventing him from opening it without a little extra effort.

He let go of the horse and walked to stand in front of Phoebe. "I'm taking the horse. Move... Ma'am."

"No."

Phoebe noticed Walter was gone, to where she did not know. Mrs. Barrett had moved to stand behind the man and raised her skillet as if to swing. "Wait," they heard someone call out from behind Phoebe. It was Will, approaching from around the front of the house, Walter in tow. "What's going on. Walter said he needed help." Will stood just outside the gate now, behind his sister. He noticed Mrs. Barrett lower a heavy skillet. And Phoebe noticed the look of disappointment on her face.

The man put up his hands in surrender. "I was sent on an errand to retrieve this horse. These ladies were preventing me from doing so." He put both palms skyward and shrugged. "Perhaps you could assist me?"

Will looked at Mrs. Barrett, still standing with the skillet in both hands, then at Phoebe. "I believe that decision is Mrs. Barrett's to make. Haven't we met?"

The man tipped his hat again, feigning politeness. "I beg your pardon, but yes, I was the one who, sadly, got your sister all in a pucker this morning. My name is Young. John Young."

"I would say it's a pleasure to meet you but I'm still considering the implications." Phoebe quickly glanced around to Will and winked at him. *Good one.*

Walter had run around the house in the opposite direction and was now entering the small corral from the other side. He quietly walked behind his mother to the horse, took hold of the reins and turned it to lead it back inside the barn. John Young knew he was outnumbered. "I'll tell Mr. Griffin he will need to retrieve his own horse, I suppose." He made a small bow to Mrs. Barrett, then to Phoebe and moved toward the gate, expecting her to move aside. "You wouldn't land another sockdolager on me, now, would you, Miss..."

"Tucker," Phoebe answered quietly. "Miss Phoebe Tucker. And I wouldn't bet on it, if I were you."

17

Gathered in the kitchen, Mrs. Barrett offered Will a glass of lemonade. Walter was skipping around the table, wound up from the excitement outside and feeling victorious. "Walter, sit down, please. You're going to make me spill something." The boy sat in one of the chairs but he sat with force and it skidded on the floor and made a screeching sound. He had the wisdom to wince and apologize.

"Thank you both for your assistance. I believe Mr. Young to be... unpredictable." She took a drink of her lemonade. "What did he mean when he said you hit him, Miss Tucker? Did you?" She seemed shocked and impressed at the same time.

Will blurted, "So that's what sockdolager means," causing all gathered to laugh. Will looked down and turned a bit red in the cheeks but Phoebe patted one of his hands, smiling at him. *It's okay to be yourself, Will.*

Phoebe briefly explained how John Young had burst through a door, run into her, and she had lost her balance and stumbled into the mud in the street. Walter was leaning on his elbows on the edge of the table, listening with rapt attention. "You walloped him good," Walter cried out. His mother hushed him but Phoebe smiled.

"I fear it was rather unladylike, Walter," Phoebe attempted to put her behavior right for Mrs. Barrett's benefit.

Mrs. Barrett surprised her with, "I am not personally acquainted him, but he seems to think he's the biggest toad in the puddle." At that Walter began hopping around the table making a comical sound somewhere between a croak and a groan.

"What are you doing, Walter, get off the floor," his mother said, but she was smiling, enjoying seeing her son smile and play.

"That's what a toad says."

"How do you know?"

He stopped hopping and said, "That's what Mary Louisa told me. She knows everything, she's nine."

Phoebe hoped no one saw how hearing that name spoken aloud had shaken her. *Mary Louisa Moore Age 20 yrs. A precious one from us has gone, A voice we loved is stilled: A place is vacant in our hearts, Which never can be filled.* J. W. had stopped and looked at her gravestone but hadn't spoken then. She had meant to ask him about it.

Now Phoebe felt sick. Mrs. Barrett responded to Walter, Will said something-or-other, but Phoebe heard none of it.

She had to change the subject. "Mrs. Barrett, who is Mr. Young to Mr. Griffin, if you don't mind my asking?"

"I don't mind." Walter had tired of hopping like a toad. His mother asked him if he would kindly go check on the gates outside and make sure they were both secure. He left, still in a bouncy mood.

"Mr. Griffin has lived here only a few weeks now. But he isn't always in Bodie. He spends time in Bridgeport and Aurora as well. I do not feel as if I'm revealing a confidence, as I know nothing of his personal business dealings." She looked to both doors to the kitchen to be sure they were not overheard. "When I allowed him to rent a room here I was led to believe it was at the recommendation of a mutual acquaintance. I believe now that I was deceived.

"However, he has been a model boarder. I have seen him speaking with that man, John Young, a time or two. I have never spoken to, or been formally introduced to, Mr. Young, so I'm unsure of their relationship. Mr. Griffin keeps late hours but never bothers any of the other boarders. I urge both of you to use caution."

Phoebe and Will exchanged glances. Phoebe said, "Mrs. Barrett, we appreciate your advice. And I don't mean to be too bold, but why are you telling us this? You've only known us a short time?"

Mrs. Barrett smiled then, a warm, genuine smile, the first the siblings had seen. She looked younger again, like Phoebe had observed earlier, and her eyes shined with warmth and spirit. "I'm well aware, Miss Tucker, Mr. Tucker. I don't know if you'll understand this, but my intuition tells me I can trust you. And it rarely fails me. Most importantly, Walter told me he saw the two of you out and about today; he likes you. And that means a great deal to me."

Phoebe liked this young woman, this young widow with a boy to raise by herself in this wild town. Later she said, "You should have seen her, Will, the way she grabbed that heavy skillet and stormed out of the kitchen. She's two inches shorter than I am but that didn't stop her from thinking she might have to whack some stranger in the head for pushing her little boy and breaking into her barn."

"Yeah, kinda reminds me of someone," he stated wryly, relaxing on his bed and staring up at the ceiling.

"What if he would have had a gun or something?"

He bolted upright, astounded. "You were standing right in front of him, keeping him from opening the gate. Yes, what if he would have had a gun, or something?"

Phoebe shrugged. "I guess I didn't think about that then. I can only hope Mrs. Barrett would have been quick with that frying pan. And I'm glad we got to talk with Walter for a few minutes. He seems like a cool kid."

"He does. But let me ask you something. Don't you think about how they are all gone now too? Why are you so annoyed talking to Newton Sanford but not to them? What's the difference?"

Phoebe was sitting in Will's chair in the corner of his room. She leaned her head back against the wall, closed her eyes and sighed. "I know the day he's going to die. It's very, very soon. And it's so sad." She sat upright and looked at him. "It's all I can think about when I see him."

"You don't know how long the rest of them have to live though. You could be talking to Mrs. Barrett for the last time at any time. Or Walter, or me." He raised his eyebrows.

"Stop that. I know, but it's not the same as knowing for sure. And oh, Will, when Walter mentioned that his friend is Mary Louisa Moore, oh, that was awful. I couldn't think of anything to say." His expression told her, once again, he had forgotten the name. "Oh really, you've got the worst memory for names. Mary Louisa Moore, the cemetery, the stone with the engraving. She died when she was only twenty."

"Yeah, I remember now. Oh geez, that's terrible."

"I wonder what happens to her."

They sat in self-reflection for a minute, realizing how tenuous their relationships here actually were.

"This is too stressful. We've got to find a way home," said Will standing up and straightening his hair before putting his coat back on. "Do I have to wear my coat to supper? Is this one good enough? How dressed up do people get for a restaurant?"

Phoebe was relieved he didn't let her dwell too long on their dismal situation. "Wear your coat, not just your vest. What you have is fine. This isn't San Francisco."

“I actually understood that reference. San Francisco was the city of the rich and elite during the gold rush.”

“So you do listen to me sometimes. Who knew? There are a couple of places like that here too, believe it or not. But I doubt we’re going to one of them. No financiers in this group.”

“If we do get stuck here we could end up really, really rich. We know what’s going to happen, we’re going to plan ahead, buy all the right stocks, land, all that stuff.”

“And leave it all to our future selves in our wills?” he asked sardonically.

Will laughed. “You said it, not me.”

“Is your tie finally straight? You’ve been fiddling with it forever.”

“I suppose. Do I have to wear this all the time. It’s choking me.”

“No, it isn’t. And no, I suppose not. But for tonight, yes. Come on, let’s go to the parlor.”

Phoebe stopped in her room first to check on her belongings. When Will asked what she was doing she replied, “I want to make sure my jacket is still there. I don’t want to lose it.” She had put it under her mattress, out of sight and not easily found.

“Who would want it?” he teased.

Rolling her eyes at him she locked her door, put her key into her bag and checked to see if her necklace with the gold horseshoe was still around her neck. She had thought it safer to keep beneath her dress while out walking on Main Street as the delicate chain made it easier for a mugger to pull from around her neck. Also because she preferred to remain as inconspicuous as possible; although small chains with charms existed, it was not the typical Victorian jewelry.

It had been a special gift that she had taken great care of for the last eight years. So for tonight’s supper at the restaurant Phoebe would wear it outside of her dress and let it shine in the gas lights. She surmised J. W. would appreciate the gesture; *darn him.*

They were seated in the parlor, awaiting the hour to meet Newton Sanford. Will was complaining about being hungry. Phoebe seemed, to her brother, nervous.

"How can you be so hungry? You ate a huge lunch?"

"I dunno. I didn't eat that much." Will looked at Phoebe who was looking out the window and squeezing her hands together. "What's wrong with you?"

"Nothing's wrong with me," she snapped. "Why?"

"Because you're acting like it's prom night and your date might not show up." Will leaned back in the chair and raised a foot to put it up on the table in front of them. He changed his mind with his leg in mid-air when Phoebe gave him a 'don't you dare' look.

"That's ridiculous." Phoebe stood up to pace the room once or twice.

The room off the parlor leading to Mrs. Barrett's and Walter's room opened behind her then, startling Phoebe. Mrs. Barrett entered the parlor wearing a dark blue skirt and lighter blue blouse with thin, navy blue vertical stripes. She carried a dark blue hat in her hands.

Phoebe glared at Will and he jumped to his feet. "Mrs. Barrett, your dress is lovely," Phoebe stated genuinely, bringing another warm smile to her landlady's face.

"Thank you, Miss Tucker. I don't get a chance to wear something 'lovely' very often. I appreciate your kind words."

"I apologize for not changing into another dress. I hope this one will do. I purchased the minimum today." Phoebe could tell Mrs. Barrett wanted to ask questions on that subject, but she politely refrained.

"Personally, I believe you chose wisely, Miss Tucker."

Walter burst from the room behind his mother, pulling at the top button of his shirt. "Do I have to wear it buttoned up all the way like this? I'm choking."

Mrs. Barrett shook her head at her son's behavior. "No, you are not." She stuck two fingers between his neck and his collar and said, "There's room, you are not choking. Now put on your coat."

He shrugged on his small coat grudgingly, slumped over to the place on the sofa Phoebe had recently vacated and plopped down, dejected. Will commiserated fully.

"Button your coat, please," Mrs. Barrett said to him calmly. He buttoned the top two buttons.

"You look very fashionable this evening, Walter," said Phoebe, hoping to cheer the boy.

Mrs. Barrett cleared her throat. Walter looked up at Phoebe and said, "Thank you, Ma'am."

A few minutes later Phoebe was seated next to Walter and Mrs. Barrett was in the other chair near the window when they saw Newton Sanford through the front window. Mrs. Barrett went to her room to retrieve her bag and returned as Newton Sanford was closing the door. "If you all don't mind waiting for me a few minutes longer, I will change my coat and return directly." They all nodded but Phoebe couldn't look him in the eye.

Walter, seated beside her, was bouncing lightly on the sofa while he talked. The others chatted while waiting for their supper escort. She eyed the calendar on the table, the previous day having been marked off accurately.

Newton Sanford walked back into the room and when she looked up he was looking at her; just her. The small smile on his face was more noticeable in his eyes, she thought, because his mustache was skilled at hiding it. Subconsciously, she hadn't taken a breath and inhaled deeply on realization of that fact. Breaking eye contact with Newton Sanford she looked to her brother, who had been looking at her, and said, "Shall we go?" and stood up quickly.

After Mrs. Barrett had locked the front door behind them all, the five of them walked down the street together; Phoebe on Will's arm because it may have looked strange for her not to have been, Mrs Barrett on Newton Sanford's arm because she had known him longest, and Walter skipping ahead and zigzagging to avoid the mud as his mother had instructed. Phoebe asked, "Mrs. Barrett, when did you say Wayanet was going to come over?"

"She was here earlier. She prepared supper for Mr. Griffin and Mr. Murphy at her home and brought it here to leave in the kitchen for a time they choose to take advantage of it."

Phoebe looked disappointed. "Oh, I was hoping to meet her. Perhaps another time."

"Yes, she comes often. She is quite friendly. I have no doubt she would enjoy meeting you as well."

Will squeezed his sisters arm that was in his grip and she looked up at him. She raised her eyebrows, *What?*

He whispered, "Taking an interest in the local people now, are you?"

"No," she denied too loudly. Then, whispering back, she said, "I was just being polite."

"Is that what you call it?"

She pulled her arm away from his, pretending to straighten the collar of her dress. She walked with her arms at her sides after that.

Not far ahead was Green Street. Just before they reached it Mrs. Barrett asked, "So, where are we going to dine this evening, Mr. Sanford? I realize it's a surprise, but can you tell us now?" They were at Green Street now, unable to turn left until the surrey ahead of them moved out of the way.

"We are going to North Main Street, to the Palace Restaurant. I couldn't let all of you walk all that way so I have hired a surrey to take us for an evening ride. I hope you all approve."

Mrs. Barrett smiled and said that was a thoughtful thing to do. Walter jumped up and down with glee. He did not often get to go on a surrey ride. Will was surprised because he didn't think walking to North Main Street was all that far even considering he wore new boots. Phoebe was delighted but resisted showing it.

Newton Sanford assisted Mrs. Barrett into the rear seat of the open surrey. She was followed by Walter who hopped in, jumped down, hopped back in and bounced around several seconds before sitting beside his mother.

Will stepped in front of Phoebe to go up next and sat beside Walter. Newton Sanford put out his hand to assist Phoebe into the front row behind the horses. She had to accept help, it would have been rude not to. When she hesitated, Newton Sanford asked her quietly, "Are you displeased, Miss Tucker?" while standing so closely that she could feel his breath on her face.

She gripped his hand for an instant, stepped quickly into the surrey, moved to the far side and sat down with a very unladylike whump, planning how she was going to get back at her brother later for putting her in this position. Newton Sanford followed next and sat beside her. He picked up the reins, glanced over at Phoebe with his smiling eyes and moved a foot closer to her to be in the center to more easily drive the horses.

Walter was jabbering behind her, a welcome distraction. Phoebe could feel his bouncing up in the front and couldn't help but grin. She could feel Newton Sanford's eyes on her and felt guilty for being rude to him. He had offered to take them all to supper, had hired a surrey, how much did that cost anyway?, to take them to the north end of town. He had been nothing but polite to all of them. And here she was...

They had begun rolling, the surrey turning immediately north onto Wood Street at a slow walking pace. "Mr. Sanford, I – I apologize. I – "

Newton Sanford looked over at Phoebe, waiting for her to continue.

She looked about and asked, "Wait, how did the surrey get here? Where's the driver?"

Newton Sanford laughed then, as if he had been waiting for her to notice. "I hired someone to bring it here. That person will take it back after we return. I'm your driver for the evening. I hope that's all right with you."

"You can do that?" Phoebe had forgotten what she had been about to say as she looked around at this part of the town. On the right there were houses along the street. On the hill were homes of the managers of the mines and stamp mills and a few other business owners. On the left were businesses and residences; not as full as Main Street but populated nonetheless.

Phoebe heard Will and Mrs. Barrett conversing in a light manner behind her, Walter interrupting occasionally to point out this or that. She turned once in her seat to see the little boy leaning forward and holding onto the seat in front of him, his mother holding onto the back of his coat to make sure he didn't fall over. She supposed kids were kids no matter where or when.

Will was laughing at him, joking with him, loosening up to their precarious and delicate situation. Perhaps putting their dilemma aside until later. So why couldn't she? Because she knew there was danger around every corner. Because she didn't know what to do to get them home. Because she was sitting next to Newton Sanford, *Died June 19, 1880. To Live in Hearts We Leave Behind is Not to Die.*

She remembered. "Mr. Sanford," she began.

"You may call me Newton, Miss Tucker, as I told you before. I don't mind."

Stop looking me in the eye when you speak to me. "Thank you, Mr. Sanford. What I was going to say before, was, I apologize. This is indeed delightful and I'm sorry if I gave you the impression I was vexed by your costly gesture." She turned away, looking ahead at the horses.

Newton Sanford laughed once again. "Vexed by my costly gesture. How eloquent."

"Are you making fun of me?" Phoebe's temper flared. "Then never mind. You needn't have wasted your money. I am perfectly capable of walking, you know."

"I'm sure you are. I though perhaps a little boy was not. And our landlady is good to us. She deserves a treat now and again, wouldn't you agree?"

Phoebe felt her face flush with embarrassment. They turned left near the mill, toward Main Street. A hotel, a hair dressing salon, a cigar store, another hotel, a barber, all before Main Street. She was missing seeing what she had longed to see, what she had poured over books to envision, because she was uselessly arguing. She was behaving less mature than the child seated, standing, behind her. And behaving like an ungrateful guest, fully aware she didn't belong. All because her guilty conscience couldn't let go of an anger from another day, another time.

She covered her face with her hands and rubbed her eyes. When she looked back up she could feel Newton Sanford staring at her, boring a hole in her head with his gaze.

They turned north on Main Street and Newton Sanford had to keep his eyes on where he was directing the horses and surrey. The mud-filled street sucked at their hooves, making the going slow. All the better to keep the wheels from spitting up too much mud from behind; but easier to get stuck.

They soon passed the intersection at King Street, Phoebe glancing back at the unrecognizable street and remembered their most recent trip with J. W. Another minute later Newton Sanford pulled the surrey over to the left side of the road and set the hand brake on the front wheel. Will jumped down with a smile on his face, looking as if he was trying to forget his problems for the time being. He helped Walter jump down.

Newton Sanford stepped down and reached to assist Mrs. Barrett first and then held up his hand for Phoebe. She moved to the edge and, before taking his hand, she said, "I'm going to try this one more time." She inhaled and exhaled audibly. "I'm sorry. I was very rude. I didn't mean to be. My words just come out that way sometimes and I..."

Newton Sanford smiled again, but he did not laugh at her.

Phoebe continued. "The surrey was indeed a thoughtful idea. Please forgive me."

Newton Sanford held his hand closer to her and she took hold of it. She stepped down onto the ground and he held her hand a moment longer than necessary, saying, "You are forgiven."

"Thank you. Newton."

18

As Phoebe rounded the side of the surrey Newton politely put his hand at the small of her back. She stiffened and tried to quicken her step but the mud at the side of the road prevented her from taking hasty steps. She nearly slipped and twisted her ankle but reached out to balance herself on the back of the surrey. Her hand landed on a splat of dirt and she pulled it away quickly. “Ew, yuck,” she said, brushing her hands together to get it off. Too late she realized her modern behavior and language habits were more difficult to hide than she realized and resolved to stop giving Will such a hard time about his.

They stomped their feet on the boardwalk before entering the hotel, knocking off the muck. Newton withdrew a handkerchief and handed it to Phoebe. Her grandfather still carried one in his pocket occasionally; she had forgotten about those. “Thank you,” she said, sounding relieved. Smiling gratefully she took it from him and wiped her hands.

“You’re welcome. It’s nice to see you smile.”

“I’ll wash it for you,” she said, turning away and putting it in her bag.

They entered the restaurant and kept to the right to walk between the bar on one side and small tables to the other. In the back of the barroom they passed through an arched doorway into the main dining room and were greeted by a young woman who took them to a round table near the center of the room. The restaurant was busy despite it being a Monday. *Vegas, baby.* Walter again sat between Will and Mrs. Barrett. A buffer between strangers who had only spoken a couple of times and had nothing in common. Phoebe sat next to Mrs. Barrett and Newton by Will.

Phoebe and Will looked around the room, as they had every building they had been in so far. Chunky ornate chairs with matching table legs, padded seats and seat backs, a large hanging chandelier in the middle of the room, smaller hanging lamps throughout the room, glass flowers in tall vases placed on tall, slender, wooden stands in the corners. *Take it all in, look while you can, memorize everything, it's all gone...*

"...Miss Tucker?" Newton had been trying to get her attention.

"I'm sorry, what?" He was grinning at her again, his mustache twitching, his blue eyes sparkling. Phoebe frowned.

He repeated himself, patiently and quietly. "I was wondering how long you'll be staying, here, in Bodie. You, and your brother?" he added.

She glanced at Will, he had not heard the inquiry, and looked back at Newton. "I, well I don't know, specifically. I'm sure I've already stated I don't wish do discuss this any further." She looked up when a man approached the table to ask if they were ready to order and was relieved she did not have to think of something else to say on the subject.

The menu was simple, printed in elegant black script on a single piece of stiff, light brown paper. As she looked it over quickly, she was annoyed to hear Newton ask Will the same question. Will looked to Phoebe, then replied, "I'm not sure of our plans. We're going to play it by – um – we're going to have to wait and see." While Newton was distracted by placing his order Will looked at his sister and shrugged.

"Do you need help in deciding? I can recommend something," Newton asked Phoebe. He had been there before, it seemed.

"I think I'll manage, thanks. Perhaps you should ask Will what I should order." He opened his mouth to speak and closed it again, taken aback by her answer.

Phoebe ordered fish, trout to be exact, the daily catch from the East Walker River, not far away. She chose fried potatoes for the vegetable, and they shared a pot of tea for the table. Everyone else made their choices, Mrs. Barrett ordering for the hesitant and distracted Walter.

The tea came. Newton poured one cup at a time for those gathered. Walter said, "I want whiskey," in a laughing voice and giggled.

His mother shushed him and said, "No, you don't. To the others she said, "Sometimes I don't think this town is the best place to raise a boy," and give her son a stern look that made him settle down in his chair instantly. "But – here we are."

Their conversation centered first around Walter, an easy subject, asking him what he liked to do and what his favorite subject was in school. There were other children and families in the restaurant, not many, but a few.

Most were men, in groups of four or more. One group Phoebe counted was twelve men at two large tables that had been pushed together. They were a loud and rambunctious bunch, beer flowing freely and hoots of laughter filling the air. Phoebe's attention was drawn to them and Newton leaned closer to her to say, "Miners."

"I see," she said, resisting the urge to say, *Yes, I know, I'm not an idiot.*

"And when they are finished they are most likely headed for the saloons," he said with an air of superior knowledge.

Phoebe stirred quicker and quicker with her spoon after having plopped in two sugar cubes. "Is that right? Imagine that, all these miners with money in their pockets in a town full of saloons, Faro tables and brothels. I thought maybe they were going to evening church services." Her comments had been meant for Newton's ears only, his attitude having gotten under her skin. But Mrs. Barrett and Will looked up at her sharply; the former with a glint of humor in her eyes and smothering a grin, the latter with eyes wide and wondering what flames he may have to put out now.

Newton stared at her, speechless. His face flushed slightly, which gave Phoebe a sense of satisfaction. He cleared his throat, sticking his finger between his shirt collar and neck, loosening the constriction there. Before he could say anything Phoebe held up her hand and said, "I'm sorry. Again. I've never apologized so many times in one day in all my life, ask my brother. That was rude. But so were you. Just because – "

Newton held up his hands too. "Okay, okay." Phoebe stopped talking. "Truce?" He held out his hand.

Phoebe shook his hand. "Truce."

Both were silent for a few awkward moments. Mrs. Barrett broke the silence when she noticed Phoebe's necklace gleaming bright in the hanging gas lights. "Your necklace," she began, and Phoebe reached up to touch it. "It's beautiful. And so delicate. Where did you get such a thing? If you don't mind my asking."

Phoebe looked down at the gold horseshoe, and suddenly missed everyone back home. Her parents, grandparents, her other brothers, little Kimberly, J. W., even Jody...

"Thank you," she replied quietly. "It was a gift. From my – from someone very special to me."

"I did not intend to cause you sorrow, Miss Tucker."

"No, no, that's not the case. I miss someone, yes, but hopefully I will see him again some day."

Newton's ears pricked up at the short conversation and he looked over at the necklace. Phoebe could see he wanted to ask her about it, but because of her previous reactions to his words he hesitated. Good. She did not want to tell him anything about herself and she did not want to lie.

Their food was delivered to the table and a neutral conversation of trivial matters ensued. *What did you order? That looks delicious. I'm so hungry.* Then Walter said, "Look," and pointed to a man walking their direction.

A well-dressed man, a gentleman on the outside at least, sauntered up to their table, stopping between Phoebe and Newton. He held his hat in his hands and bowed slightly in the ladies' direction. Phoebe could smell liquor so was sure the others could as well. "Miss Tucker," hiccup, "Newton, Mr. – Mr. Tucker, Miss Barry." Mrs. Barrett attempted to distract Walter from the man who had obviously had too much to drink.

Newton said, "Albert. How are you this evening?"

Hiccup, "On my way to Wagner's. Care to join us?" The man teetered on his feet, gripping his hat as if that would help.

"No, thank you," replied Newton. "Enjoy your evening," he said, turning away from the man and hoping Albert Griffin would be on his way.

Too much to hope for. Albert Griffin put his hat on his head, stepped closer, leaned his hands on the table near Phoebe and said, "How about you? Why don't you come with me and I can teach you how to play Faro. You can sit on my knee and pour my whiskey."

Phoebe had a tight grip on the fork in her hand, refusing to look up at the drunkard. "No. I already know how to play Faro, but thanks for the lovely thought."

"No? No? But I want you to come." He lifted one arm to put around her shoulders and leaned close to say something in her ear. The words never left his mouth. Instead he yowled with pain, gripping the wrist at the table with his other hand and causing everyone in the room to look their way. Phoebe had stabbed the back of his hand with her fork and was holding it there.

She looked up at him them. He was still yowling, more from shocked embarrassment than the pain his present drunken condition wouldn't detect until tomorrow. Calmly, she stated, "I said, no." She pulled the fork off of his hand and placed it on the table.

Albert Griffin cradled his injured hand. He said nothing more and walked quickly out of the restaurant, leaving the whispering and giggling behind.

The man who had delivered their food came directly to their table to see if there was anything he could do, not fully understanding what had just taken place. Phoebe held up her fork and asked, "Could you please get me a clean fork. This one's dirty."

Walter's eyes were wide with surprise and something that looked near hero worship. Will had a familiar grimace on his face, *Oh, geez.* Mrs. Barrett covered her mouth with her hand but Phoebe thought perhaps she was hiding a grin she didn't want her son to see. Newton was sputtering nonsensical words, his hands moving items around the table in flustered maneuvers in an attempt to put order in his brain to what had just happened.

Finally, after he had composed himself, he said, "I hope you know what you've done. Albert Griffin has a nasty temper."

"Does he?" Phoebe sipped her tea.

"And he has dishonorable friends."

"He has friends?" Another sip of tea and a bite of fish. "Eat up, Newton. Your steak is getting cold."

He stopped talking and ate without speaking again.

She saw Will shake his head from across the table. Yes, she supposed she shouldn't have done that. She, again, forgot where and when she was. Phoebe put down her silverware and said, "I'm sorry, everyone. I'm terribly sorry. I behaved miserably. Mrs. Barrett, Mr. Griffin is your tenant and now you will have to deal with him regarding my behavior. Walter, what I did was highly inappropriate."

"Miss Tucker, I am fully aware of Mr. Griffin's shortcomings." Mrs. Barrett glanced down at Walter, choosing her words carefully. "Have no fear, I am capable of handling Mr. Griffin and his so-called friends if a situation arises where I should need to do so." Remembering the incident with the cast iron skillet Phoebe had a feeling the woman spoke the truth. She was a widow, alone with a young son in a wild town like Bodie and ran a boarding house by herself. And she seemed undaunted in doing so.

Newton said, "Mr. Tucker – "

"Please, call me Will."

"All right. Will, I hope you will please try to avoid Albert Griffin from now on. He can be a pleasant enough fellow when he has not been... imbibing to excess. Please use caution."

Will wasn't sure what he was supposed to do about it. Phoebe was the expert. But to placate Newton as much as himself he answered, "I will. Thank you."

As they finished their supper Mrs. Barrett regaled Newton with the tale of John Young and his trip to the barn to retrieve Albert Griffin's horse. "I don't believe I have never met Mr. Young. Did Albert never explained the situation to you?"

Mrs. Barrett shook her head. "No. I don't believe it was complicated. He came for the horse and expected to get his way." She glanced at Phoebe. "He did not get it." Phoebe saw her chin lift and heard a proud lilt to her voice.

Walter chimed in as if he had been waiting his turn. "That old plug-ugly never woulda seen it comin' – "

"Walter!" his mother reprimanded him, cutting of whatever else he might have said.

Phoebe laughed and covered her mouth quickly. When Walter looked sufficiently rebuked they all laughed aloud, the tension of the situation relieved.

When they had finished their main meal Newton asked Phoebe if she would like dessert. She glanced up and saw Walter nodding vigorously and laughed. "I believe I should have some," she said, nodding at Walter. "I wouldn't want him to eat dessert alone." The cherry pie was heavenly.

Newton paid for their meals and desserts and they walked out the way they had come. The barroom was filling up now as night approached. Out near the boardwalk the horses waited patiently. Phoebe walked to them, stepped down into the street carefully and gently gave each one a stroke between the eyes and down to its nose. Will was assisting Mrs. Barrett and Walter into the surrey but Newton had walked to stand beside Phoebe.

"Do you like horses, Miss Tucker?" She nodded, giving each animal a pat on the side of its neck as well. One reached forward and nuzzled her shoulder in answer. "I think they like you too."

Phoebe smiled, remembering riding at her grandfather's home, racing her brothers and cousins, wandering off over the hill and stopping at the top to eat her lunch in solitary harmony. She would ride down the hill later, put her horse in the barn, take off the saddle, brush him down and give him a treat.

"At the risk of getting my head bitten off again, may I ask you a question?" Newton asked quietly, grinning.

Phoebe looked him in the eye and answered, "You may. Do not be upset with me if you do not like your answer."

He hesitated, then said, "Friday night there is a dance at the Union Hall." He paused when he saw Phoebe stiffen. Forging onward he asked, "I would be delighted if you would accompany me."

Patient 1880 Phoebe would have simply said she did not think that would be appropriate. Snarky and explosive 1980 Phoebe would have told him to jump in the lake to avoid him. But he was nothing like Rick-Rich-Honker in Iowa. Newton Sanford was trying to be kind, he was trying to be thoughtful; he was causing her heart to race as he moved closer to stand beside her...

She decided, there and then, that whatever was going to happen was already destined to be. While petting the horses, seeing the activity of this bustling town, people coming and going everywhere, music playing, wagons delivering goods, people shopping, miners enjoying their evenings off after bringing gold and silver out of the ground in record loads, Wells Fargo money leaving on stages to investors... Was she really part of it or just an observer stuck on the outside like a bug on a windshield?

She saw that his fists were clenched at his sides. He was afraid of what she was going to say. She was afraid of what was going to happen to him soon. *Maybe there's nothing I can do about that, after all. So is my avoiding him truly helping him? No; I'm only protecting myself.*

Phoebe continued to pet the horses, but turned to look at Newton. He was looking at her face, staring right through her in anticipation. "Newton, I would be delighted to go to the dance with you." She saw the surprise on his face and smiled. "I'm aware of my faults and applaud your bravery in asking. I have rewarded you with not biting your head off. This time," she teased. She walked around him to get into the surrey and waited for him to catch up so he could give her a hand up.

He looked at her closely as he helped her into the surrey, unable to take his eyes off of her. Facing forward Phoebe said, "Stop looking at me."

He took the reins and got the horses moving.

The rowdiness from the Wagner Saloon could be heard from behind them, as well as from the other saloons on either side of the street in front of them. They continued north. Newton was taking them to a place in the road, beyond the tailings from the mines, where they could turn around. They made a wide turn past the Bluff and Phoebe and Will could see more residences here on the left.

Walter was subdued now as it was getting darker outside and his stomach was full. He was usually in bed by now.

Startling everyone, Will suddenly sat forward and said in a loud voice, "Phoebe, it just occurred to me what you said back there to Albert Griffin. Exactly what is Faro, and when did you learn to play it?"

Newton turned to her, eyebrows raised, wanting to ask, wanting to comment, afraid of what she would say. He couldn't resist. "So, your name is Phoebe."

19

Phoebe turned to address Will, who sat back in his seat on seeing the look on her face. *Thanks a lot, you dummy.* "I just know." Facing forward again, she exhaled loudly and said without looking at Newton, "Yes, my name is Phoebe. I trust that doesn't disappoint." He said nothing more on the subject and drove on.

Just past King Street he had to pull the horses to a stop when several men and a few women came walking, stumbling, and running into the street in front of them. There were six saloons on both sides in the fifty yards that were ahead of them. Someone fired a gun and they heard it hit a building sign, a woman screamed, then laughed. Phoebe saw two men begin fighting and one swung to punch the other in the chin but missed when the other man swerved out of the way, slipped, and fell into the mud. The puncher jumped on top of the mud man and began choking him. A woman jumped on top of that man and began beating him over the head until he rolled over into the mud, holding the top of his head.

"Good Lord, what is going on?" Will said from the back, horrified.

Phoebe, riveted by the scene, mumbled, "They don't show pictures of this in books, now do they?"

Newton shot her a look and said, "What did you say?"

"Nothing," she answered quickly. Then, "How do we get through?"

Newton shrugged. "Wait, or go around them. Perhaps they'll get out of the way at the risk of being run over."

"You wouldn't dare."

"Do you want to drive? I have no doubt you would find it delightful to smash some drunkard's head in with a wagon wheel."

Initially shocked, Phoebe then laughed aloud. A long, hearty, unladylike laugh, holding onto her stomach as she did so. She pretended to search the crowd. "Is Mr. Griffin in there somewhere?"

Newton smiled, shaking his head. "You are an unusual person, Miss Phoebe Tucker."

"Thank you, Newton, I accept your compliment."

They moved forward slowly, Newton easing the surrey toward the side of the street, the crowd moving toward the center and the left. As he drove he watched the crowd warily, keeping his eyes open for the flash of a gun or knife. Phoebe saw him pat the side of his jacket as they progressed past the crowd.

"Do you have a pistol in your pocket?" she asked, a whimsical smile touching her lips. When he nodded she asked, "Do you know how to use it?"

"I don't believe anyone who owns a firearm does not know how to use one," was his clipped answer.

"I know plenty of people who can't shoot. Maybe you're one of them."

Will heard his sister's goading comments and wondered what happened to the person who had so far done her best to keep her comments and replies to Newton Sanford to a minimum. Remembering her so-so performance with their grandfather's Colt, he couldn't resist saying, "Perhaps if Newton has a difficult time hitting his target he can simply throw rocks."

She turned in her seat and said sweetly, "I wish I had another fork."

"Now, now," said Mrs. Barrett from the back. "No need for tempers to rule the evening. We are almost clear of this riffraff. And Walter has just fallen asleep."

They all turned to see the little boy with his head on his mother's lap. "How can he sleep with all this noise?" Phoebe asked. *Kids.*

"I don't know. As I said earlier, this is not the most proper place to raise a boy, especially alone. But he does seem to love it here. I'll never understand it."

People had come to Bodie, to California, to the gold fields all over this part of the country, from many states and many countries. Phoebe wondered where Mrs. Barrett and her husband had come from. It had been a stopping point for so many; come in, make money, lose money, break even and move on... Many had made it a home for several years, had started businesses and families, and stayed after the boom years came to an end because it was home.

They finally passed the now dissipating crowd that had begun wandering across the street into other saloons or up the street to new places. Phoebe looked back to see one man lying on his stomach in the mud, hoping he was still breathing. Newton pulled the reins and stopped the horses when they neared Green Street. The others had seen a figure crossing the street and thought nothing of it. Newton had other thoughts on the subject.

The figure crossed to them and approached Newton. It was an older man, graying hair popping out from under his crumpled brown hat. He seemed upset, flustered, in need of attention of some kind. "Newton, there you are. I – I – " The man saw that Newton was traveling with others and stopped short of finishing what he had been about to say.

"What is is Lionel? What's happened. Are you all right?" Phoebe relaxed somewhat. Newton knew this man. And they were using first names. Friends?

"I – yes, but I need to talk to you." The man looked more closely at the others in the surrey. Mrs. Barrett nodded acknowledgment when the man called Lionel tipped his hat at her and said, “Ma’am.”

“Lionel, whatever it is can wait until tomorrow, I’m sure of it.” Newton put a calming hand on the older man’s shoulder.

“If you say so. But I need to talk to you. Come see me tomorrow.” Newton said he would and the man called Lionel bobbed his head in acceptance of the situation.

The man called Lionel walked away south on the boardwalk before Newton had a chance to introduce him to the other occupants. *Perhaps another time*, thought Newton. Feeling the need to explain to a certain degree, Newton said, “I apologize for that little intrusion.”

“Does your friend need help? You can go now, you know,” replied Phoebe. The man had looked frazzled and upset.

Newton paused, finding the right words. “Friend? Yes, I suppose he is. And I appreciate that, truly. I will speak with him in the morning. I believe Mr. Bradley has a tendency to overreact.” Phoebe nodded.

They turned on Green Street, pulled the surrey around the corner of Wood Street, drove south and stopped in the road. There was a man sitting on the steps of Mrs. Barrett’s boarding house who came forward when Newton stepped down. He had delivered the surrey and was now taking it back to the livery stable near Green Street. Newton gave the man what looked like a silver coin and thanked him again for the special circumstances.

He returned to help Phoebe down the step to street level. Newton then helped carry the sleeping Walter into the house and put him on his bed while Mrs. Barrett lit the kerosene lamps in the parlor. Phoebe thought Mrs. Barrett must find him trustworthy to be allowed to do so.

“Miss Tucker, would you care to join me in the kitchen for a cup of coffee?” Newton asked politely. “I did not order any with our supper and I am wishing I had.” He was waiting patiently for a reply. Phoebe glanced at Will and

Newton mistook the gesture for something other than what she had intended. "Will is welcome to join us, of course."

Ha, thought Phoebe. *As if I need a chaperone.*

Will answered for her. "If you both don't mind, I'm going to my room and relax for a few minutes before putting my head down. I'm exhausted. It's been a long day." Will sent a questioning look in his sister's direction. *Is that okay?* With no objection as his answer, he added, "Thank you for a wonder – for an interesting evening, Newton," he shook the man's hand.

Mrs. Barrett emerged from her room behind them and said, "He's tucked in for the night. I heard what you said about coffee. I'm going to see if Wyanet left anything for me in the kitchen. I can prepare you some coffee, if you like."

Phoebe really did crave some evening coffee. And she was quite capable without her brother in attendance, in this century or the next.

After saying their goodnights to Will they entered the kitchen, lit a lamp and found a seat at the table. Newton sat at one end, Phoebe helped Mrs. Barrett with coffee and then sat at a center seat along the side. Mrs. Barrett sat opposite her. While they waited for the water to boil Phoebe said, "I want to thank you again for supper, Mr. San – Newton. It was very thoughtful of you. I also apologize for my quick temper."

"Stop apologizing," said Mrs. Barrett, surprising both of them. "What's done is done." She stood up to get cups and pour the coffee. "If I had to apologize for everything I regretted in this life I would still be talking."

Phoebe was surprised to hear such openness. Newton was grinning again, his mustache twitching, his blue eyes sparkling. Then, setting cups of coffee on the table, she said, "Don't you agree, Mr. Sanford?" and eyed him with amusement.

"Oh, certainly, Mrs. Barrett." Newton sipped his coffee. Phoebe and Mrs. Barrett exchanged a silent glance of alliance. Phoebe was growing to like this woman more and more.

"Would anyone like to move into the parlor? I'm sure it's more comfortable." They picked up their cups and walked to the doorway as the kitchen door opened and Chester Murphy walked in.

"I beg your pardon," he said politely. "I hope I'm not interrupting."

"Not at all, Mr. Murphy. We are just having some coffee. Would you care to join us?"

"That would be very nice, Mrs. Barrett."

Seated in the parlor, Phoebe and Mrs. Barrett on the settee and the gentlemen in the chairs at each side, Mrs. Barrett asked Chester Murphy if he had eaten the supper Wyanet had prepared for him and Albert Griffin. "Yes, Ma'am, I was here. It was delicious, thank you. I did not see Albert. "Not at supper."

Newton leaned forward in his chair. "Did you see him elsewhere, Chester?"

Chester Murphy hesitated, looking from one person to the next, and nodded. "Yes. I came home, saw the supper and note, ate and went back out to – "

"Go ahead, Chester" prodded Newton.

"I was on my way to the Cabinet, but I never got there." *The Cabinet Saloon. There are pictures of it...* Phoebe noticed he looked slightly embarrassed by the admission in front of the ladies present.

"What happened, Chester?"

"Albert Griffin happened." He sighed and sat back in his chair. He sipped his hot coffee and said, "He tried to talk me out of my winnings at the Faro table," he looked at Mrs. Barrett and Phoebe, "I beg your pardon, ladies. I won eighty dollars a couple of days ago and he knew I had it. He had been drinking again and accosted me. I told him in no uncertain terms that I would not allow him to take my money. I told him I don't gamble much and that when I win a little I try to save it for – I've been trying to save it. I was quite adamant about that."

Phoebe refrained from smiling at what the man considered stern treatment of Albert Griffin, especially after what had transpired at their table at the restaurant.

"That scoundrel," exclaimed their landlady. "I knew I should never have rented a room to him. There are plenty of other places he can stay. His behavior had begum to affect too many, and now in public."

"Mrs. Barrett," began Newton, "his crime is having an insufferable personality. Of course, the decision is yours alone."

Chester Murphy asked, "Has something happened of which I am unaware? What are you talking about?"

Newton regaled him with a recap of their restaurant visit. He paused when Albert Griffin entered the story and glanced at Phoebe, as if requiring her approval for the telling. She nodded and shrugged. *No more apologies. What's done is done.* Chester Murphy gasped and coughed, eyeing Phoebe warily now. *Oh, for heaven's sake.*

Just then the door on the other side of the room opened, creaked, and a small face peaked out. Walter appeared, rubbing his sleepy eyes. "You talk too loud. What am I missing?" He said, moving to stand just outside the bedroom door.

"I'm sorry we are too loud, Walter. It was unintentional. Go back to bed," his mother said gently.

"What happened to Mr. Murphy? Is he all right?"

Chester Murphy waved for Walter to come closer. "I'm sorry we woke you, my boy. Nothing has happened to me. Everything is fine and dandy." He cuffed the boy lightly on the chin. Since you are up, I brought you something." He reached into his coat pocket and pulled out a small item wrapped in wax paper. "Open it."

Walter rubbed his eyes again and looked to his mother for approval. She nodded and he unwrapped the paper, a square of chocolate fudge inside. His face lit up and he wrapped his arms around the man's neck. "Thank you, Mr. Murphy. Mother?"

"You may have it. If you go back to bed."

The boy nodded and retreated, closing his door behind him.

"That was very kind of you, Mr. Murphy," said Mrs. Barrett.

"I heard the candy calling to me as I passed by the store. It was nothing."

"I believe I will retire myself, if you all don't mind," said Mrs Barrett. "I'll see you in the morning. Mr. Sanford, thank you again for supper. Miss Tucker, thank you for the entertainment," she said with a wink.

Chester Murphy said his goodnights as well, reminding Phoebe to use caution in Bodie. She thanked him, although she was well aware of what could happen and liked to believe she was prepared more than most to handle it.

So... this is awkward, thought Phoebe. Just the two of them now, in the parlor. She reached over to the small table at the end of the settee and turned up the wick. She wanted to go to bed too, but it would look as if she were running away. She was getting a reputation in her family for running away. *No more apologies. No more running.*

Newton crossed one leg over the other and sipped his coffee, elbows resting on the arms of his chair, cup held high and in front of his face. She could feel him looking at her over the top of his cup. "What?" she asked a little too loudly, looking directly back at him.

He sputtered his last sip and covered a small cough with the back of one wrist. He uncrossed his leg, placed his cup on a table so he wouldn't spill, and coughed a couple of more times. Leaning back in his chair again he said, "You are most direct, aren't you, Miss Tucker?"

"I'm sor – no I'm not. I'm not sorry." She put her hands on her cheeks and her elbows on her lap. Will was right, it had been a very long day. "I truly don't intend to be rude. But perhaps you put yourself in the situation where that is my only choice. Did you ever think about that?" His eyes crinkled, his mustache twitched, and she was sure there was a smile under there somewhere. "Have you thought about shaving off that mustache so people can see if you are smiling, frowning, crying or laughing at them? It would be nice to know."

Newton laughed then, a hearty laugh, a belly-holding laugh, one that left no doubt that he found what she had said extremely humorous. She shushed him, pointing toward Mrs. Barrett's and Walter's door. He covered his mouth to quiet his laughter but it continued behind it's barrier. At first miffed at his reaction, she realized he was not laughing to mock her. Despite feeling the need to remain stoic she smiled, then laughed lightly herself.

Quieting down, Newton inhaled deeply and exhaled with a last quiver of laughter. He held up his hand and said, "Remember, truce."

Phoebe nodded. "I remember." They smiled at each other easily then, for the first time since meeting.

Newton fingered his mustache with a mock air of serious consideration. "Do you really think I should shave it off? You might not recognize me without it."

"Hmm, I'm not sure." Phoebe squinted at him. "I'll think about it and let you know."

Newton picked up his cup and took another sip. Phoebe did the same. The awkwardness had returned. After all, their acquaintance was new.

"Miss Tucker, may I ask you a question? If this is too forward of me, please tell me. I mean no offense."

Phoebe's cup was on her lap and she stared into it, avoiding Newton's gaze, his face, his polite voice, his blue eyes, his question. *You big chicken.*

She would have answered with, '*shoot,*' but considering the town she was in at present that would probably not have been the best choice of words. Instead, she said, "What is your question? Don't worry, if it offends me I will find a suitable answer."

"That is what worries me," he mumbled. He cleared his throat and Phoebe thought his nervousness charming. "Earlier this evening, at supper, Mrs. Barrett mentioned the gold necklace you're wearing." He paused and Phoebe's hand went to the necklace, making sure it was still there and thinking of her great-grandfather.

"Go on," she prompted

"You said, I'm sorry I do not remember your exact words, but you said that someone special had given it to you. And that hopefully you would see *him* again some day." Newton placed his coffee cup on the table once again. "Are you – Miss Tucker, are you, as they say, attached? Was it imprudent of me to have asked you to the dance at the Union Hall this Friday?"

Phoebe tried to remember just what she had told Mrs. Barrett about the necklace. *Let's see; it's special, it's from someone special, Mrs. Barrett had said I looked sad or something, I hope to see them, see him... Good Lord, he's asking if I have a boyfriend.* "Oh! Mr. San – Newton, it was a gift, it's from a family member, a very close, elderly family member. I'm not sure if I'm going to see him again."

His relief was visible. Relief that she didn't have a boyfriend, or relief that she hadn't bitten his head off at the question? "I understand. It is a beautiful gift. I'm happy that you are very special to someone."

She hadn't thought about it that way before. She had a large family, they were close, could talk about anything, would always be there for each other. They were special to her. But she had never truly considered herself to be special to them in return. She was touching the necklace, lost in thought, feeling homesick when Newton leaned forward and said, "I hope you get to see him again one day too."

20

There was a quiet knock on her door but it was growing louder, and sharper, and more annoying with every tap. Phoebe threw down her covers and said, irritation in her voice, "What is it?"

"It's Will. Let me in."

"Ugh, just a minute." *What time is it?* She rubbed her eyes and stretched. So bright outside her window. She sat upright quickly, realizing she was not at home or at her parent's house. The previous day had been an exhausting and full one and she had slept well. But it was time to wake up and face another day trying to figure out why she and her brother were here; and to try to get home... somehow.

She got out of bed wearing the dress she had worn to J.W.'s birthday party. It made a good nightgown, she supposed. She put on her Army jacket to warm her arms in her cool room, opened her door yawning and plopped back down on the bed. "Coffee."

"Yeah, yeah, we'll get you some coffee. Wake up first."

"I can't wake up without my coffee. Don't you know anything? Why are you up so early?"

"It's not early. You slept in. It's ten o'clock."

She opened her eyes and sat up straight. Sufficiently surprised at her indulgence she chased him out so she could get dressed. “I’ll meet you in the kitchen in a minute.” Placing her jacket back under her covers, she splashed her face with cold water and put her hair up like the woman, what was her name, oh yes, Mary Jacobson, had shown her. When she was satisfied with her appearance she attached her chatelaine bag and locked her door behind her.

She stifled another yawn when she entered the kitchen. Will was seated at the table and talking to Walter. There was food on plates, covered with towels. On inspection she found biscuits, gravy, scrambled eggs and bacon. “It smells so good,” she said, slathering two biscuits with whipped butter. She filled a plate with the other items and sat beside Walter.

“Good morning, how are you? And where is your mother?”

“My mama said she’d be back soon if you want to go to the market with her. She goes on Saturdays and Tuesdays.” He shrugged. “And some other days too.”

Will said, “I told her I’d be here with him until she returned.” Then he asked Walter, ” Is it less busy on Tuesdays?”

Walter fidgeted in his chair. “It’s always busy.”

With her mouth full, Phoebe was nodding an affirmation to Walter. Will made a face and said, “How can you be so hungry?”

“Supper was more than twelve hours ago. And food is always more delicious when you don’t have to make it yourself. Right Walter?”

The little boy shrugged but smiled. “My mama’s a good cook.”

“Indeed, she is,” Phoebe agreed. “You already ate, I suppose?” She asked Will, who had a cup of coffee in hand. He nodded. “Then can you get me a cup of coffee? Please?”

Will did as his sister requested and when Phoebe took her first drink and stated how good it tasted she thought of the previous night and drinking coffee with Newton in the parlor. With the light of day bringing the light of reason to her mind, Phoebe felt a rush of regret at the turn their conversation had taken.

She and Newton had spent another hour and a half in the parlor together. Awkward silence broken by a joke, a giggle, a look that made Phoebe's heart pound, a smart remark from Phoebe to ward off how she was beginning to feel inside, another silence... and the inability for each of them to walk away.

She hadn't wanted to get to know him, or anyone. See the town, experience old Bodie, listen to the hum of the people, the miners, watch the workers, feel the rhythm of an old famous town in motion; yes to all of those things. Interaction hadn't been something she had planned on. But here it was only her third day in and she now knew that was unavoidable. A people, a time, a place, a single person did not live in an impenetrable bubble never to see or be seen by another. Her heart was beginning to ache now because of it.

To get home she couldn't just go outside and sit in the barn with Will. She was sure it would not be that easy.

"What are you going to do today, Walter?" Will asked.

"I'm going to the market with my mama. Wanna come?" he asked enthusiastically.

Will glanced up at Phoebe, grinning. He did like this little boy. "Are you sure she wouldn't mind us men tagging along?"

Walter giggled. "Nuh-uh. She ain't gonna care."

They cleared the table and Phoebe heated some water to wash the dishes they had used. Once finished, Will went to his room to put on his vest and retrieve his hat. Phoebe had said he didn't always need his coat. The trio waited in the parlor.

"Walter, do you know where Mr. Murphy goes during the day? What does he do, his job?" Phoebe asked.

Walter sat on the floor tying and untying his shoes, practicing with the new, stiff leather laces. "I think he works at a bank or something. I dunno." His tongue was sticking out of the side of his mouth in concentration. "Some kind of office. Why?"

"I was just curious. He seems very nice."

"He's my friend. I think he has a girlfriend. But I think girls don't know beans."

Will smiled and Phoebe stifled a giggle.

"Except Mary Louisa, she's nine and she knows everyth – "

"I remember; she knows everything," Will finished. Walter nodded.

Phoebe glanced at Will and then asked Walter, "Is Mr. Griffin your friend too?" Will frowned at his sister but she didn't think it hurt to ask his opinion.

Still concentrating on tying his shoes, Walter said, "Phfft, he's so huffed up all the time, he ain't got no real friends, least that's what Mama says."

Will gave Phoebe a questioning look. She mouthed the word, 'angry.' Will nodded.

They heard noises in the kitchen, and voices coming through into the parlor. Mrs. Barrett entered, followed by a girl wearing a long blue and red plaid dress, with long black hair cut in bangs across her forehead and a kerchief tied around her head. The girl nodded at Phoebe and at Will, smiling broadly, when she was introduced as Wyanet, the Paiute girl that helped Mrs. Barrett on occasion. She was going along to the market.

Walter was told to go wash his face before they left. One shoe was untied and he hopped up off the floor to comply. On his return his mother tied his shoe, retied the other and asked Phoebe and Will about going to the market. Phoebe said Walter had already told them about the trip and they would both be delighted to accompany her. They locked the front door and began their walk.

They didn't walk north to Green Street this time. Instead they headed south to Lowe Street, no longer visible in Phoebe and Will's time. Phoebe was enjoying the walk, soaking in the scenery, memorizing every detail she could take in. Will was a bit confused. He didn't know the town as well as his sister and wasn't sure where he was going or the distance to their destination.

A little further on, Lowe connected with Mono Street. They continued and beyond that Lowe intersected with South Main Street. They turned right for the market, passing homes and businesses where only open fields remained for Phoebe and Will in their memories. Their destination was Kilgore's Union Market, next to the new brick Post Office building. Mrs. Barrett said, "I like this market because not only is it close, they have every type of meat one could want."

Will nodded, impressed. He whispered to Phoebe, "How do they keep anything cold around here?"

She answered quietly, "There's an ice house. Northwest, past Chinatown. Like you've seen on TV, I'm sure. They keep it in straw all year round."

Phoebe and Will enjoyed browsing the variety of fruits, vegetables and meats available. "It must be a pain in the neck to keep this stocked this way," Will said, incredulous, marveling at the inventory.

"There are a lot of people here, thousands. But there are several markets, too. They have freight of some kind coming in nearly every day."

Will looked south on Main Street then swung his gaze up North Main Street. "It really was a mile long, wasn't it?"

"Yep," she answered simply, knowing he remembered how it looked in its modern state just as she did. "Don't tell me you're becoming fascinated with Bodie," she teased.

"At least I'm not denying my interest," he shot back, stepping away when she glared at him.

They had been following their hostess as she and Wyanet chose food for the boarding house for the next few days. At one point Mrs. Barrett had asked Phoebe and Will their preferences of this or that. Will had remained noncommittal, Phoebe had lightly offered a suggestion or two but told Mrs. Barrett what she had told Walter that morning at breakfast. Her meals was delicious, and whatever she chose to prepare was perfectly fine with the both of them.

Wyanet was quiet but friendly, speaking few words but smiling pleasantly. Some people on the street or at the market openly resented a Paiute shopping with Mrs. Barrett. Others didn't seem to notice. Mrs. Barrett ignored the insults and embraced the kindness. Phoebe spoke with Wyanet a few times and received polite responses, finding her an amicable young woman.

Phoebe kept losing track of Walter. He would dart this way and that, skip down an isle, disappear, run up another. "Walter," his mother called sharply, and he instantly appeared at her side. She said nothing more but considering the look she sent his way she did not have to.

Their shopping complete, Mrs. Barrett handed Will a package to carry and Wyanet carried another. She handed a smaller one to Walter to keep him busy and to give him something to do. They walked to the Post Office to see if there was any mail that had been delivered. There was a letter for Mrs. Barrett from her sister in Missouri. "Phoebe said in a whisper, "Will, do you recognize this building?"

Trying his best to be inconspicuous, Will looked the brick building up and down and all around before opening his eyes wide. "This is still there...here... you know. Wow, it looks so new."

"It is," she said almost with pride. "To think it's been here this whole time and still welcoming visitors. If it could only talk." Phoebe was looking closely at the brick of the building and up at the windows when Walter said, "Whatcha lookin' at?" and shifted his gaze upward to see if he could see it as well.

"I think the workmanship of this brick building is wonderful," said Phoebe.

Walter said, as if disappointed, "Oh," and skipped along the boardwalk. They followed their guide and began crossing the street.

"Where are we going now, Mrs. Barrett, if you don't mind my asking?"

"I would like to stop at West and Bryant's. It's a store over at the corner, not far." Phoebe knew the store. It was another that remained to this day, her day. It had changed names a couple of times, like many that had survived had done over the years. It was a general store and she looked forward to seeing it.

Phoebe acknowledged the answer as they reached the other side of the street. She halted midstep, surprised she would see another familiar face. Walter waved at the man, smiling, and Mrs. Barrett walked a few steps closer to him. The man came out to the street to greet Mrs. Barrett and Walter. It was the older man Newton had spoken to on their ride home on Main Street.

"Good morning, Mr. Bradley," said Mrs. Barrett. "We've just come from Kilgore's. There was a fresh shipment just yesterday. Are you getting enough to eat?"

The man bobbed his head a time or two and said, "Good morning, Mrs. Barrett. Yes, I, well sometimes I forget to – it's better than we used to get back when I was..." His words trailed off as if he had not wanted to complete the comment. He noticed that Phoebe and Will were accompanying Mrs. Barrett and looked hesitant.

"Mr. Bradley, this is Mr. Tucker and his sister, Miss Tucker. They are my two new boarders."

Lionel Bradley looked down at his dirty hands, wiped one on a rag he was holding, and held it out to shake Will's hand. He thought better of it when he saw his hands were still dark and covered in ash. Will smiled and laughed and Lionel Bradley looked relieved Will had not taken offense.

"Apologies," the man said. "My hands are stained dark a lot of the time. It's difficult to wash off the soot." He pointed behind himself at his place of employment. They were standing in front of the Robson & Forest blacksmith shop and Lionel Bradley was wearing a heavy-duty apron.

"You work at the blacksmith's," Will stated, interested in the occupation. He had heard a relative on his mother's side from long ago had been one.

"Indeed. I do work on wagons and I can shoe a horse quick like." The man's smile was broad and friendly. "It's a pleasure to make your acquaintance. Ma'am," he said to Phoebe.

"Likewise," said Will. Phoebe nodded at him, wondering if Newton had remembered the promise he had made to Mr. Bradley of coming to see him today. Seeing the close proximity of the blacksmith shop and the store where Newton worked, she didn't think it would have been a difficult promise to keep.

"Mr. Bradley, would you like to join us for supper this evening?" asked Mrs. Barrett sympathetically.

Walter chimed in, "Come, come, please, please," and hopped around.

Mrs. Barrett grabbed him by the back of the shirt and pulled him to her quickly, just in time to prevent his colliding with a pair of pedestrians strolling up the boardwalk. Sheepishly, Walter stood next to his mother, motionless, her hand still holding his shirt.

Lionel Bradley hesitated, a worried expression on his face, eyes darting up and down the street. "Will Newton be there?"

"He will," Mrs. Barrett answered.

Lionel Bradley nodded. "I would love to come to supper. Thank you, Ma'am." Someone bellowed Lionel Bradley's name from within the blacksmith shop. "I'll see you this evening. When I'm done here and after I try to wash off the soot." He bobbed his head one more time and went back to his work.

They walked on toward the general store. "Have you known Mr. Bradley long?" Phoebe asked Mrs. Barrett, curious about their evening guest.

"Not long. Mr. Sanford brought him home one evening. Apparently they met when Mr. Sanford first came to town. After he became a tenant of mine he told me Mr. Bradley seemed lonely and invited him to supper. He's been over a couple of times since that first time. I feel a bit sorry for him."

They strolled to the store where Mrs. Barrett purchased a can of kerosene for the lamps, some wicking and matches, and some lye soap for laundry. Everyone was carrying something as they began the return trip home, which, Phoebe decided, turned out to be fun. They were chatting amiably, nodding to people on the street and Phoebe and Will were constantly looking around at their new environment where there was always something undiscovered to see.

They turned at the corner, walked further, waved at a neighbor sweeping her front step and reached the boarding house. "Walter, make sure the horse has enough water, would you please?"

"Yes, Mama," he said, handing his package to Will to carry into the house. They walked around the side to enter through the kitchen. Mrs. Barrett noticed the door was unlocked. Someone was home or they had left the door unlocked when they had gone out. After setting their purchases on the table, Phoebe and Wyanet were helping Mrs. Barrett sort through packages when noises could be heard coming from above them.

"Mr. Griffin must be upstairs," she said. Phoebe noticed that instead of being relieved that it was he who had unlocked the door, Mrs. Barrett seemed concerned he was in the house alone. Phoebe exchanged glances with Will.

Moments later there was a loud banging on the front door that made everyone jump at the suddenness of it. The banging continued; someone was pounding with a closed fist, yelling now. Mrs. Barrett frowned and asked Wyanet to go out the back to check on Walter. She asked Will to come with her to the front door. Will raised his eyebrows doubtfully at his sister but did as he was asked. Phoebe was close behind.

The door was solid wood so they couldn't see anyone. But it rattled on its hinges as the pounding increased and the yelling grew louder. Mrs. Barrett pulled open the door but kept her distance between herself and the aggressor. The knocker was John Young, his fist flying through the air, causing him to lose his balance midswing. "You," she said angrily, putting one hand on her hip. "What do you want?"

John Young staggered to regain his balance and slurred his words as he said, "I'm looking for," hiccup, "Albin Griffert, I know he's here, he has my, my," hiccup, "that no good," hiccup, "can't trust a man nowadays," hiccup, and John Young fell flat on his face on Mrs. Barrett's parlor floor.

Will stared at him, open mouthed, Phoebe did the same, Mrs. Barrett sighed heavily and strode back through to the kitchen to see if Wyanet had come back inside with Walter. She returned a moment later, Wyanet behind her. She had told Walter to stay in the kitchen. "I'll be right back," she said, leaving again. Phoebe saw her turn to go up the staircase and heard banging on a door upstairs, talking, a door slamming and Mrs. Barrett's return down the stairs. She was immediately followed by Albert Griffin who followed her into the parlor.

Mrs. Barrett pointed at John Young, still sprawled face down on the floor, feet hanging over the door jamb. "Get him out of my house."

Albert Griffin had the decency to look at least a little embarrassed in front of all those present. He grinned and said, "Where am I supposed to put him? Ma'am."

"He came here looking for you, yelling for you, you must have heard him, and you also ignored him. I'm sure you know better than I what he was doing here and what he wanted from you. Now get him out of my house. And when you're through, be so kind as to return and remove your belongings from my home. And do not come back."

Albert Griffin's face flushed and his eyes flashed with anger. Mrs. Barrett held his gaze, steadfast in her resolve. The man glanced around quickly, surmised he was outnumbered and dipped his chin in acquiescence. He turned John Young over onto his back, scooped him up under his arms and dragged him back outside and down the steps to the street. He'd begun to wake up in the process and was kicking his booted feet in the dirt, making it difficult for

Albert Griffin to complete his task. Mrs. Barrett left to go into her bedroom and returned to stand at the open door, waiting for Albert Griffin to do as she had ordered.

Albert Griffin stomped back into the house, glared at Will, paused to stare lasciviously at Phoebe while subconsciously rubbing his bandaged hand, ignored Wyanet and continued on his path, stomping up the stairs. They could hear banging above them, the wardrobe opening and being slammed shut. Mrs. Barrett crossed her arms, waiting. The others waited with her, refusing to leave her to face Albert Griffin alone. Five minutes later he banged his way back down the stairs with a large valise in tow.

Mrs. Barrett stepped in front of the scoundrel just before he stepped out the door. "Wait. I run an honest house. Here is the remainder of your weekly rent." She held some coins, Phoebe couldn't tell what they were, over Albert Griffin's open palm. "There had better not be any of my property in that bag of yours to make me wish I had kept this," she said as she dropped the coins. He sneered at her as he put the coins into a vest pocket and walked out the door that Mrs. Barrett slammed behind him.

21

Walter peeked from behind the door jamb and asked, "Can I come in now?"

Phoebe was looking out the front window to see where the two men had gotten to. John Young was sitting up at the edge of the road out front, rubbing his eyes and probably trying to remember where he was and what he was doing there. Albert Griffin was walking down the street, most likely angry with John Young for getting him kicked out of the boarding house. Phoebe didn't know for sure, but figured John Young hadn't been completely to blame; just the last straw.

"Is the horse still in the barn, Walter?"

"Yes, Mama."

Mrs. Barrett snorted, annoyed. "I gave him back his money and he left the horse here. I'm not boarding that beast for free," she mumbled. Then, louder, "Thank you, Walter."

"Is Mr. Griffin gone now?" the little boy asked. His mother nodded and the group returned to the kitchen. "Mr. Griffin's friend sure had a brick in his hat, didn't he?" Walter said, attempting to sound knowledgeable.

Will frowned, again, not quite catching on to what the boy had said. Phoebe stared at Walter, having the feeling she had heard that phrase before and not remembering where. Wyanet giggled and nodded, and Mrs. Barrett said "Oh, for heaven's sake, Walter. Where do you hear these things?"

"I heard Arthur's pa say that about an angry man at his house once."

Mrs. Barrett sighed. "That's not what it means, Walter. But never mind."

"Who's Arthur, another friend?" Will asked, trying to make conversation to distract Walter and forget the prior incident.

The boy nodded, smiling. Grownups didn't often ask him about his friends. "Yep. His dad's a lawler."

"A lawyer," his mother interrupted.

"Yeah. He wears fancy suits and a tall hat." He gestured high above his head with one hand.

"Walter, you're bouncing around the room and underfoot. I'm trying to put things away. I'll make you something to eat if you'll go wash up."

Phoebe realized her stomach was about to growl and wasn't sure what to do about it. Their board paid for two meals a day. They'd eaten breakfast, neither she nor Will had jobs at present, so were home midday. *How did I not think of this until now?* She exchanged looks with her brother, a look Mrs. Barrett noticed.

"You may both either stay or go to lunch, it is entirely up to you." Mrs. Barrett smiled.

"We can pay you extra, if you'd like. Especially now that you're short a boarder. I'm sorry that it turned out that way."

Mrs. Barrett waved a hand in the air dismissively. "It's just as well. Walter doesn't need a b'hoy like him around more than necessary." Will shook his head. He really needed to make a vocabulary list. "I'm sure another boarder will come knocking," she said hopefully.

Phoebe was torn between staying for lunch and offering to pay her landlady extra, or taking the opportunity to continue to explore Bodie. They were still no closer to figuring out what they were supposed to do to get home. "We can reimburse you for lunches," offered Phoebe.

Mrs. Barrett nodded. "Thank you. For today, don't trouble. Supper was at the favor of Mr. Sanford last evening."

Oh yes, I remember...

***

John Young staggered to his feet, wobbly, irritated, rubbing at the bruise that was forming on the side of his head. His hand reached inside his coat pocket for his pistol. Opening the cylinder he saw that it held six cartridges and was glad he hadn't shot off anything he might need later. Closing the cylinder carefully, he returned it to his pocket.

He didn't realize Albert Griffin had come out of the house and was walking away until he saw him in the distance. Too far to call to now. Getting to his feet with difficulty, he staggered around the house, to the back, opened the gate, entered the barn, threw the blanket and saddle on the horse without cinching it on, put the bit in its mouth and walked the horse out of the stall. It wasn't his fault if he'd lost his own horse in a bad bet. Albert Griffin had taken Joseph's horse and sold it as his own for cash after the man was shot dead in the street. They should have split the money.

This was the last time he would trust Albert. He kept putting him off, saying he had plans, would get him his share. John Young was tired of waiting, tired of trusting someone else to get what he wanted. And he wasn't waiting around to get thrown in jail again.

After he rounded the street corner he looped the reins around a railing in front of another house and saddled the horse properly. He patted the horses neck, smoothed his hand along its face, unlooped the reins and pulled himself up. His headache and lingering dizziness allowed no speed in the process.

Still lightheaded and sick to his stomach, he rode as direct and straight a line as he was able. He expected to cross paths with Albert Griffin but didn't see the man anywhere. He continued searching, shading his eyes from the bright sun. *Probably ducked in to the nearest saloon*, he thought. Feeling in his vest pockets he smiled when he heard a familiar jingle. *Faro.*

He headed to Main Street, turned north and rode to the first saloon he saw that he knew dealt Faro. He couldn't remember how much the coins in his pocket were worth, but it would get him started.

He looped the reins to the nearest post out front and stepped up to the boardwalk. As he pushed the door open he took one last look outside in case he spotted Albert. No sign of him; *where did he go?* Into one of the other dozens of saloons, *or up to Bonanza Street maybe*, he thought with a grin, pausing to reconsider his decision to gamble. *Later... I'll head there later. First, to win a few dollars.*

He pushed his way in, through several other men gathered around a Faro table, elbowing and pushing until someone pushed him back and he staggered and fell on his rump. He stood up, swearing, and a man recognized him from the previous evening. That man grabbed his friend by the sleeve and pulled him away quickly, an act repeated by another gambler at the table. They knew John Young. And it wasn't a good idea to get in his way. Especially when he already smelled strongly of liquor.

He found a spot at the table, dug in his pocket and found eight silver dollars. *That's it? That's all I've got left? What did I do last night? Or was it this morning?* With a shrug he exchanged his eight coins for eight checks and a copper. The cards were laid out in the dealing box, in two rows, Ace through King, the seven card at the end. The dealer had just shuffled a fresh full deck and announced the start of the game.

John Young put a check on the seven. The dealer turned over the soda, the first card, and discarded it. He then turned over the banker's card, the losing card, a two. He turned over the player's card, the winning card, a seven. Those who had placed bets on top of the two lost their money. John had been the only one to put a bet on the seven and won his bet, a payout of one to one.

Next round; Faro moved quickly. And if you weren't paying attention to the dealer or to the other players there was a risk of either or both cheating. John put a check on the King. The losing card was a King so he lost the bet; back to even. He put another check on the seven, it had been lucky the first time. It wasn't the winning or the losing card this time. Let it ride.

Next round, the seven was the loser. John banged his fist on the table and exclaimed his displeasure. The dealer shot him a calm warning glance and the players on either side of him flinched. Next round he bet on the four. Loser. Five. Loser. Seven again. Loser. Ten. Loser. Jack. Loser. He had only two checks left. He put them both on the opposite side of the table to indicate he was betting the player's card would be higher than the banker's card. The dealer looked up at John before he drew the cards, wary. Dealer's card ten. Player's card three. He had lost.

He banged both fists on the table then and yelled out in frustration and anger. He had wanted to buy a whiskey with his winnings. His eight silver dollars were gone. Taken by the dealer, by the saloon, by this place that tempted men with money into wasting their time and giving it away, leaving them homeless, starving and poor.

He staggered away from the table, turning red in the face, yelling, cussing, looking left and right for someone at whom he could strike out, someone to blame. Men cleared away from him like a drop of oil in a puddle of water. A couple of the men from the table he'd shared stared at him like he'd gone berserk. It was only eight dollars after all. But it had disappeared quickly, and he had no more. Not yet.

He reached inside his pocket; for what, the men in the saloon did not know. But before he could withdraw his pistol two other men nearby pulled pistols from their pockets and told him to leave now if he wanted to stay alive. John froze with his hand in his pocket, thinking better of the situation. He walked backwards out of the saloon, stumbling and bumping off chairs, people and the edge of the door. As he stepped out he bumped into a someone. "John," the man said, surprised, gripping John by the upper arm before he fell off the edge of the boardwalk.

John Young turned toward the man and, realizing it was Albert Griffin, pulled back his arm and swung it forward, slicing through air, losing his balance and falling against the exterior wall of the saloon. Albert Griffin lazily took a cigar from an inside pocket of his coat and lit it, puffing easily, waiting for John Young to balance himself. "You've had too much to drink, John." *Puff, puff.* "But I appreciate you delivering my horse from that hovel I temporarily called a home."

John Young rubbed his eyes with his hands. He wished he had some water to splash on his face and neck; and a whiskey. "I came to see you. You've got my money."

"Yes you did, and you got me thrown out, too. Now I have to find a new place to live."

"You've got my money," he said loudly.

Albert chuckled lightly. "Calm down, John. It's safe with me. If I'd given it to you last night you would have gambled that away as well, as you know."

"That's not up to you. It's my money." John Young stood close to Albert now and grabbed him by the shirt near his throat. Albert at least had the good sense to look alarmed.

"All right John," Albert said, removing John's hand from his shirt and shoving it aside. "I just came from securing a room at the Mono House. Get one for yourself. I'll meet you there later and we can divvy up what's left." When John hesitated, Albert nodded northward. "Go." John Young gave Albert Griffin one last doubtful look but he had no choice but to comply, forgetting he was penniless.

Albert Griffin stood on the boardwalk considering his options. When sober, John Young made a good partner.

When drinking, which was often, he could have loose lips and a hot temper. He would admit that their reckless behavior had already cost the life of their third associate, Joseph Hoffman. He'd been gunned down in the middle of the road by an old man claiming Joseph had been trying to kill the man's friend and that he'd only been trying to help. Albert thought the man had suffered no punishment because many thought he was addlebrained. And because Sheriff Showers was his friend.

Albert untied his horse, mounted it slowly while nursing his injured hand and rode north. At the corner he turned right toward the Mono House Hotel. He asked the man at the front desk to attend to his horse and take it to the livery on Main. It was going to cost him more than he had paid at the Barrett boarding house, thanks to John Young. And being near the middle of town put more notice on his sometimes recognizable face.

Perhaps it was time to move on, to leave Bodie. There were many profitable towns out this way where he could take advantage of other people's frailties and reap heavy rewards.

In his room now, he put his cigar at the edge of the washstand and unwrapped the bandage tied around his sore hand. The wound was red, puffy and irritated. He poured some fresh water over it. Then he dripped the smallest amount of whiskey on the four punctures in his skin. No sense wasting good whiskey. Drinking it would probably dull the pain more effectively. Grimacing, he carefully dried his hand and rewrapped it with another strip of cloth. "Damnable woman," he muttered aloud.

Albert kneeled down to pull a small poke bag from underneath the pillow on his bed. He stuck his first two fingers from each hand into the hole on top and pulled, loosening the drawstrings, and poured the contents onto the bed.. He rubbed his face with both hands, thinking about his next best move. Joseph Hoffman had been the one with the head for numbers, for accounting, for business. Unfortunately, he was dead, shot down in the street at dusk.

Now Albert had taken over fund management for the two of them.

On the bed lay a great deal of money. In Albert's opinion it was more than he and his cohorts had ever possessed all at one time before. And now it was only a two-way split. Poor Joseph. Albert had sold Joseph's horse to the livery stable on North Main Street and kept the money. John Young hadn't approved but Albert didn't care. John was a weakling, determined one day, wavering the next. When left to his own devices he became a malleable fragment of a once profitable three-way partnership.

Albert had already set aside the money from the sale of the horse. He hadn't thought John was going to be so foolish as to drink too much, get in over his head in a poker game and add the ownership papers to his own horse to the pot, only to lose. He shrugged. If John needed another horse he was on his own.

In cash there were tens and twenties totaling just over six hundred dollars. In gold coins there was one thousand dollars in twenty dollar double eagles and three hundred dollars in ten dollar Coronet Heads. Albert wondered how long it would be before John gambled and drank away his share. He grinned, remembering, with honesty, that his funds never seemed to last long either; he simply spent his in a greater number of creative ways.

John was probably here by now, at the hotel, somewhere, and possibly asking for him. He divided the cash, then divided the coins. He was fair and honest, dividing it evenly, not desirous of an ill-tempered John suspecting him of cheating. John could ask to count it all if he wanted to. But it had never been a problem before.

He was hiding the poke bag again, this time under the mattress, when there was a rapid knocking at his door. "Albert," the man called out.

Albert straightened the bed cover and his coat and went to the door. When Albert opened it John Young rushed into the room, out of breath, and slammed the door behind himself.

"John, John, what is it?" Albert asked calmly.

"I think someone followed me," he answered, going to the window and peering out.

Albert listened at the door and heard nothing of consequence. He stood near John and looked outside from his second floor window. "I think your imagination has run away with you again, John. Or maybe you're still drunk from this morning." Albert retrieved his cigar from the washstand, seated himself in the chair in the corner and crossed one leg over the other.

John continued to stare out the window, eyes darting back and forth, hands gripping the sill. Albert waited patiently. He knew John had a gun. He owned one as well but it was a few feet away on the lower shelf of the washstand. No sense in irritating him more than usual at present.

After a full two minutes John sat down on the bed and put his face in his hands. "I think I need sleep."

"Yes, so do I. Have you secured a room?"

"How can I?" John asked explosively. "You've got my money."

Albert held up one hand to quiet his partner and pointed to the other end of the bed. So absorbed had John been on the possibility of being followed, he had failed to notice the pile of cash and gold coins. Relief spread over his face. "There's your half," said Albert.

John Young quickly leafed through it, a cursory counting, and audibly sighed. He stuffed the bills inside his coat pocket and split the coins between two smaller, more secure vest pockets. He fell back against the bed and laughed.

Albert stood, puffed his cigar and leaned against the wall beside the door. He asked, "do you feel better now?"

"Oh, yes," he laughed again. "Yes, I do. I'm going downstairs to get some whiskey. Then I'm going across the street to Bonanza to find me that pretty redhead I met last week."

"John, might I remind you, that's all the money. I have held back none. So watch yourself. And don't blame me if you end up in dire straits once again."

John Young stood up with a dizzy stagger and straightened his coat. He crossed the room to Albert and slapped his friend on the shoulder. "Have no fear, Albert. I will first secure a room in the hotel before I leave. And I will see you for supper tonight at the Can Can?" He raised his eyebrows with the question.

"Sounds delightful," said Albert, nodding and opening the door.

John Young walked through and turned to Albert to shake hands. "I apologize for getting you booted from the boarding house. The whiskey was talking and I meant no harm."

Albert shook his friend's hand. "I'll make do, John, I always do. See you tonight at the Can Can. Eight o'clock?"

John nodded, grinning, and walked down the hall toward the stairs.

Albert closed the door, satisfied in the outcome of that meeting. He would wait until John was completely sober before proposing any further ventures. Until then...

Albert checked once again to confirm the safety of the poke bag and its contents. There was nothing visible from the top, and he couldn't see it if he peered under the bed. Satisfied, he retrieved his pistol, put it in his pocket, and headed out of the hotel to keep a promise to call on a lovely young lady he was sure was missing him.

22

When Walter had discovered the horse was missing his mother had been relieved. She surmised Mr. Griffin, or John Young as his agent, had come to retrieve it. She did feel bad for Walter. He had enjoyed the responsibility of caring for the horse when it was there. It had given him an important task to accomplish. But it was extra work that she simply did not have the time for. It had been her husband's idea to acquire and move the barn to the boarding house, to perhaps gain additional boarders if they offered livery services. But the barn was small and she considered the land surrounding the house insufficient space for an extended stay. Another pipe dream of the now deceased Roy Barrett.

Phoebe and Will had spent the afternoon with Mrs. Barrett, Wyanet and Walter. They had prepared and eaten lunch together, cleaned up the kitchen and planned supper. Walter had shown Will his marbles, after which they moved outside where Will was coerced into playing several games. Walter won five out of seven

Wyanet needed to get home before dark but she had time before leaving to spend some time with Phoebe and talk about her family's traditional basket weaving. Wyanet was more than honored that Phoebe was fully enchanted with her level of expertise. She used Mrs. Barrett's basket to demonstrate how the baskets were made and described other designs used by the highly skilled and more experienced older members of her family.

Phoebe listened carefully, as she was well aware of the important role weaving had played in the past and present Paiute histories. She let Wyanet speak of her family's talents and enjoyed watching the smile spread across her face when she noticed Phoebe paying close and respectful attention.

It had been an enjoyable afternoon, with the exception of John Young having fallen flat on his face on the parlor floor. When it was nearing time to prepare for supper Phoebe offered to help Mrs. Barrett. Phoebe first dressed and readied herself, checking in on Will before she headed into the kitchen.

"Hey, that looks good," said Will, commenting on dress number two that Phoebe had purchased at the dress shop. It was a deep burgundy, with a black trim around the bottom and black collar and cuffs. Eight golden buttons closed the center front.

"Thanks. The black hem will come in handy walking around these streets," she fluffed her dress. Will laughed at her. "What?"

"I think you like playing dress up. But I think tomorrow we should put our heads together to see if we can get home. I miss my tennis shoes."

"I miss my flip-flops," she said, plopping on Will's bed. "But you're right. Aside from literally looking around today, we didn't get much investigation done, did we? I don't even know where to go or what we're looking for. Maybe we should go back to the barn, where we started, to the scene of the crime."

"What a dork," Will said, straightening his crossover tie. "Scene of the crime..." he mumbled.

"Well what do you suggest we do? I don't know if we are supposed to find something, someone, figure something out... This has been driving me nuts."

"Really?" he asked blandly, turning to look at his sister.

"What's that supposed to mean?" She stood up, facing him.

He put his palms out toward her in supplication. "Chill. We haven't been here that long. It doesn't bother me that you're enjoying yourself. Being here is driving *me* a little nuts, but I'm getting used to it. Besides, I know you'll figure out a way to get us out of here."

"Me?"

"Yes, you. I think it was pretty clear J. W. sent me along for the ride."

"To what, protect me or something?"

He laughed lightly. "No, I was thinking to keep you company. Or maybe to keep you out of trouble. I'm hoping you are going to protect me," he said with humor and a grin.

"Thanks, Will. I am glad you're here with me."

After a moment's silence she asked, "So, how many times did Walter beat you at marbles?" He shook his head and buttoned his coat.

Will waited in the parlor to stay out of the way in the kitchen. Phoebe had told him to. He could hear noises coming from the room opposite and figured it was Walter washing up for supper. Another minute later and Newton Sanford came through the front door and shook Will's hand. He was home for the evening and was headed upstairs to wash up as well. Will sat down and waited.

Phoebe was in the kitchen talking with Mrs. Barrett. She set the table while Mrs. Barrett put some finishing touches on their evening meal. While she worked she said to Phoebe, "Miss Tucker, I hope this isn't too forward of me, and please tell me if it is, but what are your plans, you and your brother, here in Bodie? I apologize, but this town is different than most."

Think quick, don't be rude, you really like this lady, watch your words... "Like I said before, we were a bit lost." She paused, twisting her fingers together. "We ended up here on a family errand and now, well, now that's finished we thought maybe we would stay for a bit, you know, as long as we're here," she shrugged, "I like it here." She smiled at Mrs. Barrett.

Mrs. Barrett sat down across from Phoebe. "I'm glad. There aren't many single women around here. It's nice to have a friend to talk to."

"Thanks, I know what you mean. Mrs. Barrett, may I ask you a question in return?"

"Of course. I've most likely been asked before."

"Please tell me if I should mind my own business. You said this boarding house was your husband's idea. Is that why you keep it going? For him?"

Mrs. Barrett scoffed. "No. He had a job, like I mentioned. But so many people were here making money investing in mining and transportation, building hotels and restaurants for the miners and the workers, then all the places that came after that to support a town this size. My husband wanted a share of that but did not possess the intelligence or ingenuity to bring his grand ideas to fruition." She looked down at her hands, examining her fingernails, remembering back, shaking her head. "He was a dreamer without vision."

"I see," said Phoebe, feeling awkward for having asked. "I'm – "

"Don't apologize. You see, Roy Barrett was not my first husband. I was married before, when I was but twenty. We both hailed from Missouri. I met and fell in love with a wonderful, handsome man. He was good to me, and he loved me. I loved him in return. We thought we would spend our lives together, growing old, raising a house full of children. We married in Missouri and began our journey west. I was so happy.

"On the way we stopped a time or two. Walter was born in Virginia City. My husband, James, wanted to venture here, to Bodie. I would have followed him anywhere. We had a little house not far from here. He obtained a position at one of the mines, a good job. He was called in to deal with a problem, to help, and was killed in a terrible accident." She paused then, her face a veil of sadness, her eyes beginning to redden. Phoebe reached over and put one of her hands on top of hers. Mrs. Barrett held her chin high and looked Phoebe in the eye.

"I had money coming to me from the Miner's Union to help with his funeral, and a few families helped out like they do for some, so I could care for my little boy. Then I met Roy Barrett. He fell in love with me, was decent to Walter and we married last fall. He passed away of influenza when the cold weather came. It was a harsh winter, Bodie saw many losses. Now I have the boarding house to run. At least I have an income." She smiled.

"It may have been inappropriate for me to move on with my life so soon after Mr. Barrett's passing; but I'm on this earth a short time, do not live in proper Missouri anymore and I'll not apologize for it."

"You are an amazing woman, Mrs. Barrett. Walter will be proud of you one day, when he realizes what you've accomplished."

"I hope so. Everything I do is for him. He is very stubborn. My husband, Walter's father, said he is like me," she laughed. "I try not to preach to him, I don't believe he would listen. Demonstration is worth much more."

"And insightful as well."

"Wyanet once told me a saying that comes from her people. '*Tell me and I'll forget. Show me, and I may not remember. Involve me, and I'll understand.*'"

"It's a wonderful sentiment to pass along," said Phoebe, smiling.

"Agreed." Mrs. Barrett stood up. "You may call me Lena, if you like. That's my first name. Lena."

"Thank you, I will. Please call me Phoebe."

Mrs. Barrett smiled a genuine smile. "I'll remember that name. It's just like the bird."

Phoebe sat stunned for a moment on hearing Lena Barrett say those words. J. W. had talked about the Says Phoebe bird and it shocked her to hear it again. *Oh, J. W., I miss you, you old cuss.*

They heard an additional voice coming from the parlor. Lena Barrett untied and removed her apron and hung it on a nail by the door. On entering the parlor they saw Newton welcoming Lionel Bradley and reacquainting him with Will, whom he had met only briefly that morning. The man remained standing when the two ladies entered the room and, holding his hat in his hands, leaned his head forward in respectful greeting. "Mrs. Barrett, Miss Tucker. Thank you again for the invite."

"It's nice to have you, Mr. Bradley. Have a seat, supper will be ready soon." Lionel Bradley and Newton sat in the chairs, Will, Phoebe and Lena Barrett sat on the small sofa. In normal conditions Phoebe would have elbowed her brother to move over. Not tonight. They were squished but each plastered a polite smile on his or face. Phoebe noticed Newton looking at her again, his mustache twitching and fine lines crinkling at the corners of his eyes. She looked back to Lionel Bradley quickly in irritation.

Walter opened the door to his and his mother's room in a rush, stepped hurriedly into the parlor and nearly slammed the door behind himself. His mother shot him a look of reproachment but he did not seem to notice. "Did I miss anything?" he asked and those present that had witnessed John Young's earlier behavior knew he was remembering that he had been summarily dismissed last time.

"Walter, Mr. Bradley has arrived for supper. We will eat soon."

The boy plopped down onto the floor in front of his mother, again practicing tying with the new laces.

Lionel Bradley, Newton and Lena Barrett spoke easily for a couple of minutes. Mrs. Barrett then excused herself to the kitchen and a moment later told everyone else that supper was ready. Walter popped up from the floor with an excited, "I did it!" showing off his feet and his properly tied shoes.

"You've tied your shoes before, Walter," his mother said, busying herself. "You simply lacked the patience with the new laces. You need patience, my dear."

Walter chose the chair in the kitchen closest to the door and sat swinging his feet back and forth. "Yes, Mama," said the little boy, rolling his eyes and continuing to swing his feet. The adults grinned, especially Phoebe and Will. *Kids are kids, whenever, wherever.*

Before seating himself Newton asked, "Is Mr. Murphy joining us tonight? I thought he would have arrived home before now."

Lionel looked anxiously toward the doorway. Mrs. Barrett said, "I expected him. I received no communication from him as to his possible absence. I hope he is safe."

"Is there a reason he wouldn't be?" asked Phoebe.

"Only that he told us he had winnings from the Faro table," said Newton. "And I don't think he leaves it in his room."

Phoebe said, "That doesn't seem wise, does it? Mr. Murphy seems a rather gentle soul and Bodie has pickpockets galore." Too late she realized her mistake. "Or so I've heard." Newton glanced her way, his mustache twitched and he looked away again. Will remained oblivious to her slip of the tongue.

"He needs to find a good hiding place," said Lionel Bradley, nodding. "A really good hiding place. Out in the open but hidden in plain sight. Somewhere no one would expect to find the thing you're trying to hide. And then," he took a bite from his fork, looked at the ceiling, swallowed and said loudly, "don't talk about it to anyone. Right Newton?"

Newton sputtered and looked at Lionel Bradley with surprised eyes. His cheeks flushed, he looked from face to face to face gathered at the table, and replied, "Right, Lionel. Right," and took another bite from his plate.

It was Phoebe's turn to give him a look from which to retreat. Will and Walter were speaking together quietly now, ignoring whatever situation had just begun to develop. Mrs. Barrett was too polite to inquire of Lionel's meaning. Phoebe was tempted to ask straight out but remembered where she was. *I can be subtle, really.*

"Mr. Bradley," Phoebe began sweetly, "it sounds like you know a little bit about being crafty." She smiled at him, and glanced at Newton who would not look at her.

"Crafty? No, not really. But I'm able to manage my affairs as well as the next man, I'd say."

Surprised at his coherent answer Phoebe continued. "May I ask how you like to spend your time, Mr. Bradley?"

Lionel glanced at Newton and when he received no helpful suggestion, answered, "I work at the blacksmith's."

"Yes, I noticed that this morning when we walked past your shop and we met. But what else do you do? You do have some free time, do you not?"

"I do. A little." He glanced again at Newton who had finally stirred from his startled disposition. Newton was frowning. Lionel Bradley looked back to Phoebe. "But I don't do nothin' with it." Lionel took several bites in a row now, looking down at his plate.

"No? You don't gamble, or go to the saloons?"

"I don't believe that's appropriate conversation, Ms. Tucker," said Newton.

Phoebe's temper flared. "It's a simple enough question. And don't lecture to me, *Mr.* Sanford." She looked at their hostess. "I apol – hmph." She returned focus on eating her supper but added, "I'm happy you could join us for supper this evening, Mr. Bradley."

"I'm happy to be here. And you can call me Lionel." Phoebe nodded.

The rest of the meal was quiet and subdued. Chester Murphy was mentioned again but out of interest for his safety. "I can go in search of him later if that will make everyone feel better," said Newton as Mrs. Barrett and Phoebe cleared the table of dishes.

"I wouldn't be worried but I did expect him to be here. He's not only punctual but considerate enough to let me know when he is unable to make it," said Mrs. Barrett. "If you wouldn't mind looking I think that would be thoughtful."

"I can look on my way home," suggested Lionel Bradley.

"Thank you, Lionel. I'll accompany you." Newton said.

After having a quick dessert and a cup of coffee the front door slammed unexpectedly. Walter yelled, "It's Mr. Murphy," as he pointed toward the front door from the kitchen doorway.

All present hurried into the parlor to face a flustered and disheveled Chester Murphy. He was huffing and puffing, out of breath, so Newton steered him toward the chair nearest the door. "Chester, what's happened? Are you all right?" Newton asked, great concern in his voice and manner.

Chester Murphy shook his head 'no,' nodded, shook his head 'no' and put his face in his hands. Catching his breath he said, "I was robbed...nearly everything I've won...gone...my plans...all gone. They did it, and I can't prove a thing."

Phoebe had her own suspicions of what had happened but waited while Newton continued trying to prod the man to say more. "Chester, what happened? Who robbed you, do you know? Where?"

He nodded again. "Those two," he gestured noncommittally into the air. The assemblage looked at each other, knowing of whom he was speaking. "They knew I was playing Faro again, they waited for me. I'd won, again, I was eighty dollars ahead this time." He shook his head and grimaced in pain.

"Did one of them hit you?" Phoebe asked, angered at the effrontery.

Chester was nodding, rubbing a spot on the back of his head and kneading his knees with the other hand. "Something whacked me on the back of the head and I fell forward onto my knees." He examined his palms and showed them to her. They were scraped from his fall.

Lionel Bradley had so far remained silent. Now he asked quietly, "Who did this?"

Chester answered for himself, "I'm relatively sure it was John Young and Albert Griffin. I saw Albert on the street earlier and he was talking to Mr. Young. I've met him in the past, he's come into the bank. They had their heads together, talking. It wasn't until I was running late for supper that I hurried down the street and wasn't paying attention to my surroundings." He looked up at Phoebe. "I warned you to use caution and now I'm a victim of my own feckless conduct."

"Was there no one to whom you could turn for help? No one witnessed the attack?" asked Lena Barrett.

"I don't know. I believe I was knocked unconscious. When I woke people were stepping over me. They may have believed I was another drunk in the street, I don't know." I have a dreadful pain in my head."

Will wanted to suggest something to take for a headache but kept his mouth shut, aware what he would mention was most likely not invented and in use yet. Phoebe said, "If you could fetch some cold water and a small towel that will help." Lena Barrett nodded and sent Walter for some water while she retrieved a towel.

Lionel Bradley sat down in the second chair in the room. He was frowning. "I don't like when people hurt my friends."

"I know, Lionel. But I'm not sure anything can be done just yet. Sit tight." Newton was first trying to assess Chester's injuries and calm the man.

Lena Barrett proffered the cloth with cold water. Chester sighed. "Thank you, Miss Tucker, Mrs. Barrett, that does feel better. Thank you all for your concern."

Newton helped Chester Murphy upstairs to his room. Newton stated on his return that Chester was feeling better physically but now felt the fool for his carelessness.

"Mr. Murphy doesn't seem like the type to spend a lot of time at the Faro table, if you ask me," Phoebe muttered. "Have you any idea why he's so intent on saving money?"

Newton shook his head no. "I don't. But I've played Faro myself. Does that make me a reckless rogue who can't be trusted?" He was goading her.

"No more than it makes me one," she snapped.

Lena Barrett scuttled Walter off to their room to get ready for bed. As he was complaining she repeated the oft said statement, "You know I want you to read every night before bed. Now go. Say goodnight." He did so, sulking, fearing he was missing the action; again. "Arthur gets to stay up later than I do." Lena Barrett kissed her son on the top of his head.

"I think I'm going to take a stroll back into town tonight," said Phoebe, holding her chin high in determination. "Anyone care to join me?"

Newton and Will began to protest as one, Lena Barrett grinned and Lionel Bradley stood from his seat and put on his hat. "I'll go with you, Ma'am."

"Thank you... Lionel. Anyone else? No? I'm going to get my hat. Excuse me."

When she returned to the parlor Lena Barrett was gone and Will and Newton stopped their discussion on how to keep Phoebe from heading up Main Street. Will knew trying to stop her was useless. Newton suspected as much but said, "Miss Tucker, I advise against it."

"Good for you," she said back to him, looking at Will with a resolve he was accustomed to seeing. He shrugged.

The three of them reached the front door. Phoebe turned to look at Newton and asked, "Coming?"

He sighed and put on his hat.

23

Lionel Bradley had walked to supper. He did not own a horse. He expressed his concern for Phoebe walking the long distance into town, a kind gesture, but Phoebe reassured him she was perfectly capable and willing. She held both of her arms out to the side, elbows bent, inviting a walking escort. Newton held his arm out for her to take it on one side, Lionel did so on the other. She looped her arms through theirs and waggled her eyebrows at Will. In return he rolled his eyes, accustomed to her audacity.

"Miss Tucker, what is it you hope to gain by – "

"Shush, Mr. San – Newton. Just shush."

Lionel Bradley chuckled from her other side. "I like her, Newton."

"Shush, Lionel," said Newton.

"I like you too, Lionel," said Phoebe. "About Mr. Murphy. Do you think we'll run into either Mr. Young or Mr. Griffin while we're out?"

"I don't know," answered Newton. "I sincerely hope not. By now they've had more time in the saloons. I dislike confronting thieves, especially ones full up."

"Is there anything we can do about Mr. Murphy's money? I feel terrible about what they did," inquired Phoebe.

"Report them. But Chester will have to do so himself. Perhaps tomorrow will greet him with a sensible head and he will see his options more clearly." Newton patted her hand on his arm. "No need to worry."

She scowled at him. "I'm not worried. I want Mr. Murphy to be made whole again."

As they walked, Newton's demeanor began slowly to change. He became agitated, visibly bothered by something and surveyed his surroundings as if searching. Phoebe could feel his arm tense beneath hers and saw his spine stiffen when they heard random noises coming from nearby. Phoebe halted and unhitched her arms from both men and asked, "Okay, what is it? What's the matter with you?"

Surprised she had noticed his uneasy disposition Newton looked from person to person and back to Phoebe. Lionel asked innocently, "You didn't tell her what happened, did you, Newton?"

"No, I didn't tell her," he stated. Now he wouldn't look Phoebe directly in the eye.

"Tell me what?" She asked loudly. She turned to Lionel and smiled. Softening her voice she asked him, "What's the matter, Lionel? What is it you think he should tell me?"

Newton scowled, glaring at Lionel. Phoebe looked from one to the other and finally said, "Please, tell me."

Lionel Bradley cleared his throat, hesitant, but began his story. "I killed a man." He paused. When Phoebe did nothing more than raise her eyebrows he continued. "I didn't know his name when I shot him off his horse. He was chasing Newton, he was gonna kill him if I didn't shoot first. I don't like when people hurt my friends. Too many friends have died." He paused, looking at his feet.

Phoebe put her hand on his arm, urging him to continue. "There was a fight in town, a big one, when a man was suspected of cheatin' at a Faro table. We," he looked at Newton, "we tried to stay outta the way, but it's hard to do that sometimes. A bunch o' men started shootin', some into the air, some at each other, two saloon girls were hit in the face with something. It was a hullabaloo like I ain't never seen and it went on and on.

"This bunch o' three got on their horses and started ridin' north together. Most figured it was them that started the whole thing. They rode around and chased people that were in their way, just for fun it looked like. We were trying to get outta the way, like everybody else was. Then they rode past Newton and left.

After we split up one o' the men came back, all angry like, saw Newton and chased him down the street. I saw him pull his pistol and take aim at Newton and, well, I just couldn't let anything happen to my friend.

"I had my rifle with me, so I fired. I'm a good shot, I won a contest once. He dropped dead in the street up that way. It turned out, mind you we didn't know it at the time, the man's name was Joseph Hoffman. The constable told me he was an acquaintance of Albert Griffin and John Young."

"Weren't you arrested?" asked Will, mesmerized by Lionel's firsthand story.

"I went to the constable and told him the whole story that very same night. And one o' the saloon girls and a couple others told him what happened too. They let me go. I suppose Albert and John heard or read it was me who shot Joseph Hoffman, but I don't know if they know it was Newton he was chasing. And we don't know with any certainty if they were the other riders that evening." Lionel shrugged, looking apologetic. He was looking over at Newton now, with an expression that said, 'I hope I haven't spoiled anything.'

"I'm so sorry that happened, to the both of you. It sounds terrifying. I'm not upset with you, Lionel, if that's what you're thinking. You saved your friend. What else were you supposed to do?"

Lionel allowed himself a small smile and nodded. "Thank you, Ma'am."

Turning to Newton, Phoebe asked, "Is that why you're acting so strange? Are you afraid they've found out it was you and are after you? That they blame you?"

"I'm not acting strange. And no, I don't think they're after me. If they desired retaliation they have both had plenty of chances."

"Do you think that was why Albert Griffin procured a room from Mrs. Barrett?" asked Phoebe. She remembered when she had bumped into him outside on her first night in Bodie and had harbored doubts about his trustworthiness. She now thanked her gut for always being right. She had been on her guard against him ever since; rightly so, it seemed.

"I don't know," Newton stated more calmly. "Perhaps it was simply chance."

"Why aren't people arrested for cheating in the saloons," asked Will innocently, confused by the entire situation.

"A good cheater, once suspected, will start a ruckus intentionally. Confusion ensues, making it difficult to pinpoint the culprit, which allows them to escape under a mere cloud of suspicion," said Phoebe. All three men stared at her silently. "What?"

"Are you speaking from a place of experience, Miss Tucker?" asked Newton, his mustache once again twitching.

"Yes, that's me, the card cheater," she stated, annoyed, turning in a huff to once again grasp Lionel Bradley's arm but ignoring Newton's. "I don't know why you are so offended that I have a brain in my head."

"Oh, come on, you two, stop arguing all the time. Lionel, they can't see what's in front of their own faces," said Will, lightly laughing.

Lionel Bradley chuckled and glanced sideways at Newton.

Newton moved to walk behind Phoebe, beside Will, looking down at the ground as they walked. Phoebe walked with her chin up, staring straight ahead. Newton took the next few steps more slowly, separating himself and Will from the two walking in front. Then he mumbled, "I don't know why your sister finds it difficult to endure a jest."

Will whispered back to him, "She takes a joke just fine." Newton frowned at Will, unsure of his meaning. He explained, "I know my sister. She likes you, idiot."

Newton's eyes went wide before he asked, "How does she regard those whom she dislikes?"

Will smiled and said, "She stabs them with forks."

Music was already playing nearby and Phoebe bounced along to the rhythm. The group reached Main Street and turned north, stepping around the muck in the street and staying on the boardwalks in front of businesses when possible. "Where are we going" asked Lionel Bradley.

"Hmm, I don't know. Where can I go where they will let me in and I can show my brother how to play Faro?"

"What?" asked Newton incredulously. "You want to do what?"

"I believe you heard what I said, Mr. San – Newton."

"You can go anywhere you want; but they may mistake you for a saloon girl. Or a girl from Bonanza Street. I've heard what happens when someone does that." He was remembering Phoebe slapping the man who turned out to be John Young after he had offered to pay her brother back for interrupting his 'pleasant day.' "Won't that bother you?"

"I have nothing against the saloon girls or the girls from Bonanza Street. I was merely offended by Mr. Young's assumption and the fact that he tried to pay my brother for his error. Tonight, it is my choice and I don't care what people think. If you don't care to be seen in my company then I suggest you go elsewhere."

Newton took hold of Phoebe's upper arm and halted her forward progress. "Miss Tucker, Phoebe, please use caution." He looked as if he wanted to say more so she waited, held her tongue, and he continued. "I would be devastated if something untoward happened to you."

"Would you?" She glanced quickly back at her brother then, gently removing her arm from Newton's grip, and said, "You have you a pistol, do you not?"

"A – a pistol?"

"Yes, do you have a pistol, with you, on your person?"

"Well, yes, yes I do. For emergencies."

"Then I will consider myself well guarded." Phoebe continued walking, still arm in arm with Lionel Bradley.

"But Newton you're a terrible shot," inserted Lionel Bradley.

"Perhaps you should give your pistol to Lionel, Mr. Sanford," said Phoebe.

Newton opened his mouth to fire back a sharp retort when he saw the amused glimmer in Phoebe's eyes. "Thank you for the vote of confidence, Lionel," he grumbled. Then, "We're back to 'Mr. Sanford,' I see."

Phoebe smiled at him. "Newton. You know I was teasing you, don't you?"

Newton offered his arm to her once again and she took it. "I do, Miss Tucker. I do."

They strolled past a pair of restaurants that never closed. Hotel doors were propped open, a few people went in, came out. There was a stage coach loading passengers just ahead. The driver was hefting bags of belongings onto the top where his stagehand waited to tie them down to the roof.

"Is that stage leaving at night?" Will asked Phoebe from behind.

She nodded. "Yes. Maybe headed to Carson City. They'll travel all night and arrive tomorrow. It's about a sixteen hour ride."

"You're familiar with the stage routes, Ms. Tucker?" asked Newton.

Oops. She had forgotten whose ears were nearby. "Not exactly. I saw an advertisement." *Not really a lie; there was a lot of information in her collection of books.*

"I see. I thought perhaps that was the stage you arrived on." *He's fishing, and that was a leading statement if ever there was one,* she thought.

"No, I – we," she glanced back at Will, "we didn't come from Carson City." *Not directly, anyway.* Before either man could ask further questions on that subject Phoebe said, “Let’s cross the street,” and they did.

Newton appeared uneasy once again. “Miss Tucker, may we please curtail this expedition?”

“No, thank you. I want to experience – this – for myself,” she answered sweetly. “I understand your concern, truly I do. But I will hear no more about it.”

They walked past a saloon where they heard more music playing and a group of people singing along loudly. They crossed in front of a business closed for the evening but on the second floor above it the windows were open to the night and people were sitting on windowsills looking out. A hotel balcony ahead of them held several people drinking and singing and Phoebe was glad they had timed their walking underneath it just so; a glass bottle dropped and shattered behind them on the boardwalk.

A cigar store was open a group of men exited, lighting their purchases simultaneously, laughing and comparing and deciding where to go next. Phoebe eyed the hardware store and tinsmith back across the street and once again considered a firearm purchase.

She thought her chatelaine bag too small to carry a Colt unless the end of the grip stuck out. *Very ladylike.* She grinned inwardly as she imagined herself walking around town carrying a Winchester in her hand. A Derringer, now that would fit into her bag, but unless she intended to shoot closely it wasn’t her first choice. A Bulldog, that’s better, being a stronger snubnose revolver that would fit as well.

“Are you planning on going into the hardware store?” asked Newton with humor when Phoebe had stopped walking and was staring that direction.

“Perhaps I’ll purchase a firearm myself,” she replied.

Newton appraised her determined expression before stating, “I thought you would consider yourself well guar – ”

“We’ll be right back.” She smiled sweetly at Newton. Then she looked up at Lionel and tugged on his arm to escort her across the street to the hardware store. Will and Newton remained where they were on the boardwalk.

"Aarrgh," Newton yelled to the sky. "Your sister is the most intractable outlaw I have ever encountered." He paced back and forth.

Will frowned. "Outlaw?" he asked simply.

"I find her to be cantankerous and contrary and uncompromising and – and – and I don't know what else." He paced.

Will leaned back against the building, one leg bent, his foot against the wall. "Uh-huh," he said, having heard all of this before in one way or another.

Newton was pacing and muttering to himself when Lionel and Phoebe returned. She pointed to her chatelaine bag and smiled. "I guess my bag was bigger than I thought."

"Miss Tucker, I do hope you don't shoot your foot off," said Newton.

Phoebe looked at Newton but saw Will out of the corner of her eye. Will was silently shaking his head back and forth a fraction, telling her something, reminder her... *Newton L. Sanford, Died June 19, 1880, Aged 29 yrs 3 mo.* Her heart sank; four days, only four days left, *Oh Dear God, why have I been so callous, only four days...* "I'll be careful Newton, don't worry." She looked to Will, who seemed relieved.

She held out her arm for Newton this time and he took it.

Two women called to Will from across the street, whooping and asking him to join them in a dance. He waved his arms 'no,' embarrassed, and kept walking. Up ahead was the intersection of Main and King Streets. Will remembered where he was and was hoping his sister found what she was looking for soon, so they could get off the street.

A minute later Phoebe said, "Here, Wagner's. I want to go in here first."

"First?" Will groaned.

They walked in and a few men turned to look at Phoebe. They stared and Will hated to think about what thoughts were going on in their heads. His sister was not oblivious, she just didn't care. He thought of what his father would say to his letting her come into a place like this. No, he would know there was nothing to be done about it.

Pulling his sister aside for a instant he asked, "Phoebe, what is an 'outlaw'?"

"That's a dumb question."

"No, not the man-breaking-the-law type. There must be another type of outlaw."

"Why?" She asked, suspicious now. "Spill it."

"When Newton and I were waiting for you and Lionel he was really freaked out. He yelled at the sky and said, what was it now, on yeah, he said you were a retractable, no, 'untractable outlaw.'"

She thought about it for a moment and began to laugh. "Really, now." Her laugh got the attention of many surrounding the group of four. "An outlaw is also a horse, a horse so wild it cannot be tamed for riding. Oh, that's funny."

"Shh, he'll hear you"

"So what. It is funny, you know."

"If you say so. Personally I think you're just a pain in the – "

"Duck!" Someone yelled, and a beer bottle flew through the air. Will, slow to react, was struck just on the tip of his ear. His hand flew to cover his ear as he gasped in surprise. Lionel remained calm but scowled, searching for the offender. Newton grasped Phoebe's arm and pulled her to the side of the room.

Once there she tugged her arm free, checked on her brother's ear and declared him still breathing. "Are you sure you want to continue with this folly?" Newton asked.

Phoebe smiled broadly, said, "Absolutely," picked up her skirt at both sides and walked confidently forward through the crowd. The bar was to one side and she made her way to it, squeezing herself between two smelly, dusty men. "Whiskey," she yelled above the noise.

The two men turned to look at her and the bartender stared. Another man came up to her from behind and put his arm around her waist. She peeled his fingers off, twisted out of his way, waggled a finger at him and turned back to the bartender. Once she took a coin out of her bag his attention returned to her. He put a glass down in front of her, took the coin, poured her whiskey and winked.

Don't sputter, don't cough, and don't sip it like a so-called lady or you'll look back and regret it. Up went the glass, down went the whiskey. One drink, a third of it gone. She turned to see consternation or amusement on the faces of her three escorts. The man standing next to her called out, "Cheers," to her and she returned the sentiment, taking another swig of her drink.

She stepped to Newton, took the last swallow of whiskey and handed him her empty glass. "Shall we?" she asked, and pulled him through the room to the rear and the Faro tables.

There were a couple of empty seats at the tables in the crowded room. Phoebe plopped down in one. She kept her change from the purchase of the pistol at the top of her bag where it was easy to reach and now exchanged twenty dollars of it for twenty checks. One dollar checks; pricey. She motioned with a crooked finger for Will to come near and whispered in his ear. "You wanted to learn how, so watch. Don't call these chips, they're checks, and everybody gets a penny, a copper, to use for certain bets. Pay attention, it's easy."

The dealer was wearing a hat which he tipped to Phoebe. Two men glanced her way and ignored her after that. The others stared, elbowed each other, grinned, winked or some such similar action. Phoebe ignored the winks and grins, nodded at the dealer and waited for him to call the start of a fresh game.

She watched his shuffle carefully, making sure the cards were mixed well. Dealers cheated, as well as patrons, in attempting to cluster groups of numbers. He called all bets on the table and Phoebe placed one check on the seven. Just one, to start. The first card drawn was a six, so far so good. The next was a nine. No win but no loss. She left the check on the seven.

Will whispered in her ear, "What are you supposed to do?"

Without taking her eyes off the table and her check she said, "any bets on the banker's card, the first one drawn, lose. Any on the second card drawn, the player's card, win. I had neither. I'm leaving it there."

The coffin keeper, the man beside the dealer, had a matching set of cards as those on the table; ace through king. They were mounted on an abacus-like board. Once a card was drawn in the game the coffin keeper would slide a bead over to show which cards had already been played. Thus the strategic element entered the game if one was paying attention.

Next round, banker's card was a nine, player's card a seven, Phoebe won. She removed her winning check and moved the initial check to the jack. Next round, banker's card ace, winning card ten. She left her check in place. Next round, banker's card a two, player's card a jack, another win. She once again removed the winning check and moved the initial check to a new card. *Ahead two dollars.*

The men around her were betting small stacks of checks on the cards, making Phoebe's single check seem a pittance. But after she had won twice no one winked or grinned in her direction again. Someone put a hand on her shoulder and she could see it was Newton. He leaned down to say quietly, "Are you through with your little experiment? Can we go now?"

She shook her head 'no' and kept her eyes on the cards before her. She heard him sigh. Round after round, she would win, break even, then lose, break even, win, win... At one point she placed her check on the other side of the cards, near the dealer, and said, "high card bet." The dealer nodded and announced, "Betting on the high card." The high card was indeed a higher value than the losing card, a win for Phoebe.

After two bets with no win or loss she placed her copper, her penny, on her check on top of the card of her choice, this time the queen. Will again whispered in her ear and asked what she was doing. She held up a finger to wait a minute. The banker's card was a queen. Because she had put her copper on her check on the queen, this meant she was betting on the losing card. A win for her. Another gambler placed his check on the queen as well but without his copper. Since the banker's card is the losing card the dealer swiped the man's check off the queen. The gambler frowned at Phoebe, annoyed, but she smiled sweetly in response.

There were few cards left in the dealer's shoe at this point in the game. She kept a close eye on the abacus to see how many of which cards remained in play. The men at the table were talking amongst themselves, laughing, drinking, cheering or pouting. None of them were paying attention as closely as Phoebe.

She was waiting to see if one of the players was going to be distracted enough to place a bet on a dead card. That is, a card that had already been drawn four times, as shown by the abacus having four beads moved to the side. If that happened any player that noticed can call 'dead card' and take the bet for themselves. If any player didn't notice, the dealer could keep it. Phoebe was hoping she was the only one paying attention.

The man sitting to her left seemed to have had enough whiskey for several men. Perhaps he would be the one. Or the man sitting around the end of the table that kept staring at her after noticing her three escorts. She only hoped the dealer didn't notice before she had the chance, or that an observer didn't yell out.

Seven cards left. Phoebe placed two checks on the number nine. The banker's card was a three, the winning card was the nine. She had won two more. For the next round she had a single check on an eight.

The man on her right held a few checks in his hand, waving it over the cards, deciding where to place them. She didn't distract him, she wanted to play fair. He finally put all of his checks on the four and withdrew his hand. *Yes!* "Dead card," she said loudly, so as not to be misunderstood, and pointed to the four. The dealer looked quickly, the men present snapped their heads to attention, and Phoebe picked up the man's checks.

"Damn it!" the man yelled, startling Phoebe and giving the dealer cause to put his hand under the table to his lap, where most likely an emergency pistol rested.

Newton gripped Phoebe's shoulder tightly, a suggestion to leave. From behind she heard the alarm in Will's voice when he said, "Oh geez, should we go?"

The man whose checks Phoebe had swiped off the board gripped Phoebe's right wrist with his checks still in her fist. "You got no right. Gimme my money, tart. Go earn your own."

Phoebe dug the fingernails of her left hand into the man's wrist. When he reached with his other hand in an attempt to pull her left hand free, Phoebe leaned her head back and used her forehead to hit him in the face, hitting his left cheekbone near his eye. He yowled and both hands let go of her. She then stomped on his foot under the table and tried to move her chair back to get away. Will was standing so closely behind her the chair had nowhere to go.

At that moment a women with feathers in her hat and two shiny bracelets walked to the other side of the angry man and waved a whiskey bottle in front of his face. "Come on Harry, have a drink with me." The woman looked at Phoebe and winked. "You were supposed to buy me a drink, remember?" she said, putting down the bottle and laying her arm across the man's shoulders.

The dealer eyed Phoebe and the woman, but kept his hand in his lap. One man scooped up his checks and walked away quickly. Two of the men began to laugh, most likely at their gambling companion's foolish behavior. Angry Harry, still massaging his cheek, sighed heavily and picked up his empty glass. "Just a hooter, Doll." He held it for the woman to pour him a drink.

She had her own glass and they clinked their glasses together. "You still have winnings, Harry. Don't be so upset," she rubbed the back of his neck with her hand.

Phoebe picked up the rest of her own checks, nodded at the woman as thanks for calming the situation and stood to go. Before leaving the table she reached into her bag, retrieved the rest of her checks, handed them to the dealer and cashed them in, keeping an eye on Angry Harry the entire time. As she walked away she said politely to the table, "Gentlemen," and smiled sweetly. She saved her best glare for Angry Harry.

Lionel took hold of Phoebe's arm and they walked toward the back of the saloon, Newton and Will following closely. She glanced backwards and saw no one following them, pulled her arm from Lionel's grasp and said, "For heaven's sake, stop dragging me along."

Lionel looked sheepish. "I'm sorry, Ma'am. I was trying to keep you safe."

"It's all right, Lionel, I understand. I don't think I'm in any danger, but thank you."

"You've got what, six or seven dollars, I mean chips, um, checks left? Who's going to chase you for that?" asked Will, relieved to be away from the Faro table.

"You could have been shot for looking at someone the wrong way," said Newton, searching the crowd for danger.

Phoebe ignored him and answered Will. "Yes, at the end of the game I had four of my own and five from the gambler Harry. I know enough not to leave everything on the table in clear view of drunken, angry men. And you didn't notice what I cashed in, did you?" She checked to be sure they were not overheard and opened her hand. "I started with twenty. Now I have sixty-five. Whiskey, anyone? Drinks are on me."

24

Lionel smiled and punched Newton in the shoulder. "Ha, I told you she'd win," he said. I had a feeling in my bones."

"Phoebe, what's a hooter?"

"What do you mean, you had a feeling?" asked Phoebe.

"I told Newton – "

"Why can't you keep your mouth shut, Lionel?"

"Phoebe what's a hooter? And how can that girl drink so much and still be sober?" Will was still confused.

"I think we should pull foot. Now," said Newton.

"Phoebe – "

"But Newton, that's what you sa – "

"Enough," Phoebe stated loudly, stamping her foot at the same time. One at a time she addressed the three quiet men now staring at her. "Will, a hooter means just a little bit. And didn't you notice that girl already had a glass in her hand when she came to the Faro table? She probably had tea in it. She's here to get the men to buy drinks, gamble and spend money, not get bombed.

"Lionel, thanks for the confidence in my abilities," she said with a wink. "Newton," she sighed, "stop yelling at

Lionel. He seems to be a good friend to you, how about returning the favor."

With that Phoebe put her winnings into her bag, all except a one dollar bill, gathered her skirt, spun around and walked back to the long bar at the side of the room. Lionel followed closely behind her, on the lookout for anyone with thoughts to accost her. "Four," she yelled, holding up four fingers and waving the dollar bill in the air. The bartender brought her four glasses and she handed him the bill. "Keep the change," she said with a smile and a wave.

The bartender said "Yes, Ma'am. Thank you." His tip equalled the cost of the drinks.

Phoebe and Lionel each carried two glasses to where Newton and Will were standing. Will looked down into his drink and made a face, Newton's mustache twitched and his eyes sparkled and crinkled at the sides. "Cheers," said Phoebe, raising her glass.

A few others in the room heard her sentiment, raised their glasses in good-natured sociability and called, "Cheers," in return.

Phoebe drank down half in one gulp, Lionel took two gulps and finished it, Newton and Will stared at each other and shrugged. Newton took one swig, then another, then finished his. Will smelled it, uttered a sound of distaste, then took a drink and coughed. Phoebe took his glass from him and held it out to anyone else who cared to finish off the remnants. Lionel took it from her and drank it, Phoebe rolling her eyes at her brother.

Turning to the see the back of the saloon, Phoebe asked, "Hey, where does that go?"

"No, no, we are going out the front door, not the back," insisted Newton.

Phoebe smiled broadly, remembering. "It goes to Bonanza street, doesn't it? And we're close to King. Let's go." She picked up her skirts again and whirled around to find the door leading out the back way.

They emerged into a muddy, smelly mess. The rear door was where the drunks withdrew to Bonanza and King

Streets, to the red-light district and the opium dens of Chinatown. Snowmelt was everywhere and garbage was tossed out here, the nearest exit. "Gross, Phoebe, did we have to come out this way," said Will.

"Don't be such a baby," she said quietly. Her brother groaned and sidestepped puddles of unknown substance.

They weren't far from the next street over, Bonanza Street, and Phoebe wandered that direction, following the music and laughter. She saw a couple of windows lit with gas lamps and could smell smoke wafting through the air; cigars, opium, a few fireplaces burning as the night turned chilly. She rubbed the sides of her arms, wishing she'd purchased or borrowed a shawl.

"Are you cold?" Newton asked kindly.

She nodded. "A bit, but I'm fine."

"Why don't we go home, back to the boarding house. This is unsafe here."

"Not yet. I want to see it."

"I don't understand you, Miss Tucker. I simply don't understand you. Will, pray tell, has your sibling always been so..."

Phoebe laughed then, feeling the warmth of the whiskey and finding Newton's inability to easily articulate an accurate description of her personality extremely amusing. "Always so what?" she teased.

Phoebe's question remained unanswered. Lionel flew forward and hit the ground, covering his head with his hands; Newton ducked, exclaiming under his breath; Will turned and froze. Gunshots had rung out behind them and several men and three women rushed through the rear door of Wagner's. Phoebe heard horses hooves pounding the earth. Coming or going she couldn't tell but there were more than a few. From Bonanza Street a woman screamed and glass broke somewhere within a building or house. A door slammed and she heard profanity loud and clear in a slurred drunken voice.

Newton reached down to check on Lionel, who was fine, just startled. When he stood up he was grinning and shrugged. Newton looked at Phoebe and said, irritation plain in his voice and demeanor, "We need to go home, Miss Tucker. Now."

Phoebe glanced at Will who was nodding and looking quite worried. She supposed she was being stubborn. "Fine," she relented. She picked up her skirt and walked south toward King Street, tripping and stumbling occasionally because she couldn't keep her eyes on where she was walking when the scenery was this overly interesting.

Tiny one-room buildings, called cribs due to their size, lined Bonanza Street, the red-light district. It was a crowded place, people walking, sitting, laying on the ground in a drunken stupor. Women walked arm and arm with lonely gentlemen, some pairs were arguing with each other, other women appeared to be waiting together since the like-minded were the only company they could come by.

King Street was a haphazardly built street of patched-together wooden buildings, some taller than others, some with balconies, most built connected to the one next door. Signs of all types hung from the fronts, those of laundry, groceries, medicine shops, general store. It was its own community within a small town, not unlike thousands of others across the country.

Phoebe stopped walking for a moment and looked west on King Street. Few pictures remained of this area. She closed her eyes, listening, breathing in the smells and the feeling of the place. A light breeze ruffled her skirt. Shutting out the light allowed for mental illumination and animation of those who still wandered the street here as well as those she knew were behind closed doors gambling, smoking opium, drinking; and the families that were about to put their children to bed, kiss them goodnight and tell them tomorrow would be a better day.

When she opened her eyes again tears threatened but she quickly blinked them away.

"Miss Tucker?" Lionel asked gently, looking closely into her face.

"Yes, Lionel?"

He pursed his lips, considering his next words carefully. "They're gonna be all right, you know."

The earnest statement had caught her by surprise. At her quizzical expression he nodded at King Street and spread his hand to gesture all around him. "The folks here. They're all gonna be all right."

Not knowing any other way to answer this kind and confused man, Phoebe said, "Thank you, Lionel."

Subdued now, and satisfied she had somehow been allowed this chance in her life to see the streets of which she had long wondered, Phoebe walked east on King Street, toward Main Street and lifted her chin to the night air. Newton walked up beside her and put his coat around her shoulders. "You look cold," he said near her ear.

"Thank you."

"You're welcome."

"Is that the jail?" Will asked, pointing, amazed again, as he was every time he discovered something new here.

Phoebe nodded and Newton said, "It is." As they passed they could hear loud talking coming from within.

Silence followed a few loud thuds and Phoebe laughed aloud. "Apparently being jailed doesn't quell the need for a fight," she said.

The front door opened and a man stepped out. He eyed the assemblage but cordially tipped his hat, as did Phoebe's three companions in return. She nodded and smiled but in the next instant registered mental shock. *That face, I've seen that face before... That's it! Kirgan, John Franklin Kirgan, Constable and jail cook.* An excellent cook, or so she had read. *He's right there in front of me, in the flesh, for real, alive!*

Phoebe had to peel her eyes off of him and keep walking but found her breathing shallow and rapid. She glanced back at Constable Kirgan after they had walked on. He was not far behind them and was looking directly at her.

"Is there something the matter, Miss Tucker?"

"Call me Phoebe, would you? You know that's my name and I'm getting so tired of hearing Miss, Miss, Miss. It's so formal. And boring. You too, Lionel." Lionel nodded. Newton looked taken aback but nodded as well.

"Whatever you wish. But, is there something else the matter?"

Constable Kirgan had overtaken them now, walking quicker than they, intent on his destination. She looked at him as he walked on, noticed the fine cut of his suit, the smart hat he wore, the horseshoe mustache much like Newton's.

"No," said Phoebe quietly, her eyes still on the Constable. *Tall, about six feet, lean, handsome, moving with authority and confidence. Wow.*

At Main Street Phoebe looked left and right, seeing people peer from upstairs windows, hearing shouting from within saloons and people singing along to tinny piano music, witnessing others crossing the street and slipping in the mud. The smell of powder hung in the air, mixed with that of alcohol, cigar smoke and other smells that made Phoebe want to hold her hand over her nose.

Constable Kirgan was speaking with two other men outside the Wagner saloon, possibly in connection with the recent shooting incident they had heard from out back. When one of the men turned to walk their direction Phoebe had a feeling she had seen his face at some time as well. They began their walk south, toward home.

Phoebe held out her left arm knowing Newton was on her left side. He took the hint and looped his arm over the top of hers. "Newton, may I ask you a question?"

"Of course. Phoebe."

"Why are you here? In Bodie? There are clothing stores everywhere, safer towns than this. Why are you here?"

He did not answer right away and fingered his mustache with the first finger and thumb of his left hand. "I suppose I arrived lost as well," he said, glancing over at her.

This was the nearest she'd been to him and now looked into his eyes. They were indeed quite blue and his eyes crinkled at her again in the low light. "That's a very cryptic reply." She felt him shrug. "You didn't have any family to meet, or to greet you, or to stay with?"

He shook his head 'no.' "I did not."

"And here you remain. Why is that?" Her small smile urged him to continue. She was enjoying the small talk, but also enjoyed seeing him squirm under her questioning. Ever since arriving Phoebe she'd had the sensation of being under a microscope. Perhaps because she realized she did not belong, that she was an outsider, had funny-looking clothes, too-casual speech and mannerisms and that her head was filled with a great deal of information about the abandoned town's future.

"Why did you stay, after your, errand, was complete?" He raised one eyebrow.

"You're avoiding my question by asking one of your own. That tells me more than you think it does." Phoebe faced away from him.

"You're avoiding my question as well."

"I asked first," she said, aware of the irritation in her voice.

"You're forgetting I asked *you* first," he said.

She scowled, unlooped her arm from his and straightened her sleeve. Moving ahead of him a stride, she heard him grunt in frustration behind her.

They were passing the milliner where Phoebe had purchased her hat on their shopping excursion. She glanced at the store and noticed that the front door stood ajar and no lights shone from within. Having stopped suddenly, Lionel bumped her from behind and apologized for his clumsiness. She waved off his error and motioned for her companions to look inside.

"I don't see anyone. Why would the door be open if they aren't open for business?" she asked.

Newton reached for the doorknob and noticed that the wood was damaged near the lock. "It's been broken into," he said, sounding worried.

Phoebe inhaled sharply. "Mary," she exclaimed. She stepped back and looked up at the windows above, checking for any indication of disturbance.

"What? You know who lives here?" Newton asked.

"Yes, this is where I bought my hat. The girl, the young woman that helped me, her name is Mary Jacobson. She said she lives upstairs with her parents." She looked at Newton, worry on her face. "Do you think we should check on them?"

All present had similar thoughts. "Yes," said Newton, and the others nodded agreement. Newton opened the door and walked into the shop tentatively. Phoebe spied a lamp near the front entrance but motioned not to touch it. Lighting it might give warning to anyone lurking nearby. "But we can't see anything."

"I was here recently. I remember it well enough. This way." She led them through the store to the rear, through a curtain that separated the sales floor with inventory storage and a small office. It was very small in back, as most all stock was out front. To the side was a stairway leading up. They listened but heard no sounds from above. "What if we're the intruders?" Phoebe asked. "What if they're asleep?"

Will's eyes went wide at the thought. He was weary, Phoebe could see it in his face, in the slump of his shoulders. Her poor brother was not the adventure-seeking type. A late show put him to sleep. She could let no harm come to him.

As they contemplated what to do next a loud bang came from above their heads and they heard footsteps approaching the top of the stairway. As one they moved to the other side of the room and hid in the darkest of shadows. Phoebe put both hands on Will's arm in an attempt to calm him. She could hear his quick breaths and put a finger to her lips to quiet him.

Clunking footfalls landed on the steps, most likely drowning out any breathing sounds they might have been making. The person stumbled, caught themselves, continued, then fell onto their knees when they had misjudged how many steps remained at the bottom. A small amount of light coming through a rear window illuminated a portion of the stranger's face. Phoebe stifled her gasp and remained unheard.

Newton turned to her, making sure she kept quiet. She nodded, eyes wide with astonishment. Lionel so far had not moved a muscle.

Gaining his feet, the stranger moved through the curtain hurriedly, first looking behind him and up the stairs. No one was following. After the front door closed with a bang they waited several long moments before moving. Newton inched forward to peek through the curtain. No one was in the shop.

"What do we do now? What if he harmed Mary's family?" whispered Phoebe.

"I saw the sheriff outside not long ago. We can go and tell him. I do not believe we should venture upstairs," answered Newton, whispering as well. "They may not be home, they may be there and harmed, or maybe they will shoot us on sight."

"The sheriff? Sheriff Showers?" Phoebe asked. *That's it, that was the sheriff I saw walking south on Main. Sheriff James Showers. Van Dyke beard, the tops of his ears tipped out just a tad.*

"Yes, Sheriff Showers. He was speaking with Constable Kirgan outside Wagner's." Newton gave her a long, inquisitive look and she inwardly chastised herself for her big mouth.

"Let's go," said Lionel simply. "He needs to know something has happened here."

Cautiously they crept out the front door, closing it quietly behind them. They did not see the culprit who had escaped. But they did see the sheriff, two doors down and speaking with a man on the boardwalk. They walked toward him, Will looking around frantically, Lionel calmly strolling with large strides, Newton's eyes large and holding his hat in one hand and Phoebe frowning with determination, lifting her skirt with both hands to quicken her steps.

"Sheriff, Sheriff Showers, may we speak with you, please?" Newton began. They had met previously after Lionel had killed Joseph Hoffman.

The other man excused himself. "Mr. Sanford, Mr. Bradley, what's the trouble?"

They explained as well as they were able what had occurred, leaving nothing out.

"And you're sure it was Albert Griffin whom you saw exiting the shop?" asked the sheriff.

"Absolutely," said Phoebe. "Can you please check on the Jacobson family? Please."

The sheriff smiled at Phoebe and put a hand on her forearm. "Yes Ma'am, I will."

The group moved toward the milliner's store as one. Sheriff Showers waved across the street at someone and that man joined them at the front door to the store. He was introduced as Deputy Constable Patrick Phelan. "Please stay here," he instructed the group.

Sheriff Showers announced himself, knocked loudly once, twice, three times and stood back to look upstairs to see if anyone lit a lamp. He opened the still unlocked door and yelled into the store with the same information. Phoebe called out when, a moment later, she saw a light go on in an upstairs window.

The sheriff called out again, reassuring the occupant that he was indeed the sheriff and that he was attempting to render assistance if need be. Footsteps on the stairs, a gas lamp appearing at the separating curtain, someone coming forward, another person behind the first. Faces in the dim light, voices. Sheriff Showers spoke with the two occupants for several minutes while the others waited on tenterhooks on the boardwalk. What if Albert Griffin saw them now, talking to the Sheriff, outside the store? Would he know they had seen him?

The Sheriff opened the door and motioned for the two occupants to come meet those responsible for reporting an intruder. He introduced Mr. and Mrs. Jacobson, Mary's parents, and briefly explained the situation. Phoebe introduced herself as having met Mary recently and how she had been worried when the door was ajar. She asked if Mary was all right.

"Thankfully, she is staying at her friend's home this evening. After what she's been through lately, well, we thought it best. Apparently the timing could not have been better," explained Mr. Jacobson.

"What she's been through?"

"I will leave that to my daughter to explain," replied her father. "But I, we do thank you for rendering assistance this evening. We weren't sure what to do after that man broke into our home in search of Mary. I thought he may still be downstairs. Thank you, again, for fetching the sheriff." Mr. Jacobson nodded to Phoebe and her friends. Mrs. Jacobson put her hand over her heart and nodded at Phoebe.

Phoebe was tempted to remain on Main Street, knowing her time there might be short and wanting to retain everything her memory would allow. But it was late and it was dangerous and she felt guilty for putting Will in such an uncomfortable position.

At the corner of Green Street and Main they said their goodnights to Lionel Bradley, who said he would see Newton tomorrow. The other three continued walking to the boarding house.

"Where does Lionel live, anyway?" asked Phoebe.

"In a shack behind the blacksmith shop," said Newton with an air of unhappiness in his words.

"What? Is he all right there?" asked Phoebe, concerned.

"It is his choice. He is talented and makes a good living. I wouldn't presume to tell him what is best for him."\

"But you'll presume to tell me what is best for me?" Phoebe asked, too tired now to be truly annoyed.

At the boarding house Will said goodnight, exhausted, stating he would see Phoebe in the morning. He closed the front door quietly. Newton stepped closer to Phoebe. "Miss Tucker, Phoebe... I don't mean to interfere, I only wish to help." He put his first finger under her chin so she would look at him.

"There's no need to worry about me, I assure you."

He removed his finger and sighed.

Phoebe yawned. "I'm tired. Perhaps we can continue this conversation some other time."

He nodded. "Truce remember?" Phoebe turned to the door. He said from behind her, "If you would like to stop at my shop tomorrow, perhaps we can have lunch together."

She turned back to face him and nodded, rubbing her tired eyes. "That would be nice." Then, "Wait," she said, remembering something she had been going to ask him. "The other night, when Lionel stopped us on our way home from dinner he asked you to come by because he wanted to talk to you. Did you? Go see him, I mean?"

He took a moment to answer, mulling something over, and Phoebe wondered why. "Yes, I did."

After a moment she asked, "What did he want?" *Nosey, yes, but I want to know.*

Another pause. "We're friends, he missed my sparkling personality."

She handed him back his coat. Annoyed at his vague answers as much as she was at herself for the need to know, she said simply, "Okay. Goodnight, then. Newton." She handed him back his coat, walked through the door and left it open for him to follow.

Newton walked inside, whispered with melancholy in his tone, "Goodnight. Phoebe," and closed the door.

25

Phoebe lay awake that night, wondering what Newton and Lionel were up to and why it bothered her that he wouldn't tell her what it was. It had been a long and full evening. Trying to remember back to a part of the conversation at dinner was difficult. Lionel had mentioned hiding something in plain sight, somewhere no one would think to look. Newton had avoided her gaze at the exchange. What was he hiding from her, from them all. Something important, silly, insignificant? Could she trust him? Why did she want to?

The buzz from the whiskey had worn off on seeing Albert Griffin at the milliner's shop. What had he been up to going in to see Mary Jacobson at that hour? What had Mary 'been through' as her father had stated? So many questions that might never be answered if they were to leave soon. But would they ever get home?

She drifted off to sleep snuggled under the covers. Dreams came quickly, one of them similar to one she had had before leaving Dubuque for her two week vacation at her parent's home. The sound of horse hooves, gunshots, soggy shoes that won't dry, noise... She awoke with a start, breathing heavily, panicky, forgetful of her surroundings for a moment. It was still very dark outside; the middle of the night. She looked out the window and the world was still, at least for the time being. Walking to her door she opened it and listened at Will's door for any sound. Silence. He was probably sleeping like a baby.

Creaks sounded from above. She knew Newton and Chester were upstairs but did not know whose room was where. One of them was up and walking around. Egotistically Phoebe hoped it was Newton and that he was thinking about her. She got back under the covers with a whump and a pouting sigh. As she drifted off a sadness once again filled her heart. *Newton L. Sanford, Died June 19, 1880, Aged 29 yrs 3 mo. To Live in Hearts We Leave Behind is Not To Die.*

Phoebe woke with puffy eyes and a headache. *Not enough sleep.* She splashed cold water on her face, bending over and holding water over her eyes in hopes it would erase the puffiness. *No good,* she told herself on seeing her reflection in the mirror. Too lazy to put her hair up she did it in a simple braid down her back, tied with one of her ribbons. Then she dressed in her skirt and one of the blouses she had purchased. Hoping for a bit of luck she wore her necklace from J. W. on the outside again this morning. She could hold it and wish upon it often that way. *Lucky horseshoe, right?* Or curse him for his actions.

Will must have heard she was up. There was a knock on her door and "Phoebe," was whispered from the other side.

"Just a minute," she said impatiently and opened the door to see Newton Sanford standing there. "Oh, it's you. Good morning." Her voice croaked from thirst and lack of sleep. Leaving the door open she turned to hook her chatelaine bag to her waste. "Do you want something?"

"I brought you a peace offering." He pulled his other hand from behind his back and handed her a full cup of coffee.

"Ohhh," she said, taking the cup from him and sipping the coffee. "You really do want to be friends, don't you? Thank you." She stepped into the hall and with one hand closed her door and locked it, returning her key to her bag. "I'm sorry I was rude, I thought you were Will." Newton laughed and she realized how that had sounded.

"Your brother is in the kitchen, waiting for you, I believe. I offered to bring you your coffee."

"How very forward of you, Mr. Sanford," she said flatly, not truly offended.

He escorted her into the kitchen and said, "I found her, Will. Surly as usual."

"I have a headache, thank you very much," she said, setting down her cup and rubbing her temples.

"Can't handle your liquor?" teased Newton.

"I need more than three or four hours of sleep, if you must know. And I was so cold."

"I'm sorry," Newton said. He set a plate of bacon and eggs in front of her and pointed to the bowl of strawberries on the table.

"Thank you." She picked up a piece of bacon with her fingers and ate it.

"Very ladylike," said Will quietly.

Crap... oh well. She was tired and forgetting where she was. "What difference does it all make," she said grumpily.

Newton cleared his throat, feeling like he was interrupting. "I'm leaving now. I'll see you this evening for supper. Phoebe, will you still be joining me for lunch?"

Phoebe nodded and waved her hand in the air but turned to watch Newton as he walked out the door. "Where's Mrs. Barrett?" she asked.

"I don't know. She and Walter were both gone when I got up. You're having lunch with Newton?"

"What about Mr. Murphy? Is he still here? Is he okay this morning?"

"Haven't you turned into the doting roommate? What happened to 'don't get involved,' or 'let's just find out how to get home,' and all that stuff?"

Swallowing a few bites of eggs she hung her head in her hands and mumbled sadly, "Oh, Will, what have I done?"

"Um, I don't know. What *have* you done? Did I miss something?"

Shaking her head, she took another drink of her cooling coffee and stared into it, thinking of Newton. "At first I thought this was just all an illusion, real but like the backdrop of a play. Where we could float around inside it, observing, listening, but remaining aloof and unnoticed. I was worried we wouldn't get home. But then you told me to take advantage of this time here, to recognize this extremely rare opportunity. So I did just that." She groaned and rubbed at her eyes.

"I thought, maybe if I talk to a few of the people I will really get a feel for what it's like here, to have lived here, to be a part of this." She rested her head on her arms at the table. Will waited for her to finish. She raised her head and continued. "The next moment I'm wondering why I would go to all that trouble when I gave up caring about the past and its mysteries a long, long time ago."

"Did you? Give up caring? Because I think that's why you feel guilty for running away."

"Don't be smug."

"So why are you so... whatever this is?" He moved his hands up and down, pointing at her.

She took another bite of eggs and stuffed a whole piece of bacon in her mouth. Holding her hands palm up she said, "Dunno." Then after several more bites she said, "I'm so confused."

Phoebe looked up to see Will sitting back in his chair, his arms folded across his chest and a grin on his face. She scowled at him and stood to fill her cup again. "Go ahead, spit it out," she said, sitting back down and suspecting he had something to share.

"It's just nice to see you're human after all."

Phoebe muttered unhappily, "Oh, shut up."

"I did have a little talk with Chester Murphy this morning. He was up early and didn't hang around long."

"How is he?"

"He's got a bump on his head and a bruise on one knee. Otherwise he's feeling foolish for letting his guard down. I should have told him to take you with the next time he goes gambling," he teased.

"Ha Ha. What did you talk about?"

"Since it was just the two of us I asked him about something he'd said. I asked why he was saving his money, and why did he feel the need to gamble to get more quickly."

"You devil. And you're always telling me to mind my own business. What did he say?"

Will leaned forward and spoke quietly. "He said he's sweet on a girl and he wants to ask her to marry him." Phoebe's eyes grew large. Will nodded and continued. "Yep, but I asked him if she wouldn't prefer he earn it the old fashioned way? I mean, he has a good job, at the Mono City Bank, he told me. And maybe it would keep him out of trouble."

"Look who's becoming a considerate roommate now," she teased. "What did he say to that?"

"I believe he will take it into consideration," he enunciated carefully, mocking Phoebe's Victorian etiquette. "He is sorry he acted rashly. I think he'll be fine." Phoebe cleared her dishes, feeling a bit better after having eaten and put some caffeine into her system. "So, lunch with Newton? You must have had a nice conversation after I went to bed last night."

"Hardly. Will, how do I get rid of him? It makes me sad to think that in a few days he'll – he'll be, well you know what."

"Ha, get rid of him? As if you're trying." Will laughed then. "Phoebe, you are one of the smartest people I know. But right now you are blind and stupid."

"What the he – "

"Don't get mad at me for telling the truth. Look, Newton is a great guy. I'm trying not to think about what happens to him. But didn't you say what's done is done, and that whatever happens, happens? You read that stone in the cemetery the same as I did. It's there, it's over. You tried to brush him off, to keep from getting, I don't know, attached. But he's in this house, we can't help but run into him. You are the one voluntarily spending time with him. Now, you need to ask yourself why and to what end it's going to come. You already know the answer. To no good, that's what. We could move out, find another place to stay. That would affect Mrs. Barrett and Walter as well."

"She is already short of boarders."

"There, right there. Instead of thinking about getting home you're thinking more about Mrs. Barrett and her son. And Newton."

"No, I'm not. I'm just starting to realize they are real people. They aren't just pictures in a book. They aren't just old, scary black and white photos staring blankly back. They aren't nothings, with no meaning, no background, no stories to tell their ancestors." She held her head, which was beginning to ache again.

"They're real, living breathing people, who were born into this world the same as you and I, with parents and grandparents who love them. If they're lucky they'll have children who will pass on their stories." She paused, fiddling with her fork, thinking, remembering. She said quietly, "'The life of the dead is placed in the memory of the living.' Marcus Tullius Cicero."

Will was smiling from ear to ear now, and he waited for Phoebe to notice. "Why are you smiling?" she asked suspiciously, subdued after her prior intensity.

Will stabbed a finger at Phoebe and said firmly, "It's nice to have you back! Business major my a – "

"Good morning, you two. I'm sorry I didn't leave you a note. I'm glad you helped yourself to breakfast," said Lena Barrett as she walked into the kitchen from the parlor, startling brother and sister. "I'm sorry, am I interrupting?"

Neither spoke immediately, waiting for the other. Then, "No, you're not interrupting. You surprised us," said Will. Phoebe was still dazed by the words that had spilled out of her mouth, out of her brain.

“Will you please excuse me,” she said and left to go outside.

“Is she feeling well?” asked Lena Barrett.

“She didn’t sleep well. And she has a headache because of it. She’ll be fine.”

Lena Barrett began boiling some water to wash the dishes and said lightheartedly, “Spoken like a brother,” and smiled at Will.

“Is there anything I can do to help you?”

“Unless you have other plans would you mind keeping Walter out of trouble for the time being? That boy...”

“Yes, Ma’am, I will,” he said, glad to have a task.

Phoebe had just left the outhouse and saw Walter inside the barn enclosure. She leaned on the fence. “Good morning. Whatcha doin’?”

“Good morning, Miss Tucker. Nothin’,” he said, closing the barn door. “I was just puttin’ some stuff away for my mama. “I miss the horse.”

“You like horses?”

“Not really, they kick if they don’t like you.”

“So you miss being in charge of a horse,” Phoebe surmised, grinning at the boy.

He shrugged. “I dunno. If we lived in the country we could have other animals. There’s no room here.”

“So you like other animals then?”

“Not really, they bite and spit. But I like eggs so I guess I like chickens.”

Phoebe laughed at Walter. “I like you, Walter.”

“Why?”

“Because you’re honest; you tell the truth. That’s a good trait to have. Always tell the truth.”

Walter walked toward Phoebe and climbed the fence to sit on the top rail near her. “I know somethin’, Miss Tucker.”

“You do? Is it a secret you should keep or one you should tell?”

“What’s the difference?”

“A secret to keep is when someone asks you please not

to tell, and it's very important to them, and it won't hurt anyone not to. Like when you buy a gift for your mother and you don't want anyone to tell her what it is so it can be a wonderful surprise. The other kind is if you know something that could hurt someone or it's against the law. Then you should tell. Understand?" Walter nodded and jumped down from the fence and opened the gate. "Where are you going? Aren't you going to tell me your somethin'?"

He smiled up at her. "Nope. It ain't gonna hurt nobody," and he walked through the gate toward the back door.

Exasperated, Phoebe walked back inside, where Will was taking Walter into the parlor to read. Lena Barrett eyed Phoebe but noticed her disposition had changed after going outside. "Is everything all right?" she asked politely.

"It is now, yes, thank you. Walter has a way of cheering me up."

"He has that ability, does he not? There is a little coffee left. Would you like me to heat it up for you?"

"I would love that, thank you." *She even knows how much I like my morning coffee.*

While she worked Lena Barrett asked Phoebe about the previous evening, what they had done, if anything interesting had occurred. Feeling sheepish but wanting to be completely honest, Phoebe said, "It turned out about how I expected. There were gunshots, people running, fighting somewhere, you know."

Lena sat down at the table across from Phoebe. *Is she going to lecture me too?* thought Phoebe. "I have to confess, I spoke with Mr. Sanford for a few minutes this morning on my way out. He did not reveal much but he did say it was necessary to hail the Sheriff because the milliner's shop was broken into. By Albert Griffin, no less."

"Yes, that is true. Did he also tell you that I insisted we go into Wagner's where I played Faro, won a few dollars, made them all drink whiskey, and almost got into a fight with a gambler?"

Lena Barrett's eyes bulged and she roared with laughter while holding her stomach. A moment later Walter bounced into the room wondering what had happened. Will was behind him and leaned against the door jamb grinning. After assuring her son that everything was as it should be and telling him to continue reading, she smiled at Will and sent them back to the parlor. "Miss Tucker, you are an entertaining individual."

"Entertaining. Newton, Mr. Sanford said I was an intractable outlaw," she said with a smirk.

"Did he now? I believe Mr. Sanford finds you somewhat more than that," she said with mirth. Phoebe's brow creased. "Don't frown about it. He's a very nice man."

Phoebe heard Will and Walter laughing from the parlor. "What are they reading?" She was glad to change the subject.

"I'm not sure. I have a few books in our room." They stood to go into the parlor to see what was so comical. "You are getting your reading done, aren't you Walter," she asked with a smile.

"Yes, Mama. But Mr. Tucker told me I said a word wrong. It was funny."

"What are you reading? Which book did you choose? She sat down in one of the chairs.

Will turned the cover over. "Poems by Thomas Campbell," he said. "It's difficult for him, but we're doing all right," Will smiled at the boy.

"Read something for me, Walter," his mother said.

***

Newton Sanford assisted his third customer of the day and forgot for the third time that morning to offer to wrap up the purchases. His fellow clerk pulled him aside and asked if he was feeling well that morning. "I saw you last night, on Main Street," the man winked. "She's very pretty."

"Yes, well, I – I – "

"You are not often flummoxed, Newton. Who was the young lady, if I might ask?"

"She and her brother are passing through. I met her at Mrs. Barrett's boarding house."

"Is that right?" Newton was now using a feather duster to clean a shelf to avoid eye contact. The man leaned on the adjoining shelf on one elbow. "So you can see her at any time."

"Don't be crude."

The man slapped Newton on the shoulder and laughed good-naturedly. "I was teasing. I meant no offense." He walked to the other side of the shop to busy himself with a chore.

"I know," said Newton. Then, plopping in a chair, he sighed and said, "She's rude, irritable, stubborn, irascible, impulsive, foolhardy..." He shook his head dejectedly.

"Sounds like love, my friend," the man said, leaving his point there.

Newton let the feather duster slip from his grasp, leaned back in the chair resignedly and exhaled slowly. "Yes. It does."

26

Phoebe was dreading the lunch hour approaching. She had told Lena Barrett of her plans, of which she highly approved, and had asked what time she thought she should meet Newton. One o'clock. Should she take anything? No, there were places to eat nearby. She apologized to Will for leaving him alone with not much to do, but he did not seem to mind. He was going to do some looking around for himself. *Stay out of the saloons, Will. Don't worry, Phoebe, I asked Walter to show me the school.*

Time to go. Phoebe plopped her hat on her head and, realizing she still had her hair in a braid, decided not to change it. She wasn't very good at getting the twist to stay put without it sliding to the side anyway. Assured her Army jacket was still under the mattress where she kept it, she locked her bedroom door, stowed the key in her bag and walked out the front door.

Bang, Bang, Bang went the stamp mills, rattling wagon wheels rolled along, yelling between the men working the mines on the hills echoed down to her, the noisy sawmill a few blocks away churned out boards for building and repair, hammer-hammer-hammer. She picked up her skirt to keep it clear of the mud and dirt. Washing clothes was not easy, and sending it to a Chinese laundry service cost money.

More than she cared to spend, even after having won at the Faro table. Who knew how much longer they would have need of it? Some extra cash wouldn't hurt.

Spending money on the Colt had perhaps been a brag, almost a dare, to show Newton that she could take care of herself; she could do so without the gun. Regardless, when she thought about Albert Griffin breaking into Mary's parent's shop she was glad to have it. It was in her bag now. Heavy, but worth it.

She waved at the friendly neighbor across from them on her way down the street, as she had done before. Lowe Street connected with Fuller so she walked that way, as they'd done on their way to the market, bypassing the bustling Green Street.

There were a few people out this way, painting a house after a long winter closed in, straightening messy wind-blown yards, repairing fences, minding children. A little girl of about five waved at her and Phoebe sent her a genuine smile. What appeared to be an older sister of ten or twelve waved as well and Phoebe said "Hello," as she passed. Just like home.

No, not at all like home. In Dubuque she had no friends, drove to work, drove home, made trips to the grocery store, the bank, the library. She didn't wave at children, she didn't say hello to her neighbors. She stayed behind closed doors more than they did. But it was mostly because she hadn't had anything to be joyous about in a long time. She had become an intentionally standoffish hermit. When she'd left Carson City, friendly-hometown-Carson-City, she had left her joy behind.

Her step had begun to lag, daydreaming had taken over her brain. Snapping back to reality made her jerk her head around, aware that daydreaming here could put you in trouble. Especially when you had won at the Faro table the night before and you never knew who was watching you.

She turned on Fuller Street and approached Reinstein & Wolf. Newton was standing outside, looking up and down the street. He smiled when he saw her nearing the building and held the door of the store open for her to enter. "Good afternoon, Phoebe."

"Hello. Newton." She walked through the door. "Aren't you ready to go?" she asked, wondering why they were inside the store.

"I would like you to meet someone first," he said, holding out his hand, signaling his friend to come forward. "Miss Tucker, this is my friend and coworker, Robert Jensen. Robert, this is Miss Tucker. We are going to lunch."

Phoebe forgot to give a ladylike handshake and it was too late to unsqueeze the man's hand. *Oh well.* "It's a pleasure to meet you, Mr. Jensen."

"Likewise. Newton, take your time. I'll be fine here."

They took their leave, but Phoebe noticed Newton turn to look back at Robert Jensen before they walked out the door. *Must've been talking about me before I arrived.*

"So, where are we going?" Phoebe asked, feeling a tad self-conscious now that it was just the two of them.

Newton held out his arm and waited for her to take it. She sighed and looped her forearm under his. They walked slowly and Newton answered, "The Cosmopolitan Hotel has a fine chop stand. And, they're open all night if you feel the overpowering desire for steak and potatoes at three a.m. And I'm sure they have whiskey, who doesn't?" he inserted.

A buzz of delight spread through her and she smothered a smiled. Her first instinct had been to snap at his sarcasm, but she held back and replied serenely, "I should have purchased a bottle last night so I could keep it in my bag with my Colt."

He leaned forward to look at her facial expression, checking to see if she was joking. What he saw there made his mustache twitch and his eyes crinkle at the edges. "You should have."

Neither looked at each other as they walked. Phoebe had butterflies in her belly for the first time in her life. Newton stood taller, hoping all they met saw that he was escorting the lovely Phoebe Tucker.

The restaurant was crowded but there was room for them at a small round table near the middle. Phoebe ordered a small fillet and a baked potato. Newton had the same but a larger steak. "Tea?"

Newton chuckled. "Yes, please. How's your headache?"

"Better, thanks for asking."

They chatted of minor things, nothing of substance. The new brick building up the street, the fund raising of the proposed church to be built. Phoebe was hoping the mood stayed this way. She was finding it increasingly difficult to look him in the eye. She could feel her short temper coming back, rising from her toes, afraid it would pop out of her mouth at any moment. *Why? Newton L. Sanford, Died June 19, 1880, Aged 29 yrs 3 mo. To Live in Hearts We Leave Behind is Not To Die. That's why! Three days, only three days. I can't do this.*

She glanced up at him, having lost track of what he had been saying. She shook her head and said, "I'm sorry, what did you say?"

He looked at her closely. "I – I think your hair looks lovely like – like that," he stammered, rearranging his silverware.

"Oh. Um, thank you." *The lamps here are huge,* she thought, staring at the ceiling, a poor avoidance.

The Cosmopolitan Hotel and Chop House was on South Main Street, not far from the blacksmith shop where Lionel Bradley worked. Phoebe mentioned walking past it before Newton returned to work, if he could spare the time. "I would like to say hello."

Newton seemed skeptical of her reasons but indulged her request. When they approached the blacksmith shop they did not immediately see Lionel Bradley. After a moment he walked around from behind the shop, appearing to have come from a small building in the rear. He saw the two of them standing on the side of the street, brightened and waved. He stopped to pick up a rag on his way to speak to them to wipe his hands. He shook Newton's hand and nodded to Phoebe.

"Good afternoon, Lionel. How are you today?" Phoebe asked.

"I'm doing well, thank you Ma'am."

"We've just come from the Cosmopolitan. Phoebe wanted to say hello on her way home," said Newton.

"I can speak for myself," she said, regretting her tone. Looking at Lionel she asked, "What are you working on today?"

Newton suspected an ulterior motive for this visit. And for the specific questions. She was hunting; looking for information as to what Lionel had hinted at at supper. He tried to send Lionel a warning glance but with Lionel you could never tell if he understood the hint.

"Oh, the usual. I've got four horses for the stage to shoe, they'll be here soon. And a wagon brake that needs fixin'."

"Is that all? What about the thing you and Newton are doing together?" Phoebe asked.

Newton exclaimed, "Miss Tucker. Are you butting into my business? Isn't that unfair to Lionel?"

"Do you have something to hide? But you're right. I apologize, Lionel. I shouldn't expect you to reveal a confidence. Good luck with your tasks. I'll see you another time."

Newton suggested walking to the intersection where they would part ways, but Phoebe insisted on walking with him back to Reinstein & Wolf. They strolled in silence; Phoebe didn't take Newton's arm and he didn't offer it to her. "I'm sorry. Truly," she muttered when they approached the door. "That was rude of me."

"I'm sorry you don't trust me. You can, you know."

"Then what's going on between you and Lionel? You won't tell me, will you?"

"Why do you have to know?"

Unexpectedly, she smiled at him. "I don't suppose I do, do I? Unless you're planning on robbing the stage, or the bank, or a milliner's shop. Don't forget, I know the sheriff now."

"Miss Tucker, I did not have anything to do with – "

"You really need to recognize when I'm teasing." She said, regretting her previous questions and associated demeanor.

He grinned at her; his hands flinched, wanting to reach out to her but he stopped himself. They parted ways awkwardly, unspoken sentiment hovering between them.

She walked north toward Green Street on her return. When she'd walked a dozen yards Newton called, "Didn't you come from the other way?"

"I did," she called back.

"Where are you going?"

"Don't butt into my business either, Newton," she answered spiritedly, turning around and briskly walking away.

***

Two-thirty in the afternoon and John Young was just waking up. The knocking on his door had been going on for who knew how long. He thought at first he had been dreaming, and he couldn't take it anymore. He stood up and yanked his door open, ready to shout at the knocker, when the man burst into the room, shoving John Young aside. "Where have you been?" Albert Griffin shouted.

He pointed to the bed; *where else?*

"Where were you last night? I was looking for you."

John Young swung the door shut with a bang, rubbed his head, scratched his face and yawned. "I don't remember. I'm hungry." He splashed his face with water and started to get dressed. "First stop, food, next stop, the barber" He surveyed his appearance in the mirror.

"I believe it's time to move on from this town, John." Albert Griffin paced the small room. The more calm John Young displayed, the more frustrated Albert Griffin became.

After snapping his suspenders in place, John Young sat on the bed to pull on his boots. "What have you done now, Albert?" He stretched his arms over his head then scratched his grumbling belly. Albert stopped pacing and walked to the window to peer out. "Don't tell me you're imagining things too. Come with me, I'm hungry."

Albert pushed John back down onto the bed. "No. Not. Yet. Where were you? I met you at the Can Can, you weren't there. Where's your money? Gambled away? Spent on Bonanza? On Bodie Lightning?" If you want more, you're on your own."

John held up both hands and looked up at Albert. "Whoa, whoa, no, I didn't spend it all. Or lose it all. I went to see that pretty girl, that redhead," he grinned, remembering, "then I met some fellas in Chinatown and – "

"Chinatown? Damn it, John, that stuff'll kill you. And they'll rob you blind."

"I didn't spend my money on opium, Al. I heard a rumor that Kirgan was running raids last night and I wouldn't get caught and thrown into jail again." He rubbed his eyes, tired, hungry and irritated from the questioning. "I found a poker game. Sorry I forgot to meet you. I had a lot to drink yesterday." He scratched the sides of his face. "I really need to see the barber, Al."

"You still have your money? Good, good. Lay low, John. I mean it."

John Young stood to put on his coat. "Like I asked, what did you do?" He poured a glass of water from the pitcher and swished it around in his mouth.

Albert had his hand on the doorknob, but before opening the door he said, "I tried to pay a visit to a lady friend of mine."

"Tried?"

"She wasn't at home, if you must know."

John Young laughed at his friend's expense. "Why didn't you find another? I'm sure my redhead has a friend."

"I don't want one of *your* girls, John. I want *this* girl."

"So where was she?"

"I don't know. They wouldn't tell me."

"Who – "

"Never mind. I don't want to talk about it now. Let's go. Where's your money?"

John young patted his vest pockets and looked Albert Griffin in the eye, daring him to question him again. Albert nodded and they walked out to get John a shave and his three-thirty-in-the-afternoon-breakfast.

***

Before walking home, Phoebe headed north, crossed Green Street, and strolled through a residential area that remained from her time. There were a few more homes here, on either side, but it was strange to see them new, painted white, with new curtains on the windows and neat picket fences.

A couple of small children played on the side of one home and they were unaware of her as she passed. She was closer to the sawmill here. Smelling fresh-cut lumber reminded her just how new some of these structures were.

Up ahead was the right turn onto Union Street. Some called it Union Alley. It wasn't a long street, mainly a cut-through to Main Street. It was uneven and a bit rocky but homes were on either side here as well. The ground was slightly higher and she could get a better look across the lower roofs of Chinatown to the north.

She heard someone shout out, calling her name. Turning this way and that, and with the breeze in her ears, she couldn't tell from which direction the sound was coming. Hearing "Miss Tucker," once more she saw her. A girl was waving at her from behind, approaching now, smiling and waving again as Phoebe waited for her.

"Miss Jacobson, hello," Phoebe was surprised to see the young woman here, but perhaps the home where she had spent the night was nearby.

Slightly out of breath, Mary Jacobson smiled and said, "Please, call me Mary. What are you doing here?"

"You must call me Phoebe. And I could ask you the same question," they both laughed. Actually I was just coming from lunch with a – with – with someone I know. I'm taking the long way home."

"I see. My friend Loretta lives just over there," she gestured over her shoulder. Her parents invited me for dinner last night and I stayed the night. If you don't mind, I'll walk with you."

"Sure," said Phoebe. *Should I tell her about last night, about Albert Griffin's break-in or leave that to her parents?* If she already knew about the incident she gave no indication.

Mary chatted on about her friend Loretta, their dinner the previous evening, the books her friend read... *She's talking a mile a minute because she's distressed.* Mary had been quiet only a moment when Phoebe noticed a tension about her. She stopped and turned to her, asking, "Mary, is everything okay? I mean, you seem upset about something. You can tell me."

Mary gave a nervous giggle, her eyes searching the area. Phoebe urged her friend to keep talking. "Oh, Phoebe. Yes, yes, I am bothered. There are times when I'm alone in the shop, not often, but there is a man who watches me. He comes in to talk, and he won't leave when I pretend to be busy. He intimidates my mother. My father once chased him away. Thank you for walking with me."

Albert Griffin, I have no doubt. Phoebe realized they had walked nearly back to the milliner's when she had intended to go only as far as Main Street, turn south and return home. "I am sorry, Mary. I understand now. You need to talk to your parents."

Up ahead and on the same side of the street was the Mono City Bank, the bank that employed Chester Murphy. As it happened, Phoebe glanced up the street and saw Mr. Murphy exiting the bank.

At her side, Mary slowed her pace. Phoebe saw that she was looking straight ahead, seemingly at Chester Murphy. Chester had quickened his pace considerably and didn't take his eyes off Mary. Grinning, Phoebe remembered what Will had said. 'He said he's sweet on a girl and he wants to ask her to marry him.' *Perhaps this is one puzzle solved.*

When he approached, the trio spoke at once and laughed at the awkwardness of it. "Good afternoon, Mr. Murphy," said Phoebe a second time.

He nodded. "Good afternoon, Miss Tucker." Turning to Mary he took her hand in his and said, "I see you know this beautiful lady?"

Mary blushed adorably, mumbled an embarrassed reply, and asked Phoebe. "How is it you are acquainted?"

"My brother and I happen to be renting rooms in the same boarding house as Mr. Murphy."

"Isn't that a coincidence," exclaimed Mary, looking from one to the other of them. Perhaps we can do something together sometime. Oh, I know," the cheerful young lady nearly bounced with the idea, "Friday is the fundraiser dance at the Union Hall. Chester and I are going. Perhaps you can come as well."

"As a matter of fact, I will be there."

"You will? Oh, how fun." She gripped Chester's hand with both of hers, excited. "Are you arriving with someone? Your brother?"

And I'm hesitating to answer because...? She nodded. "Newton Sanford asked me to accompany him," she said sheepishly.

Chester smiled and said, "I'm glad. I like Newton."

Mary's brow crinkled in thought. "I don't believe we've met. You'll introduce us, won't you?"

"Of course I will."

At that moment the door to the milliner's shop opened just ahead of them and a man stepped out; Mary Jacobson's father. He was waiting to be noticed. Phoebe pointed to him and nudged Mary on the arm. "Phoebe, won't you come to the shop for just a minute? I'd like you to meet my father."

Well, see, I kind-of already met him. "That would be lovely, but I do need to explain something to you." Mary walked arm in arm with Chester, and Phoebe stated quickly,

"I met him briefly last night. I was downtown here, with my brother, and others, and I noticed your front door was not closed up tight. We hailed the sheriff to report it."

They reached the shop. "I see. I hadn't heard." Worry was visible in her expression now as she greeted her father.

"It's a pleasure to see you again, Miss Tucker. And under better circumstances, too." Mr. Jacobson smiled, greeted Chester and invited them all to come into the shop. "Can you spare a few minutes, Chester?"

Mrs. Jacobson was assisting a customer near the mirror. Mary's father took the opportunity to recount the events of last evening, again thanking Phoebe for her assistance and concern. Mary gave Phoebe a quick hug, taking her by surprise. "How frightening." *Yes, but only a little, you've never driven through Chicago during rush hour.* "I'm so happy you're unharmed." *Yeah, me too.* "Thank goodness your brother was with you," *sure, he was a great help,* "and two other gentlemen to keep you out of harm's way." *Are you kidding me? I'm the one who dragged us down here.*

Phoebe replied politely, reassuring Mary she was no worse for the wear. She stated she should be going.

"Miss Tucker," Chester hailed her as she reached the door. "Would you kindly pass on a message to Mrs Barrett for me?" Phoebe agreed. "Would you please tell her that I will not be home for supper this evening." At Phoebe's scowl he held up a hand to reassure her, "No, no, I won't be at the tables tonight. I have been invited to join the Jacobson's for supper here this evening." He grinned. "I supposed you've found out my secret."

"Secret?" she asked.

He glanced back at Mary, his cheeks turning red. "About why I've been trying to *earn* a little extra money. "It's Mary and me, I – we – I'm – "

Some secret. You told my brother and I have a feeling this information is the 'something' that Walter was hinting at. "Shh, she'll hear you. I understand, Mr. Murphy. Don't worry, your secret's safe with me." She opened the door to leave.

"Will you manage getting home on your own?" Mr. Jacobson called to her.

"I will manage fine, thank you. Mary, I'll see you on Friday."

Mary smiled and nodded and walked to her mother to give her a hug.

Well, crap, thought Phoebe. *Mary thinks I'm her new friend, Chester vested a secret in me, and I've got a 'date' for a dance. This was not supposed to happen. I just want to find a way to go home and I'm beginning to wonder if I'm ever going to get back there again.* She walked down Main Street, oblivious to the people she was nearly running into and the looks she was receiving from those around her wondering why such a lovely girl was walking with unmistakable purpose and a furious furrow to her brow.

27

Phoebe didn't walk through the front door when she arrived back at the boarding house. Instead, she went around back, opened the gate, opened the barn and walked in. She closed the door to the barn nearly all the way, leaving a little space for extra light to seep through. She peeked out each of the side windows to ensure she was alone.

A barn looks lonely without a horse, without bales of hay in overhead storage, without saddles and bridles hanging on the walls. If she ever got back home perhaps she could convince her grandfather to purchase a horse or two to ride like she used to. Then she remembered... *I live in Iowa now,* and for an instant her mood deflated.

Holding her breath in expectation, she waked to the rear corner where she and Will had re-hung the metal wagon wheel rim on the nail on the wall. Curiosity told her to check to see if it was still there. *Where else would it be? Who would want it for anything?* She reached the darkened corner, saw the nail on the wall above her head and felt her throat constrict with panic. The gold-flecked rim was gone.

She put her palms on the wall, moving them around, searching in case it was too dark and she had missed it. Nope. She then dropped to the floor and searched beneath the straw that still lay scattered about. She stood and walked the perimeter of the barn, going into the stalls, looking high and low. A narrow ladder hung from the extreme end of the loft above. Climbing this carefully, minding each step, she crawled out onto the loft and saw nothing at all on the floor or hanging on the walls at the top.

Panic welled within her. They had used the rim to get here, J. W. had known something about its use. She and Will were still trying to figure out how to use it to return home and now it had disappeared. They had been no closer to solving the mystery with it, so how were they supposed to figure out a way without it?

Phoebe slowed her breathing, remembering what her grandfather and father had taught her about keeping her head in an emergency. Besides, she wasn't going to let J. W. down. He thought she could handle this convoluted mystery and she wasn't planning on disappointing him. One last, deep breath and a slow exhale and she was ready to climb down the ladder, close the barn door and find Will to let him know. Or maybe keep it to herself for now. No sense causing him to panic once again. He was finally beginning to relax.

She exited the enclosure through the gate nearer the kitchen and found she needed to unlock the door with her key. Calling out, she found the house deserted. There was some writing paper and a pencil on the table in the parlor so she wrote a quick note to tell anyone who might read it that she was in her room, taking a nap, so please do not disturb her.

Then she boiled some water to pour into her washtub in her room for a mini bath before supper. She carried a couple of buckets of cold water in first and poured in the boiling water last. Locking the door securely she undressed, retrieved her soap and a towel and stepped into the small tub.

Water was one dollar per barrel, delivered. The barrels were large and it was included in her rent, but she was not about to take advantage of Lena Barrett's hospitality; she hadn't used much. Besides, what she poured into the tub, she would have to carry outside to dump out. She could always tell Will to do it for her, she thought with a grin. The amount didn't matter right now. Dripping the warm water over her shoulders, neck and arms felt like heaven.

While relaxing, her mind wandered. It was nice to be alone, even for a short time, to think about nothing. That didn't last long, however, when Newton's face popped into her head and she shook it to try to get it out. *Only three days.* Deciding to direct her thoughts to where she and Will could go or look next to find clues or hints as to J. W.'s intentions was a better use of her time.

Not having a clock in her room she could only guess at the time as the water had cooled and it was time to rinse and get out. Her small reserve of clean water was in a pitcher from her washstand and she poured it over her hair after having washed it with her soap and a bit of lemon juice from the kitchen. She toweled as much water as she could from her hair and hung the towel over a coat hanger in her wardrobe.

A door closed somewhere. Walter's voice was speaking to someone and footsteps were walking across the kitchen and in the hall. Phoebe leaned her ear close to her door to distinguish who was home, but Walter's voice was the only one she could make out. Staying quiet so no one would yet disturb her, she brushed her hair with the pretty brush from the Jacobson's store, missing her blow-dryer. Next, she braided it and left the braid hanging down her back to dry.

Opening her chatelaine bag, she quietly dumped the contents on her bed to take inventory. She liked to know where she stood. Pocket knife from Tony, check. Extra cartridges from her grandfather, check. Four gold, double eagles from J. W., check. Cash, check. Winnings from Faro, smile, check. Colt pistol, check. *What an idiot,* she thought. She had purchased the pistol but had not taken time in the hardware store to load it with her extra cartridges. If she'd needed it before now...

Aware there was no safety on the Colt she loaded five rounds only. Just in case. This was full, for the safety minded, as keeping the chamber nearest the hammer empty was wise when the pistol was in your possession. Hopefully she wouldn't need it, but if she did, a certain amount of comfort came from its presence.

Now reminded of her bag's contents and satisfied of its arrangement, she stood to check her appearance. Not having many clothes she dressed in the same blouse and skirt from earlier, vowing to wash the others she had worn the following day. Unlocking her door she saw Will's door open and peeked inside. He was stretching out on his bed and she knocked on the edge of the door. "Sorry to disturb you."

He sat up. "No, I wasn't sleeping, just resting. Walter had me outside all afternoon. I'm pooped. Where have you been?"

She explained about lunch with Newton, taking the scenic route home, running into Mary and Chester and speaking with Mr. Jacobson again. "You may have gotten through to Chester. He seemed embarrassed to say he was gambling for extra money. And hopefully the konk on the head helped some too."

Phoebe neglected to tell her brother that she had wheedled Newton into a visit to Lionel for her own selfish reasons. She also conveniently left out the fact that the wagon wheel rim was no longer in the barn. *Later.*

"I was going to ask you if you wanted to go for a short walk, but it you're too tired..."

"Not tired. Just," he paused, searching for the word, "weary."

"Getting lazy in this leisurely life?" she teased.

He sat up on the edge of his bed. "Leisurely? Ha. Thrust through time, people speaking phrases I don't understand, afraid of being shot at or run over by an errant carriage, looking over my shoulder for someone to bash me over the head next time I get in their way; and apparently it's legal to stab someone with a fork in a restaurant."

"Oh, calm down." She sat on the bed beside him. "Any new ideas in that weary brain of yours on what we're supposed to know, or figure out, or find while we're here?"

Will shook his head 'no,' and they sat in silence for a minute. Then he said, "Maybe it wasn't about finding something or solving a puzzle or anything like that. Maybe it was J. W.'s way of giving us a few days to experience life here. He lived here, at some point, right? Sometimes it's difficult for people to explain how a place or situation made them feel, deep down. Maybe sending us here was a way of allowing us to see it, hear it, feel what Bodie was truly like. Maybe all we have to do is stand in the metal rim again, now that we've had a few days to appreciate the place, and we can go back home."

"Not bad, little brother. You've been using that brain I knew you were born with after all." *Please don't suggest we go out to the barn right now; the rim is gone, I don't know where, and I don't want you to freak out about it.*

"Want to go try it?"

"Now?"

"Sure."

"But, if it works we would suddenly be missing. Don't you think everyone here," she gestured toward the rest of the house, "would wonder where we suddenly disappeared to? They might even call, um, notify the sheriff, thinking something wicked had happened to us, or report us as missing persons."

"Not if none of this is real."

"What?" she asked, surprised he had put this much thought into their situation.

"What if everything is just some sort of, I don't know, a delusion, a dream? What if this is just happening in our imaginations. Maybe we've both been konked in the head." Phoebe punched Will in the arm. Again. "Ouch, hey..."

"Remember when I did that the first time to see if this was real? Still think you're dreaming?"

"I don't know, maybe. I've got a good imagination."

"Don't be stupid."

"You know, you sound like you don't want to go home. I think you like it here more than you're willing to admit."

"Don't be stupid," she said, standing up and closing his door, something she realized she should have done before now, considering their risk of being overheard.

"You said that."

Phoebe began pacing the small space. "But what if it is real? If we leave, right now, without saying anything, and all of our stuff remains here, then..." She stopped walking and turned to face him. "Wouldn't they write it in the paper? Or gossip about two boarders gone missing? I don't want to become some old legend."

"I know what this is," Will said, standing to face her. "You're going to the dance Friday night and you don't want to stand up your date."

Phoebe frowned. "Don't you agree that would be rude as well?"

"Yes, I guess it would be." He scratched his neck where the collar of his shirt rubbed, then picked up his coat to put back on.

There was a quiet knock on the door. Brother and sister looked at each other, similar thoughts in their heads. *Did anyone hear any of what we had said?*

Will opened the door and saw Walter standing there, with Wyanet, who seemed embarrassed that she was interrupting, close behind him. "Wyanet saw the note on the table and couldn't understand it," said Walter. He held out the note. "And she didn't know where Miss Tucker was. She's in here, Wyanet."

Will took it from Walter and read the note Phoebe had left on the kitchen table about being in her room and not being disturbed. Will shrugged and handed the note to his sister. "Hello again, Wyanet," said Phoebe. "I wrote this note, I signed it, right here. Is everything all right?"

"Yes, I'm sorry, I didn't mean to disturb you. I couldn't read it, I'm sorry," she seemed uncomfortable.

"No, no, it's fine, Wyanet. It just says that I was in my room taking a nap for awhile. I didn't want anyone to worry."

"It's okay. Wyanet can only read a little English. And not this fancy writing." He looked at Wyanet who started to giggle.

Oh, cursive. He can't read cursive. "I should have printed it for you, Walter, just in case," apologized Phoebe, smiling at the boy.

Phoebe turned the note toward them both, pointed at her name and helped Wyanet sound it out. "Pah – hoy – boy," said Wyanet slowly, smiling. She said it quicker on the second and third try, concentrated hard and finally came out with a loud, proud, "Poor-boy!"

"Close enough for a first lesson," said Phoebe, laughing. "But it says Phoebe. Like the bird, apparently. You can call me that if you like." Wyanet nodded enthusiastically.

To Walter, Phoebe said, "I'm sorry for the confusion. I thought your mother or one of the, um, the other gentlemen might see this note. I didn't realize Wyanet had trouble reading."

The boy shrugged as if the matter now bored him. "Nobody else is home. Come on," he said to Wyanet, turning to squeeze past her and skip back down the short hall.

"Do you need any help with supper, Wyanet?" Phoebe asked courteously.

She shook her head. "No, thank you, Ma'am." She nodded at Will and turned to follow Walter. Will and Phoebe walked out as well, Will locking his door behind him.

Phoebe and Will walked out the front door and sat down on the top step in the fading sunlight and slight breeze. Daily activities were settling down. Evening activities were picking up. They were both silent for several minutes as they sat on the step, lost in thought, taking in differing details of this new world around them. Old but new, so very different but much the same, foreign yet familiar.

Phoebe sat bolt upright as a memory came to her. *Poor boy.* Her dad had told her something about J. W. What was it? That J. W. had said something on the phone that had caused her dad to worry about his state of mind? His well-being? His memory, that was it. *And just so you know, he said something strange. He said 'oh poor boy.'* Had J. W. known Wyanet? Was that a clue?

"Geez, Phoebe, your face." Phoebe looked at her brother. "You look like you've seen a ghost. Or that you're seeing one right now. What's the matter?"

How to explain? She tried, to the best of her ability, to confer to Will exactly what their dad had said on his phone call to her. She then related that to how Wyanet had mispronounced her name. He seemed less impressed than she, but the nagging feeling that it was somehow linked would not subside. "How can something that particular be a coincidence?" she asked.

"But what does it mean? Where does that get us?"

She shook her head, dejected. "I have no idea."

Walter opened the door, stepped out and jumped off the porch to the ground. He climbed back up and jumped off again. Will said, "Be careful, you're going to break an ankle." Walter climbed back up to the porch and sat down beside Phoebe, his legs swinging to and fro.

From their seats they could look across to the cemetery. It was only visible between buildings but being situated on the hill they could see the fence and a couple of the larger monuments clearly. It was relatively new now, having been moved not many years ago from the flatter, soggier part of town to the south. Walter noticed their gaze but didn't say anything. Neither did they; the boy had lost two fathers in his short life.

Phoebe stood up, curious as to what what was going on in the cemetery. The higher vantage point didn't help much. Will and Walter followed her gaze and Walter answered her unspoken question. "There was a funeral today."

Phoebe looked down at the boy sitting on the porch, swinging his legs. "There was? I didn't see a procession."

"A what?" Walter asked.

"Procession, where the family and friends, um, walk along down the street, following the, um, going to the cemetery to say a prayer. I was out having lunch and I never saw one."

The boy shrugged. "I've seen a line with the big black carriage that carries the box before. But not today. There's been a heap of funerals since the snow melted."

"A heap?" Will asked rhetorically, incredulous.

Phoebe remember telling her cousin Jody and second cousin Daniel about the building on the hill; The 'Dead House,' also known as the 'Hearse House,' where they had stored cadavers when the ground was frozen or when there had been too much snow for burials. It was June, the snow had melted, the earth thawed. So funerals were common, from either the past or present troubles. Phoebe wondered if or when there had been a funeral for the deceased Roy Barrett.

Mrs. Barrett approached the house from the street out front. When close to the house she waved and said, "Hello. I apologize for being out. I've been visiting a friend.
Fried chicken for supper tonight."

On cue Will's stomach growled and Walter laughed at him. Will stood, assisted Phoebe to her feet and Walter jumped down off the porch once more. Lena Barrett said, "Walter, stop that, you're going to break an ankle."

Will held the door for Mrs. Barrett and Walter skipped in behind her. Phoebe waited before entering and said quietly to Will, "I want to visit the cemetery tomorrow."

"You are so weird," said her brother.

Giving him an exasperated look she said, "First of all, I would like to see what it looks like without all the faded headstones and wooden name plates. Second, maybe there's a clue there."

"Good idea. But first – fried chicken."

28

After first notifying their landlady that Chester Murphy would not be at home for dinner that evening and why, Phoebe and Will kept Lena Barrett company while she and Wyanet prepared supper. Fried chicken, fresh-baked bread and a baked mixture of potatoes, onions and green beans in a light sauce. The house smelled delicious and Newton Sanford said so when he walked through the door to the kitchen. He leaned in, stating he was going upstairs but would return directly.

Phoebe's heart involuntarily gave a little flip upon seeing him and she looked down at her hands, fidgeting. Will sympathized with her. Three days.

Ten minutes later Newton entered the kitchen boisterously, greeting each of them in turn, asking if they had had a pleasant day. Lena Barrett and Wyanet put plates of food on the table, and Phoebe stood up to help pour lemonade into glasses. Wyanet was invited to stay for supper this evening and accepted gratefully.

"Walter," Newton began, "did you do some reading today? I saw a poetry book on the table in the parlor."

Walter nodded. "Yup," he said, between bites.

"What did you read?" Newton was smiling at the boy's degree of appetite.

Walter shrugged. "Tom somethin'. The words were hard."

"Thomas Campbell," corrected Lena Barrett. "It's one of my books," she said to Newton. "Don't forget to put it away later if you're finished, Walter."

"He left it for me to read, Mrs. Barrett," said Will. "We read some together, I read some to him, pointing out the words, of course," he winked at Walter, "and I told him I would like to look at it later. If that's all right with you?"

"Certainly, Mr. Tucker. Thank you for helping Walter with his reading today."

"He's doing well."

"I know it's difficult for him. I have some with simpler text and words. But I'm happy he tried that one today. Parts of the poems rhyme, which makes it easier, I believe. There is one in particular that I find quite beautiful. It's long, as many of his are. It's the poem on the pages where I have a bookmark. Did you see it? '*On Hallowed Ground*,' is the name."

"I did, yes," said Will, and Phoebe saw his features become uncomfortable, as if unwilling to discuss the subject further. No one but Phoebe seemed to notice.

"I've heard of Thomas Campbell, but am unfamiliar with that particular poem. Do you happen to know any of it to share with us all?" Newton asked Mrs. Barrett.

Mrs. Barrett smiled shyly. "Some, but not in its entirety. It is quite long." She cleared her throat. "*'For time makes all but true love old; The burning thoughts that then were told, Run molten still in memory's mould; And will not cool, Until the heart itself be cold, in Lethe's pool.'* That's not the beginning, but it is the first part I've memorized."

Walter scowled. "Who's Leeth?"

Will and Newton awaited the answer. When Lena Barrett paused, Phoebe said, "Lethe is the river of forgetfulness, a mythical river in the stories of the Greek underworld." All eyes turned to her. "When the heart turns cold in Lethe's pool it means that true love has been forgotten."

Will's eyebrows went up, impressed at his sister, and Newton stared at her, no twitch to his mustache, no twinkling of his eyes. There, instead, was a shadow, as if a sadness was now upon him, and Phoebe wanted to escape.

"Do you know more?" her brother asked and she wanted to kick him under the table.

"I'll try. *'What hallows ground where heroes sleep? 'Tis not the sculptured piles you heap! In dews that heavens far distant weep, Their turf may bloom; Or Genii twine beneath the deep Their coral tomb.'*" Lena Barrett smiled broadly.

Walter said, "See why I don't know how to read it?" and all present laughed.

Newton said, "I must apologize, I confess I don't know much about poetry. What does that part mean?"

Lena Barrett paused, thinking it through. "I believe to understand it you need a bit more. *'But strew his ashes to the wind Whose sword or voice has served mankind,-- And is he dead, whose glorious mind lifts thine on high?-- To live in hearts we leave behind Is not to die.'* But there's much more," she said, taking a bite from her plate.

Walter was shaking his head as if to say, 'see,' and Phoebe and Will were staring down at their own plates silently.

Newton said quietly, "I haven't read that entire poem, but I would like to. May I borrow your book as well, Mrs. Barrett?"

"Certainly," she replied cheerfully, unaware the poem's words had left Phoebe shaken.

"So it's saying," Newton reasoned slowly, 'that it's not the monument you leave behind," he paused, "but the soul, the life lived, that endures. That the gift of remembrance cannot be denied."

"Like I said, there is more to help explain it. But for that part I believe you're correct. Mind you, I'm no poet."

"It certainly gives one something to think about, doesn't it?" Newton said lightly.

Please change the subject, please, thought Phoebe.

"Is there something the matter, Phoebe?" Newton asked.

"No," Phoebe lied and smiled, looking up and taking a drink of her lemonade. "Not at all. I was just listening, same as you." *Stop snapping at him.*

Wyanet had been, up until now, silent, taking in the conversation, listening, learning, looking at each of them as they had spoken. On hearing Phoebe's name, Walter recounted the tale of Wyanet's mispronunciation of it. Wyanet possessed a sweet nature and ample sense of humor and received gentle ribbing without fuss. The distraction was much appreciated. *Bless you, Walter.*

With the subject off the Campbell poem and onto other topics, Phoebe relaxed. Still pushing thoughts of the missing wheel rim out of her mind, she focused on supper and this assemblage of people that she had grown fond of in so short a time.

How long had she worked in Dubuque at her latest job having only had lunch with Karen-the-houseplant-sitter a couple of times? She called Karen a 'work friend,' because they had never hung out together at any other time. At the Christmas party, yes, at the Fourth of July company picnic, yes. She had been here in Bodie for a few days and the thought of leaving them behind at any time filled her heart with sadness.

Supper was over and Wyanet was helping Lena Barrett clear the dishes. Phoebe helped too, knowing it wasn't necessary but wanting to do so anyway. Once finished, the group gathered on the porch. The men had placed chairs outside for the ladies and proceeded to sit on the steps or the porch itself. Phoebe and Wyanet brought out a tray with coffee cups for all but Walter and they relaxed, pointing out the stars in the sky. Phoebe wished she had a camera to memorialize this pleasing evening.

Cameras. There's a photography studio on Main Street. *What's the name again? Think, think.* "Hey," Phoebe blurted out, sitting upright in her chair. All turned to look at her. "The photographic studio on Main Street, Kemp's. We should get our picture taken."

Lena Barrett said, "I'm sorry, Phoebe, Kemp's recently closed. Mr. Kemp sold the hotel and studio just a few months ago. They're adding rooms to the Occidental and incorporating the top floor into it."

Now there's a fact I did not remember. "Oh," she said, disappointed.

"There's another, I've forgotten the name just now, just down the street. We can get our portrait taken there. I believe I would enjoy that." This from Newton Sanford.

"All of us?" questioned Lena Barrett, and Phoebe nodded.

"Yes. I – we," Phoebe looked at Will, "I'm not sure how long we'll be in Bodie and I would like a picture of my – our – of my new fr – " When she cut herself off those gathered looked her way. Lena Barrett smiled and Newton's gaze bored through her. Phoebe inhaled, exhaled and said slowly, "I would like a photograph to someday remember you all by. And Mr. Murphy and Mr. Bradley as well, if they are amenable to the idea."

Lena Barrett leaned close and put a hand on Phoebe's knee. "That would be lovely, Phoebe."

A member of Wyanet's family was riding up on horseback to collect her. The young man was a cousin, she said, had been working at the Kirkwood Stables and was finished for the evening. She got on the horse behind her cousin, they waved goodbye and rode south toward home.

The night was calm, only a small breeze blew from the southeast, the quiet broken by music coming from inside a saloon on Green Street, not far distant. The music began; the tinkling sound came from the upright parlor piano popular in these times. The music began and men cheered; a performer must have appeared. Lena Barrett's face creased in concern, wondering if she should hustle Walter off to bed. But her features relaxed as she recognized the song about to begin.

If everyone gathered was silent they could hear the words being sung by a female singer. As it went along Phoebe smiled.

'Oh! All of you poor single men, don't ever give up in despair. For there's always a chance while there's life, to capture the hearts of the fair. No matter what may be your age, you always may cut a fine dash. You will suit all the girls to a hair, if only you've got a moustache, a moustache, a moustache.'

The piano played an interlude and men cheered and whistled from within the saloon. Phoebe saw Will cover his mouth to hide a laugh. The second verse came along soon.

'No matter for manners or style, no matter for birth or for fame. All these used to have something to do, with young ladies changing their name. There's no reason now to despond, or go and do anything rash. For you'll do though you can't raise a cent, if you'll only raise a moustache, a moustache, a moustache, if you'll only raise a moustache.'

Lena Barrett laughed lightly. Walter wasn't paying attention at all. Phoebe was enjoying herself and was delighted there followed a third verse after the next interlude.

'Your head may be thick as a block, and empty as any foot-ball. Oh! Your eyes may be green as the grass, your heart just as hard as a wall. Yet take the advice that I give, You'll soon gain affection and cash. And will be all the rage with the girls, If you'll only get a moustache, a moustache, if you'll only get a moustache.'

Phoebe laughed aloud then, she couldn't help herself. The song was new to her and silly, and fun, and... Newton was grinning, his shoulders were shaking in silent mirth, he was looking directly at Phoebe and, although it was difficult to see in the low light from the gas lamp seeping through the window, he was blushing. As he looked at her he straightened his mustache with his first finger and thumb, as he had done before.

"What a funny song," she commented.

"Yes, that one's an old favorite. Harmless. However," Lena Barrett said, standing, "it may be time to retire before a late hour and...different...songs begin." She raised her eyebrows at the adults present and nodded her head in her son's direction. Taking Walter inside with her, using the excuse she needed to finish straightening up the kitchen and would appreciate his help, Lena Barrett said her goodnights.

"What do you two have planned for tomorrow? Anything interesting? Besides wanting to sit for a photograph?" Newton asked conversationally.

As usual, Will looked to Phoebe to answer. She replied, "I would like to picnic south of town sometime, or see the racetrack. But I know we don't have time for that. Tomorrow, though, I want to go to the cemetery."

Newton sputtered and coughed. "Please excuse me. You caught me unawares. The cemetery? Whatever for?" He had asked Phoebe but looked to Will, perhaps believing, mistakenly, that he wouldn't allow her to follow through with such a strange and unpleasant plan.

"I want to see it, that's all. I find cemeteries interesting."

"I find your interests dismal," he said, with a look of regret the minute the words were spoken.

"Then isn't it convenient that I'm not asking for your permission, or your company?" she snapped.

Will sat upright in his chair and held both hands out to his sides like a referee. "Stop. Just stop." He looked at Phoebe. "You want to go to the cemetery, fine, we'll go." He looked at Newton. "You're working tomorrow. It shouldn't make any difference to your day."

Newton stood up, picking up Lena Barrett's chair to return it to the parlor. "I apologize Phoebe. You are right. It was not my intention to dissuade you. Goodnight to you both." He took the chair inside and they heard his heel clicks walk through the room and up the stairs.

"Getting bossy in your old age, little brother?"

"You two... Why don't you just arm wrestle him and get it over with?" He sat back in his chair and sighed.

"I suppose we should learn to get along."

"What does that mean?"

"I've got some bad news," she whispered, pausing to form the words in her brain before saying them aloud. "I went out into the barn this afternoon, before we spoke in your room, to look at the metal wheel rim. I wondered if it would give me any ideas, any clues, or if I would see anything else in the barn to help us. We haven't been in there since," she looked around to be sure they were alone, "we arrived."

"And?" he asked, gripping his chair.

She played with the cup handle she was holding. "It wasn't there." Silence. "Will, did you hear me? I said it wasn't – "

"I heard you. Oh good God, oh geez, Phoebe..." He put his head in his hands and rocked back and forth. "Now what? Where is it? What happened to it? We didn't even know what to do with it in the first place. What if that other guy, that Albert Griffin took it, or his drunk friend, what was his name, John-Something? You did slap him in the face, maybe – "

"Will," she said sharply, speaking as quietly as she could. "You're rambling again. None of that makes any sense and you know it. A rusty, useless, wagon wheel rim. What use is it to anyone else?"

"Then where...is...it?" his voice rasped at her.

"Maybe we don't need it."

"Then how – "

"Maybe we just need to stop playing around and start looking harder. Tomorrow we're going to the cemetery. J. W. talked about the 'Bodie curse' in the car ride with Mom and Dad on the way home from his visit here. I don't know, maybe that has something to do with this."

"Oh geez we're cursed..."

"Shut up, no we're not. I'll explain later." She stood up and motioned for him to carry her chair inside for her. "How would it look if someone saw me doing it?" she grinned at him. "Oh, and when we get inside, I've got something else in my room you can help me carry as well," she said, remembering the tub of now very cold bath water she had left behind.

In the house, Phoebe opened her bedroom window and they managed to pour the water outside that way. It wasn't that much, after all, and only water with a bit of soap. Far worse things were dumped out windows and doorways onto the streets of Bodie. Phoebe set the tub down against the wall and closed her window.

"Will sat in the chair in the corner. "So, tell me about this Bodie curse." Phoebe filled him in on what she had been told about artifacts being taken from Bodie, bad luck following and the items being returned to the park after.

"I call it a guilty conscious, but if it keeps park artifacts safe, who am I to judge?" She shrugged.

Will frowned. "So what does going to the cemetery have to do with a curse? I don't follow."

Phoebe unhooked her chatelaine bag from her belt, pulled it open, removed the Colt and poured the remaining contents onto the bed. She moved her fingers through the items until she found what she was looking for and held it up to show Will. "This. This is why I think it has something to do with the cemetery." She was holding the pyramid-shaped piece of stone that J. W. had put into her pocket when he had hugged her before lifting the metal rim and sending them to Bodie. The piece he had said not to lose and that she nearly had. What they'd been searching for in the straw in the barn on arrival in old Bodie.

"That? Did you figure out what it is?"

She was shaking her head. "I'm not absolutely sure, but I suspect it might be a corner of a headstone. I was thinking about it in the tub today. J. W. slipped and almost fell that day in the cemetery. I think he was faking just to pick this up from the ground."

"A stolen piece of a headstone. That sounds curse worthy." said Will.

"And after that, on the way home, a couple of Pronghorn ran across the road in front of Dad's truck. They weren't close, but we joked in the car about it being the curse. So tomorrow we'll go up there and see if there are any clues, anything at all. We've got to keep a very open mind from now on."

"Okay," said Will, sighing and rubbing his tired eyes. "You know, I like the idea of getting our picture taken. All together, I mean. I'm going to miss these people."

"Yeah, me too." Phoebe gathered up the items on the bed to return them to her bag.

"How are we doing on money?" asked Will. He trusted her with their funds so hadn't thought to ask before. Asking now was simple curiosity.

She did a cursory count, already aware of the approximate dollar amount they possessed. "Not counting the money I won at Faro we still have a little over three hundred dollars left. Oh, and not counting the four gold double eagles from J. W., either."

"Why didn't you count those?"

While she answered she returned the money and other items to her bag, double-checking the pistol and the cylinder before placing that inside as well. "I was going to ask you about those." She hesitated, unsure of how he would react to her suggestion. "I want to ask you what you think about giving those to Chester Murphy. You know, since those scoundrels bashed him on the head and took his money, and he wants to get married, and, well..."

Will was smiling at her. "I wasn't aware there was a sentimental side to Phoebe Tucker," he teased. "I think that's a great idea, Phoebe, as long as he promises not to gamble them away. Otherwise we should take them back home to J. W. If we can."

"I keep going back to that. J. W. must have had a reason for putting those in my pocket. I just haven't figured it out yet."

"I don't think there's a mystery to that. He wanted us to have enough money. Plain and simple."

"Perhaps. But is it okay if we give the double eagles to Chester? With the promise not to gamble them away?" she added.

"Sure. But if we're here so long we run out of money I'm sending you back to the Faro table."

29

Will said goodnight and left to go to his own room. Phoebe heard him lock his door, after which she locked hers as well. *Oh shoot,* she thought. Unlocking it, she made her way to the outhouse as she had on that first night. She had again locked her door behind her and remembered to take her bag with the Colt. Then she unlocked the kitchen door and crept quietly down the stairs outside.

The light breeze from earlier had picked up a bit, causing uneven doors to rattle and debris to scatter. Exiting the outhouse, her eyes searched the darkness, not keen on another run-in with Albert Griffin or his cohort John Young. The metal catch on the gate clinked in the breeze, causing Phoebe to flinch and look in that direction. The thought of handling the pistol was squelched when she considered the proximity of those in the house. And the last thing she wanted was to have the pistol catch on the strings of her bag if she pulled it out quickly, an errant blast entering either the ground or her foot.

On her return, she made it through the exterior kitchen door, locked it, and began crossing to the hallway. She heard the floor creaking somewhere nearby, but as she was new to the house the exact location was a mystery. Making her way across the kitchen slowly, listening intently, she picked up a now dry dish towel from the hook near the stove, holding it in both hands. When she reached the doorway to the kitchen she heard creaking again, this time from above.

Gradually making her way down the hall she retrieved her key from her bag but moved in slow motion as several items in her bag were made of metal and clinked together as she stuck her hand inside. Cautiously, still listening to the creaking sounds coming from some unknown location, she put her key into the lock and turned, simultaneously turning the knob. Her door creaked once as she pushed it open. But there were other noises coming from within.

Her window was open. Wide open with the night breeze blowing the gauzy curtain into the room in wild swirls. Phoebe froze. She and Will had closed the window. *But I forgot to lock it. Stupid, stupid.* Hurriedly her eyes scanned the room, but it was dark and she saw nothing. She edged around the end of the bed and closed the window, believing that whoever had opened the window had either never come in or had already left. When her door creaked and began slowly to swing closed she turned around and saw the man standing there behind it.

Breath, think; he's moving slowly, you can think quickly. Just think. Breath. Maybe I can't get the Colt out quickly enough, but I can...

Slurring his words together, the drunken man said, "How lovely to see you again. Miss... Tucker." He took a step into the room and Phoebe could see his height, his clothes, the outline of his face.

Moving very, very slowly she held the kitchen towel she had taken off the hook in the kitchen in both hands and folded one corner diagonally down to the opposite flat side; the same first action as making a paper airplane. She did this while she said, distracting him from her hands, "Mr. Griffin. To what do I owe the pleasure of your company this evening?" She began rolling the folded edge of the towel as imperceptibly as possible, in the dark, her hands moving in minute increments, roll, roll, roll.

Albert Griffin hiccuped and took another step into the room. Only a portion of the end of the bed was between them and the door was behind the man. It was only partially closed and Will's door was directly behind that only a few feet. But she fervently hoped Will did not hear the intruder. He would have been ill-prepared to deal with Albert Griffin, especially since he was unreasonable, violent, drunk and most likely armed. She continued to slowly roll the towel, never taking her eyes off his face.

"I was at Wagner's watching you. I saw you playing Faro." Hiccup. "And I saw you walk away with Harry's money."

Harry? Oh... the man who's checks she had won by calling a dead card at the Faro table. It really was his own fault. Roll...roll...

Phoebe spoke calmly, "Your friend should pay more attention to his cards." Phoebe heard more creaking elsewhere in the house. She hoped it wasn't Will, maybe it was Newton and he had heard the commotion? Or perhaps it was John Young, come to join Albert Griffin. She felt her heart begin to race. *Breath.*

"I'm here to take it back."

"Why can't Harry come get it himself?" *Stall for time, think.*

Albert laughed, a single noncomedic 'ha,' filled with annoyance. "I have no intention of retrieving it *for* him. He had his chance." Albert staggered and caught his balance by leaning on the washstand near the half open door. His foot bumped the door and it swung back open. "I'm taking if for myself. Now, give it to me," he said, pointing at his chest with his index finger and hiccuping again. He extended an arm, palm upward, and the arm wobbled to and fro as if he were standing in a canoe on a flowing river.

Roll...roll... Phoebe smirked. One hand out, the other leaning on the washstand. No hand to draw a pistol, at least not with any speed. Creaking again, *Where!*

At the instant it seemed Albert Griffin had lost his patience and was about to take another step forward, trapping Phoebe on the opposite side of the bed with no way out but through the closed window she would have no time to open, Phoebe heard a creak on the floor outside her room and the unmistakable click of two shotgun hammers being pulled back nearly simultaneously. *Double hammer.*

The end of the shotgun moved into Phoebe's sight behind Albert Griffin's head. *Grip the towel, just so, like Tony and Troy showed you many years ago.*

Phoebe's pretense of calm, no matter how expert it looked on the outside, began to crack at what happened next. The voice in the hallway said, "I advise you not to move an inch, Mr. Griffin. I greatly dislike the idea of having to clean your brains off my walls." Lena Barrett was now poking the barrels of the shotgun into the side of Albert Griffin's head. He sneered, attempting to peer at her, but she poked him again to keep him from turning his head. "You are leaving my home now. And you will not return. Is that understood?" She jabbed at his head again.

Albert Griffin balled up his fists, scowled and moved his eyes as if he were going to grab the gun out of Lena Barrett's hands. Phoebe could not let anything happen to her. In the same breath Lena Barrett poked with the shotgun, Albert Griffin turned his head a fraction and Phoebe took two steps around the end of the bed. She brought the towel up in front of her, holding one corner in her right hand and the long tail end loosely in the other and snapped the towel forward with her right hand. The skinny end of the tightly rolled towel lashed out at Albert Griffin's cheek and snapped it like a whip. He yowled in pain and his hands flew to his face.

Lena Barrett turned the shotgun end over end in her quick hands and hit him in the back of the head with the steel butt plate of the gun, sending him to the floor, groaning, one hand on his face, the other on the back of his head. Phoebe lit her lamp, Will opened his door and stepped out, Newton rushed down the hallway and the four of them stood staring down at the now passed out man on Phoebe's bedroom floor.

Lena Barrett carefully released both hammers of the gun and asked Phoebe if she was all right. She nodded and hugged the woman who had come to her rescue. She asked

Phoebe, "What did you do, to his face? I couldn't see around the corner."

Phoebe held up the towel that was still in her hands and said, "It's your towel. A little torment I learned from my big brothers. They always called it a rattail. Remind me to thank them when I get back home." She laughed lightly and glanced at Will.

After a quick explanation to Will and Newton, Will said, "Now what?"

"Now we hail the sheriff or constable and report the incident," said Newton. "And Phoebe will lock her window so there will be no repeat of this remarkable occasion."

Said with amusement, Phoebe took no offense and replied. "If it does, I now know who to call." She smiled at her landlady and bowed her head in Lena's direction.

After Will and Newton had removed the drunken, and now more pliable, Albert Griffin from the house and put him at the edge of the road out front, Phoebe asked Lena Barrett if she could look at the shotgun she had used to subdue the intruder.

On picking it up, Phoebe admired the weight, the balance, the craftsmanship of the beautifully made firearm. It was a Remington Whitmore double barreled shotgun with side by side hammers and front and rear trigger releases. Phoebe admired it for its antique and rare find value, not stopping to think they were common where and when she was now. She wanted to comment on the low issue, three digit serial number but no one would understand her interest.

"This is a beautiful piece of craftsmanship. Where did you get it, if you don't mind my asking?"

Lena Barrett said, "I don't mind. It was a gift from my father. He taught me how to shoot when I was a youngster." She laughed lightly at the surprised expression Phoebe displayed. "Unusual, I know. My father was a spectacular individual and no one could tell him what to do." Quietly she said, "He passed a few years ago. I miss him."

"I'm sorry. I have a relative like that in my family as well." Phoebe touched her horseshoe necklace. He's the one who gave me this."

"I believe you have a tad of that defiance inside of you as well, if I am not mistaken," Lena Barrett suggested warmly. "It served you well this evening, did it not?"

Phoebe nodded her agreement. "I suppose it did. But I do thank you for your intervention. It was timely."

Lena Barrett shrugged. "The folks on the north end of town shouldn't have all the fun."

Will walked into the parlor and announced that Newton had walked north to find a deputy or sheriff. Will insisted on waiting outside near Albert Griffin to insure he did not leave the scene or attempt to re-enter the house. He also insisted that Lena Barrett and Phoebe wait in the parlor. Phoebe scoffed at that idea. "How very Victorian of you. What are you going to do if he wakes up and walks away?" she asked.

Smiling, he said, "Come and get you."

Phoebe sat on the top step next to Mrs. Barrett and held her pistol at the ready in case Albert Griffin decided to make an unwise decision, or in case they were visited by his associate. Neither case happened and forty-five minutes later Newton could be seen at the end of the road, walking with two other men in suits and hats.

They looked official, Phoebe knew neither of them, and they listened politely as Phoebe and Mrs. Barrett recounted the incident from earlier. A couple of questions were asked and answered, after which one of the men attempted to wake Albert Griffin by shoving at his back with his boot. When that didn't work he put his foot on Albert Griffin's rump and rolled him back and forth on the ground. The drunken man moaned and flailed his arms about as if he were fighting off invisible attackers.

Mrs. Barrett had gone into the house but returned momentarily with a small bowl of cold water. She walked down the porch steps, threw the contents into Albert Griffin's face, and walked back up the steps and into the house. As the burglar gasped for air and bolted upright

Phoebe smothered a giggle. He was rubbing the back of his head when the two law men hoisted him to his feet and announced they were taking him to jail and a good night's sleep.

Even in the low light the three inch red welt Phoebe's rattail whip had given him was visible across his right cheek. The man scowled and attempted to break the hold the law men had on his arms. He snarled at Phoebe, "Tell your box herder boyfriend to keep you in line," and one of the law men pulled on his arm sharply, shushing him, and apologizing to Phoebe.

"No harm done. Thank you for coming, gentlemen."

They turned to go, one man holding onto Albert Griffin tightly, the other aiming a pistol at his back.

Will looked at Phoebe and whispered, "Box herder?"

Newton approached Phoebe and said apologetically. "Please do not mind Albert's words, Phoebe. You know he's drunk and mean and jealous and – "

"Jealous?" she teased. "It's fine, Newton. I don't care what Albert Griffin thinks. Thank you for taking the time to hail the deputies.

He opened the front door for her and Will and said, "Please lock your window."

"I will."

"And perhaps tomorrow you could show me that trick with the towel."

After saying their goodnights once again, Phoebe and Will headed toward the end of the hall to their rooms. Will made sure Phoebe's window was locked. "I could have done that, you know."

"Yes, I know. But I did it. Now," he asked, still whispering, "what is a box herder? Some kind of insult, I've no doubt."

"Ha, I'll say. A box herder is, was, a term for the man who kept all his 'girls' in line. A sort of, wild west pimp."

"Jerk," Will replied quietly.

"Indeed," said Phoebe, yawning, clearly not as annoyed at the invective as her brother seemed to be.

Will was locking his door when Phoebe, just outside her own room, heard the front door open and close and footsteps advance through the room. She remained still, attempting to focus in the near dark. A voice greeted her from across the distance. "Miss Tucker, good evening. I'm sorry if I woke you." It was Chester Murphy so she walked forward to speak to him. She pulled him into the kitchen so they wouldn't be speaking outside of Lena and Walter's room.

"You didn't wake me, Mr. Murphy. I was up, we all were; except Walter." Chester Murphy wore an expression of someone lost to enchantment. His eyes were wide, his cheeks flushed, his smile wide and generous. He was a man who had just left the love of his life and the intensity of it was written all over his face.

"Why, what's happened?"

"Didn't you see... there were two lawmen just leaving the house..." Phoebe smiled. She didn't know what route Chester had taken to reach home but she suspected that even if he had seen Albert Griffin, in his current state he would not have noticed. "Albert Griffin broke into the house." Chester Murphy gasped. "Everyone's fine, I assure you. New – Mr. Sanford retrieved the law and had him removed to jail."

"Oh, well, that's fine, just fine." Yes, he was distracted.

"Mr. Murphy, did you ever go to Constable Kirgan and report what happened to you the other evening? That you believe Mr. Griffin and Mr. Young robbed you?" His gaze landed on various items around the room, avoiding her face. "Mr. Murphy?"

"No, no I didn't. After all, I wasn't absolutely sure it was they, and, I did win the money at the table, so..."

Phoebe waited until Chester Murphy looked up to her face before she spoke again. "Mr. Murphy, I understand, really I do. But winning money isn't as if you earned it dishonestly; like Mr. Griffin and Mr. Young seem to prefer. And if you are going to ask Mary, well, if you are going to spend the rest of your life with Mary you are going to have to be honest with her. Either you gamble a little or you don't. But don't keep secrets from those you love." She smiled and put a hand on one of his. "And I think Mary's wonderful by the way."

Chester Murphy exhaled and Phoebe noticed a slight tremble in his voice when he said, "She appreciates your friendship as well. Thank you, Miss Tucker. I've decided to stick to banking. Your brother was a source of some helpful advice as well, and I appreciate it."

They said their goodnights and parted ways at the base of the stairs. Phoebe locked her door, settled in for the night, checked the lock on her window one last time, checked that her Army jacket was still under her mattress, removed the Colt from her chatelaine bag and placed it within reach just under the edge of the mattress. Her ritual finalized, she put on her dress she had worn to J. W.'s birthday party and tucked herself in for the night.

Her last thought as she drifted off to sleep was a disheartening reminder. *Died June 19, 1880.*

30

"Shut up shu' up, shu'p, shup, shhhuu..." the drunk was yelling as he was dragged unceremoniously into the first cell on the left, waking the three other prisoners within, immediately struggling and falling off the cot onto which he'd been unceremoniously placed and onto the floor. A deputy shoved at his shoulder with his foot to assure he would not follow or attempt an assault and backed out of the cell.

Constable Kirgan spoke to his latest guest from the doorway. "I believe your arrival is long overdue, Mr. Griffin." The deputy was clear of the door and the Constable swung the heavy wood door closed, inserted the thick metal key into the lock plate and turned it. The dull thud and final metallic click put an end to any and all argument; at least for tonight.

Albert Griffin staggered to the interior window of his crowded cell and grabbed the bars, peering out. "Hey, hey ou' dere," he mumbled, his words slurred. "Lemme ou', lemme ou' n – " hiccup, "now." He tried to shake the metal bars but they were sturdy, thick and newly inset into the thick well-built jail door.

Constable Kirgan spoke to him from the small reception room outside the door. "Quiet. Go to bed. You're not going anywhere." The Constable picked up the keys, a few papers and said, "I'll see you in the morning." He walked out and locked the jail door. He could hear Albert Griffin shout a string of profanity and guttural sounds in frustration of his predicament. Kirgan grinned as he put his keys safely in his pocket, tipped his hat to a few passersby and continued on his way home for the remainder of the night.

As soon as the Constable was out of sight, the man waiting in the shadows moved forward. He approached the side of the jail where there was a small exterior window with the same sturdy bars as were built into the interior doors. Unfortunately the small exercise area with a newly installed fence, attached to the west side of the jail, prevented the man from getting too near the window. No one would notice or care if he yelled, There was enough noise coming from other places to muffle any commotion he might make.

"Al. Hey, Albert." The man picked up a few small rocks from the road and threw them toward the window where one clinked off the bars and bounced back outside, one clinked the window pane in-between, and the third was a terrible throw and clunked against the wall outside. He yelled Albert's name again and again but to no avail. Realizing Albert Griffin wouldn't be able to answer without yelling himself, he suspended his attempt to reach him.

Muttering to himself he scuffed dirt and rocks in frustration and walked past the jail with the intention of making his way to his room at the hotel. But sticking his hands in his pockets as he walked reminded him he still had money to burn and the whiskey from earlier had lost its effect considerably.

At Main Street he turned left and headed to the Pioneer Billiard Saloon. A few rounds with an inexperienced mudsill would make his money last longer than the Faro table had. And when his partner woke up tomorrow he could tell him he had worried for no reason.

The man entered the saloon, ordered a bottle of whiskey with a glass and made his way to the billiard tables. The night was just beginning for John Young.

***

As she had promised herself, Phoebe heated some water after breakfast the next morning to wash her clothes. She included the dress she had worn to J. W's birthday party that she had been wearing as a nightgown, her socks, Will's shirts and vest and the handkerchief Newton had loaned her. Having no other socks or stockings to wear in their place, she slipped on her boots with bare feet and wiggled her toes around, wishing she could go without shoes of any kind like she usually did at home.

When she carried her clothes outside to wash in Lena Barrett's washtub, she pulled off her boots and set them up on the steps to the kitchen door, hoping to keep them as dry and clean as possible. So her skirt didn't drag on the ground she bent over, reached between her feet and grabbed the rear hem of her skirt. Then she pulled it forward between her feet and pulled it up to tuck into her waistband, leaving her feet and lower legs exposed up to her knees. She giggled at her appearance, feeling rudely exposed; it was unseemly to have her legs showing.

Her last item was wrung out and she was hanging it up on the line that ran from a post near the kitchen door to the enclosure gate when the kitchen door opened. Only her dresses and skirt were on the line as she had taken her 'nightgown' and socks in to her room to dry. She was not willing to explain to onlookers why she owned a pair of white, calf-length socks embroidered with a yellow bear dressed in a red sweatshirt and holding a honey pot and a balloon on a string.

Newton and Walter stood looking at her. Phoebe said good morning, as she hadn't seen either of them until now. Walter hopped down the steps like a bunny, both feet landing on each step as he went. Newton's mustache twitched and his eyes crinkled at the corners. Familiar with the meaning of those two methods of articulation, Phoebe put her hands on her hips and said, "What are you finding humorous today?"

"You have lovely legs, Miss Tucker," he said, taking his time walking down the few steps to ground level.

She snorted and returned her attention to her wet clothes. "Don't be ridiculous. I didn't want to get wet and dirty. But I can't tell you how your reaction delights me," she replied lightly. "I'm offended you have no similar comment regarding my lovely toes." At the mention his gaze shifted downward to her feet and quickly back up to her face.

His only response was a "Hmph."

Phoebe laughed. "I was teasing you. Honestly, It's just my feet and ankles. You act as if you've never seen things like that before."

His mustache twitched. "Just my ugly old stumps." Phoebe laughed harder.

"That's better," she said, walking around him and up the steps to the kitchen door. "Newton?" she inquired, her hand on the knob. He turned to face her. "You're home. Aren't you going to the clothing store today?"

"I wanted to be available to go to the photographic studio with you. With you all," he corrected, speaking quietly. "You see, I am also unsure of how much longer I am to remain here. In Bodie." At her curious expression he continued. "People come and go here for various reasons, as I'm sure you're aware." *Is he talking about Will and me?* "I would like a photograph as well."

She felt a lump rise in her throat. If only there was a way to tell him what was going to happen to him. If only there was a way she wouldn't sound insane. She had no way of knowing exactly how or where he was to die, she had reasoned with herself on countless occasions, so telling him to stay in his room, leave town, stay at the clothing store, or what could be any number of other places she considered 'safe,' did not assure his fate would evolve differently. Did she have any right to attempt to change it? Did she possess the ability? How many other fates would she alter if she did?

'*Whatever has already happened, well, it happened, it's done...*' *That's what I said to Will when we got here. I also told him, 'We're merely accessories, observers that get to look in from the outside and go home soon...' Was that really only a few days ago?* How cold-hearted that attitude now sounded to her own ears.

"Will and I are going to visit the cemetery today. You're welcome to join us, if you like. Otherwise, we can get a photograph at any time." Newton nodded but did not reply.

She stood at the top step and unhooked her skirt from the front of her waistband, letting it fall to swing back in place, fully covering her legs once again. She picked up her boots, opened the door and stepped inside, their eyes meeting for an instant just before it closed again.

Phoebe stood with her forehead leaning against the inside of the door for a full minute before sighing loudly and retreating once again to her room and locking it. *Running away again.* She brushed and re-braided her hair, tried to pin it up like Mary had done and failed, left the braid down her back and situated her hat atop her head. The horseshoe necklace shimmered in the bright light from her window and she left it hanging outside her blouse again. *J. W., I miss you, you old bugger.*

"Phoebe, are you in there?" It was Will knocking. She unlocked her door and he opened it, leaning against it while he waited for her. Army jacket safe and sound, check. Colt in her bag, check. Window still locked, check. Lock the door on the way out, check. She asked him to help her dump out her small amount of wash water before they left. They did so and she checked on her laundry. Still there, handkerchief already dry. She put it in her bag.

They left on their trek to the cemetery but did not see Newton anywhere about, nor did she know where their other housemates were. But the others had work to take care of or chores to be done, and she was tired of wasting time.

"What is it you hope to find out by going up there?" Will asked, pointing to the slope on which the cemetery was located.

"I don't know. I brought the piece of stone from J. W. I'm just keeping an open mind and trying to remember anything that happened that day. Maybe one thing has nothing to do with the other; maybe it does. There's got to be something we're not seeing."

When they entered the intersection at Main Street Phoebe glanced south toward the blacksmith shop where Lionel Bradley was employed. She saw him, walking from the back of the building wearing a black, heavy apron and moving his head around left and right, as if searching for something or someone. Phoebe held a hand poised mid-air to wave if he looked their way. He appeared to see them, she waved, but his eyes continued their search, never acknowledging her presence.

Will questioned what she was staring at and she explained. They both saw Lionel move toward the street, continue looking, then return to the inside of the blacksmith shop. "Looks like he's waiting for someone."

"Uh-huh," muttered Phoebe, distracted now by the sight of Newton walking the same direction they were the next block over. She initially wondered if he was meeting them at the cemetery but doubted that conclusion when they crossed Main Street at the same time he turned onto it. "Newton must have made arrangements to meet up with Lionel today," she said to Will. She related the earlier conversation she'd had with Newton regarding her invitation to join them.

"Sure, because that sounds like a great place to take someone you like on a morning outing. Kind of like a picnic. You know, 'Hey, would you like to meet me in the cemetery? Honey? Darling?'" He earned a punch in the arm for his troubles.

"If he had plans all he had to do was say so." She picked up her skirt with both hands and stomped ahead of him, saying over her shoulder, "And what do you mean, a great place to take somebody you like?"

He took a couple of quick steps to catch up with her. "Oh, come on. I may be your stupid brother, but I'm still a guy. Wait... what I meant was, come on Phoebe, I know you. And I know Newton is crazy about you. Lord knows why – "

"Stop it. I don't want to hear it." She walked even quicker, staring at the uneven ground, stomping with every step.

"You're going to get a blister, you don't have any socks on."

"Shut up."

They had reached the cemetery, framed now by a wooden fence. So distracted had they been, neither had noticed the cluster of people dressed in dark clothing gathered at the south end, the Miner's section; a funeral.

Phoebe and Will kept their distance out of respect. They could hear what sounded like a passage from the Bible being read aloud, a few people crying and a mass 'Amen' a minute later. Once the crowd dispersed, the duo entered through the gate and walked toward the area of the cemetery where they remembered J. W. having picked up the stone.

Phoebe stopped and read a grave marker. "I don't remember this one. It's in wood." *It either isn't here in 1980 or no one can read it anymore. So Sad.*

They passed a few others that neither remembered seeing on their last visit. U. P. Jack, died January 15, 1878. Jack O'Hara, died August 27, 1878. James Blair, died January 18, 1878. Antone Valencis, died 1878. A. C. Robertson, died February 1880.

Phoebe commented on the last one they past. "I remember reading about that one somewhere," she said, pointing at the marker engraved A. C. Robertson. "He died from an explosion, but not in one of the mines. He was thawing out explosive powder in his oven."

"What?" replied Will, incredulous. "That really happened?"

"It did. You forget we've gained a lot of general knowledge about such things in the last century." Will nodded.

"I don't remember many of these markers," he said, looking around. It looks different now."

"In our day many are missing. I don't know if they've been moved, the marker has been stolen, it was made of wood and disintegrated, or whatever else can happen in a hundred years." They both noticed that the cemetery was kept relatively free of brush and debris. It was used more often, unfortunately.

They turned to their left when Phoebe did notice a familiar ornate stone near the border fence. "Mary Elizabeth Butler," she said. "This one is here in, well, you know. Imagine it just being here the entire time." She read one side of the stone. "*'Elizabeth my wife; wife of B. F. Butler. Died Nov. 24, 1878, Aged 30 yr., 8 mo. 8 days. Thus star by star declined, Till all are passed away. As morning high and higher shines, To pure and perfect day.'*"

"Did everybody read poetry back then? That's a poem, right?"

"Yes, stupid brother, most did. It was called a well-rounded education. It's just a change of the times, that's all. I've heard of the poets, same as you, but I couldn't say more than few lines of anything. People our age know more movie lines than poetry."

"What poetry do you know?" he teased.

She cleared her throat to make a show of it. "Let's see, 'A rose by any other name would smell as sweet,' or 'shall I compare thee to a summer's day,' both Shakespeare. 'Oh Captain, my Captain,' Walt Whitman. 'I think that I shall never see, a poem lovely as a tree,' okay, I don't know who did that one, but I know it's a poem. 'How do I love thee, let me count the ways,' Elizabeth Barrett Browning. 'Do not stand at my grave and weep, I am not there. I do not sleep.' I know that's Mary Elizabeth Frye because a girl I knew in college was obsessed with her. Weird." Her brother was staring at her. "What?"

"Your friend in college was weird?" He looked again at the Butler gravestone. "Is that marble?"

"It is. The Butler's were one of the first families in Bodie and were some of the earliest miners here."

They continued walking and saw other markers they did not remember ever seeing before. James Doyle, June 19, 1878. Andy Haggerday, Oct. 4, 1878. W. J. O'Brien, July 10, 1879. Phoebe pointed at the last one and with raised eyebrows said, "July 10, 1879. I remember that date. There was a terrible explosion in the powder magazine of the Standard Mine. Eight were killed immediately and over forty were wounded, some severely and not expected to live much longer. The fire inside suffocated some."

Will looked across the town to the other side, at the hills, the stamp mills, the equipment spread out as far left and right as he could see, imagining the chaos such an incident would induce. "How horrible."

"It must have been. Noise, smoke, worry. The Summit Mine Works nearby was blown to bits and several men there were killed. The explosion was felt as far as Bridgeport. The Miner's Union Hall was used as a makeshift hospital."

They stood in silence for several seconds, homage to those lost, so long ago to them, but only last year to the residents of Bodie now. As they walked, there were others they had never seen, and some that were not yet here as their time had not yet come.

Momentarily they reached the location of where they remembered J. W. having 'tripped' and picked up the stone. Nothing was nearby, no graves marked this spot.

"Are you sure this is where you were?" asked Will.

Phoebe searched to gain perspective on her location within the cemetery fence. "No, I'm not, but it feels to be about the right place." She turned to Will. "Think. Do you remember what we had stopped to look at when he stooped to the ground? Who's stone was there?"

Will's brow was creased in concentration. "You have a much better memory for this stuff than I do, Phoebe. I mean, I've been here before, but I really wasn't paying that much attention. Sorry."

Phoebe threw up her hands in frustration. "There's nothing here that even remotely resembles the stone J. W. left with me." She took the stone out of her bag, turned it over and over in her fingers and searched her surroundings again. "Let's walk back the way we came. And keep an eye out."

They walked back through the cemetery, past the newly dug grave where the funeral had been taking place when they had arrived, searching for any stone that looked similar in color and consistency to the stone J. W. had given Phoebe. Now uphill from the entrance and ready to leave from lack of success, Will said dejectedly, "This was a bust. Now what do we do?"

"This spot, right about here, recognize it?" Her brother was perplexed and shook his head 'no.' "This is where Newton's grave marker was. Somewhere around here. It was about this far from the fence and the entrance, if that has remained the same." She looked at the small stone in her hand one last time, before placing it in her chatelaine bag, and sighed. "Two days, Will. Only two days. I wonder what happens to him?"

"He doesn't seem sick. So probably not that. I don't know."

Walking side by side they exited the cemetery and moved down the path toward town. "He told me earlier he might not be here much longer. As if he's leaving town. Maybe he has an accident or something," she surmised.

"Could be. It looks like dangerous country for a wagon or stage to me," replied Will. I'm used to riding in a truck out here. With caution."

They were going to stop and get something to eat before heading back to the boarding house and picked a small restaurant on South Main Street. Afterward, as they walked north to Green Street they passed the blacksmith shop where Lionel Bradley would be hard at work within. Suddenly, Phoebe yanked on Will's arm and pulled him around to the back of the building. Looking over her shoulder to assure they had not been seen, she motioned for him to stay quiet.

He whispered, "Where are we going? What are you doing, Phoebe?"

"Shh," she held her finger to her lips. "I'll explain on the way home."

In the rear of the blacksmith shop Phoebe saw a small shack attached, with a window on one end, that must be the place Lionel called home. But she wasn't headed for Lionel's shack. She instead peered around the corner of the wide door at the rear of the blacksmith shop. Sticking close to the outside wall, Phoebe flattened herself against it so she could look into the opposite rear corner of the shop. Lionel was there, bent over and working on something on a bench. She didn't hear other work being conducted and he seemed to be alone. Phoebe used her arm to push Will against the wall and held him there.

She had been curious to learn what Newton and Lionel had been cryptically speaking about earlier. Now was as good a chance as any to spy on Lionel to see if there was any merit to her suspicions. Focusing in on what the friendly blacksmith was doing, she saw intermittent shimmers from something; it was hanging from the wall behind him. Her hand remained on Will's arm, her grip tightened and Will stayed motionless. The thing glinted again when a breeze blew through the front and rear open doors; Phoebe saw what was hanging on the wall.

It was the metal wagon wheel rim that was missing from Mrs. Barrett's barn.

31

Back at the boarding house, Phoebe and Will sat on the bed in his room, discussing Phoebe's explanation she had promised to give.

"It's a wagon wheel, there are probably dozens around here, don't you think?" Will offered with skepticism.

"That shine in the light? That look like they have gold in them? Seems unlikely."

"Why would Lionel have taken it from the barn? It makes no sense at all."

"I don't know. I could have asked why it was in there."

"You could have. Then explain why you were snooping around, peeking in through the back door and why you care about a rusty old wagon wheel rim. That's not suspicious at all."

"You're not helping." Phoebe stood up to pace the small room and kept bumping into Will's feet with every pass.

"Stop it, would you. That's not helping either," he said.

There was a knock at the door. Phoebe answered and it was Lena Barrett. "I thought I heard you in here," she said with a smile on her face. "I was at the market and just returned. Walter and Wyanet are outside. I was wondering if you still want to go to the photographic studio. Mr.

Sanford left me a note that he would be back about now and perhaps Mr. Murphy's supervisors can allow him to take a short break this afternoon."

She seemed hopeful of their answers. Phoebe brightened and replied, "That would be wonderful, Mrs. Bar – Lena. I'm glad Wyanet can join us." Phoebe noticed that Lena Barrett had dressed in a dark brown skirt with beige vertical stripes and a beige blouse with ruffles at the cuffs and collar. She also wore a large cameo broach at her throat. *Dressed up and ready for a photograph.* "You look lovely."

Lena Barrett looked down at her skirt and touched the broach. "Thank you, Miss – Phoebe. I don't dress properly as I often used to when I lived in Missouri. There is so much dirt here, and not nearly enough greenery. One cannot even enjoy the shade of a tree in the summer. Only if we were to go to the picnic grounds or near the lake."

Phoebe completely understood. Everyone back in Dubuque had sprawling green lawns watered regularly with rain. Here, as at her parent's house in the canyon, a lawn was hard work and watered manually or the grass would die and the dirt would return.

Phoebe wore what she had on. Not having purchased many clothes, the ones she owned were new and she had chosen colors she liked. *Besides, this is just for fun.*

"Do we have to make an appointment or anything?" asked Will, mystified by the photo-taking process that didn't involve a point and shoot camera.

"Mr. Sanford notified me that he would contact the photographer. I believe he is expecting us unless he is notified to the contrary," Lena said, eyebrows raised, hoping to hear no objection.

Will shrugged. "Let's go."

As an afterthought, Lena added, "Are you wearing your necklace? You should." Phoebe touched it, indicating she was.

Phoebe noticed Walter was dressed in a black coat and held a hat in his hands, looking self-conscious. Wyanet walked into the parlor, nodded to Will, looked at Phoebe with a smile and muttered. "Good afternoon, Miss Poh-bee."

"It's Phoebe, fff, fff," she correctly gently, smiling at Wyanet.

"Walter is attempting to teach Wyanet to read," said Lena with an apologetic tone. "Since he's still learning himself it has been an amusing morning."

"What's that mean, Mama?" the boy asked, hopping across the parlor back and forth.

"Funny. It's been a funny morning. You are a comical boy, Walter."

"Is that good?" He asked, continuing his hopping.

Lena put a hand on her son's shoulder to still his movement and looked him squarely in the eye. "Yes. Far better to have a sense of humor than grow to be a curmudgeon. Remember that."

"Yes, Mama." When released, the boy continued his hopping.

On exiting the house they were joined by Newton. He greeted the group one by one, commenting on how wonderful Lena looked today. Walter complained to him that he had to wear his suit coat but that he didn't mind wearing the hat. Newton mentioned that it did make him look the part of a grown-up, a comment Walter appreciated.

"Good afternoon, Phoebe," he said, tipping his hat.

"Newton," she said curtly. "What have you been doing this morning?" *Tell me where you were, that there is a reasonable explanation for the rim being in Lionel's blacksmith shop. Don't lie.*

"I have been visiting. I did go see Lionel Bradley this morning as well. To inquire as to whether he would be able to join us at the photographer's."

"And?"

"He will be joining us, if that suits you."

"I'm glad, yes." Phoebe walked on, staring at the backs of the others. She could feel Newton's eyes on her but he said nothing more.

On Main Street they stopped in front of the photographer's building. Newton said he would fetch Chester Murphy. They only had to wait a few minutes, as Chester Murphy had been expecting them and had been allowed to leave for a short time.

On entering the studio they were greeted by a man who introduced himself as the photographer. He asked specifics of what they desired and began to arrange a couple of chairs for the ladies present and straighten the drape that would hang behind them. As the ladies brushed their dresses down flat, Lionel Bradley walked through the door.

"I'm sorry I'm late." He held up his hands. "They are hard to get clean, sometimes."

Apology accepted, the photographer assigned a place for Lionel to stand. Since he was the tallest of the bunch he would be behind and to Phoebe's left as this was near center. Lena sat at center and Wyanet was to her left. The photographer's demeanor made it clear he was puzzled at the family desiring a Paiute in the photo, but he performed the duty he was being paid for.

Walter stood between his mother and Wyanet. Staggering the gentlemen behind the chairs, Will stood to Phoebe's right, beside Lionel, Newton on Lionel's left and Chester behind Wyanet. Hats on, dresses smoothed, breeze-blown hair straightened, ties adjusted, chins lifted, hands folded in laps; and Walter was warned to behave and hold still.

The plate was retrieved from the room behind the photographer and the subjects were told to strike whatever facial feature they chose and to hold it, as they needed to remain still for several seconds. Phoebe found it difficult not to giggle, as she did on such occasions when told she wasn't supposed to. She cleared her throat to restrict the impulse.

"Are you quite all right, Miss Tucker?" asked Newton, barely moving his lips.

"I am indeed, Mr. Sanford," *don't make me giggle.*

Ready, go. Picture one complete, time for a spare in case the first was blurry or someone had blinked. Hold still, don't move, picture two complete.

The photographer asked if they would like any other poses, groups or arrangements. Lena frowned in thought, most likely because more pictures would mean a higher cost than she had anticipated for something that was already an extravagance. Phoebe was amenable to more, but was unsure of the cost. They all looked to each other.

"How much will this cost?" she whispered in Newton's ear.

"For you, nothing, my dear. I would like to purchase a photo as a selfish keepsake for my own."

"I would like to purchase the group portrait as it was my idea, after all."

"If that is what you wish. However, it is hardly fair to you to pay for additional sittings."

Phoebe agreed somewhat and, after having quietly asked the photographer about the cost, she insisted on having a portrait of Lena and Walter taken, with Wyanet joining them if desired. She hoped it was a suitable thank you.

Phoebe also requested one of herself and Will. *Why not?*

Newton spoke to the photographer next, and the helpful and supportive man arranged the chairs once again, removing two, leaving one. "Ma'am, sit here please," he said to Phoebe.

"Me?" she asked, pointing to herself.

"Yes, ma'am. Right here. Sir, if you would stand here, just so," he said to Newton. Will had to pretend to scratch an itch on the side of his face to hide his smirk from Phoebe when she looked his way, consternation clearly written across her face. "But isn't this, um, well if it's just the two of us, I – "

"Will, I believe your sister is at a loss for words," Newton said.

"Miracles do happen," her brother jabbed.

Sputtering her objections about their picture being mistaken for a married couple, the photographer had to admonish her for frowning. "You cannot hold that face for a photo," he said, placing a new plate into the camera.

"Oh yes, she can," muttered Will.

Once done, Phoebe paid the dollar and fifty cents for a copy of the group photo for each of them, and the thirty cents each for the other individual ones they'd posed for. Newton paid for two copies of the photo of the two of them he had requested. She graciously thanked him for the gesture. *What will become of his copy someday?* she thought sadly.

The photographer said he would have the photos for them later that afternoon. Chester Murphy returned to his work at the bank and the rest of the assemblage walked toward the boarding house, stopping to chat and peer in windows on Main Street along the way.

They passed a bakery with cakes on display in the front window and an advertisement posted next to it. They stopped to admire the beautiful confectionery display and to let Walter read the sign, something he was excited he was able to do unaided. Phoebe approached the entrance and, hand on the knob, looked back to everyone. "Time for a treat." she said, opening the door.

They all had a confection of choice in hand when Phoebe paid the clerk and said, "They're on me."

Newton said, "Phoebe, you really don't have to – "

"Shut up, Newton," she said, causing him to nearly choke on his bite of raspberry tart.

Walter said, "Ha, 'shut up, Newton,'" and hopped up and down.

"Walter, that was inappropriate of me, please do not repeat it."

"Then why did you say it?"

"Because I – because I'm an outlaw, that's why," she smirked at Newton, who reddened in the face. "I'm teasing, Walter. It was rude and I apologize."

Newton shot a look at Will for sharing his private ranting, who shrugged as if to say, *You said it.*

"Miss Tucker – "

"Phoebe."

"Phoebe, I'm sor – that was – "

"Yeah, yeah. Just eat your tart."

After their dessert they returned to the photographer's studio to pick up their portraits. They stood on the boardwalk viewing them, Lena stating how clearly her cameo appeared in the photo. Lionel said he was satisfied that the residual stains on his hands did not show, and Walter stared at the photo, mesmerized that such a thing was even possible.

Newton looked for a long time at the photo of himself and Phoebe and she thought she saw his mustache twitch on one side. He then put it carefully into his vest pocket, still wrapped in the paper it had been delivered in.

Chester Murphy ate dinner at the boarding house that evening and after several games of checkers with every combination of opponents imaginable he announced he was retiring for the evening.

Phoebe had wanted to speak with him about the gold coins and had, as yet, had no opportunity to do so. She handed the coins to Will when Walter and Newton were engaged in serious checker competition and quietly nodded to the retreating Chester. "It will sound better coming from you," she whispered and nudged him with her elbow.

Will and Chester spoke in the hallway at the base of the stairs for a minute or two, they shook hands, and Phoebe saw her brother hand over the gold coins to a visibly grateful Chester. Chester looked at Phoebe and nodded. *I wonder what he told him.*

After Walter's immense 'defeat' of Newton at the checkerboard, Lena announced it was bedtime for her son. The usual wails of 'Aw, Mama,' and 'I'm not tired,' followed, but the boy eventually said goodnight to the adults present and walked into the room he shared with his mother.

Newton retired as well, picking up the book of Thomas Campbell poetry and saying he was going to read a bit before nodding off. Left alone with each other and the checkerboard, Phoebe asked Will if Chester was okay with accepting the coins.

"I told him you won it playing Faro and felt guilty about it. That you just couldn't find it in your heart to keep it and that you, we, and I as your brother," he put his hand over his heart and spoke melodramatically, "felt that since he had lost his money by the committing of a crime upon his person, that it was a fitting justification to accept our condolences and relieve you of your guilt in one fell swoop."

"Oh for heaven's sake," Phoebe said, rolling her eyes at him. "I'm glad he accepted, but I had no idea you were capable of such loquacious verbiage."

"Of what?"

"My point exactly."

As they were about to lock their doors for the evening, Will poked his head around the corner and said, "Hey, Phoebe, I had fun today. The photos, the bakery, tonight playing checkers."

With her boots off and wiggling her toes, she leaned against the door jamb. "Me too, little brother. Me, too. It wasn't much different than a day back home with the family, was it?"

"Not really, no. I always had the impression that the people in those old photos in your books were unhappy, or dissatisfied, or really, really bored. I never imagined what went on before or after the photo was taken. Or what they might have thought about their picture after they'd had it taken."

"Mm-hmm. It's difficult to put yourself into a setting from long ago. Different clothes, daily habits, hairstyles, things like that."

"But they aren't that different, are they? Not deep down," stated Will, seeing his surroundings with a fresh view.

"I guess not."

“I feel terrible about the graves we saw in the cemetery today that we didn’t even know about. It’s inevitable, I suppose, with the passage of time,” Will said quietly.

“‘*Nothing is as new as something which has been long forgotten.*’ I remember that from a class I took my freshman year; it’s a German proverb.”

“So why don’t you go back to that? To history I mean. It’s never too late, there’s always time to do what you really want. And at the risk of having my head bit off, you and I both know that’s what you really love, Phoebe. Not business.”

Phoebe looked down at the floor, at her feet, and ran her big toe along a line of wood grain on the floor. “Time. J. W. mentioned time when we were looking out the window at Grandma and Grandpa’s house. He said it was time. I don’t know what he meant. But maybe I will. You’re right, business is really boring, at least to me. There was this guy at work, ugh, what was his name, he thought it was great. For some, maybe it is. But for me...”

“Told ya,” Will said, smiling at her. “You should listen to me more often, big sister.”

Phoebe couldn’t keep her grin at bay. “Oh shut up,” she said, and closed her door on him.

32

Friday morning, fresh coffee, whipped butter from the creamery, the smell and sound of frying bacon and fried potatoes; breakfast was always delicious in the Barrett boarding house and made Phoebe and Will regret that they may be leaving soon.

"Good morning, Phoebe, Will," said Newton, coming into the kitchen a few minutes after they had.

"Good morning," each said in reply.

"I'll be home in plenty of time to walk you to the dance this evening. Will you be coming?" he asked Will.

Just then Lena walked back in through the kitchen door, having recently stepped out. A thought struck Phoebe at that moment and she wondered why she hadn't thought of it before. *Because I've been preoccupied with my own problems, that's why.* "Will, why don't you and Lena come to the dance together this evening. Lena, you need to have some fun, too, don't you think?"

Lena smiled broadly, looking to Will who was slightly embarrassed that he hadn't thought to ask her himself at an earlier time. Lena, unfortunately, mistook his apprehension for distaste at the suggestion. "Oh, I don't know, it's all right – "

Will stood. "I would love to escort you to the dance this evening, Mrs. Barrett. Really. I'm sorry I left it up to my sister," he shot her a scathing look, "to do the asking for me."

"That would be wonderful, Mr. Tucker."

"Will. Please call me Will. We are to be dance partners after all."

"Then I insist you address me as Lena. Since we are to be dance partners," her smile returned and it warmed Phoebe's heart. "What am I to do with Walter?"

"Can't you bring him with you? Are children not allowed?"

"I supposed I could, there are children at the other dances at the Union Hall. Since this is to raise funds for a good cause I believe it would be appropriate."

"Wonderful," said Phoebe, clapping her hands together. She turned to Newton. "We will all see you this evening."

He nodded to them all and took his leave. Phoebe watched him go, pushing the reminder of the date, and his fate, deep down into her gut.

Phoebe had brought in and hung up her laundry yesterday after they had returned from the Photographer and now stood perusing the items she had purchased. *Not much to choose from,* she was thinking when there was a knock on her door. Lena was standing there when she opened it and Phoebe admitted her, leaving the door open. The Army jacket remained tucked safely under her mattress but the sun dress was amongst the other items hanging in the wardrobe. She pushed it all the way to the side.

"Hello, Phoebe. I want to talk to you a moment."

"Certainly. Sit down, please," she said, sitting on the bed while Lena sat in the chair in the corner. "What is it, is there a problem?"

"No, not at all. I'm sorry to have worried you. I do hope what I have to suggest does not offend you, however." The woman folded her hands together and cleared her throat.

"I was going to offer you something to wear tonight. I have a few dresses that I do not wear often, that I wore occasionally when I was married and my husband and I would go out more often. I would like to offer one to you, if you are agreeable to the idea." She nodded toward the Phoebe's hanging clothes. "I see you are a bit limited in your wardrobe."

"I think that's extremely kind of you. And you're right, of course, I did not purchase many items when my brother and I first arrived. I wasn't sure how long we were going to be staying."

"Wonderful," Lena said, delighted not to have offended her new friend.

"In fact, I want to talk to you about something as well." *How do I put this into words?* "Will and I may not be in Bodie much longer. I'm not exactly sure of our departure date as yet, but I wanted to assure you we have enjoyed our time here, with you, with all of you," she paused, the uncommon sensation of choking up with emotion creeping into her throat. "I'm glad we had our picture taken together."

"I am, as well. And Walter and I will miss you terribly. But such is life in Bodie. I only wish the best for you both."

Now if we can't get home I'm going to look foolish.

"Mr. Sanford has recently told me a similar situation exists for him. I'll leave it at that."

"It's all right, he's told me the same thing. Do you know where he may be going? Or anything about his family? Where he's from?" Phoebe asked, knowing full well she sounded too curious.

"I don't, really. Just that he seems quite attached to Lionel Bradley, who is a very nice man. Mr. Sanford took a shine to him immediately when they met." She seemed reflective and continued. "I'm not sure of Mr. Bradley's disposition. I do know he needs help from time to time, although he is an excellent blacksmith. Forgive me, but if I'm not mistaken, I believe I detect an interest in Mr. Sanford." She was smiling conspiratorially

Whoa, wait just a minute...

Phoebe's sentiments were revealed when her cheeks flushed in embarrassment.

"Come to my room when it suits you. I'll either be there or, around, this morning." Lena stood to go and said, pointing at Phoebe's open door. "You must be reasonably sure Mr. Griffin or Mr. Young will remain at bay."

"I trust you with a scattergun more that I trust those two to behave themselves," Phoebe said in jest, but knew Lena took the situation regarding the two men as seriously as she, herself, did.

Phoebe was leaving her room when Will met her at her door. "I was in my room when I heard you talking to Mrs. Barrett, um, Lena. "Why did you tell her we might be leaving soon? Did you figure something out?"

"Sshhh, chill, would you. Come in," she said, pulling him into her room. "Not exactly. But J. W.'s words have been going round and round in my head. I think we're making this too complicated."

"Meaning what exactly?"

"We – " They heard Walter enter the house, singing a song to which he knew only half the words. "Later," said Phoebe, walking out with Will and closing her door.

"Hello, Walter," said Phoebe, walking toward Lena's room. "Has your mother told you about this evening?"

His shoulders drooped. "Yes. She said I have to wear my nice coat. But I get to wear my hat," he brightened. "Arthur and Mary Louisa may be there." He shrugged. "We can play outside while the grown-ups dance." He made a face when he said 'dance.' Will assured him he wouldn't hate it quite as much someday.

"Mama asked me to bring in some firewood. Wanna help?" Walter asked Will and Phoebe motioned for her brother to go ahead. She was headed to Lena's room anyway.

Once there, Phoebe saw the way Lena had decorated her own room. It was pretty, with photographs hanging on the walls, a stack of books near Walter's trundle bed and flowers in a vase in the corner. The room was undoubtedly the largest but it was smaller than most modern bedrooms. Sharing it with Walter made it that much smaller.

"We are very similar in height and measurement. I'm sure I have a dress that would be sufficient for this evening," said Lena, seeming to enjoy herself and the process of finding Phoebe something to wear. "This one is nice but there is too much fabric at the top for your necklace to show." She continued looking. "How about this?" She asked, holding up a gown of deep purple with off-white cuffs, buttons and petite lace sewn around the top edge of the collar. Pleats across the bust and bodice would make it formfitting on top, multiple gathers at the waist made it flowing and voluminous.

"Oh it's beautiful, if it fits me," Phoebe exclaimed, touching the soft and expensive fabric. Are you sure you won't be wearing it?"

"I've already picked the gown I'm to wear. Although a couple of years old now it was one of my husband's favorites. James had excellent taste in all things." The dress she held up for Phoebe's examination was a butter yellow with golden buttons. Lena's sentimental expression told Phoebe volumes about her relationship with her first husband, Walter's father.

As outspoken as always, Phoebe said, "If I wore that one I would spill something dark on it in the first five minutes."

Lena laughed and said, "Then purple seems the proper color for you this evening."

In the afternoon Phoebe and Will had some time to themselves and walked outside to look inside the barn. The metal rim had mysteriously returned to its prior location on the nail in the corner. Mystified and wanting desperately to ask Lionel Bradley about it, Phoebe said, "I don't understand this."

"Why question it? It's back, we probably need it, who knows? Ask if you want to, but why push it?"

She looked at Will with new appreciation of his relaxed attitude. “I want to know, that’s why.”

“Are you sure it was ever gone in the first place? Maybe you just didn’t see it?”

“Yes, I’m sure. At least I think so,” she answered doubtfully. She walked to the rim and touched its surface. “We need to try again soon. This looks like real gold to me and in a town full of people like Albert Griffin and John Young, doing anything they can to get their hands on the stuff without working for it, I don’t trust this not to disappear again. Forever.”

Will was nodding. “Okay, I agree. But how – ” She turned to him and smiled. “You know I’m always suspicious when you look at me like that,” he said. “And don’t tell me to shut up again.”

“Remember when you fainted?”

Will grimaced. “I prefer the term ‘passed out.’”

“Remember when you were freaking out when we first arrived?”

He nodded. “What’s your point?”

“I don’t feel like I did when we appeared here in the barn. I don’t think you do, either.”

Will frowned in concentration thinking back on the previous several days. “Huh, no I guess I don’t. Again, your point?”

She shook her head, her thoughts still an unexplainable jumble. “This is what I meant by telling you we’re making it too complicated. J. W. told me to be patient. He said it was time. So I’m trying to do what you said, enjoy my time here. And I’m trying, as difficult as it can be for me, to be patient. But I believe we’ll be going home soon; that we’ll know when the time is right. I can feel it.”

“Geez, you’re weird,” said Will, walking to the barn door and swinging it open. But he noticed that the noise from the stamps mills, the sound of horses and wagons and intermittent yelling from the hillside didn’t disturb him as it had before. The sun was always shining, the breeze warm with the onset of an approaching summer and he knew enough to step around the now drying mud and rushing wagons that were always filling the streets. "Coming?"

Phoebe took a last look at the wagon wheel rim hanging on the nail and walked out the barn door, helping Will to close it. She stood back and looked at the red paint and white trim and noticed its condition compared to how she was used to seeing it. "It's quite the keepsake, don't you think?"

"What?"

"The barn. J. W. said he moved it because he liked it. That's why it's on Grandpa's land now. It's one of those 'I wish these walls could talk' kind of objects, you know? I hope we get home in time to get the chance for J. W. to explain."

"We will, Phoebe."

***

"Your fine's been paid, Mr. Griffin. You're free to go, for now. You're lucky the owner of the boarding house didn't want to take this case further." Constable Kirgan walked Albert Griffin out of the jail and onto King Street, where John Young awaited his release. "Stay out of trouble, Mr. Griffin, Mr. Young. Your faces are familiar ones in Bodie."

Albert Griffin said not a word, still angry he had been forced to stay for two nights in a crowded jail with drunks, opium dealers, a jewelry store thief and a man who had pummelled his wife, all reeking of the vice of their choosing. John Young tipped his hat and offered a sardonic smile to the Constable. The lawman was not fooled, and followed the progress of the transgressors until they were out of sight.

"It's about time you liberated me," Albert Griffin said, a caustic tone to his words. "What took you so long?"

"I didn't know you were here until yesterday," John Young admitted. "I was otherwise occupied," he said, glancing back to Bonanza Street and waving at a woman standing outside in front of her crib. The woman waved back and blew him a kiss.

"Damn you, my money had better still be in my room when I get back there. If not I'm taking it out of yours. Or your hide."

John Young seemed untroubled at the prospect. "I don't have much left, anyway."

Albert Griffin's face contorted in anger and frustration. "What?" He bellowed, earning glances from others on the boardwalk.

"We each spend how we see fit. I drink and gamble and cherish the ladies, you drink and almost get your head blown off. Don't preach to me."

Albert Griffin rubbed his hand, still sore but healing from the fork stab wound inflicted by that insufferable witch. "Maybe it's time we moved on, like I said before. Fresh town, fresh resources."

"Suits me, I suppose," replied John Young. He wouldn't mind vacating the town and discovering new sources of income elsewhere. But not yet. Albert had been the one to get arrested, not he. "Soon. I know someplace we need to be this evening. And I know you won't want to miss out." He knew his partner well enough to know he would be unable to resist the temptation, so dangled a prospect of a money-making venture before him like a carrot.

Albert Griffin perked up. "Pray tell, John."

John Young proceeded to enlighten him about the event taking place in a few hours at the Miner's Union Hall and reminded him of the sort who attended those types of functions. Albert Griffin walked with renewed vigor in hopes of a fun-filled evening.

***

"Don't you look dashing," said Phoebe to Will. "Where'd the coat come from?"

"Newton took pity on me," he said. "And he suggested a barber where I went to get a good shave and a trim. You owe the man a quarter. Best deal of the century. Never mind I won't be staying in this one much longer. You look, well, you look, um, pretty, by the way."

"It almost killed you to say the words, didn't it?" She smirked at her brother. "Thanks. Lena has some pretty clothes she doesn't get to wear very often. I hope I don't ruin it," said Phoebe flouncing the skirt and spinning in a circle to send the skirt flowing widely.

"Wow, that's a big skirt. I hope Newton can get close enough to dance with you. Disco's nearly dead at home, and I'm pretty sure the jitterbug isn't around for several more decades."

They met in the parlor where Walter was pulling at the collar of his shirt and complaining it was too small. Newton came down from upstairs and his smile at Walter faded when his eyes rested on Phoebe. "Miss Tucker, excuse me, Phoebe, you, you look..."

"Lovely, I know. Thank you. Lena loaned the dress to me. I take it you approve?" She said impertinently, spinning once more to show off the gown. "And she pinned up my hair for me too, I'm dreadful at it." Newton stared and nodded.

Lena emerged from her room a moment later and rescued Newton from his speechless posture. "Oh, Lena, you look like whipped butter," said Phoebe. Never before having taken a liking to formal attire, she now felt as if she were going to a masquerade party and it was delightful.

Lena handed something to Phoebe and when she spread it wide she saw it was a shawl. A hand-knit, triangular, off-white shawl with a golden button in the front where two corners met to close it. "Oh, it's so pretty," said Phoebe, touching the soft yarn. Newton stepped forward and took it from her hands, offering to drape it across her shoulders.

As they began their walk toward the Hall, Newton offered his arm to Phoebe and she took it, no sarcastic remark included. Will offered his arm to Lena and she accepted shyly. Walter skipped ahead of them with the reminder from his mother to keep to the side of the road so as not to get his shoes too dirty.

Music emanated from the Union Hall, still a block away. People were gathering in the Street, talking to friends, acquaintances and family. Tall hats, long suit coats and plenty of lace and ruffles. Phoebe was glad to have a pretty dress to wear so she wouldn't stand out as the most plainly dressed of the gathering. Her boots weren't exactly in style, but the dress was wide enough at the bottom to hide them most of the time.

The doors to the Hall were open, allowing people to spill out onto the boardwalk and gather outside when they were not dancing or getting something to eat or drink. The Hall was decorated with streamers and hanging lamps with colored glass making colorful patterns on the wooden floor. Chairs and small tables placed strategically along the wall allowed for group seating and conversation.

Newton paid their fee at the door and their names were written down. Phoebe had given Will some money before they had left to pay for Lena, Walter and himself. Not long after entering they saw Chester escorting Mary Jacobson, with her parents coming in together behind them. Phoebe waved to her and Mary smiled and waved in return.

Newton offered to go with Will and fetch the ladies a glass of punch. Phoebe asked if they had sarsaparilla and Will screwed up his face again. She mouthed, 'root beer, dummy,' in his direction before he walked away with Newton.

"I've never been to a dance like this before," admitted Phoebe to Lena.

"No? I would have thought there would be chances where you – where you're from."

"Not really. Not like this." She didn't want to lie to her new friend so decided vague answers were best. "And I've never owned a dress like this," she said, twirling in a circle.

"Phoebe, what a delicious dress," said Mary Jacobson as she and Chester made their way over.

Phoebe laughed and said, "I must admit, it belongs to Lena Barrett, the landlady of my boarding house." Phoebe began introductions but it turned out the two women had previously met, albeit on a professional basis, at the milliner's.

The music quartet was in one corner of the room, food and drink was on a long table on the opposite side, away from the door but within easy reach. Ladies from the organization committee supervised the food and drink and their husbands manned the door, taking in admission fees. *I helped pay for the building of the Bodie Methodist Church. And I can't tell anybody about it or they'll throw a straitjacket on me.*

Lena found a table for them all with several unoccupied chairs. They would sit to begin with, knowing they would be on their feet the remainder of the evening. Newton and Will returned with two glasses of punch, two lemonades and a sarsaparilla for Phoebe. "For you," Newton said, leaning down to her and setting it on the table, earning a wide smile.

"Thank you," Phoebe said with pleasant surprise.

Walter was already antsy in his seat and looking around for friends that might have arrived. He pointed toward the door and said, "Mama, Arthur's here. Can I go?"

"In a minute, Walter," she answered patiently. "Let them proceed through the door first." When the family was further into the room Arthur waved at Walter, just as relieved to see his friend as Walter had been. The boy waved Walter over and Lena said, "You may go, but do not leave the building unless you notify me. Is that understood?" She said in a stern, motherly voice.

Walter nodded, "Yes, Mama," and he kissed her lightly on the cheek before skipping off to see his friend Arthur.

"How sweet," said Mary Jacobson, accepting her glass of punch from Chester.

"Hmm," said Lena skeptically. "He'll be outside soon, playing in the dirt and looking for mischief." She sipped her lemonade. "As long as he keeps his distance form those ruffians who were thrashed last summer for throwing rocks at the Chinese wood cutters, I believe he will remain in good company."

Will's eyes bugged out at Lena's last statement and Phoebe had to look away to hold back an inadvertent giggle..

"I'm going to go see what's at the hors d'oeuvre table if anyone wants to join me," said Phoebe, walking that direction without waiting for answers. Oysters, lemon cakes, chocolates, boiled eggs, assorted cheeses, strawberries dipped in white cream... Phoebe put a few selections on a delicate plate and turned to see Newton standing behind her. She popped a whole strawberry into her mouth and mumbled, "Mmm, delicious. Want one?"

"I do. Now that you've seen what's offered do you have any suggestions?" he asked, his eyes sparkling.

"I dunno," she mumbled; *Shoot, this strawberry was too big to eat all in one bite.* "Have one of everything."

Newton was handed a small plate and chose a couple of strawberries, a piece of fudge and a spoonful of roasted peanuts, waiting until he returned to the table to sit down before eating. He passed Will on his way to get two plates, one for Lena and one for himself.

The music grew louder, most of the attendees had arrived and Newton asked Phoebe if she wanted to dance. The organized group dance ended; individual couples remained in the center of the room. She first analyzed their movements; *Yes, nothing fancy, I think I can do that.* She nodded to Newton and took hold of his extended hand.

Not having danced a slow dance since a family wedding years ago, Phoebe moved stiffly at first. Her spine went straight and she couldn't look Newton in the eye while standing this closely. "Is there something bothering you, Phoebe?" he asked, sounding sincere.

She pursed her lips, not wanting a confrontation; not tonight. And her conscience wouldn't allow her to interrogate him about Lionel, their mysterious conversation at supper the other night and the fact that she and Will – all right she alone – had snooped on Lionel. What reason did she have for asking about a wagon wheel rim with gold flecks embedded in it? By shaking her head 'no,' and seeming to look about the room searching for someone, she hoped to avoid further questions.

"Phoebe?"

"Yes?"

"Phoebe, look at me." His feet had stopped moving and she nearly tripped over one of them, glaring at him for his clumsiness. "Stop frowning."

His right hand remained at the small of her back and his left hand tightened its grip on her right as they stood there, unmoving, drawing looks from other dancers. "People are staring," she said.

"Somehow I doubt that bothers you." He continued moving slowly around the floor, holding her close so they could converse easily.

After a moment he said, "Chester told me what Will did, what you and Will did, in giving him the double eagles to replace the money from the robbery." She said nothing so he forged on. "That was a thoughtful gesture. However, he stated it was to assuage your guilt for winning the money at Faro."

"Okay."

"You forget I was there, at the saloon. I saw you win and trade your checks in for cash, not gold. And I saw how much fun you were having."

"Did you?"

"I did. You didn't look very guilty to me."

"Tell me what point you're trying to make, please."

"Why would you randomly give Chester all that money in gold? The only reason I can think of is because you have a generous heart, and you don't care for anyone to truly see it." "They weren't mine. Someone gave them to me. I thought Chester might have better use of them."

His mustache twitched. "All that money?" He paused a moment. "You're like a prickly pear, do you know that? A prickly pear. Barbed and untouchable on the outside and soft on the inside."

Phoebe scowled. "I am not soft on the inside."

Newton laughed then, and Phoebe grinned as her words replayed in her head. "Chester is a good man. Your gesture was very kind."

Phoebe simply nodded, her only acceptance of the compliment.

The music stopped and people clapped. The musicians discussed musical selections in the few minutes break until the next song. Phoebe made to return to their table and see what the others were doing or discussing, and to get a drink. Newton excused himself when he noticed his coworker, Robert Jensen, and his wife across the room.

Back at the table Phoebe noticed that Chester and Mary Jacobson had moved on and Will and Lena were talking lightly about the food. Warmer now, she removed her shawl and put it on the back of her chair. There was a commotion near the door. Heads turned that direction and a few women scurried toward the rear of the room to separate themselves from the trouble. Someone yelled, another replied, volumes increased, men in the Hall excused themselves and moved to the doorway, voices grew louder, a woman was pushed and fell, another woman was crying...

Phoebe craned her neck to see what was going on. Will attempted to pull her down to sit in a chair, urging her to stay out of whatever situation was brewing outside. Lena's face showed concern for her son until he ran across the room and stood behind her chair, panting. His friends, Arthur and a girl Phoebe heard him address as Mary Louisa stood nearby, their parents not far from them all.

Phoebe saw Newton leave his friend Robert and run into the fray. She asked what time it was, over and over, to anyone nearby who would listen. Arthur's father slid his pocket watch out of his vest pocket and told her it was 10:45, giving her an odd look for being concerned with the hour at a time like this.

But all the while she was wondering if whoever had etched Newton's date of death into the stone that she remembered had gotten the eighteenth mixed up with nineteenth. Before midnight or after? Slightly relieved it was not yet eleven o'clock, she stood on tiptoe and searched the growing, noisy crowd for any sign of him.

Moments later gunfire erupted outside, women and children screamed and people ran for the nearest cover. Lena yanked Walter to the floor and sat under the table. Will reached out to grab Phoebe's wrist to pull her closer and down to the floor with them. But when he looked out from under the edge of the tablecloth she was gone.

33

Fighting to get through the crowd to the doorway, Phoebe was pushed and shoved in the opposite direction. Two men stepped in front of her and attempted to convince her it was not safe, another practically ordered her to return to the interior of the room. She pushed at the man, stating he had no right to demand anything from her, and managed to reach the entrance, where she was suddenly shoved from behind by others rushing outside. Keeping her balance was difficult and she took step over step, her arms reaching out to stabilize herself any way she could.

Her foot landed on the edge of the boardwalk and she twisted her ankle, falling hard into the dirt on her knees and outstretched hands. First, she examined the dress. Dirt she could wash, rips she could not. The dress had survived the fall but her knees ached from their contact with the ground and scattered rocks near the boardwalk. One palm was bleeding and she complained audibly at her own ungainliness.

A man asked if she was all right and reached out to help her stand. He then told her this was no place for a lady, to which she replied, "Thank you, but I'll be fine," and turned from him to search the crowd for Newton and a source of the melee.

A few yards to her left she saw John Young approach atop a horse, a pistol in his free hand and sneering at her. Her chatelaine bag had maintained its attachment to her waist through the pushing and shoving and fall off the boardwalk. If she reached to open it now to withdraw her Colt he would see her; and perhaps shoot at her for the action. *Bad timing.*

Someone called her name, "Miss Tucker," but when she turned toward the voice she recognized no one who might know her. John Young spurred his horse to run further down the street, directly through the crowd, firing his pistol into the air once, twice. People scurried out of his way, one man falling on his face in the street in his rush.

Atop another horse was Albert Griffin, whom John Young had run to meet. Some present withdrew pistols from their coat pockets; many appeared unarmed. "Miss Tucker," she heard again, this time seeing Chester standing across the street in the company of a few others, worry in his expression. She waved to him and attempted a small smile in the low light. She also took the opportunity to loosen the strings on her bag and pull the Colt out a few inches so the grip would be at the ready.

Other men arrived on horseback and jumped off when they approached, their horses wandering away to the sides of the street. They all appeared to have been drinking heavily and had most likely heard the commotion outside the Union Hall and come begging for trouble. Phoebe took hold of the reins of one of the horses, speaking to it softly and leading it away. She didn't want to tie it to a post to risk its inability to free itself.

The drunken men had come to disturb the gaiety and to hound the throng of partygoers. Phoebe saw one stick his hand inside a gentleman's coat and take out his pocket watch. The gentleman pushed at the pickpocket but to no avail and was slugged in the jaw, falling back on his rump on the ground. A similar incident occurred further down and Phoebe saw Albert Griffin and John Young laughing at the scene they had most likely instigated.

Phoebe saw no sign of Newton as yet and stepped back up onto the boardwalk to gain a higher vantage point. No use. The scene was mostly men and they were as tall as, or taller than, she. An increasing number of people gathered, tightening the group, some coming from inside the Hall, more from the surrounding saloons and other homes on this end of town; visibility was hampered.

So absorbed was she in her search for Newton that she made the mistake of letting the crowd move her slowly along. Even if she had wanted to, she could not, now, easily walk away. Arms were brushing her sides, pushing her from behind.

Someone stepped on the back of her boot and she stumbled, losing her balance and bumping hard into the person in front of her. The man turned around and pushed her, believing her to have been the transgressor, and she again fell into the street. Men stepped on her beautiful borrowed dress, trapping her on the ground where she sat writhing to be released, grasping at anything she might take hold of to pull herself back up.

Suddenly the immediate crowd cleared and men bolted out of her way. Stomping hooves pounded near her and she looked up from her seated position on the ground to see John Young staring down at her from atop his horse. She held quite still, knowing the horse would avoid stepping on her if he could avoid it, but not trusting John Young to keep a steady hand. "Like my new horse, Miss Tucker?" He yelled, spitting while he spoke drunkenly down to her. He inched the animal closer to her, the threat to harm her obvious. Phoebe pulled her feet in and tucked them beneath her as best she could with the yards of fabric billowing around her.

Albert Griffin had been running his own horse up the street and down again, charging people, frightening them. Other ruffians on foot or horseback joined him. John Young watched him pass by and Phoebe took the opportunity to stand up.

Out of the corner of her eye she saw Chester across the street, relief on his face at seeing she was unharmed. He was waving for her to come to him, to quit the scene, get out of the road, stay clear of the madmen. But then she caught sight of Newton off to her right.

He seemed to be searching frantically. *For me?* she wondered. Perhaps he had heard Chester call her name and knew she was outside. Taking advantage of John Young's distraction, Phoebe grabbed hold of his left arm with both hands and gave a hard pull, yanking the man off the horse to land with a thud, his pistol flying through air over both their heads. Speechless at the action and dizzy from too much whiskey, John Young stared up at Phoebe while his arms flailed uselessly to grab hold of her legs.

A whiskey bottle had fallen loose from his pocket and Phoebe stomped on it with the heel of her boot. Two tries and it broke open, spilling the remainder of its contents. John Young yelled to the sky, a guttural cry of indignation and outrage.

Taking hold of the reins of the horse, Phoebe hopped, stuck her left foot in the stirrup, swung her right leg over and urged the horse into motion. She rode far enough to escape John Young's grasp and spun the horse around to face the Union Hall, searching for Newton once again.

Gunshots rang out and she heard one land in the wall of the building closest to her. She spied John Young lying on the ground, aiming his recovered pistol directly at her. Pulling the reins around she sped off toward Green Street, away from the Hall. The move was a feint, as she had no intention whatsoever of leaving her friends and family behind only to save herself.

She turned at the Bodie House Hotel and rode quickly around the block, slowing to see if there was a shorter way to cut through. She rode to Lowe Street which came out at Main south of the Miner's Union Hall and near the 'old' Bodie Hay Yard. At a walk she turned onto Main Street.

She glanced downward and noticed a rifle holster attached to the right side of the saddle. She hadn't felt its slight bulge before due to the dress hanging between it and her leg. Moving the fabric aside she pulled the gun free a few inches and wiggled it around to see how easily it might come out of the holster. Smiling, she recognized the rifle immediately. A Winchester 1873, just like her grandfather's.

As she progressed up Main Street, there was singing, swearing and fighting in the street that necessitated weaving in and out of the sea of gatherers that had never intended to attend the dance, but instead had come to pilfer, harass and use their pickpocket skills to the highest degree.

Albert Griffin continued to ride up and down, back and forth, bumping into people, keeping them from leaving the immediate area or from re-entering the Hall. Surely Constable Kirgan or Sheriff Showers would have known this type of incident had been a possibility and would be nearby, but she had so far seen neither of them.

From a short distance Phoebe heard her name being called yet again. Her first name. It sounded like Newton but the cacophony was intense and hearing anything distinctly was impossible. *Please go into the building, keep safe, don't worry about me.* But she knew his pursuit would continue. He would not go until he saw that she was safe, just like she hadn't gone back into the building when worrying about him. *What time is it?*

John Young remained on the ground, picking at the broken glass from his whiskey bottle, mourning its loss. His pistol lay beside him, within reach but no longer in his hand. Priorities.

As she drew nearer the Hall the doorway was visible and people gathered there, heads poking out or spying through the window on either side of the door. Walter had broken free of his mother's caring grasp and was standing at one of the windows. Catching sight of Phoebe his eyes grew large and he mouthed something, either at her or to someone nearer to him.

Simultaneously she heard Newton call her name again and noticed Will standing in the doorway, wobbling back and forth, obviously standing on the tip of his toes and searching the crowd. She spied Newton so rode toward him. Someone called out, “There it is, there’s my horse,” and Phoebe noticed Albert Griffin turn and dash forward in her direction.

Phoebe ducked and pulled the horse she rode left around a cluster of men when she saw Albert Griffin aim his pistol at her. His gun fired but he missed her, the shot slamming into the post office building to her rear. He was yelling, calling out. John Young picked up his pistol, stood up in the road and searched wildly for the source of his partner’s voice.

As Phoebe finally reached Newton, notable relief on his face, Albert Griffin fired his pistol once again. A man standing several feet behind Phoebe’s horse cried out in pain and fell to the ground, shot in the upper arm. *He’s worse with a pistol than I am.* She swung her leg back and jumped down from the horse, turned the animal around with a pat on his neck as thanks for his help, and pulled the Winchester from the saddle holster in one swift movement.

An unknown man ran up behind her and took hold of the reins, talking to the animal, shushing its agitation. *So John Young is also a horse thief.* Phoebe pointed at John Young in the road and the man nodded his thanks to her. He had obviously witnessed the scene, her takeover and subsequent escape and return. As he and his horse ran from the fray Phoebe notice a name burned into the holster, Myers, and mentally promised to return his Winchester.

“Phoebe, why are you outside?” Newton asked, exasperated with her. “Go in, go back.”

“Why did you come out?” she asked. “You should have stayed inside. You left us.”

“I thought perhaps you had come outside when this started. I was worried. And I was curious. I don’t have time to argue with you about it now. We need to – ”

“Your curiosity could kill you.”

“Look who’s talking,” he said and grabbed her by the elbow to steer her away.

Albert Griffin on horseback blocked their route of escape. The moments of conversation had taken their minds off his approach. His foot kicked out at Newton but made no contact. “Phoebe, over here, come on, hurry.” It was Will, calling to her from the boardwalk. She dared not take her eyes off Albert Griffin, even to acknowledge Will’s words, so waved her hand in his direction to motion she had heard him.

Suddenly Newton fell forward, his legs kicked from behind and sending him buckling to the ground. “Newton!” Phoebe said, reaching for him. Her left arm was yanked, pulling her close to Albert Griffin’s horse.

John Young stepped between her and Newton. “This is for Joseph.” John young aimed his pistol at Newton’s face, inches away and pulled the trigger.

Empty. No more cartridges and the inability to count to six. He dropped the gun and with a primal scream of anger and betrayal he balled his hand into a fist and punched Newton in the jaw. Newton fell backward in the road, groaning and holding his face with both hands. John Young bent over and hit him again on the side of his face.

Stunned, Newton replied through the pain, “I didn’t do it – how did you know – he was chasing me – ” and immediately regretted it; Newton had no desire to bring up the past, only to put Lionel in harm’s way once again. But it was now that he knew with absolute certainty who the other two men had been that evening of the brawl on Main Street; the night they had chased him; the night Lionel had saved his life. There had been only suspicions before; he hadn’t seen their faces.

Leaning down to gain a firmer grip on Phoebe's upper arm, Albert Griffin tugged at her as he attempted to lead his horse away. "Come with me, hussy."

"No," she stated vehemently, spitting up into his face. "I won't." She pulled her arm free and slapped the horse in the rear. It started, throwing its head high, but Albert Griffin quickly gained control and circled the horse around to face them once again. Only seconds, but it allowed her time to switch the Winchester rifle to her left hand, pull the Colt from her chatelaine bag, plant her feet firmly and aim the Colt directly at his face.

Albert pulled the horse up tight and backed up a few paces. Visible beyond the horse, Phoebe could see Walter standing at the window, witnessing the entire scene. *Somebody get him away from there.*

Albert smirked, a malicious, conniving expression. "You're not going to shoot me, *Miss* Tucker."

"You didn't think I was going to stab you with a fork either, did you?" He scowled. *Oops, shouldn't have reminded him.*

John Young grabbed her around the neck from behind and Phoebe lost her balance, the pistol pointing high into the night sky. Bringing her arm down she elbowed him in the stomach. He yowled, clutched his belly with one hand and shoved her forward and sprawling on the ground with the other. The Colt spun out of her hand and landed under the agitated horse of Albert Griffin, where it was stepped on once before he pulled the horse back further, allowing John Young to retrieve it.

As Phoebe was about to stick out her foot to trip him and keep him from gaining purchase of the Colt, Newton rose up, rubbing his head to brush off the pain and flung his arms around John Young's waist, both of them collapsing to the ground. *Nice tackle.* John Young wriggled out from under Newton's grasp and lunged for the Colt. Phoebe gasped when he turned to aim it directly at Newton's chest.

A second pistol, a second chance. Phoebe saw the terror on Newton's face as his eyes darted to hers and back to the pistol. His brow knit together in bewilderment at Phoebe's confident expression. John Young pulled the trigger of the Colt.

Nothing happened and Phoebe yelled, "Ha!" *Only five cartridges, first chamber empty. No safety, Jackass.*

"Stop," yelled Chester Murphy from not far off. John Young turned the gun in the direction of the voice. Phoebe kicked at the side of one knee. There was a cartridge loaded for the next shot now, but John Young fired off balance, blindly, angrily, fury in his clenched fist and shaky gun hand. Somewhere a woman screamed, Walter banged on the glass, Will called out "Nooo," and John Young stood up and ran away, limping, across the street, taking Phoebe's pistol with him.

Chester Murphy was lying on the ground ten yards away, clutching his side. Three men ran after John Young as he weaved through the scattered people remaining in the road. Albert Griffin cheered in a boastful fashion, failing to notice Phoebe raise the Winchester and point it straight at him. When he did he froze in place, the horse no longer responding to his commands. *Never fire a gun in anger... find that quiet place in your mind... shut out the world and there is only you and the target in front of you...*

Phoebe's ears shut out all extraneous noise. Holding the rifle against her shoulder and sighting Albert Griffin down the barrel, she pulled the lever to the side to release it from the lever lock and thumbed the hammer to the full-cock position. *I hope this thing is loaded, I didn't have time to look.* Will saw his sister with the Winchester trained on Albert Griffin and jumped off the boardwalk, running toward Chester. The crowd had thinned enough for clear visibility since the gunshot that had wounded him.

Many things happened at once. Albert Griffin spun his horse around, kicked him to run and was summarily dumped into the dirt by the horse that had obviously had enough of this man he did not trust or like. Phoebe kept the Winchester trained on him. Across the street, kicking and screaming, lay John Young, face down, a large, booted foot of Lionel

Bradley pressing down on the middle of his back. The man near Phoebe who'd been shot in the arm was being tended to by another stranger. Chester Murphy was bleeding from his right side but Mary Jacobson, having seen the incident and screamed in horror, now joined another man, who was later identified as a doctor who had attended the dance, in attempting to survey the damage.

Newton stood beside Phoebe now, telling her to put the gun down or point it at the ground. "No," she said quietly and calmly. Then she yelled at Albert Griffin, "Get up." He didn't move, fear plastered onto his facial features. Phoebe kicked dirt at him as he sat on the ground. "Get. Up," she repeated loudly."

"Phoebe," said Newton. "Don't – "

"I'm not going to shoot him, Newton. Not yet," she said evenly. "But I'm not letting him go either. You're going to jail again, Mr. Griffin, and this time you're not getting out so easily. I advise you not to attempt anything foolish. Is that understood?"

The drunken man stood up slowly, restored confidence allowing a smug look of arrogance. Will came up behind Phoebe and said, "That's good advice, Albert. I suggest you take it." Newton looked from Phoebe to Will and back, stunned at Will's unrestrained confidence in his sister.

She hated bluffing, hated not knowing, hated being unprepared. And hated the smug look on Albert Griffin's face. Phoebe pointed the rifle into the soft dirt several feet to the man's right, away from anyone or anything, and pulled the trigger. A shot rang out and she pulled the lever, returning her aim to the target. Albert Griffin jumped and turned to look where her aim had taken the shot. His smug look returned.

Newton reached out to remove the rifle from her hands but Will stopped him and said, "There was no time to check, she's making sure it's loaded. Trust her." Newton nodded, confused, astonished and feeling a growing respect for this women he had grown to love despite her mysteries.

"Will," she called to her brother loudly. He was there. "My bag, the extra cartridges are inside. Reach in and get five. Fill the Colt on the ground."

"But how do you know if – "

"Do it. Now. They'll fit."

Trying not to disturb her steadiness with the Winchester, Will reached in and felt in her bag for the extra cartridges that had come from their grandfather's cabinet. Newton had retrieved John Young's empty pistol, that Phoebe had seen was a Colt like hers, and took the cartridges from Will to fill the cylinder. "Turn it to leave the first one empty." As he did so he realized now why the first shot fired by John Young from Phoebe's Colt hadn't fired. *Clever, my dear.*

The crowd had mostly dispersed, the pickpockets had lost their opportunities, the drunks were lying in the road or wandering away and back to the saloons and Walter and Lena were walking down the boardwalk in the direction of Newton, Will and Phoebe. Newton held out his hand to slow her approach as Albert Griffin was in a bind and they were all in the midst of an unpredictable situation.

"Now what, *Miss* Tucker," Albert Griffin shifted his weight from foot to foot, waving his arms, attempting to distract her. "Now you and your boyfriend take me to jail? I'll not go back. Two days was enough."

"How about two years, jackass."

"Ooh, such language from a *lady*. You should trade for another, Newton. I'll take her off your hands for – "

"Shut up, Albert," said Newton.

The man laughed without humor. The crowd staring in his direction had grown; they were waiting to see what would happen next.

Across the street Lionel Bradley had withdrawn his foot from the back of John Young, roughly hoisting him back to his feet where his futile effort at release was met with a kick in the backside of his pants. Lionel also picked up Phoebe's pistol from the ground near his feet and stuck it in the waistband of his pants. He nodded to Newton, assuring him that he had this man taken care of.

Walter ran into the road and up to Will. Albert Griffin had made an unsuccessful movement to grab at the boy. The man was tempting fate, being reckless, asking for trouble. "Walter, come back here," called Lena, unmoving. Walter shook his head 'no.' Closer to Chester now, and seeing the man further along with the wound in his arm, Walter's eyes grew wide. It was too real and unpleasant up close.

Four men, seemingly with authority, approached. Phoebe heard Newton speaking to one of them and she recognized the voice of the other, Sheriff Showers, whom she had met. He and another advanced toward Albert Griffin, one on each side. He held up his hands but simultaneously his eyes darted in all locations, scouting out a suitable avenue for escape. He waited too long, and with Phoebe's Winchester pointed at him and her unmistakably resolute demeanor Albert Griffin succumbed to the two lawmen's orders.

The other two held onto John Young. It wasn't until Albert Griffin was being led away, that Phoebe returned the rifle to the half-cocked position, lowered it and sighed. Newton rushed to stand before her, gripped her arms in his hands, kissed her quickly and wrapped his arms around her in a tight, relieved grip.

"Ew," said Walter. Phoebe squeezed him back with her free arm, touching his injured face, concerned. Will smiled and Lena went to Walter.

Many inside the Hall had come to the door, noticing the shooting had stopped and the law had arrived. They spilled out onto the boardwalk, murmuring now, pointing and gasping at what they saw before them. Those immediately involved were asked questions on what had occurred. Albert Griffin was then escorted up Main Street toward the jail.

Inexperience shows, as it did that night when the two men holding onto John Young let him wriggle free and run behind the blacksmith shop and into the dark.

The sheriff yelled at them to follow and the man assisting him with Arthur Griffin ran after the escapee as well. Taking a chance with the distraction, Albert Griffin pulled one hand free, swung his fist around and hit the sheriff in the neck. He fell, gripping his throat and gasping for air. Albert Griffin sped off up the street, avoiding Lionel Bradley who was now searching around the blacksmith shop for John Young.

People acquainted with the sheriff ran to his rescue. He would recover but his quarry was loose.

Phoebe shouted, "We can't let them get away," but no one made a move to chase or capture him. Phoebe and Newton dashed to the other side of the road, going to the rear of the shop where they saw Lionel Bradley now standing near his shack. "Did you see where he went, Lionel?" Asked Phoebe.

"No. But here's your Colt." Lionel grinned as he handed the pistol to her.

"Thank you, Lionel."

"I'm sorry it's a little banged up. The horse..."

"I know, it's okay." She examined the pistol, rubbed some of the dirt off its exterior and noticed a deep gouge on the grip. She released the cylinder and gave it a little spin, checking to see how many cartridges remained and closed it. "It seems fine, other than the grip."

"Tough little gun, those Colts," said Lionel.

"Little?" Newton asked.

Lionel held up his large hands. "For me." The trio smiled at Lionel's comparison. "Mine fit the big ones."

"What should we do?" asked Phoebe, putting her colt safely back inside her bag.

"*We* aren't doing anything," said Newton.

"Okay, what if he comes after one of us later, or just you, or just me? What then?" *Died June 19, 1880.*

"Or what if I run your friend through with this here Arkansas toothpick, just to pain you both," said the voice standing behind and to the right of Lionel, a fixed blade knife pointed at their friend's neck.

John Young had acquired a knife from inside Lionel's shack, the leather sheath discarded at his feet.

Lionel dared a glance at the man, clenched his fists and screwed up his face in the first angry expression Phoebe had ever seen him display. "Put that back. It does not belong to you."

"It does now. But I will return it if the harlot comes with me." John Young stared at Phoebe.

"No," she shouted adamantly, and she could swear she saw Lionel Bradley grin and stand taller in admiration.

Newton had taken a step back. He tugged at the back of Phoebe's dress to do the same but she shook him off and shouldered the Winchester once again, releasing the lever and pulling the hammer back all the way. *Never fire a gun in anger... find that quiet place in your mind... shut out the world and there is only you and the target in front of you...*

Having made sure Walter was safe, Will had joined them and came upon the scene to stand beside Newton. The two law men that had held John Young only minutes before rounded the building and stood several yards behind Newton, pistols in hand. Will pushed their aim downward; too many people in the way. He pointed at Phoebe and the men shook their heads in exasperation.

"I will kill him. He means nothing to me," yelled John Young in desperation.

"Then what? You'll go to prison," Phoebe replied steadily.

"But you're friend will be dead. Is that what you want? We can go have fun, just the two of us."

"No."

John Young smiled victoriously. "Then put down the rifle and walk over here. Come now, Miss Tucker. I can promise you a grand time."

Phoebe's aim and posture remained steady. "You misunderstand me. I mean no, I will not go with you, no, I will not put down the rifle. But I will shoot you, Mr. Young."

The drunken man laughed, the knife waving about in the air. Phoebe stood steady. *Breath in, breath out, eye on the target with a steady hand.* Newton was sputtering behind her, beseeching Will to intervene, to stop her before she was hurt, before it was too late for Lionel. Will shushed him.

"Put down the knife, Mr. Young. Now."

"I don't believe I will," he said as he lunged for Lionel.

Phoebe fired the Winchester, John Young's arm wheeled back, blood spurted, the knife flew through air. She brought the lever forward and back up to ready another shot and fired at the man's feet, pulling the lever once again and keeping her aim. John Young fell backwards onto the ground, writhing in pain, holding his arm with his opposite hand and screaming for help.

Phoebe returned the rifle to half-cocked, slid the lever sideways back into the lever lock, lowered it to her side, turned around and pushed it at one of the lawmen behind them all. "I borrowed this from a Mr. Myers who had his horse stolen by Mr. Young this evening. Please see that it is returned, with my thanks."

34

Will followed his sister as she crossed the street, both returning to the Miner's Union Hall. Newton had stayed for another minute to clear the matter with the two lawmen who took possession of John Young. They had been present, had seen that Lionel Bradley's life had been in danger, and concluded Phoebe's actions had been the only choice for a reasonable outcome. Chester Murphy had been placed on a wagon from the blacksmith shop and taken up the street to the office of the Doctor.

Seeking out Lena, who had taken Walter inside and off the street, Phoebe apologized profusely for the condition of her once beautiful dress. Lena interrupted her mid-sentence and wrapped her arms around Phoebe. “I am so happy you’re safe. Walter and I were worried, but when I saw the way you handled that rifle... My father would be proud of you.”

“Thank you. But just look,” she said, spreading the skirt. “I’m a mess.”

“It’s dirt. That can be remedied. But I see you’re bleeding. What can I do?” Phoebe held up arms and hands, searching. Remembering her cut palm she swiped at it with the nearest cloth napkin and winced. The cut was small but the bruise was tender and spreading. “I’ll get some water.”

“Thank you, again.”

The committee refused to allow the evening to be completely spoiled and someone rounded up the musicians to have them begin playing a quiet song. The goal; to calm everyone and remind them of why there were there. Two or three people, men and women, spoke to Phoebe, telling her they were pleased the outcome had been a safe one for her.

Newton walked through the door, seeking out Phoebe and the others. He saw her sitting in a chair at the table they had all previously shared, dabbing at her hand. When he walked up beside them he set a small bottle of whiskey at the center of the table and uncorked it. “Courtesy of Lionel,” he said, who had stayed behind, preferring to enjoy the rest of his evening in peace.

Newton had blood on his face, a swollen lip, one eye was swelling and his cheekbone and eye socket were turning purple. Phoebe gasped at the injuries but the concern as he stared down at her was for her alone. He picked up a napkin, tipped whiskey onto it and dabbed at her hand. It stung but she didn’t flinch. She held out the bottle for him to do the same to his wounds. When he finished she picked up the bottle, took a swig and sighed. Newton chuckled, grimaced, put his hand on the side of his face to still the pain and shook his head at her demeanor.

“You’re bleeding,” Phoebe said.

“Some of it is from you. You touched my face when I kissed you.” *Is he blushing? It’s hard to tell right now.*

"Oh. Sorry."

Will said, "Albert Griffin is still out there. What if they don't find him?"

"Bodie is in a valley, it's like a bowl. It's not easy to get to. Or to leave. He is without his horse, unless he steals one, and the Constable will be on the lookout for him immediately." Newton was too optimistic for Phoebe's satisfaction.

He sat down in a chair and scooted next to Phoebe. Leaning closer he picked up the napkin from the table, dipped in in the glass of water and reached to her face. She flinched and scowled. "What are you doing?"

"You've got mud on your nose. And your chin and your forehead and – "

She snatched the cloth from him and began rubbing at the places he had mentioned. "Better now?" she snapped.

"Why won't you let me do anything for you?"

"I can reach my own face, thank you."

"But you can't see it," he snapped back.

"Here, have a swig," Phoebe said, pushing the whiskey across the table at Newton.

About to give a short-tempered response, Newton bit back the words and picked up the bottle. He glanced at Phoebe, said, "Why not?" and did so. "I never took you for a drinking woman, Miss Tucker."

"I'm not. But the timing seems apropos." Her face felt less dirty now, whatever she may look like. "Tell me, Mr. Sanford, what type of woman *did* you take me for?"

She was teasing him now. It was sometimes difficult for him to tell. He took the napkin from her and dabbed at his eye with some cold water. "Ornery, cantankerous, determined..." She frowned and he put his finger between her eyebrows to smooth the crease created there. "Stop frowning. But fiercely loyal to her friends and family."

The musicians had finished the song and were beginning another, one with a quicker tempo and slightly louder, attempting to return the occasion to its previous merry atmosphere.

"Perhaps this is not apropos, but would you care to dance. One more. Please?"

He was holding his palm out to her. She saw Lena out of the corner of her eye, speaking to a couple of women she certainly knew based on her casual bearing. Will was playing thumb war with Walter. Newton stood, his hand still held out for her. "Please?"

Sighing, she took his hand and he assisted her to the floor. "You don't like dancing?" he asked.

"I don't do it often, that's all." *Oh crap, a waltz.* But she needn't have worried. Newton spun her gently and guided her around the floor.

"Be assured, they'll capture Albert. He's not nearly as clever as you."

"What's that supposed to mean?"

He pulled his head back and looked her in the eye. "It was not an insult."

Albert Griffin is a runaway. Just like me. He won't escape, but I can, I always tried to, I always have. I want to go home.

The song ended, people clapped, another began, louder than the one before. People were forgetting the trouble, moving on, reacclimating to the fun of the evening. Lena was speaking to a different group of people, of course she was, she had lived here for awhile now. Will was near her, listening only, but being polite and courteous, the fear that had been his constant companion in this new environment dwindling.

"One more," Phoebe said, remaining on the dance floor and hoping the next was a dance not foreign to her.

Newton attempted to raise an eyebrow in surprise but said, "Ouch," and put his fingers to his head.

"Do you want to sit down?" she asked.

He shook his head and his mustache twitched. "Thank you for your concern, but no. Another dance would be..." he searched for the word, "delightful."

He held her close and she closed her eyes. His hand was warm on her back and in her hand; she could feel his pulse against her palm. *One more day...or a few hours, who knows? It's time to go. I can't watch him die, I can't be here.* She caught her breath, swallowed hard and held back threatening tears.

The song ended, people clapped, and Phoebe picked up her skirt and ran for the door.

Outside in the cooler air she turned and flattened herself against the wall. *What an idiot, what am I doing?* She crossed her arms against the chill and watched the children running and playing in the street. There was Walter with his friend Arthur, outside and playing just like Lena had said he would be. Just like any other kid at home might do.

Couples stood about, talking in the moonlight. Men gathered in groups and she heard them discuss the prices of gold and silver, the rising cost of land and wood and the project of building a railroad from the forest south of Mono Lake to the north around Bodie Bluff to make the transport of wood faster, cheaper and easier. *The railroad. It isn't completed until next year.*

Life goes on: here, there, everywhere. And at home she was missing it. She also missed involving herself in subjects she had grown up studying, learning, pouring over day and night sometimes. Her books, the pictures, the people, the stories... No one listened anymore; had she ever tried to get them to?

It had never been her intention to acquaint herself with the people of Bodie. She had thought it possible to keep her distance, observe and go home with her brain full of pictures of the past. But what good is that without knowledge of the activities of those people, what they did, what they thought, how they lived. She had first run away believing none of it mattered. To some it doesn't. To her, now that she saw history firsthand, she regretted her prior decisions and was willing, now, to admit it.

Stupid, stupid, stupid. What's the matter with me? I am impatient, and rude and... J. W, was right. He asked why I left Nevada and I said I didn't know. Then he said, 'You do know why. As soon as you admit that, maybe you'll finally stop chasing away relatives that love you.' Why is he always right?

Phoebe turned to go back into the Hall. Newton was coming outside to check on her. They bumped into each other on the boardwalk. Looking up at him she said, "Good Lord, you're face looks painful in the shadows."

Newton laughed. "Your tender nature knows no bounds." Then, "Were you going back inside?" She nodded. "You're not afraid Albert will come back, are you?" His turn to tease.

"I don't have the Winchester anymore but I do have my Colt," she replied, smiling. "I'm not afraid."

"I know." he said, taking her elbow and turning to walk her in the opposite direction.

"Where are we going?"

He stopped when they were past the window of the Hall. "Out of view of prying eyes.

"Why, Mr. Sanford..."

He smirked. "Can I ask you a question?"

"Certainly. Your daring knows no bounds."

"Why did you run away?" Her eyes turned to him sharply.

"Run away?"

"Just now. We were dancing, I was enjoying myself, I thought you were as well."

"Oh, that." Relief. "I can't explain, really. But I do want to tell you something." She rubbed her arms, cold now that the excitement was over. "I'm – we're – going home. Will and I."

"Are you?"

She nodded. "Yes. I believe my business here in Bodie is finished. I need to go home now."

"Where is home, Phoebe? Where will you go?"

"I'm leaving tomorrow," she answered, intentionally vague.

"So you've found what you were looking for?"

"I never said I was looking for anything." *Did I?*

“Usually people wander because they are searching, they’re lost, and something is lacking in their lives that grounds them, gives them purpose.” He spoke wistfully, with sadness, and it was breaking Phoebe’s heart to think perhaps he was lost as well; and would never have the chance to find his way.

“Is that why you’re here?”

“I have felt lost at times, I’ll admit. I’ve been afraid I will never be able to go home. But, as they say, ‘Courage is being scared to death – and saddling up anyway.’” They stood in silence for a minute, each occupied with their own thoughts.

Wait... I’ve heard that before. Where? Think, think...

“You’re frowning again.”

She shrugged. “It’s what I do,” she said, trying to make light of the situation. “I hope you,” the words caught in her throat. “find your way home, Newton. I will – I – ” *I’ll miss you.*

He nodded, seemingly to return the unspoken sentiment. He said instead, “One never knows what tomorrow will bring.”

When they reached the door to re-enter the Hall, Phoebe said, “There’s a quote I remember that sums that up. I’m not sure who said it. ‘And so I close now, realizing that the ending has not yet been written.’”

He nodded again, finding himself unable to say the words he so badly wanted her to hear.

***

At three o’clock in the morning the last of the attendees left the Miner’s Union Hall. “I didn’t know people stayed up so late here,” said Will, yawning.

“Too bad we can’t be here for the Fourth of July festivities,” said Phoebe. They celebrate for days and stay up all night long. Sometimes Christmas Eve parties go on until morning and people all eat breakfast together.”

"I had no idea. I thought I was being bold staying up 'til midnight." He yawned again.

Making their way home Newton carried Walter, who had fallen asleep sometime around one. They all kept a lookout for Albert Griffin, suspicious at every noise, creek and rustle of sagebrush they heard along the way.

Lena said, to fill the silence on their walk, "I have some news. There were some inquiries this evening as to whether I have any rooms available for rent. I am getting two new boarders in the days ahead."

The group exclaimed on the subject and Phoebe was greatly relieved that in her and Will's absence there would be no interruption in income for her friend. Phoebe said, "That's good news, Lena. You do remember my telling you Will and I may be leaving soon, don't you?" Lena nodded and waited for Phoebe to continue. "We will be going tomorrow. As soon as we are able. I know it's sudden, but... I'm glad you have new boarders moving in soon. I feel terrible about leaving you on short notice, and I feel responsible for Mr. Griffin leaving – "

She snorted, "That man would have landed in jail before long all on his own. He didn't need any help from you. I should never have rented to him. So please don't worry about that. I'm happy for you. Walter and I will miss you."

When she said this Newton quickened his step and moved ahead of them all. Lena noticed and glanced at Phoebe. Lena Barrett was no fool.

Lena lit the lamp in the parlor and opened her door for Newton to deposit her son on his trundle bed. She proceeded to the kitchen where she checked to see if there was wood stacked for the stove in the morning. Yes, Walter had done as she had requested.

Phoebe hugged her landlady before the latter retired to her room. "Thank you, Lena, for loaning me the dress and shawl. Hopefully the dirt comes out and you can wear it again." Will noticed the hug and wondered at Phoebe's timing for their departure. "If Walter sleeps terribly late please tell him I enjoyed meeting him. And to keep reading."

"Will I see you in the morning?" she asked.

"I'm not sure. We'll have to check our travel plans," was all Phoebe would reveal. She honestly did not know.

Lena retired and closed the door.

Newton and Will were shaking hands, talking, but Phoebe hadn't heard what was said. Will looked upset, Newton appeared somber. Will excused himself and walked down the hallway to his room. Newton, holding his hat in his hands, said, "Will *I* see you in the morning?"

"I don't know. Perhaps."

"The stage left at midnight for San Francisco. So people can get some shuteye on the road. But the stage for other destinations like Bridgeport, Aurora, Carson City leave throughout the day. You can always check with the stage office and see what times – "

"Thank you, Newton," Phoebe said, holding up her hand. "I'll figure it out."

"I suspect you always will."

"Not everything, but I'm working on it." She walked past him toward her room. Turning, she saw he was standing near the stairs watching her go. "Goodbye, Newton. Be careful."

"Goodbye, Phoebe." His brow creased in a questioning gaze, taking in her words. "What do you mean, be – "

"Stop frowning," she said, grinning. She turned again and entered her room, locking it soundly behind her.

She waited until she heard the creak of the stairs, footsteps above her head and the sound of a door closing before she opened her door and tapped lightly on her brother's. He opened it and stepped into her room where she locked the door behind them both once again.

He said, "I figured you wanted to talk once we were alone. So what's going on? I didn't want to question you in front of everybody else, I would look really stupid not knowing when we're leaving or where we're going, and I really hoped nobody was going to ask what our plans are tomorrow, because I have no idea what's going on in that head of yours, I never did, I never do, sometimes you remind me of J. W. – "

She shook his shoulders. "Stop it. Breath."

He took a deep breath and his shoulders slumped. "I'm so tired."

"I know, me too. But I'm also ready to go home, if you are." He nodded and yawned.

"How?"

"Just go back in your room and get a little sleep. I'll wake you in the morning. Let me worry about it."

"Okay." He nodded and rubbed his eyes. "What about Albert Griffin? What about Newton?" She understood his meaning without elaboration.

"There's nothing we can do about Albert. But I'm sure Newton is right when he says he will be caught before too long. And Newton, well, there's nothing we can do about that either. I can't tell him his fate and I can't be around long enough to see him die. Or to read about it in the Chronicle. So we leave in the morning, either before everyone's up or when they've gone about their day. We'll see what happens."

Will unlocked and opened her door, opened his and turned back to Phoebe. "I'm sorry, Phoebe."

"Thanks. Me too." She closed and locked her door and stood listening to movements above her head. Newton was pacing, back and forth, back and forth. "Me too."

35

Worried she wouldn't wake up with enough time to prepare, Phoebe oh, so quietly opened her wardrobe and neatly folded her purchased dresses, skirts and blouses. Then she removed the dress on loan from Lena, mourning the dirt-caked hem and sorrowful she was leaving it behind unwashed. She dressed in her summer dress from J. W.'s birthday party and put her Army jacket at the end of the bed so as not to forget it. She brushed her mussed hair, put it in a braid and left the brush, extra ribbons and tin of hair pins on top of the folded clothes.

Next, she unpacked her chatelaine bag. *Newton's handkerchief; I never returned it.* After holding the small square of white cloth for a moment, Phoebe placed it in an upper jacket pocket with a tinge of guilt. It had belonged to him; she wanted it, and she hoped he would understand. She then returned her other items to the pockets of the Army jacket where she remembered them being before and checked to be sure the stone from J. W. was in a pocket as well. Assured the bag was empty she placed it on top of the clothes with the hair brush. Her straw hat sat atop the pile.

The pictures! Would she be able to keep the group photo and the one with her and Newton? And the handkerchief? Could she possibly take them back with her? She placed the pictures carefully in the other upper pocket of her jacket to keep them flat. *We'll see.*

She picked up the Colt and used a towel and some water from her basin to clean it off. Once rubbed clean the scratch may not show as much. The soft dirt under the step of the horse had kept much of the impact from taking its toll. She would leave that behind as well, but for tonight she left a single cartridge in the cylinder and placed it under the edge of her pillow.

She crossed to look out the window. The moon was growing brighter night by night and she saw shadows from the nearby buildings. *Take it all in, one last look, remember...*

Now under the covers she stared at the ceiling, wondering if Newton had drifted off to sleep yet. She was glad Lena was getting new boarders soon. Walter was doing well despite this crazy, wild town he was living in. Perhaps Lena would fall in love again and Walter would have a father. But Lena seemed an independent sort and would probably manage quite well on her own. She had done, so far.

Chester seemed only slightly injured, or so she had heard from other party goers later that night. He would make a full recovery and marry Mary Jacobson. Their lives would go on.

Wyanet and her family would continue to live nearby and blend in with other settlers in small towns. A couple of the basket weavers would become famous and make a living with their traditional weaving skills.

Families would move into and out of Bodie, from other towns and cities, to other towns and cities. Bodie would see hard times when the mining sources ceased to be as profitable as they once had been. And the people of Bodie, and other towns with similar interests, would live on, get married, have families, enjoy life.

Phoebe drifted off to sleep with visions of the Bodie she knew blending with the Bodie of her here and now. Faces drifted through her mind, smiling, happy, laughing faces, as well as violent clashes created by men, and women, that found a rough way of life befitting to their individual identity.

Dreams went on and on until finally she slept, contently, knowing that tomorrow she could finally admit to the willing desertion of her true character; and make amends.

***

Too early, Phoebe thought, rolling over and seeing the slight amount of sunlight outside. Remembering the task she had before her today she bolted upright and rubbed her eyes awake. Getting out of bed she arranged the covers, splashed her face with cold water, rinsed off the cut on her hand and folded her towel neatly on the washstand. Next she knocked lightly on Will's door, whispering his name. She wiggled his doorknob, hoping the noise would wake him, and whispered his name again.

A moment later Will opened the door slowly, trying to keep it from creaking. His hair was a mess, he was yawning, but Phoebe could tell he was ready to go. He was once again dressed in his own shoes, buttoned shirt and jeans. His new clothes were folded and on the end of the bed, along with his razor and his keys. Newton's borrowed coat was laying beside the stack. His boots sat nearby on the floor. With a wistful look at them he picked up his hat and said, "Taking it with me," and closed his door behind him.

In his sister's room he sat on the bed, still yawning. "What time is it?" he asked.

“No idea. Early,” replied Phoebe, putting her stack of clothes and other items on the end of the bed. She sat on the chair and leaned forward on the washstand to write a note to Lena on paper she had taken from the parlor the last time she had written a note.

“What are you writing?” asked Will, straightening his hair in Phoebe’s mirror.

She sighed. “This is much harder than I imagined. I’m leaving my, our belongings to Lena and Walter. What a way to say goodbye, sneaking away like this. But we can’t simply say, okay, see ya, and then walk into the barn and disappear.”

“I know, Phoebe.” His sister continued writing, pausing to form the words in her head first, and finishing it with a signature. “At least Lena will know I didn’t sign it ‘poh-boy.’” She put the note beside the pile of clothing, setting the Colt on top in case a draft blew it off. Awake now, with lucidity having swept the cobwebs from his brain, Will asked, “Now tell me why you think it’ll be possible to go home. What’s changed?”

“Everything. When we got here you were terrified. I still wish I could tell our brothers you fainted. And I was horrified that J. W. had done this to us. I didn’t want to believe it, to live it, to enjoy it, to experience it. But I did, we did. And you grew accustomed to it here, to the people. And I... I always wanted to see this place when I was a kid. I finally did, a few times. Then when I came back after high-school I found it depressing. Only a few dozen buildings remained, no people, the stamp mills and mining tunnels had been silent for so long.”

She paused, remembering. “And?” Will prompted her to continue.

“And then I left. I ran away. I put it out of my head, moved on. Stayed away to avoid reminders. I didn’t believe it mattered anymore.”

She stood to go to the window and look out. “J. W. said something about it being ‘about time,’ and that I need patience. He’s always saying cryptic statements that, I think, have some hidden meaning. He wasn't very clear, but I see it now. I see what he was trying to tell me. When you I were eating breakfast the other day, you called me 'blind and stupid.'"

"What I meant was – "

She put up one hand to stop him. "I know what you meant. And you were right. You've all been right. Dad, J. W., Tony, Troy, Mom." Returning her gaze out the window she continued. "I never should have switched to a business degree. I should have stayed my course, not let others dissuade me. Even my gut told me I was wrong, but I didn't listen to that, either."

She returned to the chair in the corner. "This town was here before we arrived, and it will go on after we leave. It will come to an end someday, but not all at once. I feel that's what people think when they hear the words 'history.' That the present is all that matters, that what's done was just a flash of memory and then it's wiped away. But just because we weren't there, wherever, whenever, doesn't mean it was all for naught. The people here deserve to be remembered. The businesses like the milliner run by the Jacobsons. The clothing store, the bakery, the photographer, the barber. The women on Bonanza Street, the people from Chinatown. They were born, they had families, they lived. And the blacksmiths." Her hands covered her face and she mumbled through them, adding sadly, "We didn't get to say goodbye to Lionel."

Her shoulders began to shake and Will heard her sniffle. "Are you crying?" Without removing her hands she nodded. "Phoebe, take your hands down." She shook her head 'no.' "I'm not going to make fun of you. I understand."

She removed her hands and brushed aside the tears running down her face. "I think J. W. was trying to get me to understand that all I needed to do was realize my mistake and admit it."

Will stewed on this thought a moment. "That's all there is to it?"

"I think so." She took a deep breath and exhaled slowly. "He lived here once. He wants it to be remembered. Yes, the park is here, they are keeping is safe. But it's not the same if you don't care about how it came to be in the first place; and what happened while it was here." She stood up and checked to see if her belongings were in order. "Are you ready to go home, little brother?"

Will stood. "I am."

Phoebe set her keys beside the pile of clothing and personal items on the bed. Unlocking her door she told Will to get his and put them on the bed with hers so there would be no mistaking their intentions. She put on her Army coat but before closing the door something caught her eye on her washstand; the two candy sticks she had purchased at the general store. *We forgot to eat them.* She pushed them into a lower pocket of her jacket and closed her door.

"Would you put these in one of your pockets for me," said Will, handing her his copy of the photos. She added them to the pocket containing hers and nodded.

They exited through the kitchen door, being mindful not to make any noise, and managed to unlatch the gate and close it back up without trouble. The barn only emitted one small squeak from its door. Once inside, Phoebe swung the door closed but couldn't latch it from the outside. *Oh well.* They moved to the corner and Phoebe was greatly relieved to see the metal wagon wheel rim hanging on the nail. Will removed it and placed it on the floor.

Will looked at Phoebe and gasped, his eyes wide. "What?" she asked, thoughts racing through her head of what she had possibly forgotten to do or say.

He pointed at her throat and wiggled his first finger. "Your necklace. Your horseshoe necklace. Where is it?"

Her hands flew to her neck and moved frantically around, searching, and not finding, her gold necklace from her great-grandfather. "Oh, no. It's gone. Last night, when John Young grabbed me around the neck, it must have come off." She turned to look at the barn door and back at Will.

Her face screwed up in anguish. “It’s gone. We can’t go back and look, it’s too late. We might get caught...”

“I’m sorry, Phoebe. Really.” He reached across the rim and held her wrist. “But right now, this is the perfect chance. Everyone’s still sleeping. We have to go.”

Knowing he was right but filled with regret and sorrow, she said, “Yes, we do.” Choking back more tears, she pulled the small pyramid-shaped stone from her pocket and stepped into the hoop.

Will stepped in next and took a deep breath. “See you on the other side,” he said, picking up the rim the way he remembered J. W. having done it, keeping it flat, horizontal with the floor and raising it as high as he could reach.

“Don’t say that, that’s creepy – ” and the darkness was upon them once again, so black neither could see, then the dizziness. She reached out to keep from falling over and brushed past Will’s arm, reaching, searching, but found no one in front of her. *Don’t panic, this happened last time. Almost there.* The air whirred around them and made a sound like an industrial fan, blowing, spinning. Heavy pressure in her ears temporarily deafened her and she tried to raise her hands to the sides of her head to clear her hearing but was unable to control her limbs. The pressure began to subside, the whirring slowed and she felt the floor beneath her once again.

Darkness, she couldn’t see and was now afraid to move. What if they hadn’t made it back? What if they were someplace altogether different? A hand took hold of her arm, let go and came back in a different spot. “Will?” she called.

“Phoebe? Is that you, geez I hope that’s you, I hate this, I’m never-ever-ever doing this again...”

Phoebe began to laugh in relief that Will was near. She could hear him but it was as if he was speaking from a great distance. “Will,” she shouted, “yes, it’s me.”

Light began filtering through to her retinas as she blinked to gain better focus. Being patient and waiting for the dim light to build and her hearing to fully return, Phoebe remained motionless. Another moment and full sight and hearing returned to them both. Will was in front of her now, holding her forearm. His eyes were wide with disbelief that they had safely arrived...somewhere.

"Well, that was fun," he said sarcastically, releasing Phoebe's arm and stepping quickly out of the metal rim. He motioned for her to step out and he picked it up, hastily hanging it back on the wall on the familiar nail and eyeing it suspiciously. "In case it decides to go off again," he said, swiping his hands together to clear the dust.

Phoebe was afraid to turn around, to investigate where they were. Moving her eyes and head she saw they were in the barn. The same barn, yes. She sent a questioning look at Will. Was she hearing voices? He nodded, hearing them too. No straw on the floor, the wood was aged and rough, no equestrian supplies on the walls, no water or feed buckets.

Turning around, Phoebe went to the window on her right, wanting to look out but afraid of what she might see there. She peered out over the top of the sill, gasped so deeply she coughed and turned around to look at Will. She turned to press her back against the wall and her hand flew to her heart. It was pounding to the touch and she could hear it aloud.

"Oh, geez, what is it, Phoebe? What do you see?" She pointed her finger over her shoulder, stabbing at the scene without, unable to articulate what was whirling in her brain. "You're freaking me out, what is it?"

Quietly she asked, "Was it real, Will? Was any of it real? Was it all a dream, a fantasy, something we made up in our heads?"

Will dashed to the window and looked outside. He saw their father playing horseshoes with their cousin Jody. Other relatives were eating, sitting in chairs on the cement block patio. Little Kimberly was running around chasing a cat. And J. W. was back in the lawn chair where he had been sitting just before he had taken Phoebe into the barn.

"Was it real?" she asked again, her hands beginning to tremble.

"If not, it sure felt real." Feeling stunned, he walked the few paces to the middle and sat on one of the crates. Phoebe sat across from him, exactly where she had been when having a talk with J. W. "We just woke up, it's early morning. I'm still so tired from last night." He yawned.

"The dance, Lena and Walter. Lionel." She sighed and closed her eyes. "Newton." They could hear talking, laughing, family members enjoying the birthday party going on outside in their grandparent's yard. "It wasn't real, was it?" Phoebe felt tears welling up and sniffled, attempting to hold them back. "I feel so stupid."

They sat in silence for another minute until Will stood up quickly, startling his sister. "Phoebe!"

"What? What is it?" She was wiping the tears away, strengthening her resolve to go back outside, rejoin the party and have a few words with J. W.

"Do you still have the stone? In your hand?" Phoebe opened her palms and shook her head 'no.' "It fell out last time, too, right? We found it in the straw."

"Your point?" She sniffled. Will practically ran back to the corner of the barn, got down on hands and knees and searched the floor. No straw, no dust, only a few cobwebs. And there it was, the stone. He picked it up and took it to Phoebe, dropping it into her open palm. "What does this prove?"

"Why would J. W. have given it to you if it didn't mean anything?" He dashed back to the corner and got down on hands and knees once more. In a moment he whooped and laughed and Phoebe thought he had lost his marbles. He rushed back to Phoebe, nearly tripping in his haste, his face red from excitement and sporting a broad smile. "Look!"

He extended his hand and shook something at her. Phoebe leaped up from the crate exclaiming her shock. "Oh, Will, I can't believe it. I don't understand how – "

"Me either, Phoebe. But it was real. It has to have been." Will plopped his Derby hat on his head. "I told you I was going to bring it back with me. It makes me look dashing."

36

Phoebe inhaled deeply, exhaled, cleared her throat, looked at Will and nodded. One last time she closed her eyes, attempting to hold onto the memories and associated emotions she had lived through. So much had happened in a short time. *Don't forget, don't forget...* She pushed open the barn door.

The early evening light was bright, the air beginning to cool after a day filled with warm sunshine. Family voices and laughter rang out. Phoebe was the first to emerge, Will close behind her and closing the barn door. Her world seemed to move in slow motion, scene by scene. Her father smiling, having hit the horseshoe stake. Kimberly squeezing the friendly barn cat and its limp limbs hanging downward. Her father's cousin, Kathleen, talking to her mother Bonnie. Her aunt Mary and uncle George enjoying a slice of pie. J.

W. sitting in the lawn chair beside her father's cousin Hugh, discussing an unknown subject.

Hugh vacated the chair and J. W.'s gaze met hers. Their eyes held each others for several moments, knowing, understanding, realizing that what had happened had truly taken place. "I have to talk to J. W.," she said to Will.

"I'll let you handle this. Be nice, Phoebe," he warned.

Jody stepped in front of Phoebe and cut off her forward progress. "There you guys are," she exclaimed. "Steve has been looking for you. He wants to know if you're ready for your rematch at horseshoes."

"Oh, Jody. Hi. Rematch?"

"Yeah, he won and you said you wanted a rematch. Don't you remember?"

That was days ago, no, I had forgotten. "Um, sure. Maybe when my dad's done, okay?"

"I'll tell him if I see him before you do."

Jody started to turn away and Phoebe reached for her arm. "Jody, when – how long has he been looking for me? I mean, I hope I didn't keep him waiting long."

"I dunno, maybe twenty minutes or something. Are you okay?"

Phoebe nodded, unable to speak. *Twenty minutes! We've been gone for days!* Will had overheard and they shared a look of disbelief. Slowly she made her way to the vacated chair beside her great-grandfather and sat down, looking out across the yard.

They sat beside each other in silence. Where to begin. Finally, she turned to him to see he was looking her in the eye. "You figured it out," he said quietly. "I knew you would." He turned to watch Kimberly drop the cat onto the grass and continue chasing after it.

"J. W., how did you know? I don't understand. I – I don't even know what to ask you?"

"What did you learn?"

"Learn?" Her hands fluttered in the air, frustrated with him, eager to know how he had accomplished such a feat. "What did I learn? Well, I – " She thought of everything she and Will had done, the people she had met, the places she had visited, all of it. She sighed heavily and sat back into the chair. "That I ran away years ago and I want to come home. To really come home. To the places and people that I love. To share the stories of those who came before us; they were real, they were special. We should acknowledge their existence, not pretend they were never here."

J. W. reached over and patted Phoebe's hand. "And there ya go."

She frowned. "I'm so mad at you. What if we had never made it home? Been stuck there? Or worse, injured or killed? How could you do that?"

He kept his gaze straight ahead and replied calmly, "I wasn't worried. I'm sorry you were, but I know what stuff you're made of, Miss Phoebe Tucker."

"How did you know what that thing would do, the wagon wheel rim, and the stone. I know you picked it up in the cemetery last week, I mean this afternoon, ugh, this is crazy..." she rested her forehead in her hands and quickly pulled them away, realizing the cut and bruise on her palm remained painful. *Yes, that had been real too.* She showed her palm to him in a 'see!' manner. He glanced at it and gave her a sideways grin.

"Do you know what I want to do? Not today, there's a party, after all. But you're not going back to Iowa right away."

"Aren't you going to answer any of my questions?"

"Not yet."

"What, J. W.? What do you want to do. One more indulgence, then I want some answers."

"Fair enough. Tomorrow, or the next day, soon, I want to do one more thing before I die. I would like you to take me back to Bodie."

"Before you die?" At the alarmed look on her face she pointed at the barn. "Wait...that way? Are you nuts?"

"No, no, Phoebe. My time in Bodie was over a long time ago. Just a visit. Won't you do that for me?"

"We did it for you today. What more is there to see?"

"For one thing, I need to return that stone. One more time, Phoebe. Please."

She looked at her elderly great-grandfather, his face weary, his shoulders drooping, his hands bent with arthritic knuckles. She leaned toward him and kissed his cheek. "Yes, of course. And I'm sorry, J. W. Whatever you want. I love you, you know, you old bugger."

"I know, Phoebe, I know." He grinned mischievously.

Later, when Phoebe had filled Will in on what she had gleaned from her conversation with their great-grandfather, he said, "He wants to do what? Oh, geez, why?"

Phoebe shrugged and said, "I'm not completely sure. There has to be more to his story than just a visit. We did that last, I mean today. This feels so weird."

"Tell me about it. I figured I was fired for not showing up to work on Tuesday, that everybody would be worried to death and file missing persons reports on us with the police. Turns out we were gone less than half an hour. I'm so tired," he yawned.

"Stop it, everyone is going to ask you why if you repeat that again."

Although their recent memories were a disruptive distraction, the siblings managed to mingle with family for what remained of the afternoon and evening. They both used the excuse that it had been a long day in answer to questions regarding their distracted behavior and inability to engage in in-depth conversation. Those they had met on their adventure were uppermost in both of their minds.

A couple of hours after returning they were all called into the kitchen to gather around the table. The family was going to sing Happy Birthday and J. W. was going to blow out the candles on his birthday cake. Another great-grandchild aided him to a chair at the head of the table.

Will sought out Phoebe and said, "I can't get them all out of my head."

"Shh, I know. Today's the day, Will. Now, sometime."

He nodded, understanding. "Think about it, Phoebe. It was a hundred years ago already. He's been gone a long, long time."

She nodded sadly. "They've all been gone a long time. My heart aches."

"Yeah, I get it. But like I said before, they didn't just come and go. They had lives before we met them that continued after we left. Some of them have kids and grandkids that remember them too."

"Not all of them," she said, choking back the lump in her throat. "I wish..."

He put his arm across her shoulders. "I'm sorry. He loved you, you know."

Tears stung her eyes. "You're not helping."

"Sorry. I thought you should know."

A nod was her only reply. Then, as the rest of the family found a spot to stand and see J. W.'s cake she said, "I want to go back too. With J. W. I want to see his stone. I can remember, and say goodbye."

With an aching heart she managed to sing along with her family and wish J. W. another happy birthday. Her second cousin, Amber, asked J. W. how old he was. He replied, "Older than you and younger than the mountains, Little Lady." He laughed at himself.

Great-grandpa, that doesn't make any sen – "

"Stop calling me that." The rest of the family laughed.

The teenager asked, "What did you wish for," and added, "J. W.?"

He sighed, lifted the single candle out of the center of his cake and licked off the frosting. Pointing the end of the candle at his great-granddaughter, he said, "Have you ever revealed one of your wishes? I didn't think so." He winked at the girl and shouted, "Cake!" After which he was served the first piece with a scoop of ice cream.

Later, after J. W. had opened a few small gifts, most family members had said goodnight, goodbye or see you later and gone home or back to hotels. Phoebe's brother

Troy had taken his wife and Kimberly home. Tony and his wife had gone as well. She and Will remained, along with their parents and a few others.

Phoebe realized, in her haste to make the drive across the country and get to Carson City before a certain time, that she had neglected to put in the time and energy to choose a suitable birthday gift for her great-grandfather. Logically she had another few weeks until his actual birthday, but it would have been nice to have it with her when she arrived at her grandfather's house in Minden. *I'll have to think about that later. It's his fault I'm distracted now,* she reasoned.

J. W. had retired to his regular comfy chair, worn out, exhausted from his day, which had been busier than usual. The party had been a good distraction for him from the pain in his knees and hips, from his weakened muscles in his back. But now the day had come to an end, his eyes drooped and he groaned when he shifted to find a comfortable position.

Several minutes later he waved Henry, Phoebe's grandfather and his own son, over and reached up to him for help in getting out of his chair. "Dad, are you okay?"

J. W. nodded but pointed toward the short hallway leading to his bedroom. Henry put his arm through his father's and walked with him slowly. When Henry returned he was rubbing his chin in thought. Phoebe watched her grandfather closely, and was also concerned with J. W.'s well-being. Henry approached Phoebe and said quietly, his worry obvious, "J. W. would like to speak with you."

"Of course. Is he in his room?"

Henry nodded. "He wanted to lie down."

More than a little surprised, Phoebe said she would go immediately.

J. W.'s door was ajar several inches. Phoebe knocked but did not push the door open or enter. "J. W.? Grandpa said you wanted to talk."

His voice sounded weakened when he answered. "Yes. Come in."

"Come in? You always said to stay out of your ro – "

"Phoebe, come in."

Doing as he said, she opened the door wide enough to enter and stepped inside. He pointed his finger at her and waved it, signaling to close the door. He was on his bed, atop the covers and leaning against a few puffy pillows. When she started to pull up a chair he crooked his finger for her to come to him and he patted the bed. She sat down bedside him. "I can come in, now, huh?"

He smiled and nodded. "Yes, now you can." He coughed, inhaled and sighed. He pushed himself up a bit so he could look at her squarely.

Now that she was growing accustomed to being back at her grandfather's farm and the shock from her arrival home was minimizing by the hour, details of her mysterious journey were becoming easier to process. "I have something for you." Phoebe reached into a lower pocket of her Army jacket and showed him the money he had sent with her and which she was now returning to him. "I spent some, but not much."

J. W. picked up the folded bills. "I know how much was here. You didn't spend much. How?"

"I went to one of the saloons. I played – now don't look at me like that," He raised his eyebrows. "I played Faro, I just had to try it. And I won."

"Hmm. Well done, my dear. But you should take that with you. This money may be worth something by now."

She shook her head. "No, I spent your money. Let's call it even. You know, you should auction that off or sell it somewhere." He looked at the money and set it aside, perhaps considering her suggestion. "You don't want to, do you?"

"I like having it. It's interesting." *He means he's sentimental, but he won't admit it.*

"I do have to tell you something and I don't want you to be angry with me." She paused, nervous, afraid her words would upset him in his fragile condition.

"Well?" He asked impatiently.

"I also found the double eagles you put in my pocket. That was gold, J. W. and worth a whole lot of money if you were to sell them now, all this time later." He waited, now, for the rest of her explanation. "I – I don't have them. I'm sorry, but I gave them to someone. He needed them and I was trying to help – "

He patted her hand and interrupted. "It's okay, Phoebe. I'm glad. I don't mind."

"You don't? All that money..."

"They weren't mine to begin with." He smiled and laughed lightly, enjoying the startled expression on her face.

"What? I don't understand."

"Someone gave them to me once, a long, long time ago. He was my friend, and he knew the gold pieces would be safe with me. But then he died, he was killed, right in front of me."

"Wait, you said that at the cemetery last, I mean earlier today." She was struggling to remember, it all seemed so long ago. "The wooden marker with the stones around it. We couldn't read the name."

He was patting her hand and nodding. "Yes, yes, that's the one."

She was confused because he offered few details. Same ol', same ol'.

He used his left hand to point to the other side of the room. "Over there," he said.

"What's over there?"

"Go. Over there. To my closet. Open it."

"You always yelled at me to stay out of your room and now you want me to open your closet?"

"Do it."

"Okay, okay." She walked around the end of the bed to the closet door and looked back at him to make sure he had meant what he said. He was waiting, so she turned the knob and opened the door. "There, it's open."

"Go in. There's a box."

"J. W., are you feeling okay, do you want me to get Grandma or Grandpa?"

"I'm fine, I'm just tired. It's been a long day. You should understand that, for cryin' out loud."

She smiled at the old man. "I do. Okay, a box." She turned to look inside the walk-in closet that her grandparents had added on for him when he had moved in. Directly inside and on the floor was a sturdy metal box. "Is this it? The metal one right here?"

"Yes, pick it up and put it here." He touched a spot on the bed.

She leaned down to pick up the box she guessed at sixteen inches long, ten inches deep and ten inches in height. It was heavy so she used both hands, reaching underneath with one hand. "What is this, anyway. Did you rob a bank or something?" She set it on the bed, close to his hand.

He indicated a small drawer in his bedside table so Phoebe opened that as well. Inside there were a couple of old keys on a ring. One looked to fit the box.

"Open the lock."

Phoebe used the smallest key to unlock the padlock, slipped it out of the hasp eyelet and lifted the rusty hasp out of the way. J. W. reached forward and lifted up the lid to the box. "I have something for you."

"For me? You're the one with the birthday and I forgot your gift. Wait, I do have something for you." Phoebe reached into a lower pocket and pulled out something she had forgotten, something she and Will had purchased at the general store in old Bodie. "Here," she said excitedly. Happy birthday!" It was the two candy sticks that Phoebe had purchased and that she and Will had been too distracted to eat.

J. W. smiled. "Thank you, Phoebe. I rarely got to have a treat like this." He looked at the two sticks a moment and set them on the table beside his bed. "For later," he winked.

"My turn," he said. He reached into the box and moved his hand around until it stopped on what he was looking for. He withdrew his hand but Phoebe did not see what he held. His fingers curled around something small and he rested that hand on his lap. "For you," he said and extended his arm to her. She put out her hand, palm up and he let go of the thing he held in his fist.

It was a shiny, gold necklace on a delicate gold chain. In the center of the chain hung a gold horseshoe pendant. Phoebe was completely speechless. Her necklace, lost only last night, but really lost for one hundred years, was here, in her great-grandfather's box, in his closet, waiting for her. For one hundred years.

She held it up, looked at it, looked it over to make sure it was still intact and that it was, indeed, the same necklace J. W. had given her when she was a teenager. Open-mouthed, she looked at J. W., saw the wide grin on his face and uttered, "How?"

"Not now. Later," he said reaching into the box again.

"Later? What? I was devastated when I realized I had lost this. I didn't think I would ever see it again. And you tell me 'later?'" J. W. began to speak but broke into a coughing fit instead. Fearing she was the cause of his growing weakness she pulled up a chair, sat down and rested her head on J. W.'s chest. "Thank you, J. W." She sighed and gripped his hand as he lay on the bed. "Thank you for saving it for me."

"I'm not finished."

She lifted her head. "What do you mean?"

"There's more. I'm not finished."

She sat up in the chair. Putting on her necklace, she asked, "Okay, you old crazy, what else are you going to tell me?"

"Crazy, huh? Hmph." He reached into the box and pulled out another item. He looked at it for an instant and handed it to Phoebe.

"Oh my gosh, J. W., what in the wor – ? I don' t understand. How do you have this? Who gave it to you?" In her hand she held a photograph. A very old, black and white photo of people dressed in long dresses and sack suits.

"I got it from a – a friend," he said mysteriously.

"What friend? Could you be more evasive?" She looked at the photo and inhaled sharply in remembrance.

She reached into a top pocket of her Army jacket, unsure of the continued existence of its contents, and withdrew the photos, including Will's, that they had had taken at the photography studio on Main Street in old Bodie. The group photo, with Will, Lena, Walter, Chester, Wyanet, Lionel, herself and Newton; it was the same as the one J. W. had just removed from his metal box. A copy she had paid for.

She focused on Newton's face. He looked so serious, they all did. But they had been joking and laughing and enjoying the afternoon together and afterward had gone to the bakery for a treat. She was amazed the energetic Walter had stood motionless for the time it had taken for the picture to be taken but he had taken his mother's instructions to heart. She stared at the picture, relishing the memories it evoked. *Oh, Newton...*

J. W. coughed again. He rubbed his tired eyes and asked Phoebe if she would get him a drink of water. She went into his bathroom and poured him a glass of water. Once finished, Phoebe sat down beside him on the bed again and asked, "You're not going to die on me and leave me with a thousand questions, are you?"

"Not tonight, my dear. Not tonight. I'm just tired."

She didn't want to aggravate him further so asked no more questions of him pertaining to the items he had removed from his box. Curiosity was killing her but she knew J. W. had his own time clock for revelations.

"So what other mysteries are you hiding?"

He picked up the bills that Phoebe had returned to him and put them inside the box. Then he sat up and swung his legs over the side of the bed and held up his arm for her to assist him to stand.

"What are you doing?" she asked, not wasting her time in telling him to stay put.

"Come with me, there's something I need to show you." He picked up the ring of keys from his bed.

"Oh, Lord, now what. I don't think I can take much more of this. You're going to give me a heart attack."

He chuckled at her dramatization of the situation. "You're going to live to be as old as I am, smarty-pants."

"And how old is that, exactly? Does anyone know? Why the big secret?"

He opened his bedroom door and turned right to enter his son's spare room at the end of the hallway. With one of his keys he opened the gun cabinet where Henry kept his guns; the ones Phoebe had learned to shoot with, the same that she had used to target shoot when they had come early to prepare for the party. *Yesterday!*

He reached in and removed the Colt, handing it to Phoebe. "Look at it."

She did so, not knowing what she was supposed to notice or see. She held the Colt pistol flat in her hands, smooth and clean, taken care of for years. And except for the long gouge in the grip it was nearly perfect. The gouge! She had known the deep scratch was there, her grandfather had mentioned it when she'd practiced with it. But now... It hit her that it was the same mark that had come from the Colt slipping out of her own hands when John Young had grabbed her neck from behind and the horse had stepped on it.

"J. W., where did you get this?" She was losing her composure. "I know this pistol, I bou – " Her hands were beginning to tremble at the excitement and mystery of what he was revealing.

He took the pistol from her grasp, returned it to the gun cabinet and locked it. He shuffled past her as she muttered in disbelief as they returned to his room, closing the door behind them both. He did not sit on his bed but went to his closet and reached inside. He picked up something Phoebe hadn't noticed before. It was long and slender and had been leaning against the corner just inside the door. Phoebe walked across the room to look at the double hammer, double-barreled shotgun that J. W. was holding for her inspection.

She picked it up. Heavy, long barrel, steel butt plate, three digit serial number. And oh, so familiar.

"J. W., this was, this is, I, oh my God, I feel so...so dazed." She began breathing heavily, feeling unable to inhale an adequate amount of oxygen. She shook her head back and forth, at a loss for words. He stood looking at her, waiting patiently. When she calmed somewhat she asked quietly, her throat constricted, "Where did you get this?"

Without further delay he answered simply, "It belonged to my mother."

37

Phoebe dropped to the floor and landed on her backside, in shock, numb, puzzling out the chaotic possibilities bouncing around in her brain. The necklace, the photo, the Colt, *I bought that Colt!,* the shotgun... J. W. shuffled to his bed and sat on the edge as his great-granddaughter remained on the floor, shoulders slumped, hands on the top of her head, unsettled.

After several moments had passed, Phoebe adjusted herself to a kneeling position, turned to face J. W. and spoke as if thinking aloud. "Your mother...Lena Barrett...she must have met someone after we left...she remarried...again. Life did move on for her. For everyone. This is amazing. And that's why you wanted me to go back, I know that now. I understand, J. W., I really do."

J. W. laughed then, a rich hearty laugh that left him breathless and holding his belly. He coughed once when he inhaled but continued laughing until his face was red and his eyes were watering. As his laugh subsided he put his hand on Phoebe's cheek and looked into her eyes, still sputtering with the lasts snickers of humor. "No, Phoebe... Think. Stop and think. You're a smart girl but right now your eyes are closed. Think."

"What are you talking about?"

"Lena Barrett was indeed my mother. But..."

"But what? Oh my God, I just realized I met my great-great-grandmother. She was wonderful, J. W. She was pretty and smart and so brave. She... I look like her don't I?"

He was nodding. "You do. And you're very much like her as well. But that isn't what I meant. Think."

Her eyes were darting back and forth, her heart was racing. *Think. About what?* "I don't understand, this is not amusing – "

"Hmm, but I can be amusing sometimes. At least I didn't grow up to be a curmudgeon. And I'm always honest. You like that, don't you? And yes, I keep secrets sometimes. But my secrets never hurt anybody so I don't have to tell." His eyes were crinkled at the corners and he appeared as if he would burst with the secret inside of him now.

Phoebe gasped, remembering the words. "J. W., what was your father's name?"

"James."

Phoebe felt her mouth go dry as her head buzzed with giddy revelation. She pointed a finger at him directly and said quietly, "You're name... It's James Walter, isn't? You were named after your father and called by your middle name! J. W.!"

"I told you you were smart. Just like your great-great-grandmother."

"The items I left in my room, at the boarding house... I wrote a note that said Lena could keep the clothes I bought, and the Colt because – because I didn't need it anymore." Phoebe stood up from the floor and sat on the bed beside her great-grandfather. "And she left it to you, and the shotgun, too. And you have the pictures now that we had taken at the photography studio." Her brain hit rewind now, trying to piece together the scenes in her memory with what she now knew.

"The barn, that's why it's here. It was yours in Bodie. Your friends, Arthur and Mary Louisa, oh J. W. that must have been so difficult to see them pass away so young."

"It was a long, long time ago."

"Not to me. It's going to take awhile for all of this to sink in." J. W. sat patiently for another minute while Phoebe sorted things out in her own time. "At the cemetery, you kicked the stones and said, 'he was my friend and he was shot dead in the middle of the road.' Who was that? Did we meet? Was it somebody I knew?"

He was nodding. "Yes, you met. Chester Murphy. He was kind to me. He bought me chocolates when he could, and loaned me books he owned. He told me he wanted to get married and I told him I wouldn't tell anybody. It was a secret that wouldn't hurt anybody." He winked at Phoebe. "He was robbed one night on Main Street. Some time after that he gave me four twenty-dollar double eagles to hold onto in case he was robbed again. He said he had gotten it as a gift and didn't want to lose it."

Excitedly she asked, "That's why you told me they were never yours. You kept them this entire time." He nodded. "I gave Chester the double-eagles. But, how did you know I would? How could you be sure?"

"I wasn't. But I know you. And after you did give them to him back then, I knew it now. Because I remember what happened."

"But it didn't turn out all right in the end, did it? You said he was killed. When? Did he and Mary ever get married?" Distressed at the thought, Phoebe's hands fidgeted in her lap.

"He was never killed in the street. You see, there was this woman, she was strong, and brave, and a tad unusual for a lady at that time. There was an incident at a dance one night, and she created just enough havoc when the man aimed at him. Chester was only wounded. I saw the whole thing through a window. A couple weeks of recovery and he was as good as new."

"Me! That was me. I – I kicked John Young in the knee...he missed his mark..."

J. W. nodded. "Mm-hmm."

"He lived? Otherwise he would have died? Oh this is terrible. No, that's not what I mean. I changed things, changed history. Isn't that, um, forbidden or something?"

"I seem to have misplaced my rule book," he teased. "It happened. Not much to do about it now, is there?"

She smiled. "I suppose not. That's why you don't have the double eagles anymore isn't it? Chester got to keep them this time. But how do you remember both ways that things turned out? That is mind boggling."

"I lived both. I expect I would remember both. You do."

"Yes, I do."

Another moment of absorbing new information and Phoebe's excitement changed to despair. Hesitantly, she asked what had been on her mind all along but had been afraid to ask. "Do you know what happened to Newton? His stone said he died on June nineteenth. That was the day after the dance, the day Will and I came home." She swallowed hard, not wanting to hear the answer but needing to know. "I couldn't stay to watch him die."

"I don't know." At her look of disbelief he continued. "He left the boarding house that morning, same as you. He packed up a bag and said goodbye. We never saw him again." Phoebe felt tears sting her eyes and her throat tighten when she said, "But he's buried in Bodie."

J. W. nodded. "There was a lot of commotion the next day, as I recall. I was a kid, of course, so nobody said too much in front of me. But you know kids, they know a lot more than you think they do. People came by to ask questions about the trouble at the dance. My mother was arranging for new boarders to move in. Chester and Mary announced their engagement." He paused to remember back. "They moved in upstairs for a few weeks after the wedding until the house they bought was ready. But I don't know what happened to Newton."

Phoebe leaned on her great-grandfather's shoulder and let the tears that had gathered there flow. "I loved him, J. W. I didn't want to, but I did. And it was so hard because I knew I would have to leave him behind."

"So now you see that history is more than a collection or artifacts and buildings and things people see. It's also what's in here," he pointed to her heart.

"I do see. I was so mad at you for sending us back there. But it opened my eyes to what I already knew to be true. So...thank you." She wrapped her arms around his neck and hugged him. "And I know I haven't said it often enough, but I love you. Great-grandpa."

J. W. didn't resist the name this time; he hugged her in return. "I love you too, little churchbell."

Phoebe laughed at her great-grandfather's terminology. "I don't talk *that* much." Wiping her eyes, she added, "So how old will you be on your birthday, J. W.?"

"Next month will the sixty-eighth anniversary of my thirty-ninth birthday."

***

Phoebe's parents were getting ready to leave and return home; long day, long evening, everybody was tired. Before saying their goodbyes, Phoebe called Will into J. W.'s room to show him the items in the metal box, the shotgun and tell him about the Colt. She enjoyed telling Will all about what J. W. had told her, even though she hadn't had long to acclimate herself to the truth.

Will had been astonished, to say the least. He couldn't believe the time he had spent with Walter, playing jacks, peeking in windows at the school house, talking about his friends and neighbors, reading, had been time spent with his great-grandfather. If nothing else it brought the two of them closer than they had ever been.

Phoebe said, "I suppose there were clues all around us, now that I think about it. You told me 'all bets are off once the shootin' starts.' I thought you were just being funny. And Wyanet, when she couldn't read my note, she thought it said pa-ho-bee, or poh-boy. That's what you told Dad on the phone when you called him to discuss the party. He told me you said something like, 'that poor boy' and laughed. We wondered if you were losing it. You were just remembering!"

J. W. smiled, remembering fondly. "Yes, Wyanet mispronounced your name many more times after that. It always made me laugh but in the end I taught her to read."

"And the phrases you said, that Walter said, you say some of those now, but why would I have assumed... And Lena told me about her first husband, James, and how much they had been in love. So Barrett wouldn't have been her name when she was married to him. She never said anything about our last name when we introduced ourselves." Phoebe continued piecing the puzzle together.

J. W. said, "There were a few other Tuckers in town. And a Barrett or two that weren't related at all. I'm sure she had other things on her mind."

"I suppose so." Will was contemplative, taking in all the facts. "Do you know what happened to Lionel? He was nice."

"He was. But no, I don't. After Newton left we didn't see him much, except when we went to the market or the post office now and then. One day that summer we stopped seeing him and that was that." He shrugged. "But that was the way of Bodie."

"It's sad to think they're all gone now. I hate to see you looking down, sometimes, J. W.," said Phoebe.

"Down? I already told you, I'm not sad. Why do you keep saying that?"

Surprised, she continued. "When you would look out the window, I would notice you talking to yourself. Or when you talk about Great-grandma Grace. I thought the past was a horrible place for you to revisit, that it hurt you to talk about it. That's one reason I didn't want to talk about the past or history anymore."

"Don't blame me for that," he nearly snapped. "I told you... I don't appreciate having to explain myself." He sighed. "I mutter to myself when I try to form the right words; for talking you into coming into the barn, to step into that metal rim. You're so danged stubborn I didn't think you'd do it." He shook his head. "I think about what I've done in the past; I like to remember it. But did you see all those faces at my party? I've been by myself plenty; but I've never truly been alone. Reflection is not the same as regret.

"And I miss your great-grandmother, I do. We had many years together. But I've appreciated the life I've lived since. She told me something when she got sick." He cleared his throat, emotion creeping up on him. "She said it was a Cherokee proverb. She said, 'When you were born, you cried and the world rejoiced. Live your life so that when you die, the world cries and you rejoice.' She was wise like my mother. So I listened."

Phoebe nodded and let the silence hang there a moment, giving all the respect due her great-grandmother.

Then, "Wait a minute. The metal rim. Where did it come from? And how did you know what it would do? You haven't said anything about that," asked Will. Phoebe felt stupid for not having asked that sooner, but there had been so many surprises.

"I found it, in that barn, many years ago. I hung it on the wall. One day, I was in there, cleaning up the barn before I moved it. It fell off the nail, down over my head, so I picked it up to put it back. Suddenly the world went dark, the wind started howling and I fell down. When the lights came back on I was still in the barn but I was somewhere else."

"In Bodie, at your old house? Whoa, how weird that would be, running into yourself and your mom and – " Will was excited and rambling and J. W. interrupted him.

"Shh. No. I was in the barn, but the barn belonged to somebody else then. I was scared to death, I didn't know what had happened. I looked out the window and saw people I didn't know dressed in old clothes I didn't remembered. I sat in the corner for along time, not knowing what to do. Then I thought about Grace. I missed her, I was afraid I would never see her again and I had to get back home. I sat inside the rim again, wishing, and lifted it over my head because I figured that's what I'd done to get me into that mess in the first place. Everything turned dark, the wind came again and a minute later I was home. I never left your great-grandmother's side again after that."

Will asked, "That's all we had to do? Wish to come home?" He glared at Phoebe. "And you made it so complicated."

"We tried that, remember? It didn't work. I knew it had to be more than that. For us."

Will conceded the point and said, "I guess so." After more consideration, he said, "Where did it come from? The metal rim."

J. W. said, "I don't know. I found it there and there it remains."

Phoebe said, "There's a tie to Bodie, somehow. It has gold flecks all over it. Maybe its Bodie gold. But, J. W., how did you know it would take us back to 1880? To the same date?"

He shrugged. "It took me back nearly that far, to what I perceived as the beginning of Bodie. I remembered you being there. When I found you two in the barn, I thought you were dressed a little funny. It wasn't until years later, after you were born and grew to look so much like my mother... I thought that was the only way to get you to open your eyes."

Hank and Bonnie were waiting patiently in the kitchen when Phoebe and Will emerged from J. W.'s room. "What have you three been up to in there, anyway? Plotting something?"

"Yes, Bonnie, I'm fixin' to rob a bank and I need their help with a getaway car," J. W. replied with humor.

"Well don't use Hank's truck. Everybody knows that old heap and you'll never get away with it."

"I appreciate your advice. Guess we'll have to keep looking, kids," said J. W. Phoebe snorted with laughter.

On the way home Hank asked Phoebe, "Is J. W. okay? I heard him coughing. Phoebe?"

"Oh, sorry, Dad. Yes, I think he's all right. For a man of a hundred and six, almost seven. He's really something, you know?"

"How did you get him to tell you his age? He never tells anybody anything."

"It just came up." *Now I know why he sent Will with me. If I didn't have somebody to share this with I would think I'd lost my mind.* "And we were just talking. Spending time with him."

"Good. I'm glad."

"Dad?"

"Yes, darlin'?"

"I'm going to move back home." She had been facing out the truck window but saw her mother turn her head sharply in her direction. "Can I move into my old room for awhile?"

Her mother looked at her dad as he drove, then quickly back to Phoebe. Phoebe saw her father look at her in the rearview mirror and smile. But her mother answered aloud for them both. She nodded energetically and said, "Of course. Of course you can."

Phoebe returned her gaze out the window, thinking back, remembering, her head and her heart full of memories. This is where she belonged, where she felt most comfortable, where she could live her life the way she was supposed to have lived it all along. No more regrets, no more apologies, no more running away.

Bonnie asked, "What changed your mind?"

"J. W. and I had a really good talk."

38

Dreams overwhelmed Phoebe's sleep pattern that night and she tossed and turned, feeling exhausted on waking the next morning. Jody was still asleep on the other side of her room. Phoebe rolled over, attempting to return to the world of the unconscious, but thoughts of Bodie and her room there in the boarding house wouldn't leave her alone. Now that she was home she could turn the lights on and off at will, walk down the hallway to easily use the shower and sink, or grab her keys and hop in her car if she felt there was somewhere she would like to go.

But it hadn't taken long for her to become accustomed to lighting her gas lamp, using the outhouse, heating coffee on the stove and walking where she needed to go. Conveniences hadn't changed the way people interacted, dealt with each other or took care of business.

Newton... What happened to you?

Perhaps she could drive to the historical museum in Bridgeport, look through the newspaper collection and find the death records from that summer. *It was a stranger from a hundred years ago. Let it go.*

Phoebe was up before anyone else and made a pot of coffee. She went to the patio, wrapped in her comfy sweater, and sat in the early morning sunlight, listening to the morning birds. Her father joined her half an hour later, surprised to see his daughter already up and about.

"Have you changed your mind since yesterday?" he asked from the chair opposite hers.

She shook her head 'no.' Then, "You were right, Dad," was all she said, but it was enough.

"It's about time." He sipped his coffee and grinned at her over the top of his cup.

She returned the expression and said, "I'm probably not going to say that again, so don't get used to it." After ten minutes of silence she asked, "Can I make you some breakfast? Eggs? Pancakes? What'll it be?"

"That was some talk you and J. W. had. Are you feeling all right?"

"Oh hush. I don't always sleep late, you know." She stood up to go inside. "If you don't decide, you're going to have to suffer through whatever I make for you."

"I'll suffer." Hank smiled at her and reached for her hand as she walked past him. "Phoebe?" She stopped to look down at him. "Whatever's going on that head of yours... I'm glad you're coming home."

"Thanks, Dad. Me too."

Phoebe made her father a stack of pancakes and heated some sausage patties she had found in the freezer. She poured two glasses of orange juice from a carton, relishing the cool taste.

The telephone rang. It was J. W., requesting to speak with Phoebe.

"Good morning, J. W. Did you get some sleep last night? We kept you up late."

"Of course I did, or I wouldn't be calling you." Typical J. W., back to normal. "I would like to go today. Come get me when you're ready."

“Okay. But can’t you tell me why – ”

“I’ll see you at eleven.” *I guess I’ll be ready before eleven.* “And pick up your brother on the way.”

“Will?”

“Who else? I’ll see you at eleven.” He hung up the phone.

Without going into details, Phoebe attempted to explain what she and Will were going to be doing that morning. “He wants to go back again? Why? Never mind,” Hank said, taking a bite of his breakfast. “I know you’ll be here the rest of the week. And more. Hopefully J. W. won’t monopolize all your time while you’re home.” Knowing he was joking, Phoebe kissed him on the cheek and went to shower and get dressed.

Ahhh... a hot shower. Okay, there were some things she had missed.

When she was dressed, this time in jeans and a Pink Floyd t-shirt, she called Will to tell him she would be picking him up in half an hour. Today? Yes. This early? Yes, get over it. She told her parents, aunt and uncle and cousin Jody she would see them later without explaining much about what she was doing. No one was greatly surprised.

Phoebe stopped at a supermarket and picked up some donuts and a danish. After picking up her brother, the two of them rumbled down the road toward Minden in Phoebe’s International-Harvester Scout II. J. W. had already called her car a hunk o’ junk. What would he think about traveling to Bodie in it?

Will yawned from the seat beside her. He rolled his window down part way, slouched low and was resting his head against the high seat back. “Why does J. W. want to go back to Bodie again? He didn’t say?”

“Just that he needs to return the stone, that’s all. Are you really that surprised?”

“No. But he was doing a lot of talking last night. More than I remember in a long time.

"I think he'd been looking forward to that conversation for a long time. A really long time," Phoebe added.

Will nodded, after which they rode in silence until the turn off to Henry and Julia's farmhouse in Minden.

They knocked lightly and walked in through the kitchen door. Through the large window in back that they saw their grandparents outside on the brick patio enjoying the morning sun and some late morning coffee. She greeted them with the danish and donuts, telling them she and Will were there to see J. W.

Henry said, "We know. He told us." Henry stood up to walk back into the house with his granddaughter. "Promise me something, Phoebe."

"Anything, Grandpa."

"That when I get to be his age, which isn't all that far off," he chuckled, "you'll be just as straight forward and accommodating. You're special to him because you see him as he's always been." He kissed her on the cheek and said, "Off you go now."

As they walked through the kitchen to the living room, Will whispered, "If he only knew just how we see him now." They shared a laugh of secrets kept.

J. W. was sitting in his favorite chair, dressed and ready to go, his walking stick in his hand. "It's about time you got here."

Phoebe looked at the wall clock and said, "It's two minutes before eleven. We're on time. And I brought some danish and donuts. Want one?"

"I didn't live to be as old as the hills by eating that junk. Bring one with and I'll eat it in the car."

Phoebe loaded his wheelchair into the rear of the Scout and helped J. W. into the front seat, Will sitting behind him in the second row.

"I hope we get there," he said, poking fun at Phoebe's car.

"If not I'll push you the rest of the way in your chair. Don't think I won't." She saw him attempt to hide a grin.

Same road, same hills, same sagebrush, same turn-off, same paved portion, same dirt road, same drop-offs, same ruts, same curves... Different Bodie.

They curved around to the left and Phoebe slowed down. She knew what it looked like ahead and for an instant closed her eyes, keeping the way she had seen it not long ago, complete, painted white, populated, fresh in her mind, not wanting to forget the way she had experienced it.

The race track was off to her right, barely visible now; *I wish I'd had a chance to visit that while I was there, here, ugh...* People used to picnic south of town, travel to Aurora or Lee Vining or Bridgeport for events and parties. Phoebe knew all of this, had read and studied so much of the place. She smiled, realizing she could admit now that she loved her old books, could and would move them back home where they belonged. And no, they were not going to end up in her first bonfire.

They paid their entrance fee and circled around to park in the lot. J. W. leaned over to touch Phoebe's hands on the steering wheel. They'd been sitting in the car nearly a minute and Phoebe hadn't realized her hands were frozen to the wheel, that she was unable to move them, and unwilling to see Bodie the way it looked now.

"You won't forget, Phoebe, how could you? How could we?" Will said. "J. W. hasn't forgotten."

She looked over at her great-grandfather. "You're right, Will. It's so fresh in my mind. I don't want to forget. This place is – it's – "

"Special," Will finished. "We know. Now we know."

The siblings assisted J. W. into his chair and started down the path to town, past the first house on the left, and stopped at the church. They stood looking around, each remembering in their own way. To the right had been Fisher Street. Ahead on the right the Bodie House Hotel. So many buildings, so many homes, so many miners and tunnels, so many stamp mills quieted.

Phoebe closed her eyes and smiled, putting her chin in the air and smelling the warm breeze blowing through the valley. She laughed and laughed some more, drawing curious looks from passersby until Will asked what had come over her.

"I can see it now, in my head. I can hear it, all of it. Listen, the banging of the stamp mills. The wagons coming up and down the road. There are kids running in the street and throwing rocks and getting into trouble from their parents. The piano is playing in the saloon, playing the mustache song, the sheriff is raiding the opium dens and the people in the jail are yelling it's too crowded. The girls on bonanza street are lonely and just want to fit in, the horses, the hay, the fires in the blacksmith shop. I can hear it now, J. W., I can feel it, I can smell it." She opened her eyes, her heart was thumping, adrenaline pumping in her veins.

Will smiled and he and J. W. looked at each other. "She's gone crazy, J. W., she's finally lost it."

"Yep. And it's about time. When you come back to earth, push me. Take the path, up to the cemetery. I assume you know the way. If you don't I'm walkin'. I may not make it so you'll have to bury me where I fall," he added.

It was uphill so Will stepped in to push. "Did you bring the stone with you?" J. W. asked.

"I did. But unless we return it to exactly the same location it's useless. Anything historic removed from where it was originally found no longer has – "

"Don't lecture me, I know that. I'm the one that accidentally broke the corner off that headstone in the first place. So I'm taking it back where it belongs."

"When did that happen?" asked Will, picturing his great-grandfather as the boy Walter. When he did so it was easy to imagine him doing such a thing.

"It's from the headstone marker of the McQuaid family. I went to my friend Arthur's burial and memorial. Then when my friend Mary Louisa died I went to hers. I picked up a rock to throw it on the ground in anger. It hit the corner and a piece broke off. I regret that. Not long after, I met your great-grandmother. She said life goes on and that while we miss old friends, they will always be with us." He shook a finger at his great-grandchildren. "You know that now."

They made their way to the cemetery, passed through the gate and walked along the clearest route nearest the fence on the left. J. W. showed them the way as they moved between the grass and stones. Soon they reached the McQuaid memorial stone and J. W. was assisted out of the chair. "There, right there, see the depression in the earth? That's where I picked it up. Wanting to return it himself, Will helped the old man bend over and place the stone carefully into the shape in the dirt. He pushed it down lightly with the toe of his shoe so it would stay in place and returned to his wheelchair.

Having to cross back the way they had come to exit, they detoured further uphill to find an easier path. Nearer the main gate and at the northernmost Ward's section, Phoebe stopped suddenly. Somewhere nearby had been the wooden marker and oval of stones that had signified Chester Murphy's grave. Knowing his outcome, that it had changed from the last time they had been here, Phoebe wanted to look and see if there was anything in that location now. Perhaps it was Chester and his wife, later in life.

"J. W., do you know anything about Chester Murphy and his wife. About how long they lived, whether they stayed in Bodie, or moved, or – "

"You want to know if he and Mary are here," he stated. I moved away from Bodie before he did, so I'm not sure. We can look."

Phoebe was hesitant to continue further. She and Will had glanced at other stones and markers on their way back to the main gate, to show due respect to those buried here and to see the changes from their memories of their last visit. She did not want to see Newton's headstone. Not again, being that only yesterday she had left old Bodie; that a day and a half ago, in her mind, she had danced with him at the Union Hall; that she had begun to love him and he had felt the same. That she would never see him again.

Will moved onward, leading them uphill to see if Chester's marker was near what he remembered as the same location as last time. With J. W.'s help they found the spot; there was a marker near where the stones and wooden slab had been but it was not for a Murphy. "That's good news, right?" asked Will.

"It could be. Perhaps he lived to a ripe old age, like somebody else I know, and moved or chose to be buried elsewhere, perhaps near other family. In any case, it's not right here anymore." Phoebe spun to take in the surrounding area and saw no Murphy's at all. "And I don't see anything labeled Bradley either." *I wonder what happened to Lionel.*

She looked slightly up the hill and to her left, but saw nothing familiar. "Wasn't that where Newton's tall marker was?" asked Will.

Phoebe swallowed hard and nodded. Will urged her further over and uphill, noting her hesitation. "Maybe you need to see it, Phoebe. Isn't that the point of a memorial, so you can say goodbye and move on?"

As difficult as it was for her, she acknowledged that he was right. They walked the steps she remembered to reach the dark stone marker that was Newton's. The one with the poem by Thomas Campbell, read aloud from a book that had belonged to Lena.

They reached the spot. Nothing but smaller markers were on this part of the slope, space in between them all and no marker with an engraved poem. Phoebe stepped around quickly, searching, searching, reading engravings, searching. Several feet away now, she called back excitedly, "It's not here. I don't see it, it's gone." She walked back to her family and repeated herself.

"We heard you. What do you think happened, J. W.? Do you know?" asked Will.

"I told you I didn't. Asking me again won't change what I know." His voice sounded grumpy but he leaned forward in his chair, searching, as mystified as the others.

"Maybe he didn't die on the nineteenth," Phoebe said hopefully. Her tone deflated. "Maybe he died elsewhere, maybe he was all alone."

Will felt for her, for them all. "Phoebe – "

She tried to adopt a positive mood. "And maybe something changed that night at the dance. He said he was leaving soon; maybe he lived a long, long life somewhere else."

Will wanted to support her. "Yeah, and maybe he met somebody else and you went to school with his great-great-grandkids," he said lightly, cuffing his sister on the elbow.

"Gee, thanks. I feel better now," said Phoebe with a grin. "But if he did live... I'm glad. I'm very glad." The others allowed her a moment to mourn her loss, and their own, and when they moved on she was renewed. Time marches on.

While at the park, the three of them took the time to slowly walk the streets, each memorializing in their own way. The Standard mill, rebuilt but in the same location; the scars on the hillsides and slopes where the miners had dug tunnels, stored explosives and brought out tons of rock and millions of dollars in gold and silver; the jail that had been overcrowded most of the time; a trail that marked Bonanza Street; the vault from the Bodie Bank that had survived the fire, just north of the bank where Chester Murphy had been employed; the schoolhouse where Walter, J. W., had gone to school with Arthur and Mary Louisa; the slender road where the boarding house had once stood.

As they stood in the spot where J. W. had pointed with his walking stick and stated he had once lived nearby, Phoebe asked, "J. W., didn't you live in two different places here? That's what Lena, your mother," she smiled, "my great-great-grandmother told me anyway."

He nodded. "Yes, That's why last time I just pointed 'over there.' I lived in a little house on Mono Street when we first moved here. Then, after my father died we moved to the boarding house."

"You were intentionally vague. So we didn't catch on that Walter was, is, you."

He nodded and pointed to his temple. "Yep. I used my thinker on that one."

"I agree, that would have been quite the distraction," said Will, shaking his head at the coincidence of it all. "Did Phoebe tell you how helpful I was?"

"Did I tell you that Will fainted in the barn," she replied quickly.

They enjoyed a moment of conspiratorial humor then, a closeness Phoebe would profoundly miss when the day came that J. W. was no longer with them.

Walking back along Green street, they turned left on Main Street and stopped in the middle of the road. The Miner's Union Hall was on their right, the empty space where once had stood a blacksmith shop on their left. In a long few minutes of reflection, they stood in silence, images fresh in the minds of Phoebe and Will, fuzzy images remembered from so long ago in the mind of J. W. They walked onward, past the post office, and turned back around. That was the end of the street now with the exception of a few scattered homes further on. The rest was gone; moved, torn down for lumber and bricks or burned.

A stranger was walking toward them. He appeared to be in some sort of official capacity within the Park and Phoebe wondered if it was the ranger from their last visit. *Jeremy-the-ranger-who-had-never-said-his-last-name. The one that had somehow offended J. W. and had asked him if he ever wanted to share stories to let him know.*

As he approached, Phoebe noticed J. W.'s grip tighten on his walking stick. She put her hand out and patted his shoulder. The man advanced but slowed considerably. Had he seen the look on J. W.'s face and changed his mind about talking to them? No, this wasn't Jeremy-the-ranger. This was somebody else altogether. The man removed his hat and ran his hand through his hair, straightening it. He stopped walking when he was twenty or so yards out.

Phoebe was about to suggest they simply keep walking and continue when Will gasped and his hand flew to his throat.

"Will, what in the wor – "

J. W.'s shoulders began to shudder up and down, just before he laughed aloud, a snorting guffaw of extreme humor and delight. He slapped his knee with a hand as his head tilted back in uproarious laughter. "What! Why are you laughing?" Phoebe asked, seeing Will, now recovered from shock, wearing one of the biggest smiles she had ever seen. Feeling left out and possibly the butt of a joke, Phoebe scowled at the two of them. "Tell me. What am I missing?"

Prying an answer out of the two of them was proving to be a waste of time. When she returned her gaze to the man in the street he was much closer now, having resumed his forward progress. The man was smiling, a wide, joyous symbol of acknowledgment. "Would somebody please tell me – " And she saw him, recognized him.

Now only a few feet before her stood a man she had known for only a short time, but someone she thought she would miss terribly for the rest of her life. Her breathing was shallow as she gasped for air and felt herself getting dizzy from lack of oxygen. "Newton!"

39

"Hello, Phoebe." he said simply, unable to look away.

"You're – you're – but – " she sputtered.

"Well spoken as always, my dear," he teased.

She ran to him and flung her arms over his shoulders and around his neck and held on. He was here, in the Bodie of her today. Here he was, in the flesh, in front of her. She could touch him, speak to him, he wasn't gone.

Pulling back, embarrassed at her instant reaction, she looked into his eyes, the same sparkling blue, the same crinkling at the edges, but...

"You shaved off your mustache."

"Do you approve? You weren't around for me to ask."

"It is you, isn't it? I'm not dreaming?" Will stepped beside her and punched her in the arm. "Hey..."'

"You wondered if you were dreaming. What do you think now?"

"Newton..." she stared up at him and his eyes crinkled. With his stick, J. W. whacked Phoebe in the side of the leg. "Ouch, what was that for?"

"Move outta the way and let me say hello," J. W. said cheerily. Will helped him out of the chair to a standing position. "*Mr.* Sanford. It's been a few years, but I'm glad to see you well."

Newton was more than a little surprised but shook the elderly man's hand. "I'm sorry, I'm afraid I'm at a loss."

"You don't recognize me," J. W. said. Newton shook his head. J. W. turned his head this way and that, letting the man get a good look at him and finally said, "Are you sure?"

"Phoebe, what's wrong," Newton said with concern.

She was staring at him and did not realize that tears had streamed down her face. She whispered, "I thought you were dead. Gone. But you're here..."

He walked to her and wrapped his arms around here. "I'm here. I can't believe *you're* here! And I don't believe in ghosts, so I'm relatively sure I'm not dead." He released her and stepped back.

She turned and pointed at the cemetery. "Your headstone, up there, we saw it, it was, it had, it said – "

"Geez, Phoebe," said her brother, having never before seen his sister so completely lose her composure.

Shaking her head and rubbing her face to clear the cobwebs, she blurted out a string of somewhat more cohesive words. "We came here, only, when, yesterday, only yesterday. We were walking, me and my family, and my cousin, Jody, read a headstone with a poem on it. It said, '*To Live in Hearts We Leave Behind is Not to Die.*' I know what it said, I've had it echoing in my head for days and days, yes I know that doesn't make sense. It said, *'Newton L. Sanford, Died June 19, 1880, Aged 29 yrs 3 mo.'*"

Newton gazed at the slope and looked back at Will, Phoebe and the elderly stranger. "What? I don't understand."

"You died," she practically shouted at him. "The day after the dance, sometime that day. That's why we left. I couldn't stay around and see you killed. I couldn't stay."

"The day..." Newton's brain was working overtime, remembering, analyzing. Then he asked quietly, "...I died?"

Phoebe was nodding her head in the affirmative. "But you're here." She held up her hands in wonderment.

J. W. interrupted, "If I complained about dressing up, or asked for a whiskey, or read poetry, badly, to you, then would you recognize me?"

"Geez, I can't believe this is happening. You should be over a hundred by now, no offense, J. W., " said Will.

Everyone's words were overlapping, reliving differing points of memory and not understanding any of what they were seeing and hearing.

Newton took hold of the elderly man's upper arms and said with excitement and disbelief, "Walter? Is it really you?"

J. W. was grinning from ear to ear and bobbed his head once. "Yes. And I would introduce you to my great-grandchildren, Phoebe and Will Tucker, but I believe you've met."

"Walter... I've thought about you often." He hugged J. W. and Phoebe winced, but the greeting was accepted wholeheartedly. The words J. W. had spoken had taken a moment to register before Newton took a step back. "Introduce me to your – what!"

"How are you here? I don't understand," said Will, shaking Newton's hand warmly but distractedly.

"It's a long story," said Newton, sighing and finding it difficult to take his attention from Phoebe. "What do you mean I died?"

"For one thing, you should be a hundred and twenty-nine, so how are you here, like this, like we remember you? And for another, we saw your grave in the cemetery. I read your stone before we ever showed up at Lena's boarding house." Phoebe began gesturing wildly with her hands while her voice rose in a frantic pitch and her words spilled forth quickly. "And then I met you and you said your name aloud, and I knew, I knew," she pointed at him with her index finger, her eyes squinting in recollection, "I had heard that name before, ask Will," she pointed at Will, "I told him, I read your stone, it said you were going to die on the nineteenth, then I got to know you, and you were so... But then I couldn't stop thinking about you, and then Lena read that poem in the Thomas Campbell book, it was the one that... I couldn't stay, I knew how to get home then, and I couldn't stay..." she inhaled sharply and wiped the tears from her eyes.

Will took hold of her shoulders and shook her. "Phoebe, stop panicking. Can I slap you now?"

"I'm not panicking," she nearly screeched. "This is a perfectly reasonable reaction to the most unbelievable situation."

"At least you're not panicking."

"I need to sit down." Phoebe was breathing hard and walked over to the boardwalk in front of the Miner's Union Hall to sit down. She sat with her head in her hands for several seconds while Will, Newton and J. W. talked without her. Will then helped J. W. back into his wheelchair and they all joined her at the side of the road, Newton sitting beside her.

"Phoebe?" Newton inquired quietly. Then louder, "Phoebe."

She looked up. "How are you here?"

Newton inhaled, as if readying himself for his forthcoming explanation. He pointed across the street. "Do you remember what was over there?" He asked, waiting patiently.

Phoebe nodded. "The blacksmith shop. Where Lionel Bradley worked and where he lived."

"Yes. I met Lionel near there. I must have looked bewildered and I think he took pity on me. He was kind and gentle, and seemed a little lonely himself at times. But he was my friend. He would ask me over from time to time; Once when you were with me on the ride home from dinner that night at the restaurant. Do you remember?"

"I remember he asked you to come and see him. You didn't want to talk about it."

"No, I didn't. Mostly I didn't want anyone to hurt Lionel." Newton shifted, considering what to say next.

"I asked you about that and you behaved very secretively."

"But it wasn't only my secret; I couldn't talk about."

"If it don't hurt nobody then you don't have to tell," chimed in J. W., garnering a quick glance from Phoebe.

"I also asked you why you were here...then? If you had family or friends. You said you were lost, just like I said we were."

"I remember," answered Newton.

"Where did you come from?"

"My name is Newton L. Sanford, and I was born March 29, 1951. I'm from now, Phoebe, if that's what you're asking."

She frowned in thought and said, "I should have known. When we were at the dance you said, 'Courage is being scared to death – and saddling up anyway.' That quote is attributed to John Wayne; long after Bodie. How did you get...there? And what was Lionel doing?"

Formulating his words carefully, Newton explained. "Lionel told me he wasn't really a blacksmith." He stuck up a finger to keep her from interrupting. "He told me his father and grandfather had been and had taught him simple skills. That's why he did the smaller jobs when he arrived in Bodie, why he needed assistance and advice.

"After my arrival, Lionel saw me outside the blacksmith shop. I was wearing jeans and a plaid shirt and he loaned me a coat. It was huge and hung on me. He also loaned me some money until I bought some of my own clothes. I went door to door looking for a place to live. I knew there were boarding houses around, and I found Lena Barrett's place.

She had a room and it wasn't a costly place. She let me stay and directed me to Reinstein & Wolf for employment. Her husband had previously worked there and she gave me a recommendation."

Phoebe remembered her conversation with Lena about her husband having worked there before setting up a boarding house. "So you got a job and earned money to pay her and Lionel back." He nodded.

She turned to Will. "And you were horrified when I suggested you get a job. What a baby." Will crossed his arms and scowled.

Newton continued. "I believe Lionel suspected I was out of my element, didn't quite fit in. Probably because of the way I spoke initially, and the way I dressed; just like I suspected when you two came to the boarding house that first night and stayed for supper." Again he kept her from interrupting. "I'll get to that."

"We spoke often; when felt he could trust me, he took me to his shack and showed me something. He asked for my help in fixing it properly. It was then that I explained to Lionel exactly how I had gotten here."

"What did he show – how did you get he – "

"No interrupting, Miss Impatience," said J. W.

Phoebe grunted and he continued. "He showed me a rusty wagon wheel rim. It had speckles in it, gold speckles that shined in the light." Phoebe, Will and J. W. gasped simultaneously and Newton smiled at the secret. "He showed me where it had cracked into two halves. He told me it was broken and he needed to fix it before he could go home; and that it was a difficult task. That's when he admitted he was an ironworker, not a blacksmith; and wondered if I had any suggestions."

Phoebe turned to J. W. and said excitedly, "There's more than one." Then, "Go home where? And when?"

He pursed his lips momentarily, said "I don't know," and quickly continued. "But because I understood his predicament I felt an obligation to help. And to keep his secret."

"You understood? How exactly?" asked Will.

"Yes, I did." continued Newton. J. W. rolled his wheelchair closer and Will sat down near Phoebe to listen to more of the story. "You see, I was on a trip to see the ghost town of Ruby, Arizona. It's an old mining camp. While I was there I was hiking, exploring the desert. I came upon some artifacts. While I was taking pictures of them and logging their locations I saw something shiny, half buried in the sand.

"I dug it out, it took awhile, and it was a rusty wagon wheel rim. It had some chips at the edges and a couple of cracks running almost all the way through. I tried to be careful with it so I stood in the center of it to lift it up evenly, to take the pressure off the cracks. I attempted to lift it up to set it on a large boulder nearby so I could look at it more closely and take some better pictures of it.

"As I set it on the boulder everything went dark and this terrible wind started blowing. I felt off balance and thought I was falling. I grabbed at whatever was in reach, but when the mysterious wind stopped and the light returned the wheel rim was what I had grabbed and it fell and came apart at the cracks. I broke it." Newton looked down at his hands, remembering, regretting some of the things he had done. He looked back at Phoebe.

Phoebe realized her eyes were wide and she was holding her breath, listening to his story, understanding how he felt when his world went dark and the wind howled; and when he woke up in a strange place. "Where were you, when the light returned?" she asked, suspecting the answer.

"Here, well, back then, in Bodie, in Lionel's shack. On May 10, 1880. The same day I had been hiking in the desert, but one hundred years earlier. It looked like somebody lived there, I was scared and tucked the halves of the rim behind a wardrobe in the shack."

"Hold on. If you cracked a rim in getting here, there, and he showed you a rim...?" Phoebe was finding it difficult to form the right questions to ask.

"After Lionel mentioned fixing the rim to go home, I realized he must have one himself." The three others looked at him with incredulity. Newton nodded affirmation. "I was only responsible for the one I had used to get here – there. I had cracked the one I found in the desert when I landed in Lionel's shack. He had another he was trying to fix for himself." Newton smiled in reminiscence.

"When he found you he didn't realize you would have needed your own?" asked Phoebe.

"I appeared different at first, but he had no idea why. And you knew Lionel; I don't know how much thought he actually put into it. When he invited me back to his shack to show me his rim, he also showed me the rim he had found behind his wardrobe. I told him my story then, explaining that it was I who had placed it there."

"J. W., where did your wheel rim come from?" Phoebe asked suspiciously.

"I found it. It was just in my barn one day."

"And you don't know who built the barn, or where it came from originally?" Will asked. J. W. shook his head 'no.'

"Newton, why were you in Arizona?" asked Phoebe, attempting to piece together this puzzle.

"I took a couple of vacation days from work. I was there exploring, that's all."

"Is Ruby anywhere near, what was it called again, J. W., the Doorway to the Gods? Have you heard of that, Newton?"

"That's it," said J. W.

"It is, it's not far at all. I had heard stories about an arch that leads through time and about lost gold. I didn't believe it, but now I'm reconsidering. I wanted to go to Ruby to see the old town."

"So what happened with you and Lionel; and the rims? We saw you, Will and I, when we were walking to the cemetery. You were on your way to see Lionel again, weren't you?"

"I was. He told me that day that he was almost finished fixing one of the rims. He may have been quicker had it been a plain rim, without the gold, but I think he finally knew what he was doing. I also think he was enjoying living in Bodie. That's why he gave me the first one he fixed."

"I have a confession to make," she stated sheepishly. "After the day Will and I went to the cemetery we walked around to the back of the blacksmith's and peeked in to see, well, to see what we could see. I knew you were hiding something and I wanted to find out what it was."

"I was talked into it, I assure you. I told her to leave well enough alone," Will said.

"Oh, hush," said Phoebe.

"Don't worry, Will, I believe you," said Newton with a smirk.

"You know, it *is* easier to see what expression you're making without that mustache of yours." Newton raised an eyebrow. "Anyway, I saw Lionel in the corner," she glanced across the street. The scene was still so very real in her head. "I saw something shiny, and there was a rim hanging on the wall. That was after I had discovered that the one hanging in J. W.'s barn, I mean Lena's barn, was missing.

"I thought Lionel had taken the rim, but I didn't know why he would do that. He must have used it to figure out how to fix his, and yours. And the other one was back in J. W.'s barn not long after I saw Lionel with it." She paused a moment, thoughtful. "He knew we weren't from here, there, either. He knew, and didn't say a word."

"He was minding his own business," said Newton, eyeing Phoebe.

"Lionel started it," she said defensively. "He talked about finding a good place to hide something."

"Okay, you two. Can you ever *not* argue?" asked Will, wanting to hear the rest of the story.

"Let the man finish," said J. W.

"Sorry," said Phoebe.

"He may have suspected, yes. But that's something I hadn't completely figured out at the time, even when he told me he needed to find the other one to see how to fix his. I didn't know what he was talking about. Maybe after meeting the two of you he thought to look in Lena's barn. You were newcomers, after all.

"The worst part was, after you said you wouldn't be here, there, much longer, that you were leaving soon, I no longer wanted to stay myself."

Is he blushing?

"I felt guilty for leaving Lionel behind. But I finally had a reason to come home and get on with my life. If I could. You were no longer here."

"That's when you told me you were leaving soon, too. It was because of me?"

He nodded. "Yes, Phoebe. At first I enjoyed seeing Bodie the way it had been, first hand. It was fascinating and enlightening. Then I met you. I wondered if the same thing had happened to you. But I didn't know where or when you were from. I didn't know anything, really. Lionel told me he had fixed the rim I'd broken and that it was in his shack. I met him in the morning, shook his hand, told him thank you and goodbye."

"Why didn't you say something about it to us?"

"What was I supposed to say? 'Hi, Miss Tucker, I'm from the future, so perhaps we have something in common after all...'" Phoebe and Will exchanged glances and smiled conspiratorially. "What did I say?"

"We had a similar conversation about saying that to you. Except we thought we knew the day you were going to die," said Will.

"About that," Newton's brow creased. "What's this about a poem on my gravestone?"

"I told you, we saw it. It was right up there," she pointed. "I couldn't stay to watch you... get killed. I knew the day, and every time I saw you and got to know you made it more difficult to be around you. Every day I had a countdown going in my head and it was terribly stressful. I was rude to you, I'm sorry."

“That’s why you told me to be careful,” he remembered. Phoebe nodded. “I wonder what changed.”

“What did you do that next day, after we got home from the dance?” Will asked.

“Well,” Newton stared off into the distance, it’s been a few weeks but – ”

“A few weeks? This is so bizarre.”

“Yes, Will, it is. I was here for over a month but when the rim was fixed and I wanted to go home, I arrived back in the desert only a short time after I had dug up the rim from the sand. I didn’t have a watch or anything, but by the time I hiked back to my car and drove to my motel, I discovered I had been gone from the desert for about twenty minutes. I was very confused. At least you two had each other.”

Phoebe and Will both turned to look at J. W. He looked at each of them in turn and gave a little sideways grin.

Newton continued. “The day after the dance; I was up earlier than I expected to be. The sun was up and Lena was in the kitchen heating the stove. That’s when she told me she had knocked on your door, Phoebe, and found it unlocked and with a note on your bed. I didn’t get to tell either of you goodbye. I asked you and Will where you were from, how long you were going to stay, trying to get some hint to your story. That morning, I didn’t think I would ever see you again.”

Phoebe reached over and took his hand in hers. She felt sure they shared the same feelings at this point, and had no reservations about such an act. “After I had eaten, the sheriff knocked on the door and wanted to let me know he had intercepted Albert Griffin on Main Street. After questioning, he admitted he and John Young had robbed Chester on the boardwalk. The sheriff also thought he was trying to catch a stagecoach out of town. Apparently, Mary Jacobson had been on her way to the the office of the Doctor on Main Street and had seen him attempting to disguise his identity.”

“That’s it!” said Phoebe. Albert Griffin, he killed you. You know what I mean.”

"But why am I here and not up on the hill," he pointed, confused.

"Because Chester Murphy didn't die," Phoebe felt giddy at how what felt like a minor turn of events had changed everything. "When we were here before and saw your stone, Chester Murphy's marker was not far from it. We didn't know it then, because his headstone was made of wood, his name obscured and the grave circled by stones. But J. W. knew. He mentioned that it was a friend of his who had been nice to him; and had been shot in the street.

"It was Chester. His marker isn't in the cemetery anymore either. He didn't die that night. Because of me. Because I kicked John Young in the knee and Chester got shot in the side instead. Because Chester survived, Mary went to see him and noticed Albert. Otherwise he was probably going after you and then leaving town."

"So that's what happened to Chester. That's wonderful. I didn't know. But how do you know I didn't die that night in the street? The night of all the fighting? John Young tried to shoot me, twice."

"That was before midnight. Wrong date. I *was* worried someone had possibly mixed up the dates, though."

"Okay, so why would Albert have come after me?"

"Revenge. You didn't recognize them from when Lionel Bradley shot and killed their cohort, what was his name?"

"Joseph Hoffman," said Newton, furrowing his brow, attempting to make sense of it all.

"Yes. But the two of them knew who you were, because they had seen you with Lionel. And I had thwarted Albert's efforts more than once. He was angry for so many reasons and was probably going to take it out on you. I knew the date but not what would happen to you. I thought perhaps Albert, or John Young, or – "

"John was still in jail that morning the last I heard. Courtesy of you, I believe."

"I suppose so. But I, we, didn't know if your death was caused by either of them or an accident or if it even happened in Bodie or in another town. I just knew I couldn't bear to think of you being gone. Then...now...ever."

Newton squeezed Phoebe's hand. "I'm here now." She nodded. "But... explain your relationship to Walter. I mean... J. W. is it?"

J. W. explained. "Yes. My father was Lena's first husband, James Tucker. My name is James Walter, something Phoebe found out not long after she and Will arrived back home in my barn. I was called Walter by my mother." He shrugged.

"In your barn? You mean with the third rim?" said Newton.

"Yes. When I was an adult and left Bodie, with my mother and my new bride, I had the barn moved with us."

"You married Grace in Bodie?" interrupted Phoebe, having never heard that story before.

"She was from Bridgeport. We married there. We lived here for awhile before we left. Bodie was slowing down.

"Anyway," he said, glancing at Phoebe and resuming his story, "I liked it, the barn. It was my little piece of home. The metal rim was inside it. Like I already told these two, I had the same thing happen to me once. I was brought back to old Bodie when the barn belonged to someone else. I was terrified and wanted to go home immediately. And it took me home. It was horrible and I never touched it again. But then – " he looked at Phoebe, "my great-granddaughter here caused a stir by not being true to herself. I'll let her explain that to you one day. She needed a nudge and I sent her here through the rim. With Will."

"But we all got sent back one hundred years. You didn't," said Will.

J. W. shook his head, and said. "If the rim has Bodie gold in it what reason is there for the it to bring me back before Bodie existed. 1880 was an important time here, the population was at it's peak. I returned before that, I could tell. Maybe when it was newer and just beginning."

"But where did the rims come from?" asked Phoebe.

"I think I know," said Newton. "Lionel's family had something to do with it. He told me his grandfather had been a blacksmith and had also prospected gold. He had a small vial of gold dust in his shack. I saw it there. His father's family had lived in the west during the earliest gold rush. That's all I can tell you."

They sat in silence for several seconds, gathering their thoughts, reliving what they had been through together and remembering those they would never see again.

40

They meandered back the way they had come, toward the parking lot and the Scout. Newton strolled beside Phoebe, Will pushed J. W. in his chair behind them. "Do you work here now?" asked Phoebe.

"Occasionally," he said. I help maintain the buildings, make sure the road is safe for travel, answer questions. As you know, Bodie doesn't fix anything up. They simply make sure things don't fall down," he laughed lightly. I was helping put a proper roof on one of the winter staff homes a couple of weeks ago."

"Does Jeremy still work here? I didn't see him today," asked Phoebe.

"I don't know anybody named Jeremy," said Newton. The staff here is small. I would have met him."

She slapped herself in the forehead, garnering J. W.'s and Will's attention. "I didn't think about that changing too. When we met a Jeremy last time we were here, you were dead. You couldn't have been working here. Now you're here, so... no more Jeremy-the-Ranger."

"Weird. Geez, having to remember two outcomes is making me hungry," said Will.

"Newton, do you remember when we were dancing and – "

"Yes, dear, I do."

"Let me finish. Do you remember telling me that Chester had told you about Will and I giving him gold double eagles?" Newton nodded but kept silent. "Will made up the story about my feeling guilty for gambling."

"No kidding," he said dryly.

"Hmph. Anyway, it was because I already had money when we got here. J. W. had stuck some in the pocket of my Army coat I was wearing but I didn't know it until later. The gold double eagles were in there too." She could tell he wanted to ask something but he let her continue. *Yes, he is much more patient than I.*

"When things, um, were the way they had turned out before, Chester had given four double eagles to Walter after he'd been robbed. It was for safe keeping. Chester never got them back, before, because he was killed. Years later, J. W. gave them to me. He was hoping I would have a heart and share them with Chester. Which I did. He used the money for a fresh start with Mary. They got married. J. W. told me the story."

Newton wrapped his left arm around the top of Phoebe's shoulders. "I'm happy for Chester. And also that you *do* have a heart," he teased. "And I'm glad I have somebody to talk about this with. I thought I had lost my mind."

“You were going to finish telling about how you suspected we didn’t fit in when we came to the boarding house. What did you mean?”

They had reached the Scout now and Will was helping J. W. into his seat and putting the wheelchair in the back. “I loaned Will one of my coats to wear to supper your first night at the boarding house. I thought your clothes were from, elsewhere, but I couldn’t come right out and ask you.”

Phoebe leaned against the side of her car with Newton facing her as he continued. “All I could do was wait and see what you said, what you did, how you behaved.” Will came around to the driver’s side of the car to listen. “Then, when you seemed in accord with your surroundings, and the next time I saw you you were shopping, wearing normal clothes, I wondered if I had been wrong. I waited. And waited. You knew things, about Bodie, about the nineteenth century. And you behaved accordingly. Most of the time,” he grinned.

“I had no idea what was going on,” said Will. That’s why I let Phoebe do all the talking.”

“You warmed up soon enough,” said Newton. To Phoebe he said, “You, on the other hand... You behaved properly one moment, and then – ”

“I wasn’t that unusual for the times. My great-great-grandmother bashed a burglar in the head with a shotgun.”

“...And then stabbed a man in the hand with a fork, without nerves or regrets,” he finished.

“Get used to it, Newton,” muttered Will.

“I think I already have.”

Phoebe scowled at both of them. “Are you through?”

Will opened the passenger door to get into the Scout.

Newton laughed at her once again. “Phoebe, how can I contact you? Where do you live? Where are you from?”

“My home number and address is in Dubuque, Iowa.”

“Iowa? That’s so far.” She caught the disappointed tone.

Her tone softened. "But I'm from Carson City. I was born there. That's where most of my family lives." She looked into his eyes. "And I'm coming home."

"You are? Why? When?"

She glanced in the back seat at J. W. "Soon. Because my great-grandfather taught me a valuable lesson."

They hugged and Phoebe didn't want to let him go. She wrote down her number for Newton to contact her. Will did too; they had become friends.

Before getting behind the wheel, she said, "I see your black eye and fat lip have both healed up fine. For me that was only a day and half ago."

He touched his cheek, remembering. "It's been a few weeks for me, but no permanent damage done. Someone asked me about it after I returned and I used the excuse that I fell while hiking." He laughed lightly. "I'll call you, Phoebe."

She got in the Scout, closed the door and rolled down the window. He said his goodbyes to Will and J. W. through the window and put a hand under Phoebe's chin. "I'm glad to have found you again. Miss Tucker."

***

That evening, after dinner and while having coffee on the patio, the Tucker phone rang. From the kitchen, Bonnie called Phoebe to the phone and whispered, 'it's a man calling.' Phoebe smiled and waited for her mother to go back outside with the others before speaking. "Hello?"

"Hello," was all he said.

Phoebe sat down and absentmindedly laid a towel on the table, folded over one corner and slowly rolled it up tight. Newton said, "Are you there, Phoebe?"

She smiled contentedly and replied, "I'm sorry, I'm here. It's weird to talk to you on the phone. I'm picturing you in a hat and sack suit. And a mustache. I'm glad you called."

"When can I see you?"

"When are you not working?"

"Tomorrow. Lunch? I'll pick you up."

Phoebe smiled into the phone. "Okay." She gave Newton the address to her parent's house and they arranged a time. "See you tomorrow."

When a distracted Phoebe, towel still in hand, strolled back out to the patio, her brother's Troy and Tony, visiting while she and some of the other family were still in town, mentioned Phoebe's altered disposition. "What's up with her?" Troy asked.

Will answered, defending his sister. "I'm pretty sure she's got a boyfriend. But don't yank her chain about it."

"Why not, that's we're here for," said Tony.

"Because she's holding a kitchen towel in her hands, and what you taught her just may come back to bite you."

***

Newton arrived at the Hank Tucker residence the next day around eleven thirty. Introductions were made and white lies where they had met before were told. In the car, Newton told Phoebe, "I hope you don't mind but I called Will this morning."

"Why should I mind?"

"Because we're stopping to pick him up, too."

Phoebe said nothing.

"Does that bother you?"

"Nope."

"Really?" He teased.

"You're goading me, and I don't appreciate it. If you've got something to tell me, come out and say it. Like I told Chester, you shouldn't keep secrets from those you lo –" She quickly looked right, out the passenger side window.

"What was that? What did you tell Chester?" When she didn't reply he said, I'm sorry, Phoebe. I was just teasing you. I have something to show you before lunch. And I want Will to see it too. Trust me."

She nodded, still feeling foolish for what she had been about to say.

Phoebe reached into her Army jacket pocket and withdrew something. She spread it flat on the seat between them and patted it to get his attention. Newton chuckled when he looked down and saw the small, white handkerchief he had loaned Phoebe when she had gotten mud on her hand outside the Palace Restaurant. "I washed it for you," she said. "I'm sorry I'm so slow in returning it."

Newton smiled and put his hand atop hers. "One hundred years. You are slow," he said, winking at her. He drove one-handed until they arrived at Will's.

Will's apartment wasn't far and when they arrived to pick him up he was waiting outside. He got in the back seat of Newton's pickup and said, "This sure is different than a buggy, um, carriage, um, whatever it was we rode in before."

"Technically it was a surrey," said Newton. "But 'carriage' will do just fine."

"What do you do, Newton?" asked Will. "Specifically, that is."

"I mainly work in historic preservation and reconstruction. Fixing up old houses, buildings. Historic renovations, things like that."

"Cool." He then muttered under his breath, "You two are made for each other," but they had both heard him nevertheless. Phoebe covered a smile with her hand and Newton laughed aloud.

"So where are we going?" Will asked.

"You'll see," Newton replied, turning out of Will's neighborhood and driving north on Carson Street before taking a couple more rights and lefts to their destination.

As the drove, Phoebe asked Newton, "Where are you from, by the way. I know when, but not where." She looked at Will. "I heard it, it sounded weird, I know."

"I was born in Sparks. My family moved a couple of times when I was a kid. My parents moved to Reno a few years ago."

“But where do you live? Now?” She just had to know.

“Just outside Gardnerville. I have an old house with a couple of acres.”

“So close,” she whispered in disbelief, explaining that her grandparent’s farmhouse and J. W.’s barn weren’t far from there.

“How did you end up in Dubuque, Iowa?” he asked.

“I ran away.”

“You ran away from home!”

“Not exactly. I moved to go to college. But I ran away from what I loved.” She leaned back in her seat and told him a shortened version of how a series of wrong decisions had culminated in J. W. tricking them into his barn and the subsequent trip to Bodie.

“That’s how Walter, sorry, J. W. taught you a lesson, then.” She nodded as he considered her words.

“I can admit it now. I think that’s all my family ever wanted. J. W. told me I needed patience. I heard Lena tell him the same thing. But I didn’t know what he meant. Now I know he meant with myself.” She glanced back to Will. “Bunch o’ buttinskies.” Newton was grinning.

Newton turned left into the Lone Mountain Cemetery, drove a short distance and pulled to the side. Phoebe asked, “What are we doing here?” and opened her door to get out of the truck.

“You and Will went for a walk in the Bodie Cemetery. I thought this would be a great place for a second date.”

“Ha, second date? What about the first?” Phoebe asked.

“We had our first. The benefit dance.” To Will he said, “Is she always this forgetful?”

Will was shaking his head at them as he exited the back seat. He remembered telling Phoebe the cemetery was a silly place to ask a person you had feelings for to join you.

“So why are we here?” she asked again.

“Shh, and I’ll show you.” He reached and took her hand in his to pull her in a specific direction. They walked to the next section in the cemetery, each separated by drives and walking paths. He stopped when he found what he was looking for, took Phoebe by the shoulders and turned her toward what he wanted her to see. He pointed down.

"There. Read it. Aloud."

"Okay, but I hope you can explain, because this is – "

"Read it."

She sighed. "Okay, okay. '*WWII Veteran, 41st Infantry Division, SGT Bradley Lionel, b. Oct 21, 1908, d. Nov 19, 1979.*' I don't understand who this – wait a minute– Bradley Lionel?" Phoebe gasped and turned to face Newton. "Is this... Lionel? Lionel Bradley?"

Newton was grinning. "It was difficult to keep this from you yesterday. I told you that was all I could tell you. I'm sorry for the fib. I wanted to show you in person." He turned to look down at the grave marker. "When I got back I tried to find out what happened to him. I couldn't find anything at first and thought I would never know. But... then I remembered. When I met him he introduced himself and said, 'I'm Lionel, sir,' and shook my hand very seriously. As if he were introducing himself military style. You know, last name first, adding the 'sir.'

"So I searched records with the names switched around. I found him, but he's still Lionel to me; it doesn't feel right calling him Bradley. He had been an ironworker, employed in various places, and had joined the Army in the spring of 1942.

"There was a missing persons report filed for Lionel in Silver Springs in the fall of 1977 by his son." Phoebe and Will exclaimed and Newton, nodding acknowledgment of their reaction, continued. "The newspaper article mentioned that Lionel had been last seen in a desert town in Arizona; he was on his own, a private adventure, searching for lost mission gold. It stated that his family had lived near there at one time, it didn't say when. According to another newspaper article he notified his son of his whereabouts a couple of days later. Meaning he made it back; back from Bodie."

"I wonder how long he was there," said Will wistfully.

Newton answered. "Almost two years. He was there during the big strikes. He told me so."

"So he's actually two years older than his headstone implies." Will smiled broadly. "Good for him."

"Newton, you found the wagon wheel rim in the desert and Lionel was already in Bodie when you got there... That's three rims. We have J. W.'s; where are yours and Lionel's?"

"And where did they come from?" asked Will.

"Initially, I thought Lionel had made the rims. Embedded with Bodie gold. But he was having a difficult time mending the cracks. Then, like I told you yesterday, I wondered if his grandfather had made them, being a blacksmith and prospector. I kept searching and found a record that said a Jonathan Lionel had lived in Bodie in its early years. His great-grandfather.

"Before and after living in Arizona, where quite a bit of gold was prospected, Johnathan had lived and worked in Bodie. He was recorded as having been a carpenter and blacksmith. I think he was the original owner of J. W.'s barn, perhaps its builder.

"After I found the Arizona information, I wondered if there had actually been four rims, you know, to outfit a wagon. It's quite the egotistical status symbol, so why have only three metal, sturdy wagon wheel rims to show off? He probably made the rims in Bodie, used the wagon for transportation and prospected in Arizona."

"So he just left a wagon with expensive wheels sitting in the desert to rot? How does that make any sense?" asked Will.

"It doesn't," answered Newton. "I believe the Doorway to the Gods is responsible for the wagon having been lost for a time. Or part of it. People and belongings are suspected of reappearing in locations different from where they had originally disappeared. I believe all but one of the rims went missing at the time and Jonathan brought it with him back to Bodie. If nothing else he could have extracted the gold. Perhaps it was he who hung it in the barn.

“I told you I never believed such things, but now...” he aimed his gaze pointedly at Lionel’s grave. “I think Lionel heard the family story and went in search of the wagon wheels made with gold. He found one and appeared in Bodie, the same as I did, from the same location, to the same location.

“Why not into the barn?” Asked Phoebe.

“Your guess is as good as mine. Perhaps it has to do with where each rim was lost or who was in control of the Bodie destination at the other end.” He shrugged. “If I’d known what I didn’t know, I would have asked Lionel more questions,” joked Newton. “At the time I didn’t pay much attention to some of the things he said because he didn’t always make sense. I confess, I thought Lionel was a little, sorry my friend, a little addlebrained. Turns out he had several injuries during the war and never returned to service after that.”

Phoebe’s eyes popped, remembering. “When shots were fired behind Wagner’s saloon... he dove to the ground. And he said he didn’t like when his friends were hurt. And the knife with the leather sheath that John Young held on him; everyone was issued one of those in World War Two. Oh, and he said my Colt was too small.”

“His records said he was an expert with the M1 Garand Rifle, standard military issue at the time. He saved my life with that skill,” said Newton, reminiscing.

“Newton,” said Phoebe, her brow creasing with concentration and frustration that her previous question had yet to be answered, “where are the two rims you and Lionel used. And what about the fourth?”

“This keeps getting better and better,” muttered Will sarcastically, crossing his arms.

Newton knelt down and brushed away the sand and small rocks that constantly blew over the area surrounding Bradley Lionel’s grave marker. He brushed and brushed and brushed, and what was revealed shocked Phoebe and Will.

There, on the ground and framing the stone were strips of metal, end to end, bolted and held in place. Other strips, straightened out like the others, outlined the grave itself, driven into the ground on the thin edge like a garden border. Newton reached over and cleared the stone on the right with the same results.

"Who's that?"

Sigh... "Read it." Newton pointed.

Phoebe read the second stone. "Violet Lionel, born in 1909, died in 1974. His wife." She put her hand on her heart. "A wife and a son. I'm relieved; and so happy for him. He wasn't all alone after all. And the metal pieces," Phoebe leaned down to touch them and peer closer. "They all have gold dust in them. It's the wagon wheel rims, flattened out and in pieces. Never to be used again."

"I think he fixed the broken ones with his great-grandfather's prospected gold; the vial I saw. Maybe when he arrived back in Arizona three years ago he found the fourth one and brought it here with him. Also, I think he didn't want what happened to him, to all of us, to happen to anyone else. On finding the fourth, he knew they were all accounted for. This is a lot of metal, several feet. I believe there is enough to make two rims here."

"That only accounts for three. We have J. W.'s, two are here. Where's yours, the one you used, the one Lionel fixed for you?" asked Phoebe, afraid there was a final rim in an unknown location.

I brought it back with me. It's something that belongs in a very, very safe place, don't you agree?" Brother and sister nodded.

"Where did you put it?" asked Phoebe.

"I'll show you later," he said with a grin. "I think the one in J. W.'s barn should stay there. We all know what it does. It's the safest place for it," said Newton dropping his arm casually across Phoebe's shoulders. "This was exciting. What are we going to do for our third date?"

***

The next day Will had to return to work. He didn't mind, since he felt he had been on a long, though stressful, vacation. He was looking forward to normalcy. Phoebe was going to be around for several more days so he would see her later. Her aunt and uncle, Mary and George, and her cousin Jody, were staying for another day before returning to Albuquerque. Jody's brothers James and Roger were leaving the next morning.

In the afternoon, Phoebe was helping her mother sort through a few more photographs, putting them in order in albums, when they came across a few of her father and grandfather when her dad was a kid. "Mom," said Phoebe, choosing her words carefully, "do you have any pictures of Grandpa when he was little? With J. W. and Grace?"

"Hmm, I don't think I do. If there are any they're most likely at Henry and Julia's house. "Hold on, I do have..." She remembered, searching the pictures in the small box on the table. "This one." She put it in front of Phoebe. It was a very old photo, small but clear. In it were two women, one man and a baby. Phoebe stared at it, studied it, but she knew instantly who the subjects were. J. W., *probably called Walter at the time*, her great-grandmother Grace in a pretty dress, a baby, *that would be my grandfather Henry,* and... *It's Lena! Older now, Walter grown up and married.* Phoebe hadn't asked what had happened to Lena; she hated to think of her as deceased. But she'd had the chance to be a grandmother. *Time to play dumb.*

"Mom, is this J. W?" Yes. "This must be his mother, then, right?" I suppose so. "Her name was Lena wasn't it? She's pretty."

"And full of fire, according to J. W. She would have to have been to raise him, in my opinion." Phoebe laughed, remembering the boisterous but respectful boy. Bonnie took back the photo and said, "You look like her Phoebe. How about that."

"Yeah, how about that," echoed Phoebe, loving the fact.

What were you talking about before this picture, J. W.? Where did you go after? Old pictures no longer left her feeling as if the past had been static, boring, monotonous.

There was a knock at the door and Bonnie went to answer it. She came back with someone following behind. "Newton," Phoebe exclaimed, more than a little surprised.

Bonnie had some laundry to take care of and left them alone. Newton sat beside Phoebe and she showed him some family pictures, saving the one with Lena for last. He said aloud the same thing she had wondered; "Phoebe, do you still have the picture we had taken? At the photo studio in," he checked to see that they were alone and whispered, "in Bodie?"

It shocked her that she had forgotten about them after J. W. had shown her the copy he had in his box. Racing to her room and checking the upper pocket of her Army jacket, worrying it was no longer there, Phoebe withdrew all three photos from within, along with Will's copies. She plopped down beside Newton excitedly and said, "They're here. With everything going on they slipped my mind." He had removed his own copies from his wallet and was looking at them now.

"You have yours too," She said, delighted.

"Of course I do. I wasn't going anywhere without them."

In the one taken of Newton and Phoebe alone, Phoebe was upright, stoic; she had been afraid to move. Newton wore a slight sideways grin; typical. "You're smiling."

"I was having my picture taken with you. I was going to keep it with me to remember you." He held the picture. "I still love this picture, but now I have you." He paused and said, "Don't I?"

She wrapped her arms around his neck. "Since I tend to turn most people off and I can't seem to get rid of you... you win." She kissed him timidly.

"Would you prefer I grow back the mustache?"

"I would always know you were smiling under there anyway. Oh," she exclaimed, racing back through the kitchen and disappearing. Newton craned his neck to see where she had gone. She returned a moment later with something in her hand. "Here," she said handing him a coin. "Will told me I owe you a quarter for a shave and a haircut. Sorry, I didn't add interest."

"A hundred years of interest is a lot of interest," he joked, laughing. "Thanks."

They looked through a few more pictures and Phoebe remembered something she had meant to ask earlier. "Newton, you've heard of the Bodie Curse, haven't you?"

"Sure. There are items there that people have returned over the years. Why?"

She explained about J. W. putting the piece from the grave marker in her pocket. J. W. thought that had something to do with the rim working. What do you think?"

He politely considered her point. "I told you I don't believe in ghosts. And I don't believe in curses. But I never would have believed a crazy story about stepping inside a metal rim and zooming to another place and time either. So..."

"Then why did your rim – "

"The rims have Bodie gold in them. I'm thinking that's a sizable souvenir, whether we knew what we were taking or not. And if a curse worked for J. W., then who's to say?"

"Maybe he was making sure we got there," she speculated. "Or maybe the stone was J. W.'s way of getting me to take him back out there after Will and I returned from old Bodie. To make his own amends and have a story to tell us." She explained about his having broken the headstone years ago. "He doesn't tell anyone much about what's in his head. We weren't even sure about his age. I don't think he wanted us to suspect that he and Walter are one in the same."

He stared at the group picture of all of them. "I want to see you tomorrow."

"Do you?

"I'll be in Bodie. Would you meet me? I know it's another long drive, but I have a surprise for you. Unless you have plans. I don't want to take you away from your family."

She put a finger on his lips and grinned. "Another surprise? I'll meet you there."

***

Rounding the last curve in the dirt road, Phoebe's nerves started to prickle and her heart began thumping. That feeling she hoped wouldn't fade was still with her. But up ahead she had an added bonus. Newton was waiting for her.

She parked and got out of her car. As she walked down the path and rounded the curve that turned into Green Street she saw him, standing by the Methodist Church. He was wearing work clothes; jeans, boots and a flannel shirt. As she walked a breeze blew her hair, sending it fluttering around her head and into her eyes. She brushed it away and held it to the side with one hand.

A guide was standing near the church and giving a brief history of Bodie before she took them to a few select buildings. Others had a map with descriptions and were walking a self-guided tour.

"Good morning, Miss Tucker." Newton held out his arm and she wrapped hers around it.

"Good morning, Mr. Sanford. Where are we going on this wonderful summer day?"

"Not to the cemetery. I believe a third date should be a tad more delightful." She giggled as they strolled toward Main Street.

Newton asked, "Can you believe the noise this morning? And the mud... watch your step." She took a hop over an imaginary puddle. "I heard there was a fight in town last night."

"Really? What happened?" asked Phoebe.

"There was this man, and he was in a jealous rage over a man dancing with his wife. He went out to Main Street, south of the post office, and shot the man dead, right there in the street."

"Wait, that really happened," said Phoebe. "I remember reading that he – "

"Really? Huh. There was also a stage robbery just outside of town and the driver was killed."

"That happened too."

"Do you remember, just last year, when there was an explosion near the Standard Mine? And that the snow this past winter was over the rooftops."

Phoebe stopped him when they reached the intersection of Green and Main Streets, and pointed. "Look, Newton. Up north to the curve, and south as far as you can see. Buildings, businesses, people, carriages. I *can* see it. I *can* hear it. Can you?"

He nodded. "I can. Come this way." He walked with her south to the Miner's Union Hall. Waiting outside was a horse-drawn two-person buggy. The attendant nodded to Newton as they approached. Newton held out his hand to help Phoebe step up into the buggy. "Would you care to go for a ride with me today? I promise to be a gentleman."

"I would love that. But you don't have to be too much of a gentleman." she replied lightly. Newton set the horse walking at a slow pace. "This is a wonderful surprise. I love it. Where are we going?"

"I may have once thought your visit to the cemetery was an unpleasant location to visit. But now I understand. You wanted to see what was the same, and what was different." She nodded. "You never got to do the other activities you mentioned. You said you wanted to picnic south of town or go to the racetrack."

"You remembered."

The lake is a bit far and the racetrack is deserted now. So how about a private picnic near the racetrack."

"That's a wonderful idea. But we don't have – "

Newton reach under the seat and pulled out a basket. "Look inside." Phoebe found a picnic lunch for two, packed and ready to go.

"You devil," she said, laughing and closing her eyes to the breeze.

They rode down what remained of Main Street, parts of it no more than a path now, and turned left at the fork at Cottonwood Canyon Road. "I never told you, J. W. was the one who gave me my horseshoe necklace. And I lost it when John Young grabbed me in the street that night."

Newton looked and saw she was wearing it once again. He pointed at it and Phoebe cut him off before he could ask about it. "Walter picked it up in the street. He kept it this entire time, in a locked metal box in his room. He gave it back to me when I came home."

Newton moved his head back and forth. The outcome of all they had been through was sometimes too much to absorb.

They traveled onward, slightly uphill, and continued until they saw the outline of what had once been the racetrack of Bodie. Newton pulled the buggy off onto the side of the road at a clear, flat spot and staked the reins into the ground. He took the blanket off the seat and spread it on the ground.

"Newton this is a beautiful spot for a picnic."

He laughed and said, "But there's no lake, no shade."

"It's perfect. I'm moving back home, I got to see J. W. and my family again, I know, and now admit, why I was so unhappy, I met you... And I didn't lose you." He passed out wrapped packages from the picnic basket while Phoebe poured drinks from a thermos.

"I know why I was ready to come back, too. Without you there was no adventure."

A while later, Phoebe took an apple slice to the horse for a treat and seated herself, once again, on the blanket. She stretched her legs out in front and leaned back against Newton; both faced the old town.

"Look at it, Newton." She turned to look northeast, back along the road they'd traveled. "It's still here. It's not gone, it's not dead, not at all. Bodie needs people like us, to share the stories, to keep it safe, to help people see the relevance of what came before us, to remember. If you open your eyes and your ears and your imagination... Bodie is alive and well.

"Lena told me a tribal quote that Wyanet told her once. I think it's fitting, for this place that we were fortunate enough to witness firsthand. *'Tell me and I'll forget. Show me, and I may not remember. Involve me, and I'll understand.'*"

Epilogue

Bodie, California, 1981

The couple emerged from the Green Street Methodist Church amid cheers and congratulations. Family and a few friends gathered around the bottom of the steps to hug them and wish them well.

Newton received handshakes from all three of Phoebe's brothers and Will said, "Good luck," with a wink of levity.

Newton turned to watch his bride greet family members, smiling contentedly. "I may need it," after which Phoebe joined her new husband.

"What do you need?" she asked.

"A good luck charm," mumbled Tony. "Or a lead room to hide in, in case you decide to go off." The brothers and Newton laughed at her expense.

"Ha ha, very funny," she said. holding up a fist in a threat to punch him.

"See..." he said, pretending to duck.

"How far away is this spot you picked, anyway?" Will asked in regards to the outdoor reception Phoebe and Newton had planned.

"Not far, that direction." She pointed southeast in the direction of Sugarloaf.

"Isn't that off limits? Because of all the old mines?" asked Will, who garnered a quizzical glance from his older brothers because never before had he shown much interest in, or knowledge of, Bodie.

"We're not going that far, just that direction, and we're certainly not climbing the hill. We have a canopy and some chairs. And a singer and a fiddle player."

"Geez, you're so weird," said Will, smiling at his big sister.

The assemblage made their way east on Green Street, turned south on Wood Street and continued. It wasn't long before they passed the location where Lena's boarding house and barn had been and the new bride and groom, walking hand in hand, exchanged conspiratorial glances. They continued south and turned to the left, off the path and through the sagebrush, just past the curve in the road.

There were four canopies staked out at the base of the hill, shelter for tables and chairs. Coolers and warming bins had been packed with their meals and drinks and an attendant was sorting through and arranging food onto one of the tables as they arrived. Whiskey bottles with sprigs of flowering sage were the decorations for each guest table. Pitchers of lemonade and tea were on a small table near the attendant.

Family and friends gathered and chatted while the early supper was arranged.

"How much have you got left?" asked Phoebe's uncle Charlie, Hank's brother.

"One more semester. Then I graduate and get my promotion at the Nevada State Museum in Carson City." Phoebe replied.

Tony's wife, Clara, was standing nearby. While holding the couple's newest addition to the family, Phoebe's three-month-old niece, Lena, she said, "We're happy for you Phoebe. No matter how Tony teases you. And I'm glad your great-great-grandmother's name came up in conversation. I love it."

"Me too," replied Phoebe, letting the little girl grab her pinky finger and shake it."

Newton came to stand beside Phoebe and made faces at the baby. Soon, Clara and baby Lena walked to find a seat beside Tony and Newton wrapped his arms around his new bride's waist, facing her. Quietly, he asked, "So, Mrs. Sanford, how are your guard duties coming along?"

Phoebe laughed. "Great. And after my promotion, the only person who will have access to it will be me. You know, for a fourth date that was quite a shock."

"I couldn't think of a better place to put it, at the time."

After arriving back in the Arizona desert, Newton had, with telepathic apologies to Lionel Bradley, re-broken the metal wagon wheel rim that had whisked him to old Bodie. In six pieces, with broken edges scraped rough, he proceeded to donate it to the Nevada State Museum in Carson City.

I found it in the desert, scattered beneath the dirt in several pieces. Was it already beyond repair? Sure... Sorry about that. But look how old and unusual it is, with gold dust in it. It belongs here in your museum...

"I promise to take good care of it. Maybe if we find a relative of Lionel's he or she can put it back tog – " she started to tease.

Newton put a hand on either side of her face and kissed her.

Phoebe pulled away, laughing. "Don't start thinking that's always going to work, Mr. Sanford."

"We've still got one rim to worry about. We don't need two," said Newton, smiling.

"Do you think anyone will ever find out what it does? And use it again?"

He pulled her close. "I don't know. It caused enough problems, don't you think?"

"It also solved the mysteries it created in the first place." She looked up at him and whispered, "How about a honeymoon in old Bodie?" Newton groaned, closed his eyes and rubbed them with a forefinger and thumb. "Just kidding, geez..." and she scooted away from him, laughing, before he could say more.

Soon the bride and groom called the reception to order. Phoebe's father gave a short speech, Newton's father did the same and anyone who wished to say a few words was invited to speak. Phoebe was last, because she had something special to add.

She poured a glass of lemonade, not tea, and held it in front of her, taking a moment to gather her thoughts. She cleared her throat and everyone quieted down. "I would like to raise a toast." Most people expected what she would say next. Phoebe touched her horseshoe necklace and said, "To J. W., James Walter Tucker, my, our great-grandfather, who would be here, right next to me, if he could be."

Phoebe's words faltered and tears stung her eyes. "He was my great-grandfather, but he was also always my friend. It's difficult to imagine life going on without him. In a way, it won't." She put a hand on her heart. "Because he's here, with me, beside me, in my thoughts and my actions, just like my grandparents and parents are. I owe him more than I am able to put into words today." She looked at Newton. "It's a complicated story, but without him I never would have met Newton." Her tears were flowing now, unheeded, unchecked, and she didn't care who saw them.

"He taught me to not let important moments pass you by, don't let opportunities slip through your fingers, to be grateful for what life has to teach us. And don't forget to always be true to yourself." She cleared her throat, sniffled and looked at each family member present. "He loved us all, in his own way, and I certainly loved him. I'm glad I took the time to tell him so." She raised her glass and said, "To J. W."

"To J. W.," everyone echoed.

Newton held her after that, knowing how difficult it had been to say goodbye to James Walter Tucker.

The gathering ate their meals, helped clean up and mingled, and the Tuckers got to know the Sanfords a little better.

Phoebe snagged one of the white cloth napkins off the table before an attendant removed it and waved it at Newton. He frowned in her direction, wondering what she was up to, but kept watching her as she put it flat on the table, folded one edge over and rolled it up tight.

She then searched the group for the perfect target, spying Will as he passed in front of her. She snapped the towel out at him, nicking the edge of his sleeve. He jumped and scowled at her and she and Newton laughed aloud at his expense. Newton shrugged an apology to Will, said to his bride, "So that's how that was done," and wisely removed the napkin from her grip.

Phoebe instructed the fiddle player to begin the song she had chosen as their first dance as a married couple. Newton had no idea what song she had picked, so when Phoebe said, "It's not a slow song, sorry," he was neither heartened nor disappointed. He expected his life with her to continue to be atypical and was prepared for the adventure.

The fiddle player was joined by the singer, their only entertainment for the event, who winked at Phoebe when the music began. Phoebe had been rehearsing the words as well and sang quietly to Newton as he took her by the hand to dance near the fiddle player.

Will hung his head and covered his eyes with his hand.

Hank and Bonnie displayed astonished expressions.

Tony and Troy smirked, accustomed to their sister's penchant for individualism.

As the song rolled along, the crowd got the giggles and started laughing. This was a joyous occasion, after all. Phoebe sang the last verse loudly, happily, and Newton blushed.

> "*'Your head may be thick as a block, and empty as any foot-ball. Oh! Your eyes may be green as the grass, your heart just as hard as a wall. Yet take the advice that I give, You'll soon gain affection and cash. And will be all the rage with the girls, If you'll only get a moustache, a moustache, if you'll only get a moustache.*'"

After several other songs had been played, genuine slow songs or upbeat fun songs, Phoebe, Newton and Will took a break from the party to slip away. Phoebe led the trio up the hill, sidestepping holes and rocks and uneven ground as they progressed higher and slightly north. When they were as high as they dared, due to dangers of century-old mining hazards, they turned to face northwest and looked down upon the town itself.

The warm summer breeze was blowing from the southeast, from over their shoulders, and swooping down over the town as it always had. It swirled the dust and settled it in new places, only to pick it up and set it down elsewhere.

Phoebe's great-grandmother, Grace, J. W.'s wife, had been buried in the cemetery in Carson City. J. W. had been cremated, at his request, and his ashes were to be interred beside Grace. But he had had one additional request that he had put upon Phoebe to carry out. He knew she would do it.

Phoebe opened the small canister she held containing a portion of J. W.'s ashes. She held it high in the air, looked at Newton and Will, nodded, waited for the breeze to pick up and blow from behind them and tipped the canister over. The ashes blew downward with the breeze, following the contour of the hill, racing toward Bodie, and dispersing across the wide expanse of sagebrush-covered land spread out before them.

Phoebe said, “Return to Bodie, J. W. You’re home.”

Author's Note

Facts and fiction: You might want to finish the story first.

I would like to thank Virginia City, Nevada; Carson City, Nevada; Bridgeport, California; Lee Vining, California; and Bodie State Historic Park, California. Thank you for useful information; you made me feel right at home.

Bodie, California is one of the finest gems of protected property in the west. It is maintained in a state of arrested decay, to be enjoyed in the natural state in which it was eventually abandoned.

In the beginning of this story, Phoebe Tucker drives on a portion of Highway 50, Lincoln Highway; all information regarding Highway 50 is true. It was a great feat of engineering at the time of its dedication in 1913.

All locations in Bridgeport, California, are accurately described. It is a delightful town.

The Says Phoebe bird is factual.

The tour Phoebe Tucker takes with her family through Bodie is accurately described. All streets and businesses spoken of were and are real; old maps are intriguing as some streets are now barely visible.

In the cemetery, the graves of Solomon Burkham and his wife Kathryn, William Hick, Arthur and Hugh McQuaid and their Mother and Father, Peter Noonan and Mary Louisa Moore are all as described.

The Doorway to the Gods in southern Arizona has been chronicled as a continuing mystery.

Through the years, many items have been returned to Bodie, blaming an individual's bad luck on the Bodie Curse.

It is difficult to imagine now, but there were once seven ore crushing stamp mills in Bodie by 1879. Two years later there were an additional two stamp mills atop the surrounding hills. Originally the stamp mills were so busy they operated around the clock, as well as many restaurants, saloons, brothels and opium dens in Chinatown.

The factual businesses are as follows:

The three cemetery sections named Ward's, Masonic and Miners Union; Standard Mill, Pioneer Brewery; Bon Ton Lodging House/Schoolhouse; sixty-five; saloons; Boone Store; Gilson & Barber; Bodie House Hotel; Mortuary on South Main Street; Big Red Barn; Fuller Street; Methodist Church; Reinstein & Wolf; Nevada Restaurant and Chop House; Palace Restaurant; Cabinet Saloon, Kilgore's Union Market, Ice House, Brick Post Office, Robson & Forest blacksmith shop, West &

Bryant's, Mono House Hotel, Wagner's Saloon, Bodie Jail, Cosmopolitan Hotel and Chop Shop, Kemp's Photography Studio, Occidental Hotel, Kirkwood Stables,

Pioneer Billiard Saloon, Mono City Bank, Bodie Hay Yard, Bodie-to-Benton Railroad; Bodie Standard Chronicle, Nevada State Museum. If an associated location is given, it is genuine.

The Barrett Boarding House and Lionel Bradley's shack are fictional, although many boarding houses existed.

The nearby East Walker River was an excellent source of fish for the town.

The winter of 1879 was a record snowfall for Bodie. Many deaths occurred and burials were stalled until spring.

There were many dances held at the Miner's Union Hall on South Main Street. It also housed church services for Methodists and Catholics, each service taking place at a different time of day. Members of the Miner's Union were allotted a burial payment for funeral services.

Paiute basket weaving is a unique art. Many have sold at auction for thousands of dollars. The Mono County Museum in Bridgeport houses a collection of the baskets. If you have a chance, do a search for them yourself; you will be amazed.

Constable John Franklin Kirgan did indeed do occasional raids in Chinatown in an effort to reduce opium usage and addiction. He was aided by Sheriff James Showers and Deputy Constable Patrick Phelan. King Street and Chinatown were the main targets of the raids as opium was a prevalent vice in that part of town.

The Thomas Campbell poem is as quoted. It is much longer than what I used; obviously I chose my favorite parts.

The song, *'If You've Only Got a Moustache,'* is an original song and the lyrics are accurate. It was written by Stephen Foster in 1864 and became a popular, lighthearted ditty in the post-Civil War climate.

On Phoebe's and Will's visit to the cemetery in Old Bodie, the individuals mentioned and the information given are true; U. P. Jack, Jack O'Hara, James Blair, Antone Valencis, A. C. Robertson, Mary Elizabeth Butler, James Doyle, Andy Haggerday, W. J. O'Brien were all Bodie residents.

The July 10, 1879 explosion of the powder magazine is well documented; it was a devastating event in Bodie.

Lone Mountain Cemetery is located in the northeast of Carson City, Nevada.

In Phoebe's and Newton's conversation when they revisit Bodie, the incidents in their reminiscent conversation actually took place; a man was killed south of the Miner's Union Hall after dancing with a jealous man's wife; a marker remains to commemorate the incident. A stagecoach driver was killed outside of Bodie in a robbery attempt. The explosion of the powder magazine and record snowfall were previously clarified.

All author's quotes are given their due. However, the quote attributed to Wyanet, *'Tell me and I'll forget. Show me, and I may not remember. Involve me, and I'll understand,'* is, in truth, attributed to an anonymous author from the Cherokee Nation.

The quote, *'And so I close now, realizing that the ending has not yet been written,'* is by an unknown author.

Bodie produced millions of dollars of gold, drawn out from the hills by workers earning four dollars per day, a good wage then, on par with the silver miners in Virginia City. Bodie owes a debt to their tenacity and determination, as well as to the brave and independent business owners and entrepreneurs; and their families. Rapscallions and opportunists were common. Yet, without this combination of citizens Bodie would not have become the memorable slice of mining town history that it is has.

Final Note: Four metal wagon wheel rims; metal rims created a sturdy finish to wagon wheels, greater so than those made of wood alone. While I manufactured the story of the rims, I cannot say with all certainty that similar rims do not exist. Also, if you happen to come across one, I cannot say with what unique qualities and/or abilities it may have been imbued. What I can tell you, is to be true to yourself, follow your dreams and never forget from whence you came.

Lastly, please do not forget the cardinal rule when visiting any historic site, monument or place of remembrance; take only memories, leave only footprints. Or you may find yourself the victim of a mysterious curse.

Made in the USA
Las Vegas, NV
18 July 2021